Like W.P. Kinsella's "Shoeless Joe," Jerry Jac̶
fashions fanciful fiction from hardball ign̶
everyone from Sir Francis Drake, the brill̶
brilliant stealer of merely bases. Jacover take̶ ̶ ̶ ̶ ̶omp
through the Cubs' long stretch in the desert— ̶ ̶ ̶ ̶ ̶er than the
Israelites'—and gives us a North Side version ̶ ̶ ̶ ̶rs of Solitude."

Jeremy Schaap, best-selling author of Cinderella Man:
James J. Braddock, Max Baer and the Greatest Upset in Boxing History,
and Triumph: The Untold Story of Jesse Owens and Hitler's Olympics

Where else can you find a cast that includes the Roman General Trajan, Simon Bar Kochba, Christopher Columbus, A.G. Spalding, William Howard Taft, Babe Ruth, Arnold Rothstein, Jackie Robinson, William Tecumsah Sherman, and Ernie Banks?

"Merkle's Curse" is a terrific read that gives new meaning to the term "fantasy baseball." You don't have to necessarily be a fan though to enjoy a wonderful book that craftily blends history, sports and whimsy.

Mike Leiderman Award-winning
Chicago sportscaster and producer

"At last, the truth! Thank you, Jerry Jacover."

Ellen Wright, author,
Pressing On: The Roni Stoneman Story

This is a fascinating tapestry to enthrall both baseball fans and readers who loved The DaVinci Code. The author embeds a treasure trove of little known baseball lore and historic play-by-plays in his tale of a 100 year curse on the Cubs. But the dazzling origins of the curse take readers back to the court of Constantine and then to Dracula's Transylvania. There a band of heroic orphans originates the bloodlines that carry the power to bless and curse, and whose families' separate and rejoin and eventually include Babe Ruth and Jackie Robinson. A great read for baseball fans, history buffs, and lovers of great big yarns.

Jean Ward, online magazine editor;
former book reviewer, Pioneer Press

MERKLE'S
CURSE

MERKLE'S CURSE

why the Chicago Cubs have not won a world series since 1908

A NOVEL BY

JERRY JACOVER

TATE PUBLISHING & Enterprises

Published by Tate Publishing & Enterprises, LLC
127 E. Trade Center Terrace | Mustang, Oklahoma 73064 USA
1.888.361.9473 | www.tatepublishing.com

Tate Publishing is committed to excellence in the publishing industry. The company reflects the philosophy established by the founders, based on Psalm 68:11,
"The Lord gave the word and great was the company of those who published it."

Book design copyright © 2008 by Tate Publishing, LLC. All rights reserved.
Cover design by Jonathan Lindsey
Interior design by Benton Rudd

Published in the United States of America

ISBN: 978-1-60462-935-4
1. Adventure-Special Interest-Baseball
2. History
08.03.24

To my Dad,
who taught me how to play baseball;
and my Mom,
who let me play until the street lights came on.

ACKNOWLEDGMENTS

How does one properly acknowledge those who have provided me with the baseline of information that was needed to write this book? To the multitude of authors and other creative people of society—along with countless teachers, friends and family members—an impersonal "thank-you" hardly seems sufficient. Yet the passage of time and the limitations of memory prevent me from recalling what I learned from whom, when I learned it, and under what circumstances it entered my consciousness. As such, an impersonal "thank-you" is about the best that I can realistically offer.

Some of the factual information that appears in this book can, however, be attributable to specific sources. These sources include: Myers, Doug, *Essential Cubs* (1999), Snyder, John, *Cubs Journal* (2005), Robinson, Jackie, *I Never Had It Made* (1995), Overy, Richard, *Complete History of the World* (2004), Dimont, Max I., *Jews, God and History* (1962), Rubenstein, Richard E., *When Jesus Became God* (1999), Hertz, J.H., *The Pentateuch and Haftorahs* (1964). In addition, I consulted eclectic material that was made available on the Internet by many writers and compilers. I do not know how to properly acknowledge these people other than to mention them generally, and note that I kept a hard copy of almost all of the material that I used as a reference.

Certain individuals also warrant a heart-felt thanks. Foremost among them is a distinguished man of letters, Theron Raines. Not only did Mr. Raines provide initial encouragement for this project, he volunteered constructive criticism and thoughtful insights that pushed me toward the highest standard of excellence. To the extent I approached this standard, I must thank Mr. Raines; to the extent I came up short, I blame only myself.

My wife, Judi, and my three sons, Aric, Evan and Brian, also warrant special mention. Judi read and re-read the manuscript, never failing to provide helpful observations and needed encouragement. My sons did the same. In addition, over the years we watched, listened to and attended so many Cub games—including the Bartman game—that many of our baseball experiences must have found their way into the pages of this book. I can't thank my family enough for all they have done for me.

Numerous friends and other family members also took the trouble to read the manuscript in various stages of completion. Each, in their own way, provided me with welcomed encouragement. My parents, my sister, Renee, and my friends Ward Katz, Neil Baum, Bob Gilhooley and Steve Nasatir, are among the many who contributed in this way. I must also acknowledge my partners and friends at Brinks Hofer Gilson & Lione. Ellen Wright, an accomplished author in her own right, edited the transcript and corrected countless grammatical errors.

I must also thank the volunteer word processors who converted my initial drafts into a properly formatted, readable manuscript. These capable and cheerful professionals include Sandra Manolas, Chris Hernandez and Pam Ward. A final and sincere thank-you is also extended to my dedicated and loyal secretary, Lori Peterson. Lori has been my friend, aide and confidante for over seventeen years. Her good nature, thoughtfulness and competence has helped me through the most challenging times, and for that I will be eternally grateful.

CONTENTS

GENEALOGY

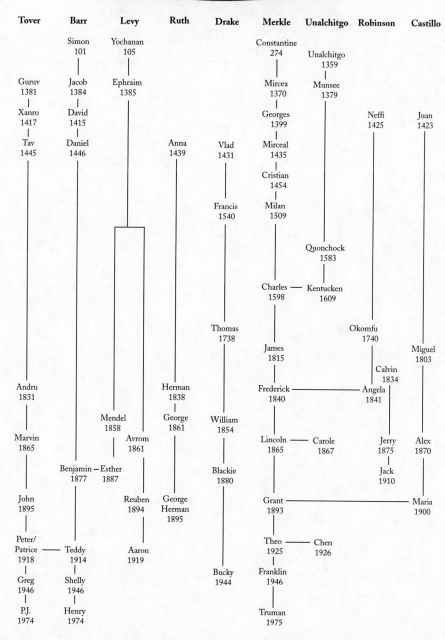

Tover	Barr	Levy	Ruth	Drake	Merkle	Unalchitgo	Robinson	Castillo
	Simon 101	Yochanan 105			Constantine 274	Unalchitgo 1359		
Guruv 1381	Jacob 1384	Ephraim 1385			Mircea 1370	Munsee 1379		
Xanro 1417	David 1415				Georges 1399		Neffi 1425	Juan 1423
Tav 1445	Daniel 1446		Anna 1439	Vlad 1431	Mirceal 1435			
					Cristian 1454			
				Francis 1540	Milan 1509			
						Quonchock 1583		
					Charles 1598	Kentucken 1609		
				Thomas 1738		Okomfu 1740		
					James 1815			Miguel 1803
							Calvin 1834	
Andru 1831			Herman 1838		Frederick 1840	Angela 1841		
		Mendel 1858	George 1861	William 1854				
Marvin 1865		Avrom 1861			Lincoln 1865 — Carole 1867	Jerry 1875	Alex 1870	
	Benjamin — Esther 1877 1887			Blackie 1880		Jack 1910		
John 1895		Reuben 1894	George Herman 1895		Grant 1893			Maria 1900
Peter/ Patrice 1918 — Teddy 1914		Aaron 1919			Theo — Chen 1925 1926			
Greg 1946	Shelly 1946			Bucky 1944	Franklin 1946			
P.J. 1974	Henry 1974				Truman 1975			

PROLOGUE

Greg Tover emailed a high-importance message to his partner's Blackberry: "Got the tickets; P.J. and I'll meet you and Henry on the Wrigley side of Clark and Addison at 6 p.m."

Seconds later, Shelly Barr felt a vibration on his left hip. He removed his wireless from the plastic case, scrolled to Greg's text message, and grinned. Using the same device, he telephoned his son, Henry, who worked as a software engineer at a small start-up on the northwest side.

Henry noted the caller i.d. "Did we get 'em?" he asked.

"All four," Shelly answered, trying to restrain his excitement. "We're meeting the Tovers at the ballpark at six." Shelly glanced at his Timex. It was almost 3:45. "I'll pick you up at your office in an hour."

"I'll be outside," Henry said, his enthusiasm muted by a nagging feeling of uneasiness. But then his spirits rose. "What could be better than Wrigley in October?" He smiled when he contemplated the difference between the Cubs and the Florida Marlins. "Do their fans even know where their team's playing?" he asked himself. He shook his head. "They don't deserve a pennant." Then he smiled again, comforted with the knowledge that if the game was close, it would be the exuberant hometown Cub fans who would determine the outcome.

The moment Henry hung up, Shelly sent an email to his partner.

"Confirmed." By then Greg was already on the phone with his son, P.J., an orthopedic resident at Mt. Holyoke Hospital in north suburban Evanston.

"You still on?" Greg asked.

"I've traded rotations for Thanksgiving and Christmas. Wouldn't miss it for the world." P.J. momentarily put his hand over the mouthpiece of his phone, and turned to a nurse who was looking at him impatiently. "I'll be right there," he told her. Then he uncovered the mouthpiece of his cell. "Gotta go now, dad. I'll meet you at the Howard El around five. We'll take the train—like old times."

Greg grinned. Then he looked at his watch—not for the time, but for the date. "October 14, 2003," he said to himself. "This is gonna be one of the greatest days in Cub history," he thought, brushing aside the nagging worries he and his son had been harboring throughout the summer.

The platform on the Howard El was overflowing with Cub fans. Not all of them had tickets; some just wanted to be in the vicinity of the "friendly confines" when the Cubs would win the game, and their first trip to the World Series in almost sixty years. Greg and P.J. Tover sidled their way onto one of the cars, and the train lurched forward.

At each stop, additional fans squeezed onto the train. At one stop the Tovers came face-to-face with a station sign that read, "Foster Ave—5200 North." It reminded Greg of his many childhood trips to Wrigley. It was a happy childhood, marred only by the painful futility of his favorite team. P.J., meanwhile, reached under his green scrub shirt, grabbed an old bronze medallion that hung around his neck, and squeezed it for good luck.

Shelly Barr arrived at his son's office five minutes early. He stopped his Grand Cherokee by the curb in front of the loft building where his son worked. A few moments later Henry emerged, a blue Cub hat propped on his curly, auburn hair.

Shelly knew the expressway would be at a standstill, so he opted for the less congested city boulevards. Suddenly he veered off onto a narrow one-way street. Henry started to protest, but bit his lip instead. It was only after Shelly pulled up in front of a red brick bungalow that Henry nodded with recognition. It was the home where his father grew up.

"I stopped here for good luck," Shelly told his son. Then he looked nostalgically at the front porch of the tiny house. "Every day, after I read the morning paper, I hoped I'd live long enough to see the Cubs in the World Series." Shelly paused for a few more moments before putting the car back into gear. "This is gonna be the year!" he said as he pulled away from the curb.

Shelly parked the car in a surface lot that was over a mile from Wrigley Field. As he and his son walked toward the corner of Clark and Addison, Henry unzipped his jacket and reflexively clutched a bronze medallion, identical to the one worn by his cousin, P.J. Like P.J., he had received that medallion from his father on the day he got married.

Over 40,000 ticket holders converged on Wrigley Field; tens of thousands of ticketless fans spilled onto the neighboring streets and sidewalks. All of them, and the countless millions of Cub fans who would watch the game on TV or listen to it on the radio, shared a rush of excitement in expectation of a glorious Cub victory.

Unlike that of their fellow Cub fans, the excitement of the Tovers and the Barrs was tempered by a dark feeling of apprehension. Their anxiety was well-founded. They, alone, knew that the Cubs were *really* cursed, and they, alone, were in possession of the clues that could alter their team's fate.

PART I
TRANSYLVANIA

VLAD'S SPEAR

In the second year of the second century of the Common Era, Roman legionnaires under the command of General Trajan crossed the Danube River, scaled the thickly wooded crests of the Carpathian Mountains and looked down upon a valley of pastoral splendor. Trajan called the valley Trans-Silva, Latin for "beyond the woods." Roman citizens colonized the land, intermarried with the indigenous Dacian stock, and substituted a Latinized language for the native tongue. In due course the valley and its environs became known as Transylvania, and this "land of the Romans" was called Romania.

In true Roman fashion, Trajan began building roads through the woods and bridges over the streams. Then, thirty years later, Trajan's legions were abruptly reassigned by Hadrian, Emperor of Rome. This left the land pregnable to attack by barbarians from the north.

In the ensuing centuries the land fell prey to successive waves of Goths, Vandals, Angles, Saxons, Huns, and Slavs. They invaded, pillaged, and withdrew with a regularity reminiscent of the ebb and flow of the Black Sea tides. And though the Romanians had, by then, embraced the Eastern Church in Constantinople, it was too distant, and too weak, to offer any assistance against the pagan hordes.

In the fourteenth century there arose from the south a more ominous threat—the Ottoman Turks, carrying the green banner of Islam.

The land became rife with rumors of the terrible fate that befell those martyrs of the Eastern Church who had earlier rejected their conquerors' edict that they "convert or die." After centuries of poverty, cruelty and war, "hope" among the Romanian people did not exist as a realistic expectation of a better future; it existed only as an amalgam of prayer, superstition, loathing, and revenge formed in a crucible of fictional legend rather than factual history.

It was in those days of despair that there arose a man who would successfully lead the Romanians through this crisis. He was known to his subjects as Mircea "the Old," King of the Romanian Principality of Wallachia. The local people pronounced the first syllable of their sovereign's name as if it rhymed with "birch," the majestic, white-trunked trees that forested the local hillsides. Mircea traced his royal line all the way back to the first Christian Emperor of Rome—Constantine the Great.

Mircea's strategy was simple enough. He would form an alliance with the greater German Empire that exercised hegemony over the realms to the west. Such a pact had, of course, the potential to cause great controversy at home because of the existing schism between the German's Church of the Pope and the Romanian Church of the East. Mircea was nonetheless convinced that the risk was warranted. If all went well, the alliance would give Romania a veneer of strength that would discourage the Ottoman invaders from attacking Wallachia; instead they would prey upon more vulnerable targets in the south Balkans.

Mircea knew, however, that even if this tactic were successful, it would only be a matter of time before the Turks would cast their imperialistic eye toward the Principalities of Romania. He planned to use this time to create a disciplined army that could defend the homeland. Toward this end Mircea recruited a cadre of Wallachian youth, including his son Georges, heir to the Wallachian throne. He sent them for military training in Black Forest Baveria at the Fraternal Order of the Bund of the Ruth—which meant "Bond of the Red" in the native language. It was there that they would learn the chivalry, honor, and methods of war perfected over the centuries by the German Empire.

Georges left a boy, but returned a knight. His shield bore the frightening image of an upright dragon holding a spear in one claw and a cross in the other. His brigade was appropriately known as the Royal Order of the Dracul, "dracul" meaning "dragon" in the local Wallachian tongue. The Draculs wore blood red garments, emblematic of their Ruthian bond, and green cloaks, symbolic of a dragon's scales.

Several years after his return to Wallachia, Georges succeeded Mircea as king. He ruled wisely, and was adored by his subjects. Among other things, he inculcated a culture of cooperation among the three Romanian principalities of Wallachia, Transylvania and Moldavia. It was in that spirit of Romanian brotherhood that he moved his capital from the southern province of Wallachia to a more central location in Transylvania. In the process, he implemented a revolutionary way of creating freedom and prosperity which he called "The System of Pebbles."

In order to protect his people, Georges used his disciplined brigade of Draculs as the foundation of a formidable army. Thus, just as his father had hoped, when the Ottoman Turks resumed their inexorable march into Eastern Europe, the three Principalities of Romania were spared from the murder, carnage and forced conversions inflicted by the Turks on the less organized Bulgar populations that lived south of the Danube.

In Transylvania, Georges and his wife Sofia built an enormous stone castle with strong ramparts and lofty spires. It was there that their three children were born—a son Vlad in 1431, a son Mirceal in 1435, and a daughter Anna in 1439. The middle-child's name was a common variant of that of his grandfather, the revered King of Wallachia.

As the children grew into young adults, it was apparent to all that they bore no resemblance to each other but for a head of thick black hair. Vlad was tall and angular. He had a long face punctuated by dark, deep-set eyes, a large nose, and thin lips. His complexion was chalky in color and texture.

Mirceal had much softer features. He was somewhat shorter than his brother, but considerably more muscular and athletic. His cheeks also bore a distinct pallor, though his smile and demeanor were warm and comforting.

Anna, unfortunately, was a rather homely girl. She was thick-boned, had a stout neck, and a large head. Unlike her brothers, Anna had a ruddy complexion and thick, full lips. She was strong of body, and filled with the exuberant spirit of youth.

On his twenty-first birthday, Vlad was given a Dracul shield and ceremoniously inducted into the Royal Order. It was an honor he had not earned. Nonetheless, the young prince relished in the accoutrements of knighthood. But his penchant for bullying and cruelty soon became renowned throughout the kingdom. He became estranged from his father, and no longer considered himself the son of Georges, but the son of a militant sect within the Dracul Order. As a result, Vlad became known simply as Dracula, the suffix "a" in the local dialect meaning "son of."

Ironically, the word "dracul" meant both "dragon" and "Satan" in the parlance of the Wallachia. It was by this curiosity of language that Vlad became in words what he was to become by deed—the son of a dragon, and the son of the devil.

Vlad's powerlust was of grave concern to his parents. Four years following his son's investiture into the Royal Order, Georges discussed the matter in the sitting room of his castle with his wife, Sofia.

"I fear our sons are like Esau and Jacob of the old bible," said the king.

"In what way, My Lord?"

"Vlad is hostile and rash, like Esau; Mirceal is resolute and pensive, like Jacob," he answered.

"Who, then, would make the better king?" Sofia inquired.

"Solomon the wise was a better king than David the warrior," he replied, "and so it is that Mirceal would be a superior king to Vlad."

"But is not Vlad, by primacy of birth, the lawful heir to your throne, My Lord?"

"Perhaps," said the king, "but does not the old Bible also tell us that the older brother shall serve the younger?"

Vlad, standing outside the sitting room door which was inadvertently left ajar, had eavesdropped on his parents' conversation; his veins now pulsed with anger and hate.

"I will never serve my brother," he growled under his breath. "On my oath as a knight, the blood of Mirceal, and that of his proponents—even if they be my own parents—will drip from my spear." Vlad was already plotting his vengeance as he retreated stealthily down the corridor.

"And what shall become of your daughter?" Sofia continued, unaware that their conversation had been overheard.

"Anna will be blessed with children. The fruit of her womb will be acclaimed for his feats of strength and skill throughout the world, and remembered across the generations."

Sofia smiled. "And what will be our fate, My Lord."

"We will die as we have lived; embraced in everlasting love."

The king's prophecy came true that evening. An enraged Vlad violated his parents' chambers and murdered them with Mirceal's sword as they slumbered together in each others' arms. Through the open window, Dracula saw a comet light up the moonless night as it moved lazily across the October sky. Vlad thought this was a good omen— a signal that his deeds were sanctioned by the gods. By right of birth, his act of patricide made him King of Romania.

Dracula deliberately left the bloody sword at his parents' bedside in order to frame Mirceal for his own cowardly crimes. He then sped to the room of his brother whom he intended to slay in alleged retribution for his parents' murder. Inexplicably, neither Mirceal nor his sister could be found. Incensed, Vlad awakened his knights, whose obedience to the new king they were bound to by both oath and law.

"They murdered the king!" he bellowed." Find them and deliver them to me, dead or alive."

Mirceal and Anna had spent the late evening hours in the castle garden watching the comet as it progressed through its perihelion—the point of closest approach to the earthly sun. They were interrupted by a tumult coming from within the walls, and then horrified to hear the orders emanating from the lips of their own brother. Mirceal reached for his sister's hand, ran with her across the garden, and scaled the stone wall that defined its border. Moments later guards began fanning across the garden precincts, torches in hand. Mirceal and Anna pressed themselves against the cold granite courses and held their breath. Eventually the guardsmen directed their search elsewhere.

"We must flee," whispered Anna.

Mirceal nodded. He grabbed her hand again, and together they ran into the night. They moved swiftly through the royal orchards, past the harvested fields, and along a cart path that led into the dark, forbidding woods. There they collapsed into a clump of bushes, exhausted.

By morning, news of the murders had spread through the land. Grief for the beloved king was sincere. A sense of vengeance for their murderer was palpable.

Mirceal and Anna could not be found despite a kingdom-wide search. This infuriated the new monarch even more, resulting in a royal edict that anyone aiding or abetting the siblings would be summarily executed by impaling. This cruel form of torture involved spearing a victim through the buttocks until the pointed lance emerged through the mouth of the condemned. The spear, with the impaled body still attached, would then be implanted in the earth as a warning to any who dared to offend the new king.

Because of Dracula's bloodlust, the death sentence was enforced even in the absence of evidence. Mere rumor or suspicion would be enough to effect this cruel decree. It was enforced against men and women, boys and girls—even babies. The Transylvania countryside became a forest of writhing bodies and disintegrating corpses.

It was in this way that the light of the comet would forever be remembered as an omen of misery and tears, and Vlad's spear would stand as a permanent reminder of torture and death.

GURUV'S AXE

Fifteen hundred years before the Common Era a fair-skinned race of people left their native land and swarmed into the valley of the great river that drained the northwest border of the Indian sub-continent. These people were called Aryans, which means "nobles" in the ancient Sanskrit language. Their place of origin, therefore, became known as Iran—land of the Aryans.

Upon their arrival in the Indus valley, the Aryans encountered a straight-haired, dark-complexioned people who called themselves "Dravidians." The Aryans believed they were a superior race to the Dravidian natives. They imposed strict rules of separation between themselves and the brown-skinned people with whom they shared the land. Over time, this primitive form of segregation evolved into a rigid social hierarchy. It was in this way that the Indian caste system was born, determining each person's station at birth and lot in life.

Through the centuries, the Indo-Aryan peoples fragmented into a multiplicity of tribes, linguistic groups and sub-cultures. One such sub-culture that arose in the northwest Punjab region of the Indian peninsula was a swarthy and superstitious people known as the Romani, named for their peculiar Hindi dialect. Though the Romani engaged in numerous caste-prescribed occupations, they were most renowned for their skill as metal workers. Because they were so talented at making swords, honing weapons and fashioning horseshoes, the Romani became a necessary adjunct to the Indian military. And so, when Muslim armies marched into the Indus Valley in the fourteenth century of the Common Era, the Romani played a major role in their defeat.

The Romani were justifiably angry and bitter when they returned from the holy wars to an ungrateful, even antagonistic, Indian nation. This, in turn, led to a momentous decision by leaders of several Romani clans—they would leave the Indus Valley, which had been home to their people through the millennia. The ensuing Romani migration initially followed the trade routes west through south-central Asia. It then passed across the Ottoman lands and ultimately into the Balkan Peninsula.

Throughout the generations, wagon after wagon, pulled by horses or water buffalo, delivered Romani families into the continent of Europe. One such family was headed by a blacksmith named Guruv Tover. In the Romani language, a "tover" was a two-headed axe of the type Guruv was expert in making. Guruv's wife, Kali, made a drawing of the axe-head which the family painted on their wagons and many other belongings. Guruv and Kali believed that the "sign of the tover" would ward off evil.

Over the years the Tover family had drifted throughout the Balkan Peninsula. Nowhere had they found acceptance, much less peace. By the mid-fifteenth century they had driven their wagons along old Roman roadbeds, over the Carpathian Mountains and into the Transylvania countryside.

Prohibited from owning land, and prevented from taking up residence inside the limits of any Romanian village, the Tovers could establish no permanent home. They resigned themselves to living in their wagons and eking out a living by sharpening knives, shoeing horses, and otherwise tinkering in metal. When that failed they resorted to fortune telling and omen reading.

The fact that the Tovers learned the local language and adopted the faith of the Eastern Church did nothing to diminish the animosities of the indigenous population. Indeed, all the Romani were maliciously referred to as tramps, beggars and thieves. Because of their swarthy complexions and superstitious ways, the local people erroneously believed that the Romani had originated in Egypt. It was for this reason that they were referred to as 'Gyptians, or more derogatorily—gypsies.

One morning Guruv Tover awoke at the first light of dawn and went to the bushes to urinate. To his astonishment, he saw a young man and woman sleeping in the weeds beneath his feet. Their royal garments at first gave him pause. But the oddity of the circumstances and the fact that their clothing was dirty and torn made it clear that the couple was on the run.

Mirceal and Anna were startled out of their slumber by the gray-haired stranger standing above them. He had a long, thick mustache that did not follow the downward curve of his upper lip, but extended in a straight line from the bridge of his nose all the way to the bottom of his cheekbones. A two-headed axe hung from his belt.

Anna's face turned ashen with fear.

"Do not be afraid," Guruv said softly. "You will come to no harm while you are with me."

Anna was immediately comforted. "What is your name, kind sir?" she inquired, after picking herself up and embarrassedly brushing the grass and leaves off her ankle-length dress.

Guruv introduced himself.

Mirceal did the same. "And this is my sister, Anna," he added quickly.

"From whom do you flee?" Guruv asked.

Mirceal and Anna exchanged cautious glances, but instinctively felt that the man could be trusted.

"Our brother is Vlad Dracula," offered Mirceal. "Last night he murdered our parents and declared himself king. His guard is out to kill us even as we speak."

"Then henceforth you shall be in my protection," said Guruv, extending his hand to Mirceal.

Mirceal hesitated momentarily when he saw a strange tattoo on Guruv's forearm. It was in the form of two equilateral triangles meeting at one of their apices.

"It's the mark of the axe—our family sign," Guruv explained. He pulled the wood-handled weapon with its glistening double-bladed axe head from his belt, and showed it to his new acquaintances. "We are expert in axe-making," he said proudly. "Come, you will now meet my family."

Mirceal and Anna followed Guruv to a little clearing beside a cart path. Four large wagons, each adorned with Tover's sign of the two-headed axe, were parked by the roadside. Several horses were tethered nearby.

Rustling from inside the wagons indicated that the Tover clan was rising to greet the new day. Voices of babies, children and adults could be heard above the clatter. From one of the wagons emerged a thin woman, wearing a long, fluffy white skirt and a colorful long-sleeved blouse. Her dark hair was parted down the middle and covered by a red scarf which was tied in a bow under her chin.

Guruv introduced the two visitors to his wife, and recounted the siblings' story.

"I told you that comet was a bad omen," she said tersely. "And what are we going to do when the Dracul guard comes to our camp looking for them?"

"They will dress as we do, and hide among us," Guruv said firmly.

"If we are caught, they will kill us and torture our children," Kali argued.

"I promised them my protection. Now take them and go," he ordered.

Mirceal and Anna disappeared into different canvas-covered wagons for their transformation into Romani garb. In the meantime the Tover clan came out from their wheeled homes and began their morning chores. There were actually four families in the clan, each occupying its own wagon. One wagon belonged to the patriarch Guruv; the others were occupied, in turn, by Guruv's three sons, and their respective wives and children. Like his father, Guruv's oldest son, Xanro, bore the joined triangle tattoo of the Tover on his right forearm. He also carried a double-headed axe in his belt.

Within fifteen minutes, Mirceal and Anna emerged from their wagons in colorful Romani costume.

"What should we do with these?" Kali asked Guruv, pointing with her chin to the siblings' soiled clothes, which were piled on her outstretched arms.

Guruv motioned her to the fire where his smithing work was done.

"In there," he said.

Kali dropped the garments into the fire. Guruv gave his bellows a few energetic pumps and the clothing burst into a bright, orange flame. Moments later, the clatter of hooves could be heard from the road. Two Dracul guards appeared, and galloped into the Tover camp. Guruv approached them on foot.

"We are looking for two members of the Royal House," the taller guard announced imperiously. "Prince Mirceal and his sister have disappeared. Have you seen them?"

"What would royals be doing in a place like this?" Guruv asked.

"Your place is to answer questions, not ask them, beggar," snarled the guard.

Guruv fidgeted nervously. "A thousand pardons, Your Worship," he stammered.

The smaller guard, meanwhile, had made a quick survey of the gypsy camp, but saw nothing that aroused his suspicion. "There is nobody here but tramps and thieves," he announced. Then he turned his steed in the direction from which he came, but the horse reared uncontrollably.

"He's thrown a shoe," Guruv warned.

The shorter man dismounted and inspected the animal's left foreleg. Then spotting the nearby fire and smithing tools, he ordered Guruv to make the necessary repairs.

The Draculs sat by the fire as Guruv did as he was told. When Xanro's wife came to add coal to the flames, the taller man eyed her lasciviously. She caught his gaze, but looked away immediately.

"The job is done," Guruv announced, leading the newly shod horse to its rider.

The Dracul inspected Guruv's work and appeared to be satisfied. "Let's be off then," he said, mounting his steed.

"We bid you farewell," said Guruv, anxiously wiping the soot-laden sweat off his brow with the back of his hand.

"Not so fast," interrupted the taller man, who was still standing by the fire, transfixed by the flames. With that, he pulled his saber from its sheath, poked it among the anthracite, and fished out a charred piece of blood-red cloth from among the embers. "Just how might the remnant of a royal blouse find its way into a gypsy fire?" he asked accusingly.

"It is our custom to wear red as well," Guruv countered, casting his eye toward Xanro's wife who was dressed in a bright red skirt.

The Dracul turned menacingly toward the woman and thrust the tip of his saber against her jugular. "The only red you will wear is blood!" he roared. "Now bring me the royals."

No one in the camp moved.

"Bring them to me," he repeated, twisting the saber until it drew a small stream of blood from the woman's neck.

Again, no one moved.

"Do it now," he threatened.

Suddenly a cry from a young woman cowering near one of the wagons broke the silence.

"Here I am," Anna wailed. "Take me and spare the woman. She knows nothing." Anna walked haltingly toward the Dracul, her hands raised high in the air.

The smaller Dracul approached Anna, grabbed her wrist, and pulled it painfully behind her back.

"She will bring us a fine reward on our return," he said gripping her arm more tightly.

"And this apple blossom will bring me a fine evening of comfort," said his companion, ogling Xanro's wife.

"I would sooner die than spend even a minute with the filth of you," she said through her fear.

"You will die either way," he sneered.

"Then I prefer to die now," she said, and mustering up whatever strength and courage remained in her trembling body, spat in her tormentor's face.

The tall man's jaw stiffened and the veins in his neck turned an ugly purple. "Then die you will!" he screamed, plunging the saber into the woman's throat, causing a geyser of blood to erupt from the wound.

Reflexively, Mirceal grabbed a spear and threw it with great force at the attacker. It struck the tall man between the shoulder blades and buried itself in his spine, killing him instantly. He fell in a heap on top of his dying victim. Simultaneously Xanru's two-headed axe whizzed through the air hitting the shorter Dracul in the middle of his forehead, cleaving his face like a cracked walnut.

Guruv Tover ran to the shorter Dracul, pulled his son's axe from the dead man's skull, and stared at his mutilated face. "This is bad," Guruv said quietly. "This is very bad. We must bury our child and leave this wretched land immediately."

By noon, the four Tover wagons were lumbering along the narrow cart path. The path intersected with a somewhat wider lane which merged into a well-traveled road leading to a nearby village. It was there that the Tovers could obtain the supplies needed for their long journey out of the country. As they approached a stone bridge that arched over a swift running brook marking the village limits, they saw over a dozen Dracul guards galloping toward them from the rear. The lieutenant of the platoon commanded them to stop.

"Search the wagons," he ordered. "The prince and his sister are hiding in them."

Simon's Coin

Almost 4,000 years ago, a Mesopotamian nomad the world now knows by the name of Abraham, had a brief encounter with God. It resulted in the first recorded exchange of promises between man and an incorporeal, monotheistic deity. For his part, Abraham agreed to accept this invisible deity as his one and only God. God, in turn, promised to make of Abraham a great nation and give his people a land that they would have as an everlasting possession. As a sign of this covenant, Abraham took a sharp stone and cut off a piece of his flesh at the fountain of his manhood—a rite of circumcision that his male heirs follow to this day.

Abraham and his extended family wandered through the Near East for many years. Eventually they crossed the Euphrates River and made their way to the Promised Land—a patch of desert that hugged the Eastern shore of the Great Sea. This insignificant clan of Abraham spoke a Mesopotamian dialect, the name of which later morphed into the word "Hebrew." It was in this way that the House of Abraham became known as Hebrews.

Abraham begot Isaac, Isaac begot Jacob, and Jacob begot twelve sons. Jacob's eleventh son, Joseph, became a viceroy in the powerful Kingdom of Egypt. In the midst of a great famine, Joseph invited the clan of Jacob, which was then known by the revered name of "Israel," to temporarily reside in the Egyptian Province of Goshen. Food was plentiful in Goshen, and so it was there that the Hebrews grew in numbers and prospered.

Some generations later there arose in Egypt a pharaoh who knew not Joseph. Fearing the growing strength of the Goshen Hebrews, this Pharaoh put them to work in mortar and brick. A few hundred years later, the Hebrews were liberated from bondage by a prophet known only as Moses. Moses led the Hebrews to the brink of the Promised Land. En route, he came into possession of a body of statutes and ordinances which became written into, and intermingled with, the long history of the Hebrew people. This document was sometimes called the Law of Moses, but the Hebrews referred to it more reverently as their "Torah," or teaching. The last book of the Torah teaches that, before they entered the Promised Land, Moses forewarned his people that they would be the object of both a blessing and a curse. How this prophecy would be fulfilled—and through whom—would remain a deep mystery.

Under the leadership of Joshua, Moses's chosen successor, the Hebrews re-conquered the Promised Land. The land was then parceled out among the twelve familial tribes who traced their lineage through the sons of Jacob. About 1000 years before the Common Era, the Hebrews named a warrior from the Tribe of Judah to be its king. David's shield bore the sign of a six-pointed star formed by two oppositely extending, but overlapping equilateral triangles. This Star of David soon came to symbolize both the Nation Israel, and the peculiar form of monotheism practiced by its people.

As Georges of Romania would do almost 2500 years later, David wanted to move his capital to a more central location. This, he hoped, would forge a bond of brotherhood among the Tribes of Israel. Eventually, he chose a dusty hamlet surrounded by hills, and called it Jerusalem—which meant "City of Peace" in the Hebrew tongue.

David's vision of brotherhood was short-lived. Upon the death of his successor, King Solomon, the Hebrew nation fractured into a Northern Kingdom and a Southern Kingdom. The Northern Kingdom consisted of ten of Israel's twelve tribes. In the year 722 before the Common Era, the kingdom of the north was defeated by Assyrian invaders. Its people were carried off into exile where they became "lost" in the greater populations of the Near East.

The Southern Kingdom, which included only the powerful clan of Judah, and its confederate, Benjamin, fared much better. It persevered off and on for almost another 700 years before being occupied by the armies of Rome. In the course of this long history as a nation, zealots under the leadership of Judah Maccabee, defeated even the Seleucid Greeks who introduced idolatry into the precincts of Jerusalem. This military victory is still celebrated today as the Festival of Hanukah, or "rededication," of the Holy City.

Because of its dominance by the Tribe of Judah, the land became known as Judea, the tribe's monotheistic religion became known as Judaism, and its people became known simply as Jews. The Jews had a fanatical loathing of Rome. With its Pantheon of gods, maniacal emperors, and culture of human sacrifice, torture and cruelty, the Roman Empire seemed an embodiment of blasphemers and barbarians. Jewish zealots believed the shackles of Roman tyranny could be broken only by war; the pacifists believed their freedom could be won by appeasement. Both, however, prayed that this was the moment for the arrival of the Messiah, harbinger of an era alluded to by the prophets, when each man would sit under his own fig tree and learn war no more.

It was into this hotbed of civil unrest that there emerged a Jewish preacher called Jesu, a common diminutive for the name of the Jewish hero, Joshua. When, on a hillside strewn with bleach-white stones, Jesu proclaimed that the law of the Torah went through him, the zealots believed he, too, was a blasphemer. Some of the pacifists, on the other hand, believed he was the Messiah—the anointed one—or in Greek, "the Christ."

The Jewish elders realized that the zealots were hoping to turn this controversy into a rationale for their longed-for revolt against Rome. The elders were also certain that this was a revolt that the zealots could not win. Indeed, the sages knew what the inevitable outcome would be: death, destruction and exile—the same fate that befell their brethren of the Northern Kingdom centuries earlier. And so it was hoped that when the Romans executed Jesu, the crisis would subside, and a cataclysmic confrontation with the armies of Rome would be avoided. Unfortunately, that is not what happened.

Less than fifty years later, the zealots had their revolt. The outcome was exactly that predicted by the Jewish sages a few decades earlier. Hundreds of thousands of Jews died in their unsuccessful battle for freedom, and its bloody aftermath. In the process, Jerusalem was sacked and the Holy Temple was destroyed. Nonetheless, sixty-two years later, in the year 132 of the Common Era, the zealots regrouped and revolted again. They were led by a charismatic leader known to history as Simon Bar Kochba—Simon, Son of a Star. Bar Kochba's enormous strength and magnetic personality was exceeded only by his supreme self-confidence—some would say arrogance.

Miraculously, the zealots defeated the vaunted army of Rome, and the Nation of Israel was reborn. Rumors spread that this seismic event presaged the coming of the Messiah. Indeed, many believed—including the revered sage Rabbi Akiba—that Bar Kochba was the Messiah incarnate.

With the Romans gone, Bar Kochba began organizing the framework for a secular civil administration. One of his first tasks was to re-establish Jerusalem as the eternal capital of the Jewish state. He also minted coins which had a Star of David on the obverse and the following message, framed by olive branches, on the reverse: "Year One In the Revolt to Redeem Israel."

But that year Bar Kochba's thoughts were primarily focused on war.

Daniel, Son of Asher, entered Bar Kochba's Jerusalem headquarters, beat his fist onto his breastplate, and proclaimed, "The people of Israel live!"

"So they do," Bar Kochba answered. "What news do you bring me?"

"It is not good. The Romans will never accept our independence."

"What choice do they have? Their legions are reduced to corpses rotting from the Galilee to Beersheba; their chariots are rusting on the field of battle; the statues of their gods lie in ruins."

"They will regather. They will bring legions from Gaul, and from the lands bordering the barbarians on the Danube."

"That will take years," Bar Kochba surmised. "In that time can't we fortify our defenses and reinforce our armies?"

"We have begun to do so already," said Daniel.

"And what can you report?"

"Our sons will fight like lions."

"How about the followers of Jesu?" Bar Kochba inquired.

"They hate the Romans as much as we do," Daniel answered. "But only those who bear the mark of Abraham will join us because only they still consider themselves Jews."

Bar Kochba sensed hesitation in the manner of his confidante, and gave his friend a reproachful look.

"The Romans will return," Daniel said with deep resignation. "If it takes two years, three years, four years ..." His voice trailed off.

"They must know that taking legions from the hinterlands will lead to their demise; the barbarians will ultimately overrun Rome itself."

"They must take that chance," warned Daniel. "If they don't crush our revolt, they will be facing insurrections in every province of their empire. They will either destroy us, or destroy themselves trying."

"Is there no chance that they will accept our terms for a peaceful co-existence?"

Daniel shook his head. "Tyrants are motivated by greed, cruelty, and power. Anything else, much less the peaceful world envisioned by our prophets, is simply beyond their imagination."

Bar Kochba's disappointment was betrayed only by an imperceptible tightening of the muscles in his chiseled beard-covered jaw. He knew, however, that his comrade spoke the truth. "Thank you for your candor, my friend. That is all for now."

"Shalom Aleichem—go in peace," Daniel said as he took his leave.

"Aleichem Shalom," Bar Kochba responded.

The young officer left the room, leaving Bar Kochba alone with his thoughts. Within an hour this Son of a Star knew exactly what must be done. And so, later that very afternoon, Bar Kochba sought out his mentor, Rabbi Akiba, to confirm that his plan was grounded in the religious law of his people. He found the great scholar on the Mount of Zion—the place where the Holy Temple stood before it was destroyed by Rome at the end of the first rebellion. Enroute up the steep slope, he passed a huge retaining wall, the only remnant of the Temple compound. Many Jews were praying at the Wall—their supplications being distorted by the wind as moans and wails.

Bar Kochba found Akiba and his disciples sitting among the broken pilasters that once formed the esplanade leading to the Holy Sanctuary.

"Peace unto you," Bar Kochba greeted the scholar.

"And unto you," said Akiba in a strong voice that belied his ninety years of age.

Two marmots chased each other through the rocks and debris where the inner sanctum of the Temple—the Holy of Holies—once stood. "Woe is us," said one of Akiba's disciples. "How sad it is to see that this holy place has been reduced to a playground for varmints and vermin."

"It is an occasion for joy, not sadness," reproved the great rabbi. "For is it not written that, as hope is born from despair, so the Temple will be destroyed and rebuilt? How could it be rebuilt if it were not first destroyed; and how could we have hope if we do not first have despair?"

"So the destruction of the Temple should give us joy?" the disciple asked.

"It gives us far more," Akiba explained. "It gives us the Messiah."

The disciples looked bewildered.

"I ask you this," the rabbi continued, "if the holy writings are so accurate that they foretell such a calamity as the Temple's destruction, will they not be equally correct when they predict such a delight as the advent of our Messiah?"

The great rabbi turned abruptly toward Bar Kochba when he spoke the word "Messiah." "And what brings us the pleasure of your company?"

"I, too, have a question, rabbi. Is it a sin to take a scroll of the Torah out of David's City, out of the land itself?"

"Not only is it no sin," he answered, "it is a commandment that we spread the word of God to all the peoples of the earth. As it is written: 'from Zion shall come forth the Torah, and the word of the Lord from Jerusalem.'"

That night Bar Kochba met again with Daniel, Son of Asher.

"You are to take my wife and my young son, along with your own family, and leave this land. You are to be accompanied by six of your most trusted soldiers, and their families. Joining you will be Yochanan Levi, one of Akiba's disciples, who will bring with him a copy of our holy scrolls. You are to take horses and provisions for a long journey, and go to a region beyond the great River Danube—beyond the reach of the Roman fist. There you will form a community where the visions of our prophets for a better world on this earth may take root and flourish."

Daniel was about to protest when Bar Kochba put up his hand. "This is my order; it is commanded by our law according to Akiba, himself."

The next morning Bar Kochba met with his wife and family for the last time. He took a coin from his realm and fashioned it with an eyelet and a chain. Somewhat clumsily, he placed the chain around the neck of his wife.

"Remember me by this," he said adoringly, "and give it to my son when he comes of age. Now go, and may God be with you."

"And with you," she said through her tears.

The caravan followed a well known road through the Judean Hills into the coastal plain, and then along the Great Sea toward the Carmel Mountains near Acco. The only exit through the mountains was via a pass at Har Megiddo—the word "Har" meaning "Mount" in the local language. After passing through the gap at Har Megiddo, it was relatively easy to follow the Sea to the ancient cities of Tyre, Sidon, and Antioch. At Antioch they left the coast, and proceeded north into the province of Galacia. After a difficult trek through rugged inland terrain, they finally arrived at the great Black Sea straits. It had taken them over a year to reach that place.

At the Black Sea straits they encountered a massive Roman army, under the leadership of General Trajan, marching in the direction from which they had come. The army consisted of thousands upon thousands of Roman soldiers, each armed with sword and shield. Following the foot soldiers came the cavalry; following the cavalry came the war chariots; following the war chariots came the engineers; following the engineers came the wagons of provisions. It took days for the army to pass.

Daniel, Son of Asher, quickly learned that Trajan had been ordered by the emperor to leave the place north of the Danube where he had been stationed for over three decades.

"That, then will be our destination," Daniel concluded. "We will be safe there, just as Bar Kochba had predicted."

Daniel shuddered, however, when he learned Trajan's destination: Judea, renamed Palestina in an effort by the Roman emperor to forever blot out the name of the Jews in their own land. Daniel told no one in his company of travelers where Trajan was headed. If Bar Kochba's wife knew, she had the good sense not to say.

After traveling two years, and covering a distance of a thousand miles, the caravan crossed the Danube, passed through the Carpagian Mountains, and found itself on a well-worn Roman road. In the distance Daniel saw that the road crossed a rushing stream via a Roman built stone bridge.

"We will make our new home here," he announced. "The stream will provide our water, the land will provide our food, and the God of Abraham, Isaac, and Jacob will provide us with whatever else we may need."

As Daniel, Son of Asher, was offering these words of hope, the legions of Trajan were attempting to make their way into Judea via the pass at Har Megiddo. They were cut down and annihilated by Bar Kochba's army. First hundreds, then thousands, then tens of thousands of Roman soldiers were slashed to pieces. The pass became a repository of blood and gore.

But when one Roman legion was destroyed, it was replaced by another, and another. In the end, Rome's greatest general was called in from Britannia, leading an army of 35,000 legionnaires—far more than Alexander had needed to conquer the entire world.

It was in this way that Rome finally defeated Bar Kochba, and reconquered Judea. Instead of blotting out the name of the Jews, however, it marked the high-water mark of the Roman Empire before its precipitous decline, culminating with the sack of Rome by the Visigoths in 410. And the battle at Har Megiddo became synonymous with a final cataclysmic struggle between good and evil. Today it is known as Armageddon.

EUSEBIUS'S EPIPHANY

In the spring of 325, over 250 bishops from all over the Roman Empire began congregating at the summer residence of Constantine the Great, Emperor of Rome. The residence was located on the Lake of Nicaea, about 200 miles east of the metropolis growing on the opposite side of the Bosporus that the locals had already begun referring to as Constantinople—Constantine's City. History would refer to this congregation of clergy as the Great Council of Nicaea.

Twenty-three years before the Great Council convened, Constantine formally adopted the religion of his Christian mother, Helena Augusta. This occurred after he saw a fiery cross in the eastern sky. At the time, Constantine was leading his army from Britannia to Rome where he intended to challenge Maxentius for control of the western half of the Roman Empire. Shortly before the competing armies clashed on the banks of the Tiber, Constantine changed his army's standards from the sign of Apollo to the sign of the cross. In the ensuing battle, Maxentius's army was soundly defeated. Twelve years later, Constantine routed the forces of Licinius at Hadrianopolis, and thus became Caesar Augustus, supreme ruler of the entire Roman Empire.

Though Constantine accepted Christianity, he refused to be baptized. He made that decision in an effort to avoid an eternity of dam-

nation that he believed his sin-filled duties as emperor would necessarily cause. Only on his deathbed, after being relieved of his kingly
obligations, would he allow the baptismal waters of Christianity to
touch his body. In that way he could die without sin, and achieve everlasting life, through his Savior, Jesus Christ.

It was to resolve a theological dispute about the very nature of Jesus
that the Great Council of Nicaea was originally convened. Though the
dispute began in Alexandria—then the largest city in the world—it
was causing turmoil and dissension from Libya to Syria. If immediate action wasn't taken to remedy the problem, the divisiveness could
spread to all the other Greek-speaking provinces, and thereby fracture
the empire.

On one side of the dispute were the followers of an Alexandrian
priest by the name of Arius. Arius was a tall, handsome and scholarly
man, then in his sixtieth year. Arius represented the long-held and
wide-spread belief that Jesus was born a person, but elevated to the
divine by God because of His sublime life on earth, and His supreme
sacrifice in death.

On the other side of the dispute was a passionate, red-haired priest,
also from Alexandria, whose name was Athanasius. Athanasius was
considerably younger than his antagonist, but every bit his intellec-
tual equal. It was Athanasius's position that Jesus was not merely the
adopted Son of God. He was God incarnate who came to earth, suffered, and was crucified solely to show people of faith the path to eternal life. Since the path to eternal life could be provided by nothing
less than God, any denial that Jesus was the Lord on earth rendered a
Christian's salvation impossible.

Not a scholar himself, Constantine could barely distinguish the
difference between these two theological positions. Nor did he com-
prehend why they caused such civil unrest throughout such a large
part of his empire. As a sovereign, however, Constantine instinctly
understood that such civil unrest represented a clear and present
danger to his imperial rule. He also knew that it would be best to
resolve this internecine controversy conclusively, but peacefully.

For the dogmatic Athanasius, the controversy was not merely one of
semantics. Its outcome would determine the future of Christianity and
the fate of countless human souls. In an effort to discredit Athanasius's

arguments, Arius attempted to discredit Athanasius, himself. He did so by publicly accusing the volatile priest of corruption, extortion, licentiousness, vulgarity and outright violence. The bishops arriving at Nicaea in 325 were well aware of these allegations.

As each of the bishops and their lieges entered the precincts of Constantine's residence, they were warmly greeted by a cadre of the emperor's soldiers and servants. Many of the arrivals bore scars from the terrible persecutions of Constantine's predecessors, which took the form of gouged eyeballs, torn limbs and grotesquely burnt skin. Nonetheless, it was with a feeling of triumph and jubilation that the clergy settled into their comfortable guest quarters. They were, after all, being welcomed into the residential compound of the world's first Christian monarch.

In the first session of the conclave, the clergy assembled in the Great Hall of Constantine's summer palace. The bishops entered first, and seated themselves on wooden benches in the front of the hall; then came the priests, followed by the deacons and the servants. After a deliberately long wait, Constantine made a grand entrance, adorned in royal robes and a gold crown. Everyone rose, and remained standing until the emperor seated himself on a three-legged wooden throne facing the benches.

With a nod from Constantine, the emperor's friend and confidant, Bishop Eusebius of nearby Nicomedia, made some brief opening remarks in which he profusely thanked the emperor for his hospitality. The emperor, in turn, gave a short, impromptu welcoming address, urging the bishops to reconcile their differences for the sake of the empire and their church. He concluded with an admonition that disorder is the work of the devil. "Do not let him achieve by discord, what your tormentors could not achieve by torture."

Then the business of the Great Council began in earnest.

Being only a priest, Arius was not permitted to speak for himself. It was Bishop Paulinas of Tyre who spoke on his behalf. "To argue that God and Jesus are one is to deny the truth of our own Gospels. Do they not tell us that when Jesus was suffering on the cross, He cried out in his anguish, 'My God, why hast thou forsaken me?' Are we to believe He was talking to Himself?"

Bishop Alexander of Alexandria joined the debate on behalf of

Athanasius. "God was not talking to Himself, but to us. For the Creator to enter the realm of the flesh and blood to show us the path to salvation by experiencing pain and suffering is the ultimate demonstration of love and compassion."

"It is inconceivable that our omnipotent, omniscient God—the creator of the universe—could experience pain."

"It is inconceivable that our good and benevolent God, creator of all flesh, would do anything less for the purpose of showing us the way to everlasting life."

"God created Jesus and made Him divine."

"Jesus was begotten, not made."

"They are both divine, but of a different nature."

"There cannot be two natures in the same divinity."

Over the course of two weeks, Constantine listened patiently to the arguments of both sides. In the end, however, he knew that there could not be one God of two natures any more than there could be one Caesar Augustus having two heads.

"God and Jesus are homoousios, of the same essence," he concluded.

And so a draft of the Christian Creed with nothing more than these words distinguishing the anti-Arians from the Arians was put before the assembled bishops for their consideration.

When all but Arius and a few of his most head-strong supporters fixed their signatures to the final Creed documents, it was their host whom the bishops lauded and cheered.

"Long live Constantine," Bishop Alexander shouted.

"May he live a hundred years!" Bishop Eusebius exulted. "May his kingdom on earth last for twenty-five generations!" he exclaimed.

It was then that Arius rose to his feet in anger, and in one final effort to yet have his way, falsely accused Athanasius of the vilest and most contemptible deeds. Though Arius's outburst was not a crime against the state, it was a grave insult to the Great Council—and it warranted retribution. The retribution came swiftly. Arius was expelled from the conclave and excommunicated from the church. Nonetheless, Athanasius remained deeply troubled, and confided his concerns to Bishop Eusebius that very evening, after the day's session was adjourned.

Eusebius looked pensively at the young priest, nervously brushing his palms across his graying temples. "Are you suggesting that Arius should have been arrested?" he asked.

Athanasius shook his head. "That would only make him a martyr and thereby further his cause," the Alexandrian priest replied.

"Then what course of action would you suggest?"

Athanasius's eyes darted left and right. "Curse his name," he answered angrily.

The bishop's jaw dropped. Then slowly his expression morphed into a wry smile. "Curse the name of Arius," he whispered, slowly brushing his hands through his hair once again. "Of course," he said to himself, his eyes now sparkling with understanding and purpose. "Curse the name of Arius," he repeated, this time with more resolve.

"Then it can be done?" Athanasius asked hopefully.

The bishop gave a distinct but distant nod, still overwhelmed by his epiphany.

"Then if I may be so bold," Athanasius continued, "there is yet one more thing that I must request."

Eusebius's eyes were momentarily fixed in space, as if he were looking for some celestial object.

"My good name is being ruined by lies and innuendoes," Athanasius began to explain.

Eusebius raised his hand, momentarily silencing the priest. "You want your good name blessed and your reputation restored," the bishop said placidly.

Athanasius looked down.

The bishop patted Athanasius on the head. "I understand," he said. "And if you will place your trust in me, it will all be done, just as you have wished."

Athanasius raised his eyes.

Eusebius briefly smiled, and then turned his gaze toward the clear, evening sky. The sun had just dipped below the western horizon, casting a bright crimson hue across the heavens. "Meet me at the Church of Helena Augusta when the pole star appears in the north," he said, turning in the direction of the large stone chapel that the emperor had named for his mother. "Wait patiently, and tell no one of this conversation."

Athanasius bowed, then took his leave.

Later that night, when the two celestial lights of the great dipper could be seen pointing to the star that had guided sailors across the Mediterranean for centuries, Athanasius made his way to the church. He sat in a front pew and waited for the bishop as he was told. When no one appeared even after the passage of half the time needed to empty an hour glass, he feared that he had misunderstood the bishop's orders. He began to doze off after the passage of yet another half an hour.

He was startled out of his dreams by the voice of Eusebius. "You are a man of patience and faith," he said. "And for that you will be rewarded."

Athanasius turned, and in the dim torch light saw the shadows of several men moving toward him. He was shocked to discover that one of them, resplendent in his purple robes and golden crown, was the emperor himself.

Athanasius's Elevation

Athanasius bowed nervously before the king

"As you were," Constantine ordered.

Athanasius straightened. It was then that he recognized two other figures from the council proceedings—martyred priests from Miletus and Ephesus. The former carried a crutch because he was missing a leg. The latter's face was terribly disfigured from what must have been a painful test of his faith; he wore a black patch to cover the socket where a living eye once dwelt.

"Follow me," Eusebius commanded. The bishop then walked briskly up the steps to the altar and through a black curtain that hid a small space at the rear. Thick, white candles illuminated the area; the pungent odor of incense was unmistakable. The candlelight revealed a simple oaken table on which stood a magnificent two-handled silver pitcher resting in a matching silver bowl. On the far wall hung a large Greek cross fashioned of silver and inlaid with precious stones. The cross bar and upright were of equal size; their ends were flared into intricately-worked, pointed tips.

It was Constantine who spoke next. "On the day I witnessed the fiery cross in the sky, and accepted the religion of my dear mother, I also saw something else: the words, *Touto nika*—By this, conquer. And so I conquered." The emperor paused so that the others could acknowledge his accomplishment. Then his expression turned grave.

"On the very day that this Great Council convened, I saw the fiery cross once again." The emperor waited for the murmurs of surprise to subside before continuing. "But this time the words were different. They said, "*Nomen Maledicto*—Curse the Name, followed by the numeral 'C.'"

Athanasius gasped.

"I did not know what this message meant so I asked Bishop Eusebius to interpret it. Unfortunately, this he could not do."

Eusebius acknowledged the emperor's comments with a conspicuous nod.

Constantine then continued. "The next day the cross of fire again appeared, but again the words were different. This time they said, *Nomen Benedicto*—Bless the Name, followed by the numerals 'XXV.'"

"Once again I consulted Eusebius, but he did not understand the meaning of this message any more than he understood the meaning of the words of the night before."

Eusebius nodded again. Athanasius's face turned white.

"It will be all right," Eusebius whispered to him.

Constantine looked into the faces of the holy men that stood beside him before resuming. "Each night after that, throughout the entire course of this conclave, the fiery cross reappeared. But the message alternated from one day to the next: first, 'Curse the Name,' then 'Bless the Name.' I knew not what they meant," he confessed. Constantine paused to take a sip of water from a bejeweled chalice.

"It was only this evening, after Bishop Eusebius met with our brother, Athanasius, that the meaning of these words was revealed." The emperor took another sip of water before continuing. "I now understand that God has given me the power to bless and to curse— the power to bless those nations who perfect the world by spreading the word of God, and the power to curse those nations who defile God's creation. Why God chose me, and how this imprecation will ultimately fulfill His master plan, is part of His mystery. But I will not shirk from the responsibilities that destiny has placed upon me." The emperor took a deep breath, then proclaimed in a strong deep voice:

"I hereby curse any nation which defiles God's work, and bless those nations that struggle to perfect the world that God has given us."

It was, unfortunately, beyond the imagination of even a Caesar Augustus to understand that the Roman way of spreading the word of God through conquest, tyranny, and forced conversions did not perfect God's creation, but defiled it. Constantine had, unwittingly, cursed his own nation. In accordance with that curse, the barbarians would overrun the Roman legions, and reach the gates of the capital city less than a hundred years later.

Amidst some muffled "oohs and aahs" at the pronouncement of his curse, Constantine turned toward Eusebius, Bishop of Nicomedia. Eusebius, draped in a white tunic embroidered with golden threads, stood beside his emperor overcome with pride and emotion. Visions of grandeur played in his mind.

"Tonight I saw the flaming cross myself," Eusebius began. "It was supported by two martyrs of the church, each carrying evidence of their suffering—in this case a crutch and an eye patch. They spoke in Greek of the need to punish their tormentors and heal the victims."

Constantine believed that the bishop saw the cross of fire only in his imagination, but did not reprove Eusebius. "While the cross of fire gave me, alone, the power to conquer the world, our new Church will need both formal ritual and the trappings of power in order to persuade the skeptics and awe the masses," he said to himself. "It is only for this reason that I will allow Eusebius to conduct the ceremony that he desires."

"And so," continued Eusebius, "with proper witnesses, symbols and incantations, the curse of Constantine can also be imposed upon those blasphemers who have defamed the good name of a loyal son of his church. It also bestows upon us the power to restore the reputation of the person defamed."

Constantine nodded. The others murmured in astonishment.

"In view of the manner in which the name of Athanasius has been viciously slandered and maligned, it is now time for us to act," Eusebius continued. "We must curse the heretic Arius, and restore the good name of Athanasius."

"Amen," responded the martyred bishops.

Eusebius then turned in the direction of Athanasius. "Are you ready to proceed?" he asked.

Athanasius was unsure what to do next. Then a thought occurred to him. "How long will the curse last?" he asked the bishop.

Eusebius smiled. "As the numeral 'C' illuminated by the cross of fire told our emperor—one-hundred years unless undone," he answered. "But the numerals XXV also tell us that the power to re-make the curse of Constantine will remain in his descendants for twenty-five generations from the curse last made."

Athanasius paused to catch his breath. He looked first at the emperor, then at Eusebius. "I am ready," he said at last. And so began the imprecation ceremony with the witnesses, symbols and incantations directed by Eusebius. Constantine knew, from his visions of the cross of fire, that the power of the blessing and the curse resided in his royal line, not in the priestly line of Eusebius. Constantine also knew that he should not put his imprimatur on the ceremony conducted by Eusebius, and thereby formally effect the curse on Arius and the blessing on Athanasius, until the day of his own baptism. Thus, when Eusebius concluded his ceremony, it was the emperor who spoke next.

"For reasons that will remain sealed in the memory of my confidante Eusebius, the curse and the blessing which he has just pronounced, will not take effect until after my death. But when that fateful day comes, and salvation is upon me, it will restore the good name of Athanasius, and bring ruination upon the heretic of our church."

Twelve years later, Constantine became seriously ill. When prayers and supplications failed to bring on a cure, the emperor visited his friend, Eusebius of Nicomedia. "It is time," the emperor said calmly.

Eusebius helped Constantine exchange the purple robes of his kingship for the white robes of his baptism and absolution. The bishop then poured purifying waters from an ornate, double-handled silver pitcher into a matching basin. And with that water the emperor cleansed himself for his first and last communion with God.

When Constantine died in 337, he was succeeded by his son, Constantine II. Constantine II was born when his father was a month shy of forty-five years. The twenty-five generation power to re-make the curse of Constantine would therefore last 1,120 years—until 1457.

At the time of Constantine's death, the philosophical battle between the Arians and the anti-Arians was still going strong, and the scurrilous accusations against Athanasius remained rife throughout the Roman world. Fifty years later, however, the Creed formulated at the Great Council in 325 became firmly fixed as the foundation of Christian belief. About the same time, the name of Arius became a synonym for heretic, just as the name Benedict Arnold would, much later, become a synonym for traitor. By then Athanasius, the passionate priest of Alexandria, had long since been elevated to sainthood.

DAVID'S PEBBLES

Sometime in the first half of the fifteenth century, Jacob Bar Kochba bent down and scooped up a handful of dirt from the cold, black earth beneath his feet. His ancestors first set foot on that ground 1300 years earlier. They named the place Gesher—Hebrew for "bridge"—because the only object in sight was a stone bridge that spanned a nearby stream. Though Gesher began as a mere encampment for a tired, bedraggled band of Jews who had left Judea during the Bar Kochba War, it now covered over 500 hectares—a large tract for a clan that had no royal blood. Jacob did what he had done on every Sabbath since he learned the story of how his forbears had come to this place. He said a prayer of thanks as he let the handful of dirt slip slowly through his fingers.

It was the first day of the Festival of Hanukah, a celebration of Judah Macabbee's victory over the Greeks, and rededication of the Holy Temple in Jerusalem. That time seemed so long ago, and Jerusalem seemed so far away, that for a fleeting moment Jacob wondered if any of it had even happened. And yet, he wore around his neck proof of an even more improbable event—Bar Kochba's defeat of the Romans. He put his hand under his blouse and rubbed the Bar Kochba coin between his finger and thumb to make sure it was still there. On the day his eldest son, David, got married; Jacob would pass the coin on to him, just as the Bar Kochba family had been doing for centuries.

David, aged twenty, and his brother, Jonathan, younger by a year, were seated around a wooden table in the common area of the family's modest, frame house. The brothers' hands were severely calloused from a day of splitting wood and sawing it into lumber. With the day's work done, and the family dinner concluded, the brothers and their parents were amusing themselves with a traditional Hanukah game called "dreidel," named for the four-sided top with which the game was played.

Each player had a pile of pebbles which served the purpose of modern day poker chips. After anteing a pebble into the pot, participants would spin the dreidel, and depending on which side it landed, would either receive a portion of the pot, or add to the pot from their own pile. As the game progressed, the pile of pebbles in front of Jonathan was depleted. It came his turn to spin.

Jonathan turned to his older brother and said, "Loan me a pebble, David, so that I may continue to play."

David assessed the situation and refused to do so.

"If I loan you a pebble, the chances are even that you will lose, and be unable to repay me. Even if you win the entire pot of four, you will still be out of the game because, after you repay me, you will have to spend your remaining three pebbles on antes before your turn comes around again. Therefore nothing good can come to either of us by my making the loan," he reasoned.

Jonathan accepted the logic of his brother's answer, but Jacob did not. "There must have been a way for both the lender and the borrower to profit from the loan," Jacob mused. He spent a restless night struggling with the problem, and was still thinking about it when he was eating breakfast with his wife, Leah, the following morning. So immersed in his thoughts was he, that he failed to take notice of his sons, who had gathered around his chair to solicit his advice.

"Jacob, your sons are talking to you," Leah said, interrupting her husband's thoughts.

Jacob turned his gaze to David, and the eldest son began to speak.

"We have an idea, Papa," David began. "We have observed the miller who owns a small tract of land downstream. He was kind enough to show us how he has diverted water onto a mill race and used it to turn a large wheel. The wheel, in turn, causes a great millstone to rotate over a stationary stone. Kernels of grain are placed between the stones, and in this way the germ of the grain is separated from the chaff."

"I am familiar with this machinery," Jacob said. "It saves many hours of labor."

"Precisely," said David, his face brightening. "Well, I believe I could harness the same power to saw our logs into lumber."

Before Jacob could ask how he intended to do this, Jonathan produced a cart wheel and a hand saw and set up a crude demonstration.

"Pretend this cart wheel is turned by the water, just as in the grist mill," David continued. "The saw is connected to the wheel, not by a center axel as with the mill stone, but by an eccentric rod."

Jonathan produced a wooden rod from a broom stick, and held one end near the circumference of the wheel, and the other end near the top of the saw. "See how the rod converts the circular rotation of the wheel into an up-and-down movement of the saw?"

Jacob looked in disbelief. "Yes," he said. "The wheel turns around, but the saw reciprocates." But then his expression soured. "This is nothing but dreams; it can never be done."

"Did not our patriarchs also have dreams?" Leah interrupted. "Did not Joseph have dreams that led him to become the Prince of Egypt?" she added.

"It is a dream that I can achieve, Papa," David said enthusiastically. "Look," he continued, forming into a mound the pebbles that remained on the table from the previous evening's dreidel game. "Suppose each year of my labor is worth one pebble for the work I do as a free man, and one pebble for the produce formed by the sweat of my brow," he said, taking two pebbles from the mound and placing them on the table directly in front of where he was standing. "And suppose further, that it will take me two years to build my saw mill." He added two more pebbles to the original two. "It will also cost the equivalent of two years of labor for me to hire an artisan who can obtain the iron and then fashion the saw and gears and machinery that I will need," he continued, putting another two pebbles in the pile he had created in front of himself.

"But we must deal with money, not pebbles," Jacob said impatiently.

"Let me finish."

Jacob nodded.

"When my mill is completed I believe I can produce four times as much lumber with the same amount of labor that I use today. Therefore, only four years after my mill is in operation, I will have sixteen pebbles." David counted out sixteen pebbles from the mound and put them in a separate pile in front of his mother. "Assuming it still costs me one pebble per year in which to live, I will have accumulated twelve extra pebbles four years after my mill is in operation." With a flourish, David removed four pebbles from the pile in front of his mother and returned them to the mound.

"Where do you get the six pebbles you need to begin this enterprise?" Jacob asked, motioning to the pile that was still sitting on the table in front of David.

"That's the most creative part," David said. "I borrow the six pebbles from you at the outset of this venture. Six years later, I not only repay my loan," he said counting out six pebbles from his pile of twelve, and then putting them in front of his father, but I give you six additional pebbles for having taken the risk of loaning me the first six. David took the remaining six pebbles from his pile and placed them in front of his father.

"But now you have nothing," Leah observed.

"Not true, mother," David smiled. "I have my mill, and with it I can produce three more pebbles a year than I need to live. It will create great wealth for me and my family."

"Your family?" Leah asked.

"Well…" David avoided his parents' eyes. "Rachael Asher and I want to marry. We agreed that we will formally seek her parents' blessing, and yours of course, if father agrees to loan me the money for my mill."

"You are telling us nothing that we hadn't already discerned," Leah smiled. "And, of course, your father will give you his blessing. We have already discussed this matter. But I have a question. Last night you would not loan your brother even a single pebble to play dreidel; why should your father now loan you the equivalent of six years of labor?"

Jacob's face, prematurely wrinkled after toiling on the land since the age of five, brightened with sudden insight. "There's a difference," he said enthusiastically. "There's a big difference. In dreidel there is always a fixed amount of pebbles. One person's gain is always balanced by another person's loss. In David's plan, the number of pebbles actually increases; there will be more pebbles for everyone. In six years we will have doubled our money, and David will have a mill of his own which, itself, is worth six pebbles. We will have turned six pebbles into eighteen without the expenditure of any additional labor."

"Then you will loan me the money?"

"You are my son, and I would surely give it to you as a gift if you had asked," Jacob said.

"I believe you would," David replied. "But it is not a gift that I seek—just the opportunity to make something of myself."

"I will give you that opportunity, not only because you deserve it, but because I am eager to see if such a system of enterprise can actually work."

"Is there a person in these precincts sufficiently skilled to fabricate the machinery you need?" Leah asked.

"I have already discussed this with Xanro Tover," David continued. "The son of the blacksmith who Papa allows to squat on our property. The Tovers are confident that they can make the saws and equipment we need."

"We have known the Tovers for fifteen years," said Jacob. "Their ways are peculiar, as some would say are ours, but they are honest, hard-working people. You made a good choice."

"Thank you, Papa." David said appreciatively. "With your permission, I would now like to share the good news with Rachael."

"Tell her that you have our blessing."

Five years later David had built his mill, and a small cottage beside it. It was there that he lived with his wife and son, Daniel. On the eve of the Hanukah Festival, David and his family arrived at the frame house of his parents. It was at that time and place that David gave his father double the amount that he had been loaned.

"This is a year early," Jacob said with astonishment.

"Everything went better than planned," David said. "And there was one aspect of the project that I hadn't predicted."

"What was that?" Jacob asked.

"I worked harder and with more enthusiasm than I ever thought I could."

"You had the encouragement of a fine, strong wife," Jacob said.

"No, Papa, I counted on that. What I didn't count on was the feeling deep inside that I was working for myself, that whatever I was building would be mine, that I would have an overpowering feeling of pride when I was finished."

In the short time that the mill had been in operation, it had produced the best quality lumber in unheard of quantities. David also made his lumber available at such a low cost that it became more economical for freemen to obtain David's products through purchase or barter, rather than hew the timber with their own labor. Word of David's mill, and how it was built through Jacob's financial wizardry of turning one coin into three, spread through the land. It was in this way that King Georges learned of the Bar Kochba family. A short time later Jacob received an announcement on royal parchment that an emissary of the king wanted to visit David's mill.

On the appointed day, Jacob, his sons David and Jonathan, and Bar Kochba family confidante, Rabbi Ephraim Levi, were greeted by a distinguished advisor to the king—and head of the Romanian church, the Right Honorable Bishop Mathieu. The clergyman was accompanied by a retinue of aides and lieges. After some awkward introductions and pleasantries, the bishop asked if some of his aides could visit the mill itself. Jonathan escorted them to the mill, while the clergyman and the rest of his attendants remained with Jacob, David, and the rabbi.

"Actually," the bishop began, "the king is less interested in the mill's operation than the method in which it was financed. It would please his Royal Highness if you could explain it to me."

"It would be my pleasure," Jacob answered. Then bringing forth a box of pebbles, Jacob gave the clergyman the same demonstration that he and David had gone through several years earlier. The bishop was an intelligent man, and quickly grasped the concept.

At one point in the explanation the bishop pointed a long bony finger to six of the pebbles in a pile that Jacob had placed before him and asked, "These, then, would be interest on the original loan of six, would they not?"

Jacob nodded.

"This the church would not allow," he announced dogmatically. "I was under the assumption that the law of the Jews does not permit interest either," he said.

Jacob cast a nervous eye toward Rabbi Levi, hoping he could provide an answer.

"Our law does permit interest," the rabbi explained. "What it prohibits is usurious interest."

"Aha," said the bishop. "But how does one distinguish permitted interest from that which is usurious."

The rabbi was quick to answer: "The test of proper interest depends on the risk of the investment," he said. "Thus, if the risk is high, the rate of interest may be high; but if the risk is low, that same rate of interest may be usurious."

Bishop Mathieu stroked his beard with great deliberation because he wanted to choose his words accurately. "The concept may work well in a close knit group of people like your own," he finally said, "but it is unworkable in the larger realm of the king. We are better off not being involved in the mechanics of interest altogether."

"The System of the Pebbles creates more than wealth for both the lender and borrower," reminded Jacob. "By investing in better tools and machinery, the entire realm benefits from better products obtained from less labor."

"I agree with you," answered the bishop, "and more importantly, so does the king whom I revere more than any except the Christ Himself. Therefore, it will be you who will charge the interest, not the king, not his aides and certainly not the church."

Jacob's blank look prompted further explanation.

"The king intends to give the Bar Kochba family a patent on the charging of interest. In return for this royal patent, you will give the king nine coins for every ten in interest that you collect. By receiving money in return for the patent, rather than receiving money directly from the interest that the king's patent allows you to collect, the Royal House benefits without doing that which offends the church. In the process, you will become a wealthy man and a trusted liege of Georges the Wise."

"I am flattered by the king's offer," Jacob responded. "But it is not wealth that I seek. The System of Pebbles may create a class of freemen—artisans who could become better wheelwrights and wainwrights, better tanners and coopers and tinkers—artisans who work for themselves and not another."

"And so it will be," the bishop concluded. "You and I no longer have any choice in the matter because this is what the king desires. My aides will finalize the arrangements at a later time. I thank you all for your patience. Good day, gentlemen," he said nodding to Jacob and David. "And good day, rabbi; I think there is much we can learn from each other."

"I welcome the opportunity," the rabbi said.

After the bishop and his entourage took their leave, the rabbi spoke candidly. "This is bad for us, Jacob. We should not participate in a scheme that singles us out in this way."

"You heard the bishop," Jacob countered. "We have no choice. Anyway, we are being singled out to receive a great benefit, not as victims of an invidious decree."

"Any decree which singles out a minority such as us, no matter how beneficial in intent, will prove to be invidious in fact," the rabbi warned.

Jacob's thoughts had already drifted into a different realm. He saw the world around him as a hierarchy of noblemen, each superior to the one below him in rank. At the bottom of this pyramid of humanity stood the serfs—slaves to the land on which they lived. Human progress could not exist in such a feudal arrangement because it was essentially a zero sum system, just like the game of dreidel—a never-ending circle of life, misery, and death. He understood that a financial system based on risk and reward was the only way in which ordinary people could achieve both freedom and a better station in life. If it also meant that the rich would get richer, so be it—the rich will always get richer until their heirs squander their wealth.

In the course of his dreamy meanderings, the words of the ancient prophets hit him like a hammer. This is what they meant when they foretold that each man shall sit under his own fig tree. And this is what it meant when it was written that the words of the Torah would go forth out of Zion. It was to fulfill these mystic prophecies that his family was sent to this place so long ago. Now understanding his purpose in life, Jacob sat down at the wooden table in the living room of his house, cupped his head in his hands, and wept with joy.

TAV'S HEADACHE

David Bar Kochba had an idea for an improved saw. Though the reciprocating saw that he installed in his mill had been working well for a number of years, it was subject to certain drawbacks. The most annoying was that the gearing between the water wheel and the connecting rod would frequently break or malfunction. David believed he had devised a remedy: substitute a circular saw for the reciprocating saw, and thereby eliminate the connecting rod altogether. He couldn't wait to discuss his idea with Xanro Tover.

David arrived at the Tover camp just as Xanro's axe cleaved the face of the shorter Dracul guard.

After the initial shock of the violence had subsided, David tried, without success, to console his friend as together they laid his dear wife to rest.

"I will fight the Dracula with my last breath," Xanro vowed. "I will not rest until a torrent of blood erupts from his heart."

"We must all leave this place," Guruv pleaded. "Do so for the sake of your son."

"For the sake of my son we shall stay here and fight."

"We and the royals are in immediate danger. We must flee at once," Guruv repeated.

David agreed with Guruv's assessment that the Tovers had no

choice but to leave the country immediately. If Xanro would not go with them, he and his son could stay in his mill cottage deep in the woods. David disagreed, however, with Guruv on one important point. The royals must not accompany them.

"Your wagons will be searched at every town; the guards will find them and kill you all," David argued.

Guruv insisted that they remain under his protection.

"We have imposed on your family enough," Anna said determinedly. "David is right; if we go with you we will only cause your family more hardship."

"Then what will become of you?" Guruv asked.

"They will stay with me as well," David interrupted. "The Bar Kochba family has lived on this land for over a thousand years. They will be safe with us."

"We know of your family," Mirceal informed David. "Our father talked of the Bar Kochba's often. Your father has done much for our people."

"Your father did much for us all; we will miss him dearly," said David. "But we have no time to lose."

Xanro and his eight year old son, Tav, said their final farewells to the Tover clan. When Tav waved a teary goodbye, David noticed that the boy, like his father, bore the double triangle sign of the Tover on his right forearm.

"You will be in our prayers," Xanro said to his parents.

"And you in ours," Kali said as the wagons began moving down the cart path in the direction of the main road.

When the first wagon disappeared around a bend, David led Xanro, Tav, Mirceal and Anna in the opposite direction toward the mill. Under Rachael's directions, they busied themselves arranging both the mill house and the cottage so that sleeping quarters could be provided for the guests. When that task was completed, Rachael served everyone some porridge and bread.

After their repast, Tav tugged on his father's trousers. It was an obvious signal that the boy was afraid, and needed comfort. Xanro excused himself, took his son by the hand, and led him outside where they sat down on a fallen log.

Tav looked at his father with wide-eyed innocence and asked, "Do we have the power to tell the future?"

Xanro was startled by the inquiry, but tried not to show his surprise. "Why do you ask?" he said simply.

"Grampa Guruv once told me that our people have such a gift, and now I wonder if it is true," the boy answered.

"Your Grampa spoke the truth," Xanro assured him.

"Then tell me what will happen to Grampa Guruv and Gramma Kali."

Xanro put his arm around his son and tried to answer. "Our powers are not that straight forward," he said. Tav gave his father a quizzical look. "Signs and symbols of future events exist in nature, and are sometimes even fashioned by humans. But though they are there for all to see, only some people have the gift to interpret their hidden meaning."

"Do I have that gift?" the boy asked.

"If you do, it will surely be made known to you."

"How will I know?" Tav persisted.

Xanro looked lovingly at his young son. "Grampa Guruv told me that the gift came to him on only one occasion. And when it did, it was preceded by a painful noise in his ears, and strange lights in his eyes."

Young Tav failed to hear his father's explanation. He had clamped his hands over his temples to block out an uncomfortable buzzing sound inside his head. Then he closed his eyes to hide the ghoulish sight of recognizable faces melting like wax in a hot flame, and familiar bodies being cut to pieces and soaked with blood.

"Now let's join the others inside," Xanro said comfortingly.

Tav nodded. His headache had subsided as abruptly as it had begun.

While Xanro was explaining the Romani tradition to his son, a platoon of twenty Dracul guards had picked up a trail outside the castle garden. They followed it through royal fields and orchards, along a narrow cart path, and into a small clearing. It was there that they discovered the warm bodies of their fallen comrades, and the recent marks of heavy wagons moving in the opposite direction from which they had come. The wagon tracks appeared to have stopped in front of a modest frame house, before moving on toward the main road.

"Kill the traitors," the Dracul lieutenant ordered.

The Draculs dismounted and stormed into the house, swords drawn.

In the ensuing fight, Jacob and Jonathan killed two of the attackers before being overpowered and murdered. Leah was taken captive and interrogated at knife point. All she could say was that the Tovers passed by a short time earlier to tell her husband that they were moving on, she knew not where. They thanked him for his years of friendship and kindness, and left. She knew nothing about the death of King Georges or the missing royals.

When the lieutenant was convinced Leah could give him no further information, he slit her throat with an air of complete indifference, and then threw her body to the ground like a sack of grain.

"Burn this place," he ordered, and within moments the frame house was aflame.

The lieutenant watched the blaze only long enough to satisfy himself that the dwelling would be entirely consumed.

"Justice has been done," he pronounced. "This is what comes of money changers and usurers."

The Draculs followed the Tovers' tracks to the main road, and saw the dust of their wagons in the distance. They kicked their horses into a gallop, and quickly overtook them.

After the wagons were stopped, the occupants were ordered to disembark. Then they were disarmed and assembled into a line along the roadside. The lieutenant approached Guruv.

"Where are the royals?" he demanded.

"We know no royals. We are alone, My Worship; I swear we are alone," Guruv pleaded.

"You are a liar," the lieutenant screamed. "They are in your wagons, and we will find them." The lieutenant motioned to a subordinate. "Burn them," he ordered.

Within a few minutes all the earthly goods of the Tover clan were in ashes, but Mirceal and Anna were nowhere to be found.

"What shall become of us," wailed Kali.

Certain that the Draculs were going to kill his entire family, Guruv made a desperate leap at the throat of the lieutenant. His sons did the same.

"Kill them," the lieutenant commanded, plunging his sword into Guruv's chest. And they did.

The lieutenant looked at the corpses. "Impale them," he ordered. "This shall be a warning to anyone who dares offend the king."

CONSTANTINE'S PITCHER

David Bar Kochba walked out of his cottage to collect his thoughts. In the distance he noticed a dull orange tint in the blue sky; his nostrils twitched at the smell of smoke. He mounted his horse and sped in the direction of the fire. He arrived to see his parents' home in flames, and his mother's lifeless body lying on the ground. David knelt down beside her, and tenderly touched her cheek. He gagged at the cockeyed angle of her head, and blood-caked wound that circled her neck.

David gently straightened his mother's head, and then ran into the burning house. He saw four dead men inside. He pulled the bodies of his father, then his brother from the inferno, and placed them next to his mother.

"Must warn the Tovers," he thought, leaping on his horse, and galloping toward the main road. He arrived at the stone bridge too late. The Dracul platoon, having completed its grisly task of impaling and implanting the bodies of innocent men, women and children—some of whom still possessed the breath of life—were in the process of removing the charred remains of the Tover wagons from the road. A large crowd of locals had gathered to stone the corpses and curse the gypsies.

The Dracul lieutenant addressed the small crowd. "Last night Mirceal killed our great king, and tried to murder his brother so that he could wear the crown of our country. He escaped with his sister, and the two are now in hiding. We will find them, and make them pay for their treachery,"

"Death to Mirceal," yelled one of the bystanders.

"Death to gypsies," yelled another.

The lieutenant, pointing to the impaled bodies that lined the side of the road, continued: "These thieves were hiding the usurper, Mirceal, and were punished accordingly. Let this be a warning to anyone else who gives comfort to the pretenders to our throne."

David shuddered as the crowd cheered in approval. He remained on the scene even after the Dracul platoon rode off and the crowd dispersed. Kicking through the pile of rubble by the side of the road, he saw Guruv's axe among the ashes and debris. He decided to give it to his friend Xanro in memory of his father. As David put the axe into his belt, he feared that he had no such memento of his own father. Then he put his hand under his shirt and touched the Bar Kochba coin that hung around his neck. He wondered whether he'd be the last Bar Kochba to wear the sign of the star.

The next day the community of Gesher Jews, with the assistance of Rabbi Levi, gathered to bury Jacob, Leah and Jonathan Bar Kochba in a clearing among the thick woods near David's mill. As this was happening, Bishop Mathieu was meeting with the new king and his trusted lieutenant. Dracula made it clear that things would be different under his administration. The System of Pebbles was over, the plan to create a class of freemen would end, taxes would be raised, his personal Dracul guard would be increased and the professional army would be reduced.

"This may make us pregnable to attack by the infidels," the bishop warned.

But this logic only angered the new king.

"Traitors are a greater danger to us than infidels," he argued. "The traitors are already on our soil."

"But the traitors have no army, Your Highness. How will we stop the invaders who have one?"

The muscles in Dracula's jaw tightened with anger. "Did you not see the sign of the comet last night? Was that not an omen of my invincibility? Am I not one of the gods?"

The bishop looked at the Dracula incredulously. "Has the king gone mad?" he asked himself.

Dracula was unfazed by Mathieu's pained expression.

"Lieutenant," he snapped. I want the coins of the realm changed immediately. Henceforth they shall bear the sign of the comet on one side and my visage on the other. Indeed, henceforth the sign of the comet shall be the honored symbol of this kingdom itself, replacing all previous symbols and representations that now exist."

"Even the cross?" protested the bishop.

"Even the cross!" bellowed the king, his face flushing with emotion.

Bishop Mathieu cast a nervous glare toward the Dracula, then quickly looked away without making eye contact. "Dracula is worse than a madman," the bishop concluded. "He is Satan." Bishop Mathieu then returned his gaze in the king's direction. "As you wish, Your Highness," he said, hiding his look of anxiety by bowing deep at the waist.

By the time the bishop righted himself, Dracula's face had turned yet a deeper shade of red. "You may take your leave," the king responded curtly.

Bishop Mathieu needed no further prompting. He quickly left the castle of Dracula and returned immediately to his church. It was a large Gothic structure made from gray limestone. The flying buttresses and narrow, arched windows, gave the building a defiant, but eerie look.

The congregational priest and several deacons bedecked in brown hooded robes were quietly going about their appointed tasks when the bishop entered the sanctuary. He walked past them with uncharacteristic brusqueness.

Then, with a backward glance at the priest, he said in a tone of great purpose: "Father Stephen, accompany me to my office immediately. We are not to be disturbed, Alexandru," the bishop admonished the deacon superior.

"Of course, Your Worship," Alexandru replied obsequiously.

With that, Bishop Mathieu and Father Stephen entered the bishop's office and locked the massive oaken door behind him. The bishop's lips tightened with a look of concern. Then, taking a deep breath, he began to speak in carefully measured tones.

"Father, I believe the Dracula has gone completely mad and, as a result, the great Romanian Order of our church is in considerable danger. Therefore, what I am about to say and do must remain our secret until death."

"It will be so, Your Worship," the priest whispered.

"With Christ as our witness," the bishop pronounced.

"With Christ as our witness," the priest repeated.

The bishop said a silent prayer, then with renewed strength of purpose, pushed his desk to the side of the room, rolled the carpet into a corner, and searched on his hands and knees for a latch concealed in the stone floor. Finding it, he pulled up on the iron lever which, in turn, caused a cantilevered trap door to rise above the floor, revealing a steep, dark staircase. With an oil lamp in hand, the bishop and the priest descended the stairs, and followed a narrow stone path until it terminated at another oaken door. The door was a decoy to lead trespassers into a room that contained no secrets.

On the stone wall adjacent to the decoy door was an alcove containing an icon of Jesus. Behind the icon was a camouflaged keyhole. The prelate inserted a key into the lock. A portion of the wall swung free revealing a hidden chamber. Hanging on the far wall of the secret room was a large Greek cross fashioned in silver and inlaid with precious stones. The cross bar and the upright were of equal size in accordance with the eastern tradition; the ends flared into intricately-worked, pointed tips.

The bishop removed the cross, and where the center of the sacred symbol had been, searched the wall for a concealed lock. With yet another key, he turned the lock which opened the door to a deep, walk-in safe embedded in the wall. The bishop's hands trembled as he removed the contents: a two-handled silver pitcher bearing the seal of the Emperor of Rome, Constantine the Great. The pitcher rested in an ornate basin which, in turn, rested on a plain oak table.

"The water of the Baptism of Constantine rested in these sacred vessels," whispered the bishop.

"I have heard the legend of Constantine's pitcher with my own ears," Father Stephen acknowledged with a sense of awe, "but never did I think I would see these icons of our faith with my own eyes."

"They are not legends," corrected the bishop. "They are as true as the Gospels themselves."

"I beg you to share with me this sacred truth, Your Worship."

Bishop Mathieu looked at the eager expression on his loyal friend and liege, then began to speak in a slow, deliberate manner. "In the beginning God created the Heavens and the Earth. The Earth was created to provide a home for people like us. The Heavens were created to give people like us a sense of wonder." The bishop's pace then began to quicken. "God wanted us to wonder because He believed it would help us understand that we are here for a reason—to perfect the world by spreading His message of 'peace on earth, good will toward men.'"

"It is the truth, just as you say!" exclaimed the priest.

The bishop continued without acknowledging Father Stephen's comment. "From time to time God revealed himself to different people in different ways. He did that so His prophets could remind us of the lofty purpose for which we are here. Ultimately, of course, He gave us His own flesh that showed us the way by performing acts of loving kindness toward our fellow man."

"So He did," Father Stephen interjected.

"But Jesus's message initially failed to take root," the bishop reminded his disciple. "It was then that Helena Augusta, mother of Constantine, was visited by God. It was through her influence that the Emperor of Rome embraced our church and then formulated our Christian Creed. At the Great Council of Nicaea, and again in the course of his conversion, the Holy Spirit touched this pitcher from which the waters of Constantine's baptism poured forth."

"That I have lived to see the imprint of the Spirit of Christ before my very eyes," marveled the priest.

"At first both the Nicene Creed and Constantine's conversion were ridiculed by the citizens of Rome," the bishop explained.

"No," whispered Father Stephen.

"But within a century it was the walls of Rome that began to crack while the walls of Constantine's City remained strong for a thousand years. It is for all of these reasons that the waters in the vessels before us have the capacity to restore the good name of one who is maligned while bringing a curse upon the house of his maligner."

Father Stephen put his hands together in prayer. "May the water that these vessels now hold, give us wisdom in this crisis," he entreated.

"May your supplication be heard," the bishop added, "for I fear our king and Satan are one and the same."

The priest's face turned ashen.

The bishop continued: "It is for this reason that you must go as my emissary to the church Congress in Vienna. You must take these sacred treasures with you and put them in a place where they will be safe from the devil, just as years ago they were brought here to keep them safe from the infidels who now threaten Constantine's City itself. I will stay here to ward off the Dracula myself."

"But Vienna is in the hands of the Roman Church," Father Stephen objected.

"At least it is in Christian hands," Bishop Mathieu reassured him.

"Some say Constantinople will soon fall into Muslim hands. And after that the Muslim armies will reach the gates of Vienna itself," the priest continued.

Bishop Mathieu put a hand over his eyes and rubbed them in painful thought. When he removed his hand a moment later, his eyes glimmered with hope. "I will trust you, in the name of our Lord, to find a safe home for these icons of our faith until they can, one day, be returned to the Church of the East," he said decisively.

"It will be done," said the priest.

"Then let us pray."

The two clergymen washed their hands, whispered some incantations, and made the sign of the cross.

KING GEORGES'S CROSS

David, Xanro and Mirceal built their own secret chamber inside the mill where the royals could hide. Anna had great difficulty adjusting to her life as a fugitive. Mirceal mostly brooded in anger over their helplessness. He was certain that neither his sister, nor his country, could persevere through many more weeks of Draculan tyranny.

After some months of growing frustration, they all became convinced that they had to take action. Their first priority was to ensure Anna's permanent protection and well-being by smuggling her out of the country. As Anna's health and spirits noticeably diminished, the urgency to do so grew. Despite their best efforts, however, no alternative to that of keeping her in hiding at David's mill could be devised. Instead, their discussions invariably devolved into an animated expression of their loathing for Vlad Dracula.

"He has destroyed the System of Pebbles, and with it the opportunity for freemen to improve their lot in life," David angrily complained.

"He panders to the masses by blaming their poverty on the hardworking Romani," Xanro said bitterly.

On this point, however, it was Mirceal who was most vociferous. One afternoon, as the three men were walking from the woods to the mill, the emotion spilled uncontrollably from Mirceal's lips. "My brother murdered our parents and left all of us as orphans; he has ruined our lives and endangered the only loved ones we have left. The cruelty of his Dracul guards has terrorized our nation, and the proliferation of his comet symbols has blasphemed our church. To me alone, however, he has done something even more unbearable: it is Dracula who has committed these horrific crimes against our people, but it is Mirceal who the people blame. I can accept poverty, misery, torture and death, but I cannot bear the thought that throughout eternity my countrymen will be cursing my name for something I did not do."

Until that moment, neither David nor Xanro had appreciated the extent of their friend's torment.

Mirceal picked up a long stick from the forest floor and, with a running start, hurled it in anger. It soared like a javelin through the air, landing upright in a tuft of weeds near the edge of the mill stream.

"Were it a spear in the tail of Dracula's comet!" Xanro yelled.

"Were it a cross in the flesh of Dracula's heart!" Mirceal screamed, his face contorted by rage.

David, however, was preoccupied with a handful of pebbles that he had scooped out from the water's edge. "I have an idea," he said suddenly. "I think I know somebody who can help us."

His two comrades looked at him inquisitively.

"Bishop Mathieu," David suggested. "I met him once several years ago. He seemed like a reasonable man; someone who would not countenance Dracula's evil deeds."

"He was a trusted aide to my father," said Mirceal. "I know him well. But I fear he has been intimidated into cooperating with my brother. In any event, the Draculs will be watching his church night and day. I could never go there without being noticed."

"But I can," David smiled. "And I will."

The next day David rode to the bishop's church. He tethered his horse to a hitching post on the expansive church grounds, and walked tentatively up the wide stairway of the Christian holy place. He had never been inside a church before.

David stared nervously at a pair of Gothic-style doors that were at least twice his height. He pushed one open and found himself inside a large vestibule closed off from the main hall of the church by three pair of smaller inner doors. Cautiously, he opened one of the doors and looked inside. He saw no movement so he entered the sanctuary and proceeded past many rows of pews to the place where the nave of the church met the transept. Several brown-robed deacons were engaged in quiet conversation at the altar. One of the clergymen, distinguished by black, shoulder-length hair and a long, drooping mustache, was the first to see David.

"My name is David. I came in the fervent hope of meeting with Bishop Mathieu."

"He has given me strict orders that he not be disturbed," Deacon Alexandru replied unsympathetically.

"This is a matter of great urgency."

"He is now attending to a matter of great urgency."

"Would you be kind enough to at least inform him that I am here?"

"That would be quite impossible."

"May I at least make an appointment with him?"

"The bishop is not taking appointments."

They were interrupted by the tintinnabulation of iron bells from the church tower. When the last of the twelve mournful percussions tolling the noon hour faded into silence, David continued: "If you see Bishop Mathieu, please tell him that David Bar Kachba was here, and that I will return tomorrow at this time in the hope that he will see me then."

"I can assure you that your visit tomorrow will be quite futile."

David took a few steps toward the door, then abruptly turned and faced the deacon. He withdrew six pebbles from his pocket and handed them to the clergyman.

"When you see the bishop, would you be kind enough to give him these?"

The deacon frowned, and emptied the pebbles into a silver collection plate that was resting on a maple stand that stood near the first row of pews. A statue of a comet, with its tail rising from the ground, rested on an identical stand that was placed across the aisle from the first.

David retraced his steps through the nave of the church, and disappeared inside the vestibule.

"That deacon is hiding something," he thought. "And I intend to find out what it is."

At that moment, Bishop Mathieu emerged from his office, located at the far end of the transept.

"I heard voices," he said to Alexandru.

"One of the Jews from Gesher came to see you. I turned him away, of course."

"Of course," the prelate repeated. "You can always be trusted to carry out my wishes."

"Thank you, Your Worship," Alexandru responded.

The bishop was about to return to his office when he noticed the collection plate.

"What are these?" he asked.

"Pebbles, sir. The visitor asked me to give them to you. I planned to discard them the moment he left."

The bishop emptied the contents of the collection plate into his palm, and rolled the pebbles around in his hand.

"Pebbles," he mused, now recalling the ingenious young man he had briefly met several years earlier. "Did he say anything else, Alexandru?"

"He said the matter was urgent, and that he would try to see you again tomorrow at this time. I told him that would be quite futile, Your Worship."

"To the contrary, Alexandru. I can think of no reason why he'd come here on a matter of urgency unless, perhaps, he knows something about the royals." The bishop's lip momentarily quivered in sadness at the loss of King Georges. But then the cleric's resolve returned, and he looked squarely at the deacon. "Now be off, my loyal friend. You know Father Stephen departs for Vienna in the morning. Please go to the supply barn immediately and make certain that everything is in order for that important journey."

Alexandru took his leave and headed for the supply barn as directed. His furtive glances to his rear, however, betrayed a strong sense of insecurity. Taking one last look back at the church, and seeing nothing suspicious, the deacon abruptly changed his direction, and ran to the stable. There he saddled a horse and rode off in haste toward the castle of Vlad Dracula.

Several minutes earlier, when David was still in the vestibule of the church, his eye caught the sight of several deacons' robes hanging in the cloak room. Impulsively, he slipped one of the brown garments over his clothing and re-entered the church sanctuary. He did so in time to hear the tail end of Bishop Mathieu's conversation with Alexandru. And so, when Alexandru left the church, David followed him in stealth to the stable, and saw him ride off in the direction of Dracula's castle.

Emboldened by his discovery, David ran back to the church, returned his brown robe to its hook in the cloak room and walked briskly through the great hall of the sanctuary. He took a deep breath before knocking on the thick oaken door of the bishop's private office. The door creaked open, and David stood face to face with Bishop Mathieu himself.

"You are in grave danger, Your Worship," David warned.

A few moments later the two men were walking briskly to the supply barn to ascertain whether there was any merit to the suggestion that Alexandru had betrayed the bishop's trust. When they found the supply barn empty and a horse missing form the stable, David's accusations were confirmed. The two men rushed back to the bishop's office to formulate a plan.

"Dracula is mad," the bishop said. "He will kill you and your family if he has the slightest suspicion that you are hiding the royals. You must bring them here immediately where I will provide sanctuary to you all."

"The Dracula will not hesitate to kill you for your efforts."

"We will leave my well-being in the hands of the Lord. Now go in haste."

David turned, but the bishop interrupted.

"Give Mirceal this," he said. Then putting his hand under his vestments, he removed a chain that he wore around his neck and handed it to David. Attached to the chain was a silver Latin cross with the ends of the crossbars and the top of the vertical post flattened into decorative squares.

"It belonged to Mirceal's father. I removed it from the body of my revered king the night Dracula murdered him."

"Then you know it was not Mirceal," David whispered.

The bishop nodded. "Now go," he ordered.

XANRO'S MEDALLIONS

Shortly after David left for the church in an attempt to meet with Bishop Mathieu, his wife, Rachael, had an idea of her own.

"Daniel and Tav need some playmates," she told Xanro. "They can not spend their entire lives hiding in the woods. I am going to take the wagon and ride to the other side of Gesher and spend a day with my sister and her children."

"There is too much danger," Xanro cautioned. "David would never approve."

"I am not seeking his approval," she insisted, raising her jaw defiantly.

Xanro realized that Rachael's mind was made up. "Then I will follow you there," he said, "but I permit this on one condition: that you do not return here alone. David or I will come for you at the three o'clock hour. If, by chance, we get delayed, you must give me your promise that you will spend the night with your sister, and await our arrival the next morning."

"I appreciate your concern, and it is for that reason only that I make such a promise," she said.

When Xanro returned to the mill cottage, he spent the remainder of the morning at his smithing fire. Inspired by the sound of bells and the dazzle of sunlight, he fashioned four identical bronze medallions with skill and artistry. Each was rectangular in shape, and designed to be worn as a pendant around the neck. He intended them to be a talisman of eternal friendship and good luck among Mirceal, Anna, David and himself. Each of them suffered the horrible fate of their parents being brutally murdered by the hand of Dracula; now each would have a shared symbol that justice would be done.

Xanro carefully cut into the face of each medallion, beginning near the bottom, center, the outline of a comet's tail. The tail traced an expanding arc toward the top left corner, terminating in a circular comet head adjacent to the earthly sun. An oversized spear with an exaggerated pentagonal tip partially bisected the medallion along its length. The tip of the spear pierced the comet at the origin of its tail. Along the long side of the medallion, opposite the comet head, Xanro had engraved the words, "Spear in a Comet's Tail."

"An enduring symbol of my outrage of yesterday," Xanro said to himself with great satisfaction.

Mirceal arrived with an armful of firewood, and looked over Xanro's shoulder as he was polishing one of the medallions.

"You are a fine craftsman, but a poor theosophist," he said.

"I don't know such words," Xanro confessed.

"All you need to know is that your medallion lacks the spirit of God. Can you modify these pieces so that a Latin cross overlies the spear? As my father once explained, 'It is the spirit of the Lord that controls the arm of man.'"

"It can be done," Xanro said, amidst a recurrence of the same sound of bells and flashes of light that he had experienced a few moments earlier.

"But can it be done thus?" Mirceal asked, taking a stick and drawing a cross with squared tips at the ends of the crossbars and at the top of the upright.

"It can be done," Xanro repeated, "but why do you insist on this particular shape?"

"It resembles the cross that was given to my father by the Bavarian Brotherhood where he trained as a knight. It is of the Latin style, an uncommon icon in our Church of the East. My father wore it in the hope that one day the great schism between our churches would end. He promised me it would be mine someday, but regrettably that did not come to pass."

Though the ringing in his ears reached a painful pitch, Xanro immediately began making the modifications that Mirceal had requested. When the work was completed, he fastened a chain to each medallion, and placed one around Mirceal's neck, and another around his own. At that moment his world suddenly became quiet.

As the two men were admiring their new medallions, Alexandru was halting his lathered horse in front of Dracula's Castle, and bounding toward the entrance. He was stopped immediately by the Dracul guards.

"I must see the king," Alexandru cried. "We will all lose our heads if there is any delay."

Despite his pleas of urgency, Alexandru was escorted into the drawing room where he waited impatiently for almost an hour.

"The king will see you now," one of the guards finally announced.

To his great disappointment, however, Alexandru was ushered into an empty anteroom where he waited alone in frustration. After what seemed an interminable time, Alexandru was eventually taken into the throne room to meet the king.

"To what do I owe this impertinence?" the Dracula said with arrogant sarcasm.

"I have news of the usurpers."

The king suddenly became attentive. "Proceed," he commanded.

"They are hiding with a miller in the woods of Gesher."

"This information best be true, or it will be the death of you."

"On my honor as a loyal subject of Your Highness, son of the revered Georges the Wise, I swear that everything I tell you is God's truth."

The Dracula suppressed an urge to reprimand Alexandru for mentioning his father in the same breath as himself. "Continue," he said.

"The miller, David Bar Kochba, visited our church at noon today on a matter of alleged urgency. He wanted to meet personally with Bishop Mathieu, but I refused to disturb His Worship. When I mentioned this to the bishop, he surmised that the purpose of the visit pertained to the whereabouts of Mirceal. The miller promised to return to the church tomorrow at noon in a second attempt to meet with the bishop."

"Anything else?"

"I suspect the miller was serving as an intermediary for Mirceal and Anna, who hope to find sanctuary in our holy church. I came here as fast as I could to share the news."

"I suspect you are correct," said the king. "Now return to the church immediately before you are missed."

Alexandru did as he was told.

"I want that man killed the day we find the fugitives," Dracula told the captain of his guard, a moment after Alexandru departed. "For now, take a first contingent of the guard to the Gesher mill, find my siblings and bring them here alive. Take a second contingent and surround the church. For all we know the miller is already on his way there with my brother and sister."

"It shall be done," said the captain.

———————————

While Alexandru was waiting in the sitting room of Dracula's Castle, David Bar Kochba arrived at the cottage by his mill in time to see Xanro put a pendant around Mirceal's neck.

"Get Anna, get Rachael and the children!" he screamed without dismounting. "We have no time to lose."

Mirceal and Xanro were bewildered by David's sense of urgency.

"Dracula knows you are here. We must leave this place immediately."

"How does he know? Where will we go?" Mirceal stammered.

"I will explain after we are on our way," David answered. "I saw the bishop; he has offered us sanctuary, but we have no time to lose."

"Are you sure he can be trusted?" Mirceal implored.

David reached into his pocket and grabbed the silver Latin cross once worn by King Georges.

"Do you trust this?" he answered, dropping it in Mirceal's hands.

Mirceal recognized the icon immediately, and looked at David with a sense of confusion.

"The bishop knows that it is your brother who is the guilty one; he removed this from your father's body the night he was murdered."

Mirceal hugged Xanro.

"Your talisman has already worked magic!" he exclaimed. "The spear in the comet's tail will be a charm for us all."

David looked at Xanro for an explanation.

"I fashioned medallions for all of us this morning. Here is yours," he said, handing a pendant to David. "Your wife and our children are at the home of Rachael's sister; they will be safe there for now. I can explain everything. Now let us get Anna, and leave this place with the dispatch that you have requested."

The three men galloped the short distance to the mill, but Anna was nowhere to be found.

Instinctively, they spread out in different directions to search for the princess.

Mirceal was making his way through a tangle of mountain laurel and rhododendron when he saw the late afternoon sun reflect off a metal object. He dismounted, and raced through the underbrush. He saw the dagger first, then his sister.

"No!" he screamed at the top of his voice.

He reached Anna before she could do harm to herself in the manner she was contemplating. He hugged his sister and whispered in her ear: "God is at our side. Look what He brought us just a few moments ago." Mirceal opened his shirt and showed her the Latin cross.

His sister gasped.

"I will explain later," Mirceal promised, "but now we must go."

She nodded obediently.

"This will give you comfort and protection," he whispered, draping Xanro's talisman around her neck. "I will explain this as well."

Mirceal, Anna, Xanro and David followed the narrow paths through the woods of Gesher, past the charred remains of the frame house where David was born. David paused a moment to reflect on the crimes that had occurred there.

"Better put these on before we turn onto the main road," David advised, removing some brown deacon's robes from the pack that was behind his saddle. "You never know who we might meet along the way."

The trio donned the brown robes as David had suggested. Moments later a contingent of Dracul guards sped past them en route to the church. To the few who even noticed, all they observed were four deacons on their way home after a day of tending to the poor and providing comfort to the afflicted.

MATHIEU'S IMPRECATION

Despite the cordon of Dracul guards surrounding the church, Mirceal, Anna, Xanro and David calmly and uneventfully rode their horses into the church compound. They followed David to the stable where they dismounted, removed the saddles and led their animals to empty stalls. The four of them then walked inconspicuously into the church and knocked on the bishop's office door.

Bishop Mathieu suppressed his surprise when he recognized Mirceal beneath his deacon's hood. He quickly ushered him and his companions inside and locked the door. The four removed their brown robes and surveyed the dark, windowless office through the dim light of a solitary oil lamp. They were shocked to discover that there was another person in the room.

"Father Stephen," said the bishop, clearing his throat, "this is Prince Mirceal and his sister, Princess Anna."

Father Stephen made a deep bow.

"Gentlemen," said Mirceal proudly, "these are our friends, Xanro Tover and David Bar Kochba. We owe them our lives."

The bishop raised an eyebrow that bade Mirceal to continue.

"The Dracula did more than murder Georges the Wise and his queen, my dear mother. He murdered the parents of David, and then murdered the parents of Xanro. He murdered their families as well.

Nonetheless, through their suffering, and at great risk of torture and death, these two men have provided aid and comfort to Anna and me."

Father Stephen made a deep bow before David and Xanro.

"You are among the righteous," said the bishop. Then turning to David, he said, "It is an honor to see you again. When I saw the Dracul guard around the church, I feared you would be discovered if you attempted to return. I should have known that your ingenuity would see you through the danger."

"Danger is all about us, Your Worship," answered David. "I suspect that Deacon Alexandru has already informed the Dracula of my promise that I will return here tomorrow at noon. It is then that the guard will be poised to intercept us."

"One thing we have all agreed upon," interrupted Mirceal. "Anna must leave the country. And based on what David just said, it is imperative that she leave here before noon tomorrow."

"Better I should die on my native soil than flee to a foreign land," Anna countered.

"Your protestations will not be heard," rejoined Mirceal. "One of us must survive to preserve what is good in the blood of our family. You will go, not only for your sake, but for the sake of our parents."

"But how will she go?" Xanro asked. "The church is surrounded."

Suddenly Father Stephen raised his hands in a plea for attention.

"She will go as she has arrived," the priest said softly. "Tomorrow morning I leave for Vienna. She will accompany me as my aide, wearing the same deacon's robe on her way out that she wore on her way in."

Everyone nodded approvingly.

"May you walk with God, sweet princess," added the bishop.

"We all walk with God," Mirceal blurted. "Xanro, show the bishop our medallions."

Xanro removed his pendant and handed it to Bishop Mathieu. The cleric looked at the engraving with great interest. "It shows a spear, beneath a likeness of King Georges's cross, which pierces a comet's tail," he observed.

"It is a depiction of my anger of yesterday afternoon," responded Xanro.

Bishop Mathieu's perplexed expression prompted Xanro to explain the origin of the medallion's design. "The likeness of King Geoges's cross, however, is the result of Mirceal's anger, not mine," he added.

The bishop looked inquisitively at Mirceal.

"I loathe my brother. His soul should be damned and his name should be cursed."

Mirceal's words ignited a fire of insight that caused the bishop to close his eyes and thank the Lord. He had been schooled in the legend of Eusebius's ceremony condemning Arius at the Council of Nicaea. Like his predecessors, he mistakenly believed that the power of the curse was effected by priestly ritual rather than through the family line of Constantine the Great. Now the bishop believed God had given him the opportunity to put his power to good use. Bishop Mathieu turned toward Mirceal. "And what would be your curse?" he inquired.

Mirceal gave the bishop a look of uncertainty.

"What would be your curse?" the bishop repeated.

Mirceal paused for a moment before the answer came to him. "I call on the Holy Spirit to send permanent injury onto my brother's name," he said angrily. "And..."

"And..." the bishop prompted.

"And I want my good name, and that of my family and my church, returned from my brother who defamed it," he continued.

Bishop Mathieu gave a fleeting glance at Father Stephen, who responded with an understanding nod. Then the bishop turned toward David and Xanro. "This curse can only be done—or undone—in the presence of the martyred families of Tover and Bar Kohba." Are both of you willing to swear an oath as to your family's martyrdom?"

David and Xanro nodded.

"Even then," the bishop continued, "the imprecation can be effected only in the presence of an iconic symbol of each family, and a tangible sign of the reason for the curse itself. Is that understood?"

Mirceal's expression now turned serious. "It is, Your Worship."

"The curse will last for a hundred years, unless undone within that time. And it may be reinstated by your heirs under the same circumstances I have described, for twenty-five generations." The bishop then looked purposefully at Mirceal. "Is that also understood?"

"Yes," Mirceal whispered.

"Then hereafter your name shall be a blessing. As such, it will be in your name that the peoples of the world will come together as family—just as our Lord Jesus told us it would."

"No family can hope for more, and none should strive for less," Mirceal responded humbly.

"It is a blessing that you can make and God can fulfill," the bishop added.

Mirceal's eyes flashed with hope. "Then it is a blessing that I hereby make—in this holy place—before God and man. It is a blessing that I make, not for myself, but for my heirs—and not because of the despair of the present, but the promise of the future."

"May God hear your plea," whispered Father Stephen.

"Amen," intoned the bishop.

"Amen," echoed Anna, Xanro and David in unison.

A moment later, Bishop Mathieu abruptly broke the uneasy silence. "Lest we forget," he began, "here on earth, God's work must surely be our own." Then his eyes darted in the direction of the priest. "That being the case, Father Stephen, would you be kind enough to assist me?"

The four companions watched with great astonishment as the bishop and the priest, moved the desk and carpet, then opened the trap door in the stone floor.

"Have them wait here, Father Stephen," the bishop said, taking the oil lamp and descending the stairs. Several minutes later he reappeared at the bottom of the stairwell. "Follow me," he ordered.

The bishop led them down the dark corridor into the secret room. The double-handled Pitcher of Constantine was resting in its basin on an oak table.

"Acts of unselfish courage for the protection of strangers, without expectation of reward, are the noblest deeds of man," the bishop began. "This is the example of our Lord and Savior Himself."

The bishop then turned to David and Xanro.

"Through your words and deeds, this imprecation I am about to make for the good name of Mirceal may be done, but only upon your uncoerced acknowledgement and approval. If you accept these conditions, then say 'I accept.'"

"I accept," Xanro and David said in unison.

"Do you have a personal item by which you will so swear this oath?"

Xanro withdrew his father's axe from his belt, and handed it to the bishop. "This is the axe of my father. It was found among the remains of his wagon after he was murdered by the fiends of the Dracula. It embodies the double triangle sign of my family." With that Xanro pulled up the right sleeve of his shirt and showed off the sign of the Tover tattooed on his forearm. "In the name of my deceased parents who were murdered by the Dracula, I so swear."

The bishop poured water from the pitcher onto the axe and into the basin. He returned the axe to Xanro and looked at David.

David withdrew the Bar Kochba coin from around his neck, and showed it to the bishop.

"Can you read the inscription?" the bishop asked.

"It is in a language I cannot read and do not understand," David answered.

"It is in Aramaic, the high Hebrew language spoken by the Jews during the Roman period. It was the language in which Jesus preached," explained the bishop.

"I was told it harkens back to the days when my ancestors rebelled against the Roman Empire itself."

"So it does," said the bishop. "The inscription says: 'Year One in the revolt to redeem Israel.' How fitting, since we are in year one of the revolt to redeem our country from the hands of the Dracula. Now please make your oath."

"This coin is the coin of my fathers. It embodies the sign of my people, which coincidentally, is also a double triangle. In the name of my parents murdered by the Dracula, I so swear."

The bishop poured water from the pitcher onto the coin and let it drip into the basin. He then returned the pendant to David.

"Do you accept the oaths of your friends?" the bishop asked, turning toward Mirceal.

"I do," he said.

"And by what personal item do you so swear?"

Mirceal pulled the Latin cross from around his neck and handed it to the bishop.

"This is the cross of my father that he earned as a knight and wore as a king. It is by this sign that he ruled our kingdom as Georges the Wise. It was removed from his body after he was murdered by my brother. In the name of my parents who were murdered by the Dracula, I so swear."

Again, the bishop poured water from the pitcher onto the cross and let it spill into the basin. When the ritual was completed, he handed the wet icon back to Mirceal. "And what tangible evidence do you offer as a reason for the curse that you are about to make?" he asked.

Mirceal put his arms around David, Xanro and his sister. "We have all been orphaned by the treachery of Dracula. What more compelling evidence can there be?"

The bishop nodded, then offered some incantations in a language that was foreign to all but the priest. He concluded in the local tongue, "We bear witness to the imprecation to restore the good name of Mirceal for a hundred years lasting twenty-five generations from year one in the revolt to redeem Transylvania. It has been subscribed and sworn under the honored signs of Tover and Bar Kochba, as tradition requires."

The bishop paused and looked directly at Mirceal. "The curse is now yours to pronounce. Choose your words carefully."

Mircea squinted demonstratively, as if asking the bishop to explain his admonition.

This the bishop was quick to do. "The curse you are about to utter will come to pass with surprising literalness," he began. "A stilted phrase that departs even slightly from your conscious intent could have disastrous consequences."

Mirceal nodded, then bowed his head and began to speak, "I, Mirceal, son of Georges, in accordance with the holy power now vested in me by the Orthodox Church of Christ, hereby curse the name of Dracula and bless the name of Mirceal. By this curse the name of Dracula will forever be the subject of loathing and scorn, and by this blessing the good name of Mirceal will be restored."

As Mirceal uttered his blessing and his curse, the bishop poured the water in the basin back into the pitcher. He then held Mirceal's head over the basin and, as in a baptism, washed the contents of the pitcher onto Mirceal's head and face.

"The blessing and the curse now live," the bishop said solemnly. "Let us pray"

In their own words, each of the participants asked God for His blessing. In so doing, however, Mirceal extended his curse to include all enemies of the Creator who defiled God's earth. As a direct descendant of Constantine, it was Mirceal's words, not the priestly rituals that would effect this Old Testament curse.

"The four of you will spend the night in this room with Father Stephen. You will all be safe here," the bishop said. "I will call for you at sunrise."

"Your Worship," Mirceal interrupted. "At great risk to yourself, you have provided me and my companions with more than we could have ever asked for. It now troubles me that earlier today I doubted you. I beg your forgiveness for such lack of confidence."

"It was not confidence you lacked, but hope. You have it now. You are forgiven, my son."

While the others rested from their long, exhausting day, Xanro collected the four medallions he had made, and meticulously etched on the back of each the imprecation of Mirceal, as recited by the bishop.

It read:

Imprecation

To Restore

The Good Name of

Mirceal

For 100 Years

Lasting 25 Generations

From Year One

In The Revolt

To Redeem Transylvania

Subscribed and Sworn

Under the Honored Signs

Of Tover

And Bar Kochba

ALEXANDRU'S PRAYER

While Xanro was etching the four medallions with the imprecation of Mirceal, David voiced a concern that had been troubling him all evening.

"The likelihood is high that the Draculs will not allow the small entourage of Father Stephen to leave the church compound without being searched," he said. "If that occurs, I fear Anna's thin disguise will be exposed."

"Fear not," Mirceal assured him. "We now have the comfort of the medallions and the power of the curse."

"But would we not have additional comfort if there were a plan that denied the Draculs of any purpose in even making such a search?"

"From whither could such denial of purpose come?" asked the bishop.

"From the Dracul guards themselves," suggested David.

"I beg you to elaborate," said the priest.

"We know that Alexandru is providing information to the Draculs," David began. "I suspect his ear is at your office door even as we speak."

Everyone nodded.

"So if the bishop confided in his trusted deacon that I will be delivering Mirceal and Anna to the church tomorrow at noon, as he thinks we plan to do anyway, would he not immediately inform the Draculs who are congregated outside?"

Everyone agreed.

"And would not a Dracul guard immediately inform the Dracula himself."

Again, everyone concurred.

"In that event, would neither the guards nor the Dracula see any purpose in interrogating the priests' entourage when they leave the church at dawn tomorrow?"

"It is a worthy plan," said the bishop, "except for one problem. It will ensure that the church is stormed at noon, and that you and Mirceal will then be apprehended."

Mirceal resolved the dilemma. "The church will be stormed in any event. What becomes of us is in God's hands. But if we increase the chances of Anna's escape, then I urge that it be done."

"I follow the path of Jesus, not Thespis," said the bishop, "but if playing the role of one who discloses confidences is what is required of me, then that is what I shall do."

"I have one other request," continued Mirceal. "I fear for Anna even in Vienna. I am convinced that there is only one place on earth where she will be safe, and that is with the knights who trained our father. I beg Your Worship to allow Father Stephen to take her to the place in Bavaria where the Bund of the Ruth has its Holy Order."

The bishop looked at Father Stephen.

"We can follow the Danube from Vienna to Munich. From there it will be easy enough to search out the place Mirceal described," said the priest.

"So it will be done," said the bishop.

"Thank you, My Worship."

"God be with you," the bishop replied. "With all of you."

Bishop Mathieu left the secret room, climbed up the stairs, and closed the trap door in the floor of his office. He returned the rug and furniture to their proper place. After assuring himself that everything was in order, the bishop left his office, locked the door, and mopped his brow with a deep sigh.

Alexandru was loitering in the hall.

"A trying day, My Worship?" the deacon inquired.

"I fear tomorrow will be more so," answered the bishop. Then lowering his voice to a whisper he confided to the deacon, "Our suspicions were correct, Alexandru. The miller will be bringing the royals here tomorrow at noon. They will be hiding in a wagon of hay, and it is in this church that they will find sanctuary."

Early the next morning, Anna, disguised in deacon's robes, left with Father Stephen's entourage exactly as planned. Upon exiting the church compound, the horses carrying the small party of clergy walked slowly past a cordon of disinterested Draculs. Anna's horse chose a poor moment to relieve himself, arousing the ire of the nearest guard. He called out at Anna, but she ignored him. When he called out again, with a similar result, he approached her horse in a menacing manner.

Father Stephen perceived an impending calamity, and quickly intervened: "The deacon is on a vow of silence, my good sir. I apologize for his apparent impertinence, but it would be a bad omen at the start of such a long, arduous journey if that vow were to be broken."

Placated, the Dracul muttered an oath under his breath, and allowed the entourage to pass without further ado.

Throughout the rest of the morning, and into the early afternoon, the Draculs were on the look-out for the anticipated hay wagon, but no wagon of any kind was forthcoming. Frustrated and angered with each passing minute, the Dracula decided to inspect the church in person. Flanked by two guards, he walked through the vestibule and into the sanctuary itself.

"Where is the bishop?" he demanded of the first deacon he encountered.

The deacon pointed in the direction of the bishop's office without comment. Dracula found Alexandru standing near the door.

"He's in there," Alexandru said. "I've heard many strange noises from inside, like the moving of furniture. I suspect there is a hidden door."

Dracula pounded on the door demanding that it be opened. When he heard no response, he ordered his guards to break it down. At the first sound of axes tearing away at the oaken timbers, Bishop Mathieu unlocked the door and pulled it open.

"Where are they?" Dracula demanded.

"I am alone," the bishop said calmly.

Dracula's eyes darted around the room.

"Move the desk," he ordered.

Moments later, his guards were on their hands and knees, searching for the latch to the trap door.

They found it soon enough.

"Show us the way," demanded the Dracula, touching his sword to the bishop's back in a menacing manner.

The bishop descended the stairs and proceeded down the narrow corridor until it dead-ended into the door of the decoy room.

"Open it," ordered the Dracula with growing impatience.

The door swung open to reveal an empty chamber.

"Enough of these games!" screamed the Dracula. "Guard, fetch me the woman."

"Yes, Your Highness," one of the guards responded.

He ran off with purpose in the direction from which he came. A few minutes later he returned gripping David's wife, Rachael, tightly by the wrist.

Dracula put his sword to her throat, but looked at the bishop.

"I will kill you both if you don't give up my brother," Dracula threatened.

"Say nothing," she stammered bravely. "He will kill us anyway."

"Haven't you killed enough?" answered the bishop. "First your parents, then your subjects, and now us?"

Alexandru summoned up his courage and angrily faced the bishop. "You are mistaken, Your Worship. King Georges was murdered by Mirceal."

Dracula sneered at Alexandru and then lashed out, "You pitiful idiot. I killed the king, and it will give me great pleasure to kill you as well." With that he plunged his sword into the deacon's chest.

As he writhed on the floor in pain, Alexandru realized that he had mistakenly betrayed both his king and his church. He prayed that he would not die with the recognition of this terrible sin as his last worldly thought.

"Now kill the woman," Dracula ordered.

But before the order could be obeyed, a painful wail came from behind the stone wall.

"Enough!" Mirceal cried. "Stop the killing."

A side of the wall moved exposing Mirceal, Xanro and David.

"Death to them all," Dracula ordered.

The two Draculs stormed the chamber. Xanro's axe hit one of the Dracul's a glancing blow before he was cut down. David fended off the other Dracul with an oak table before he, too, was slain by the Dracul's sword. Mirceal had removed the silver cross that hung from the wall and flung it at his brother, but it fell harmlessly to the ground. Dracula now advanced on Mirceal with a look of loathing and vengeance in his dark brown eyes.

"Beg me that I let you die without pain," he hissed pressing his sword against his brother's chest.

"I beg only to serve the Lord," Mirceal answered.

"You will beg only to serve me."

With his last measure of strength, Alexandru raised his body from the floor, picked up the silver cross that was lying on the ground and lunged with all his might at the Dracula.

"Long live King Mirceal," the deacon yelled as the weight of his body pushed a pointed bar of the cross entirely through Dracula's torso.

Dracula dropped his sword and touched the tip of the cross that speared his heart and protruded out of his chest.

"King Mirceal?" he gasped, choking on his own blood.

"You die in my service," whispered Mirceal.

ANDRU'S SCARS

Word of Dracula's treachery spread rapidly throughout the kingdom. True to Mirceal's curse, his brother's name was reviled throughout the land. Indeed, the very word "Dracula" became synonymous with terror and cruelty—not just in his native Transylvania, but throughout Europe and the Near East.

The name "Mirceal," on the other hand, was elevated to genuine approbation among his people. In his day, Mirceal was admired above all others except Mircea the Old and Georges the Wise. As such, this aspect of the curse was fulfilled exactly as it was sworn.

The land was also cleansed of the sign of the comet. In its place was substituted the traditional Eastern cross, albeit with decidedly untraditional pointed cross bars. The bravery of Mathieu and the martyrdom of Alexandru were celebrated as part of annual holidays by a reinvigorated Orthodox Christian community.

Mirceal was astonished at both the rapidity and the literalness with which the words of the curse took effect. Nonetheless, Dracula's demise came at a cost. One of the most immediate was that, during the melee in the church basement, Mirceal's abdomen had been lacerated by his brother's sword. The wound quickly became infected and Mirceal lay near death for weeks before making his recovery. By then a Dracul knight claiming lineage through Mircea the Old assumed the Romanian throne and moved the gravitas of the kingdom back to Wallachia. In his weakened condition, and for the sake of his country, Mirceal chose not to challenge his successor.

As he lay recovering in the castle of his birth, Mirceal learned that, during his brother's brief reign, Dracula had sired a son through one of the Moldavian handmaids who had been brought there to labor. Infuriated that the product of such a licentious relationship was begotten on the bed of his murdered parents, Mirceal banished both mother and infant from the kingdom. Several months later he learned that the two were living in England under an Anglicized version of his brother's name—Drake.

About the same time Mirceal received word concerning the Drake family's relocation in England, Father Stephen returned from Vienna with news about Anna.

"She was well received by the Ruth," he reported.

"It is ironic," observed Mirceal, "that the reason for her departure ceased to exist less than a day after she departed."

"It was not irony, but providence," corrected the priest.

"Call it what you wish," Mirceal conceded. "But after my brush with death, I considered dispatching a detail of soldiers to Bavaria for the purpose of bringing her home."

The priest arched his brow.

"But much as I miss my sister, there is little here for her now except misery and grief."

"Then you will be pleased to know that she has found happiness in her adopted land."

Now it was Mirceal who raised his brow.

"She met a man named Hermann from the Brotherhood of the Red," the priest explained. "He is a good man, who seeks your blessing on the occasion of their betrothal."

"If this man you call Hermann is so good, why do I detect hesitation in your voice?" Mirceal inquired.

"Though he is both good and honorable, he is nonetheless an adherent of the Roman Church."

"Yet he makes my sister happy?"

"Does conversion, even for the purpose of personal happiness, absolve disobedience to church doctrine?" the priest challenged.

Father Stephen had raised a profound question to which Mirceal had no immediate answer.

"When our creed says that the Holy Spirit comes through the Father, can the Roman clergy insist that it also comes through the Son?" the priest continued.

Mirceal's thoughtful response startled the priest: "The church chooses its doctrine, but the people choose their church. The freedom of the church to choose the former, and the freedom of the people to choose the latter, while the king remains indifferent to the choices of both, must supersede everything."

Father Stephen was aghast. "That is blasphemy," he said.

"That is our Bible," Mirceal responded. "Was it not the prophet Malachi who reminded us, 'Have we not all one father?'"

"Hath not one God created us all?" Father Stephen whispered, completing the verse.

And so with great happiness, Mirceal messengered both a greeting and a blessing to his beloved sister and her betrothed. Over time he sent her much correspondence in which he recounted his confrontation with Dracula, his wounds and his miraculous recovery.

Mirceal was also happy, though loathe to admit it, that it was the new Wallachian king, and not he, who inherited the many challenges that came with the Crown. Among other things, the disciplined army built by his father was now in complete disarray and the productive economy based on the System of the Pebbles was in a total shambles. Even worse, most of the population lived in abject misery—bound to the land in a perpetual and hopeless circle of life called serfdom.

On another front, the dormant threat from the Muslim East had reappeared. In response, the king agreed to pay tribute to the Ottoman Turks, thereby reducing the land to a Muslim suzerainty. It was only in this way that the king was able to maintain the peace and allow Romania to remain a Christian enclave amidst the advancing sword of Islam.

Being at a crossroads between Europe and Asia, between Islam and Christianity, and between the Eastern Church and the Church of Rome, the land saw little respite from war, civil strife, and tyranny during the centuries that followed. In the process, Mirceal's son, Cristian, saw the Jews of Romania herded into small rural communities, like

Gesher, from which they could not leave without dispensation from the authorities. It was in those communities that they were subject to frequent raids resulting in looting, rape, and even murder.

In 1488, Cristian watched the transgressions against the Jews unfold in helpless horror. "They did so much for our people, and this is how we repay them?" he asked the confidante of his late father—a now gray and wrinkled Father Stephen.

The elderly clergyman shook his head defiantly. "It is not the world of grace and mercy taught by our Saviour," he answered.

"Yet our people defile the world and profane our Lord by doing these terrible things in our Saviour's name," Cristian responded.

Father Stephen gave Cristian a fatherly pat on the head. "It is the gravest of sins, my son." Cristian knew not how to reply, so the cleric continued. "Taking the Lord's name in vain is the only sin that God will not forgive," he explained. "The Decalogue is without equivocation on this point."

Cristian now regained his tongue. "Taking the name of the Lord in vain?" he asked. "I thought it was merely a prohibition against profanity."

The priest shook his head. In the process, his long hair and heavy beard swung out of phase with the movement of his chin. "This commandment is a strict injunction against using God as an excuse for wrongdoing—such as harming the innocent," he elucidated. "God will never forgive one who blasphemes His name in this way because it falsely suggests that such sins are sanctioned by the Lord." Father Stephen paused to let the impact of his words sink in. "By these acts, our people are accomplishing precisely the opposite of what God wants from us."

The priest's explanation now became clear in Cristian's mind. And it rekindled the legend of an ancient family curse placed on the nations of Western Europe after the Jews had been unjustly expelled from their homes 200 years earlier. Anger welled up inside him until he could control it no longer. "Then let there be a similar curse upon my own people—and any other people who behave in this way," Cristian said aloud. He paused for a moment to contemplate the words he had spoken. Then, dissatisfied that his curse would bring sufficient retribution on the peoples of the earth who defiled God's creation, he added a further denunciation: "Let them enjoy a brief period of grandeur, so they may taste the world of the righteous; then let it be followed by a lengthy period of defeat, humiliation, and misery so their pain will be that much more severe."

The fate of the Romani was even worse than that of the Jews. Cristian's grandson, Milan, saw them sold into chattel slavery, and in a burst of anger, repeated the curse of Cristian. But it was Milan's great grandson, Charles Mirceal, who ultimately left the gray stone castle in Transylvania, and moved, as had his distant Aunt Anna many generations earlier, to the land of the Germans. It was there that he met an engaging gentleman by the name of Peter Minuit.

Minuit was interested in Mirceal's ideas regarding investment and risk; Mirceal was interested in Minuit's ideas regarding religion and good works. The connection between faith and prosperity was wholly new to Charles Mirceal. He found the philosophy so consistent with his previously unarticulated thinking, that he began attending services with eagerness and regularity. Soon enough, Mirceal became a congregant at Minuit's church, which was presbyterial in organization and Calvinist in doctrine.

In 1622, less than a year after Charles Mirceal's conversion, he and Minuit fled to Holland in an effort to escape the religious violence that was consuming the rest of Western Europe. It was there that the two men learned of a business organization that seemed to be a practical embodiment of their religious beliefs: the Dutch West India Company. They invested heavily in the company, and because of their business acumen, soon became principals. It was in that capacity that they were sent across the Great Ocean to an aboriginal-occupied place in which their company had a huge, but risky, financial stake. And it was also there that Charles Mirceal changed his name to the more phonetically-friendly and Dutch-looking spelling of "Merkle."

In a new place, with a new religion, and a new name, Charles Merkle could finally cast off the suffering his family had experienced in his homeland. He would never again return to the land of his birth.

For those who did remain, it wasn't until the early summer of 1863 that Romania awakened to the enlightenment that had long since shone on the more westerly nations of Europe. And it was only then that the institutions needed for a modern Romanian state began to formally take shape. This, in turn, resulted in a program of land reform, the liberation of the serfs from their feudal lords, and freedom for the Romani slaves after centuries of bondage.

One of the Romani who saw the light of freedom in that day was Andru Tover, twenty generations removed from his patriarch, Guruv. Andru was a rebellious lad whose back bore the scars of repeated lashings by his former master. On his belt hung an old two-headed axe and around his neck hung a bronze medallion. On one side of the medallion was a strange diagram. On the other side was an even stranger imprecation that was subscribed and sworn in both his family name and that of another which he did not recognize.

The descendants of the three other Transylvania families who owned identical bronze medallions also wore a second family heirloom around their necks. The progeny of Merkle and Ruth wore a silver cross of the Latin style; the Bar Kochba heir wore a pendant made from an old coin taken from the Holy Land.

Andru Tover absent-mindedly gripped the handle of his axe, then his bronze medallion. Both, he was told, had been fashioned by his forebears centuries earlier when the Romani had sufficient freedom to express their creativity. Now, however, he envisioned freedom and prosperity, not for his ancestors, but for his son, and not in Romania, but in America. For reasons he did not understand, such thoughts caused his temples to ring, and his eyes to burn.

PART II
NEW YORK CITY

Munsee's Arrow

About 10,000 years before the Common Era, Asian nomads began migrating across the Upper Siberian land bridge to North America. As aboriginal peoples had done throughout history, the extended families of these wanderers banded together both for protection, and to better provide for the necessities of life. Over the ensuing millennia, these familial clans coalesced into tribe-based communities that became scattered across the American continents.

Those tribes that could adapt to the brutal forces of nature and successfully compete for food with neighboring clans would survive in this harsh environment; those that could not would perish. In the process, the inexorable forces of heredity, environment, and luck caused these tribes to become differentiated by physical features, language, and customs. Of the ten million natives that would eventually inhabit the pre-Columbian Americas, perhaps as few as a million lived in what would become the United States; perhaps only a hundred thousand lived in the sliver of land between the agitated waters of the great eastern ocean and the majestic blue-ridged peaks that loomed above the Piedmont as little as a hundred miles to the West.

Centuries before Vlad Dracula seized the Wallachian throne, and cast the Romanian lands back in the direction of the Dark Ages, three of the tribes on the great American land mass would not merely survive, but evolve into highly advanced civilizations. They were the Incas in what later became known as Peru, the Aztecs in what is now called Mexico, and the Maya who lived in places that would one day be called Yucatan, Belize and Guatemala. As in their European counterparts, war, slavery, and torture were endemic to them.

The Maya built great cities, developed a storehouse of knowledge based on the written word, and progressed further in mathematics and astronomy than anyone else on earth. Unfortunately, and for reasons still unknown, the great Mayan civilization started to decline at the very moment Portuguese seamen had begun exploring the west coast of Africa. By the time these Iberian adventurers turned their ships westward, and reached the New World, the Mayan cities were in ruins.

On the other hand, the Aztec city of Tenochtitlan, inhabited by a dominant tribe called the "Mexica," continued to thrive. Indeed, Tenochtitlan had a population of over 100,000 Aztecs. This far exceeded the population of the largest city in the most powerful country of Europe—Spain.

Not all the native peoples in the Americas were as advanced as the Maya. In those lands that would one day become the United States, the tribes had barely progressed past the Stone Age. Thus at the height of the Mayan Empire these more northerly tribes had no written language, no implements of iron or bronze, and no means of land transportation other than walking. Beasts of burden had not been tamed, the wheel had not yet been invented, and species of the equine family, all destroyed in the last ice age, would not return to the New World soil until brought there by Spanish conquistadors over a century later.

Munsee was the eldest son of Unalchitgo, chief of an eastern tribe called "Mana-hat-tan," which meant "Isolated-in-Water," in the native tongue. Though part of the much larger Wappinger Confederation, the Mana-hat-tan controlled extensive lands east of what would be later called the Hudson River, but was then referred to as a "Quinnehutek" or "long tidal water" in the language of the Wappinger. Most likely, the Mana-hat-tan tribal name was derived from the fact that the far southern tip of its holdings was actually an island formed by a triangle of riverways including the Hudson.

Unlike his father, who could wield a stone axe with prodigious strength, yet shoot an arrow with sublime skill, Munsee was frail and uncoordinated. He was a terrible disappointment to both his parents and his tribe. Although already sixteen years of age, Munsee inexplicably showed little interest in tracking and hunting. He preferred, instead, to spend his time experimenting with different woods and flints in an attempt to devise an improved hunting bow and a more accurate flying arrow.

Through trial and error, Munsee determined that willow was the best wood for the bow and beech was the best wood for the arrow. He used a conventional length of deer sinew for the bowstring, but lubricated it with beeswax to prevent it from drying out and shrinking. Since bowstrings tended to break, he got the idea of making a spare bowstring, and wrapping it around the center of the bow where it could be used as a "grip" for the weak hand until needed. He also realized that even the supple willow bows tended to warp under constant pressure from the bowstring, so he deduced that one end of the string should be unfastened from its bow notch when not in use.

The problem Munsee could not solve was how to make the arrow fly straight. After much experimentation, he assumed that the speed of the arrow at release from the bowstring had a favorable effect on maintaining the direction of its flight. This was why a strong man like his father could pull the bowstring back further, discharge the arrow with greater speed, and hence achieve somewhat better accuracy. But even arrows released in such a manner tended to dart and flutter off course long before reaching their intended target.

One afternoon in early spring, Munsee contemplated the problem for the umpteenth time. He was alone, as usual, sitting chin in hand on a stump in a grove of maple trees that reached high above the bluffs overlooking the Hudson River. The double-winged seeds of the maples were falling from the tree limbs like rain. Munsee soon became obsessed by the flurry of descending samara, each spinning furiously on its wings as it dropped to earth. His eye traced the path of a single seed through a fifty-foot fall, and marveled at the straightness of its path. The seed then hit the soft ground and augured itself into the soil.

It was at that moment that the idea hit him. "It's the spin that keeps the seed on its path," he said to himself. "If I can make an arrow spin along its length as it soars through the air, it too will not float or flutter."

Munsee picked up a few maple seeds and rubbed the wings between his thumb and fingers. They were dry and brittle. He pulled an arrow from his quiver and studied it from the flint tip to the notched end that accommodated the bowstring. He envisioned the arrow flying through the air, and wondered whether it would spin around its long axis if he could attach the seed wings onto the surface of the shaft at a slight angle to the direction of its flight.

"The seed wings would catch the air, and cause the shaft to rotate," he surmised. "And the faster the arrow flies toward its target, the faster it will spin."

With that, he removed a flint arrowhead from one of his arrows, and used it like a knife to make three diagonal slots around the circumference of the arrow shaft, halfway between its ends. He then gently pushed a seed wing into each slot, inserted the notched end of the arrow into the bowstring, took aim at a tree trunk and let the arrow fly. To Munsee's disappointment it floated and fluttered exactly as arrows had done in the past. When Munsee retrieved the experimental arrow, however, he realized that the seed wings had fallen out of their diagonal slots the moment the arrow had been released from the bow.

Munsee thought for a moment, and was soon struck by another idea. With his flint, he scratched through the bark of a healthy tree branch, extracted several drops of sap from beneath the bark, and then used his finger to guide the sap into each slot. He then carefully placed a seed wing into the three sap-laden slots, and waited impatiently for the sap to dry. Cautiously, he put the arrow into his bowstring, and again shot the arrow in the direction of the same tree. To his great delight, the arrow flew straight and true before embedding itself in the center of the tree trunk.

In the ensuing months, Munsee spent many hours testing his arrows. In the process he substituted carefully cut turkey feathers for the brittle maple seed wings, and moved the slots cut into the periphery of the arrow from the center of the shaft to the rear. When he had perfected his design, he fashioned scores of arrows by hand. Then one evening he invited several Mana-hat-tan braves of his age into the woods to show them his invention, and explain why it worked. His presentation was interrupted by noises coming from the village.

The young braves arrived to find their village under attack by a rogue clan of the Delaware Nation which had crossed the Hudson under cover of darkness. Munsee led the counter-attack, and with the aid of his new arrows, he and his young comrades warded off the invaders. One was killed, two were captured and enslaved, and the rest fled to their canoes.

The following afternoon a feast was declared in Munsee's honor. Women of the tribe began work on a wampum belt, made from whelk and clam shells, to commemorate the occasion. The men competed in archery contests using Munsee's arrows. Centuries later an ingenious German gunsmith would duplicate Munsee's idea by rifling the inside of a musket barrel with a spiral groove. The groove imparted spin to the musket ball allowing it to fly in a straight path. It was in this way that sharpshooters would be able to accurately hit a target at three-hundred paces. Their muskets with grooved bores became known as "rifles."

The generations that followed Munsee remembered him with fondness and pride. The stump by the maples was maintained as a shrine. Periodically, of course, the tribe suffered attacks on the lower parts of their lands by the Delaware, periodically they faced difficult winters, and periodically they had trouble finding food, but they always persevered. When canoes of unimaginable size arrived at the mouth of the Hudson, however, and alien people emerged carrying exploding sticks and riding huge beasts, most of the Mana-hat-tan knew that they faced the greatest challenge of their long history. All they could do was pray to their holy spirits that someone with the wisdom of Munsee would guide them through the crisis. Their prayers would be answered by a chief they called Quonchock.

MIGUEL'S HACIENDA

In the middle ages, the monarchs of Europe urged their warriors and adventurers to travel east, recapture the Holy Land, and forcefully convert the infidels. En route the Crusaders found a savage diversion from their original mission. It took the form of brutally murdering every Jew that they could find along the way.

When the Crusaders finally returned home with their pillage and plunder, they brought with them something else as well: the living bacilli of the Bubonic Plague. By the end of the fourteenth century one fourth of Western Europe's entire population succumbed to this Black Death. Those who survived asked their kings to explain what curse was upon them that could cause such a scourge of pain, suffering and misery. By then, however, their kings had turned their eyes from the East to the West.

In 1492, after King Ferdinand expelled the Jews from Spain, he sent Christopher Columbus off in search of gold. When Columbus made his historic voyage, however, he discovered neither gold nor America. What he did discover was a group of islands in a sea later named for a tribe of cannibals known as the Caribs. Though he was over 10,000 miles from the Indian sub-continent, Columbus referred to these Caribbean Islands as the West Indies, and referred to their native inhabitants as "Indians."

Within twenty years after Columbus's voyage, Spain had colonized the islands, subjugated the Indians and began importing African slaves in massive numbers to work newly created tobacco and sugar plantations. Other European nations quickly followed suit. Eventually, over eleven million Africans arrived in the new world as slaves—all but 500,000 of whom ended up in the European colonies of Latin America and the Caribbean.

The most successful of the European imperialists was Spain, whose mission was to exploit the West Indies for the purpose of financing King Charles's wars with England. When a Spanish bureaucrat heard persistent rumors of additional wealth that existed on the continental mainland controlled by the Mexica tribe of the Aztec Nation, he conquered the Aztecs, and converted them to Christianity. Ironically, it would be the progeny of the converts who would teach the true message of Jesus to the descendants of the proselytizers.

The land of the Aztecs was renamed New Spain, and its treasures were loaded onto galleons and sent to Madrid. In London, Queen Elizabeth had an alternative plan for funding her war against King Charles: whatever the Spanish stole from the Indians, the English would steal from the Spanish. To facilitate this plan, the Virgin Queen secretly financed privateers to prey on Spanish settlements in the New World, plunder their wealth, and sink their ships.

One of these privateers was a flamboyant sailor with a shadowy past by the name of Francis Drake. Drake was such a successful pirate that he was knighted for his efforts. Nonetheless, he died without a legitimate child to whom he could legally bequeath his fortune. It was rumored, however, that Drake had fathered offspring—some of whom knew of his secret family history.

Despite the British privateers, Spaniards from New Spain sailed freely up the Pacific coast of North America in search of more wealth to exploit, and additional souls to save. In the process they became familiar with an elongated land mass, thought to be the mystical island ruled by an Amazon Queen named Califia. The Spaniards, therefore, called the place California. In due course, California and the vast lands stretching eastward for over a thousand miles to French Louisiana, were annexed into the Spanish colony of New Spain.

Spain's initial success in the New World emboldened its king to launch a full-scale invasion of its arch-enemy—Protestant England. To do so, he assembled an unprecedented armada of 130 ships carrying over 30,000 men. In 1588, the armada was annihilated—not by the British, but by a perfect North Sea storm—leaving Spain to ponder who was responsible for the execration that forced them off of the world stage.

Spain's humiliation was compounded a little over two centuries later when Indian peasants in their colony of New Spain revolted against the ruling class of criollos—descendants of Spanish nobility born in the New World. Eventually the colony wrestled itself free from its Mother Country and renamed itself Mexico. Unlike the revolution that began elsewhere on the American continent in 1776, Mexico had no "founding fathers" who could create a democratic republic tempered by a series of "checks and balances," much less envision one in which "all men are created equal." As a result, the new country experienced struggles for power resulting in a succession of unstable, repressive and often dictatorial governments. This, in turn, led to internal revolts on the part of the more distant provinces which desired independence from Mexico itself. In the course of one of these revolts, Guatemala freed itself from Mexico in 1823. Texas did the same in 1836.

By then, the descendants of the criollos had gained control over sizeable rancheros that were carved out of twenty-one Spanish missions that Franciscan padres had established along the California coast. These California criollos understood that one day soon they would have to decide whether to remain in the Mexican union with their Spanish-speaking brethren, or fight for independence like the Texans and the Guatemalans. It was to discuss these alternatives that, in the spring of 1844, the leaders of seven powerful criollos families met at the 12,000 acre ranchero of Miguel Castillo Chavez. The Castillo hacienda was located a few miles north of the San Gabriel Mission complex in a California community that would later be called Pasadena.

The criollos were seated around a heavy wooden table decorated with hand painted tiles. Each man was impeccably groomed and fastidiously dressed. All wore rich leather boots customized with artistic tooling, colorful shirts having intricate embroideries on the chest pockets and sleeves, and matching trousers with the same embroidered patterns continuing down the outside seam of each pant leg. Silk ribbons, festooned into elaborate bows, were knotted around their shirt collars, and a matching sash was tied around the waist with the loose ends falling over a hip. Black cloaks and black felt sombreros having a low, cylindrical crown and a wide flat brim were hung on wooden pegs anchored into a plaster wall for that purpose. Above each peg was a large wooden crucifix. On the opposite wall was a colorful fresco of the Archangel Gabriel, wings spread, horn raised, gold halo shimmering against puffy white clouds.

As to the issue at hand, three of the criollos favored continued union with Mexico, and three favored independence. Only their host had not yet taken a position. Juan Carlos Gonzalez de Soto spoke for the union. Not only did he own thousands of acres of arable land outside the original Franciscan Mission of San Diego de Alcala, but he controlled much of the commerce flowing into and out of the Pueblo of San Diego itself.

"Everything I am, everything I have, and everything I believe in are attributable to two immutable facts: I was born in Mexico, and I am of pure Spanish descent. Would not each of you gentlemen admit the same?"

Bautista Cabrera Gomez, representing the advocates for independence, spoke next. Senor Cabrera owned 100,000 acres near Mission Santa Clara at the southern tip of San Francisco Bay. His holdings were almost 500 miles north of those owned by Juan Carlos. Cabrera concluded that the further one lived from Mexico proper, the freer one was from government bureaucracy, and the stronger one's desire for independence became.

"I acknowledge with reverence and humility the words of Senor Gonzalez," Bautista began thoughtfully, "and I accept them for the truth that they are. Indeed, it is only with deep reluctance that I speak at all."

Juan Carlos tipped his head in Bautista's direction, appreciative of his words of respect.

"Nonetheless," Bautista continued, "the gravity of the situation and my sense of duty to my fellow countrymen, compels me to express a different point of view."

The two criollos who also advocated independence acknowledged Bautista's comment with a barely audible, "*Si, si.*"

This emboldened Bautista to continue, "It is therefore with deep regret that I must acknowledge yet another truth. The government of Mexico is corrupt and incompetent, and if we cherish our liberty we must disassociate ourselves from the tyrants who run it."

Everyone looked at Juan Carlos for rebuttal. The gentleman cleared his throat, and then forthrightly answered his friend. "Independence will lead inexorably to union with the Americans. Are we not better off in union with our own people rather than the Anglos?"

The two criollos who agreed with Juan Carlos mumbled, "*Si, si.*"

"Yet Texas still remains independent," Bautista rejoined.

"It will only be a matter of time before she is annexed," Juan Carlos countered.

Indian servants periodically brought food and drink as the discussion continued throughout the afternoon and into the evening. One of them, a woman who bore a red birthmark on her back which was hereditarial proof of her Mayan descent, wondered if these gentlemen from aristocratic families would consider the fate of people like her in the course of their deliberations. "Freedom and opportunity supersede language," she thought. "If given a vote, my people would choose the Americans." Then she quickly made the sign of the cross to assuage her guilt about even thinking of siding with the Protestant Anglos.

Despite strong differences of opinion and the seriousness of the subject, the discourse among the criollos was polite and amiable. Throughout the entire debate, Miguel Castillo remained silent. After another round of maguey tequila, Juan Carlos turned to Senor Castillo. "You have been quiet all day," he observed. "Do you not have an opinion that could break our deadlock?"

The six criollos turned toward Miguel with great anticipation. He had an impeccably smooth, tannish complexion, a youthful smile and a lithe, athletic body.

"I am your host," he tentatively began, "and for that reason I believed it would be ill-mannered to express my views on this sensitive subject."

"We are no longer so sensitive," one of the gentlemen laughed, pouring another glass of tequila and consuming its contents in a single swallow.

114

"Nor would we be offended by ill-manners," smiled another, who did likewise with his own glass of spirits.

Miguel blushed. But when he began to speak, his compadres listened attentively. "My friend Juan Carlos is absolutely correct when he predicts that Texas will be consumed by the American nation. Indeed, the same fate would befall California shortly after our sons spilled their blood for Californian independence."

Three heads in the Juan Carlos camp nodded approvingly.

"But," Miguel continued, "my friend Bautista is also correct that the Mexican government is corrupt and incompetent. We would leave our grandchildren a regrettable legacy if we consigned their fate to these Mexican dictators."

Now three other heads nodded in agreement. But then all realized that Miguel had presented them with a conundrum: Juan Carlos and Bautista could not both be right when they were recommending distinctly different courses of action.

Miguel tried to choose his words carefully. "Anglos are coming to California in increasing numbers, just as they did in Texas. Soon these headstrong people will raise the flag of rebellion. As a result, America and Mexico will go to war over California. Each side will promise us much to join them in their struggle, because we can help determine the outcome of that war. In the end, neither will keep their promises. Therefore the question we must answer is, regardless of their promises, would our grandchildren fare better with the experiment in democracy offered in English-speaking America, or the experiment in tyranny offered by Spanish-speaking Mexico. For their sake, I would side with the Americans, even if that means becoming one of them myself."

The six gentlemen shook their heads in unison, and mumbled, "No, no."

"Join the Anglos? You must be loco," Juan Carlos responded, half jokingly.

Now it was Bautista who spoke. "I don't know if my friend Miguel is right or wrong, but he has opened my eyes to a matter of great importance. The decision we make today is not for us. It is for our grandchildren. Yet who among us is wise enough to predict what would be best for our progeny in the next century."

Bautista's comments were followed by another round of drinks, and then a prolonged reticence on the part of any of the criollos to speak at all.

Juan Carlos finally broke the silence. "If we join the American nation, our grandchildren will speak English."

"If we join the American nation our grandchildren will have freedom," Bautista countered.

"How will our grandchildren retain their heritage in the dominant American culture?" one man asked.

"People from other nations have retained their heritage in the American culture," another man answered.

"Our grandchildren will not be accepted in America."

"Our grandchildren will prosper in America—and then they will be accepted."

"In the names of our grandfathers who first explored these lands, we must remain Mexicans."

"The names of our grandfathers will forever remain associated with these lands even if we become Americans."

And so the criollos, like every other group that came to America, evaluated the compromises to their native culture that American citizenship would entail. In the end, the criollos decided to cast their lot with the Americans. So, when the inevitable war with Mexico came, the American triumph was made easier because, to the surprise of the Mexicans, Spanish California had little enthusiasm for the Mexican cause. A couple of years later, California followed Texas into the American union. Eleven years after that, California and Texas found themselves on opposite sides in a war that would determine whether the American union would continue to exist.

ANGELA'S VOW

The Gher N-Gheren River—which meant "River Among Rivers" in the native tongue—was renamed "Niger" by the European sea captains who began exploring the coast of West Africa in the fifteenth century. The Niger River originates in the Foula Djallon Mountains about 200 miles from where the western bulge of Africa juts into the Atlantic Ocean. Ironically, this great river begins its long journey to the sea by flowing in the opposite direction. After traveling about a thousand miles farther inland, the Niger makes a sharp right angle turn to the south, and then continues for yet a greater distance until it empties its waters into the Atlantic at the bight of the African Continent.

The area drained by the Niger is immense—about the size of Western Europe. In the latter half of the fifteenth century this land was home to hundreds of different ethnic groups. Each group was distinguished by different linguistic dialects, tribal customs, and religious ceremonies. Like their brethren in Europe whose complexions ranged from fair to swarthy, the complexions of the Niger Africans ranged from copper to ebony. Nonetheless, when Iberian seamen began exploring the west coast of Africa in that day, they referred to any person of the Niger as a "Negro"—which simply meant "black" in the Portuguese tongue.

Portuguese ships hop-scotched from port to port along the southern coast of the great bulge of the African Continent. In so doing, these European explorers came into contact with the Black African kingdoms of Mali, Mossi, Ashanti, Oyo, and Benin. North of these kingdoms was the dominant empire of Songali, which was forcefully converted to Islam in the aftermath of the Muslim invasions of North Africa centuries earlier. Because of their location, the Songali controlled the lucrative trade routes between the Black African kingdoms to the south, and the prosperous Arabian states that hugged the Mediterranean in the north. And so it was that for many generations the Black African kingdoms obtained textiles and manufactured goods from the Mediterranean states, and in return, the states of the Mediterranean obtained ivory, gold—and slaves.

Initially, there was a genuine feeling of mutual respect between the nobility of the Iberian and Niger kingdoms. Neffi Kerekou, the King of Benin, was welcomed to the Portuguese Court in Lisbon, and treated in the same manner as any comparable monarch of Europe. As a result, some of the Benin learned the languages and customs of Western Europe. And while they admired the magnificent cities and wondrous buildings, they viewed the purposeless cruelty which permeated European societies with quiet disdain. For his part, Prince Juan Castillo de Leon, one of several cousins in line to the Spanish throne, was awestruck by the colorful flowing robes, exquisite sculptures, and exotic dances that were introduced to his court for the first time by these peaceable, well-mannered African guests. The intricate carvings in wood, ivory, and bronze exceeded in creativity and skill any works of the same genre made by pre-Renaissance European artists.

This cordiality came to an abrupt end when European explorers discovered immense new lands on the west side of the Atlantic. These lands had enormous mineral and agricultural wealth which could be exploited only with vast amounts of manual labor. Initially, the Europeans tried to use the indigenous populations for that purpose. This effort failed miserably, however, because the people native to the Americas lacked immunity from diseases carried to the New World by the Europeans. As a result, they died en masse.

Europeans next tried to bring their own populations, still mired in serfdom, to the New World as slaves. This too failed for a number of reasons. Chief among them was the fact that people from such northerly latitudes were unsuited to labor in the tropical climates of the Caribbean Islands and the Portuguese Colony of Brazil to which they were brought.

Soon the Portuguese began purchasing men and women from the kingdoms of West Africa and shipping them to the New World as chattel slaves—by far the most cruel of the many forms of involuntary servitude that were extant throughout the world. These people of the Niger had the strength, stamina and intelligence to perform the required labor in the steaming environs where they were held in bondage. But unlike either the native populations or the European serfs who were initially enslaved, they could not obtain their freedom by escaping from their owners and then melting, inconspicuously, into an existing population.

For the next 200 years, the Portuguese had a virtual monopoly on the African slave trade. In due course, Spain, France, Holland, England and Sweden, as well as many privateers, were participating in this lucrative business. The latter were particularly greedy, ruthless and cruel.

One hot July afternoon sometime in the second half of the eighteenth century, Osei Kerekou, Prince of Benin, relaxed in the shade provided by the roof of a stone watch tower and scanned the western horizon through his spyglass. The two-masted schooner first appeared as a disembodied dot moving slowly toward him. Soon the huge foresail became faintly visible against the bright blue sky. When the visage of a fire-breathing dragon emblazoned on the foresail could be made out—spear in one claw, cross in the other—Osei knew that the privateer, Thomas Drake, would arrive in Benin exactly as planned.

Osei descended quickly from the tower. He went straight to the holding pens located on the edge of the beach. Over three-hundred souls—men, women and youths—had spent the past week there, chained together in groups of ten. Their ankles were shackled and their wrists were manacled.

"We'll load them tonight," he told his younger brother, Okomfu. Though bigger and stronger than Osei, Okomfu had always shown great deference to, and respect for, his older brother.

"Do you still trust Captain Drake?" Okomfu asked.

"Drake is a scoundrel," Osei answered, "but at least he is my scoundrel. I get what I want, and so does he."

Okomfu shuddered that the fate of so many human beings could be discussed so matter-of-factly.

"Now ready the canoes so we can begin the transfer at dusk," Osei ordered.

Later that afternoon Drake's schooner anchored a quarter mile offshore and several four-oared skiffs were lowered into the calm waters of the Gulf of Guinea. One of the boats carried Captain Drake; the others carried the cargo eagerly awaited by Osei. When Drake walked ashore, his pale complexion, framed by his long dark hair and full black beard, seemed eerily ghost-like.

Drake was tall and thin. He wore high black boots, breeches, a long blue coat, and a matching three-cornered hat. A pistol and cutlass hung from his belt. The handle of a dagger was visible under his vest.

"Welcome to Benin," Osei greeted him in English.

"The welcome will be all the sweeter when you see what I have brought," Drake answered, extending a bony hand in the direction of the prince. Osei grabbed it in his, and shook it firmly.

As Drake spoke, the sailors unloaded four wooden chests from the rowboats. The captain beckoned his mate to unlock them. With little fanfare, Drake threw open the lids of the first two chests. One contained colorful glass beads; the other held semi-precious stones that sparkled in the sunlight. The Kerekou brothers were not particularly impressed.

With greater showmanship, however, Drake thrust up the lids of the remaining two chests, and smiled triumphantly. Each was filled to the brim with shells of the Cowrie—snails that lived in the warm, shallow waters off of the African coast. Osei beamed with approval. The shells were of high quality. Some were six inches across. All were shiny and colorful. Used as currency among the Niger kingdoms, as well as many of the neighboring Bantu communities, the shells would bring great wealth to the Benin royalty in the form of ivory, grain, cattle, and human souls.

As dusk approached, and the water of the gulf blazed in the reflection of the setting sun, Captain Drake unloaded skiff after skiff of valuable cargo and set it upon the beach for the Kerekous' approval. There were bolts of fine linen and cotton cloth, piles of iron stock in the form of sheet and bars, bottles of brandy and barrels of rum. Osei was overjoyed at this ostentatious display of wealth, but expected more—crates filled with muskets and pistols, kegs of powder and bags of lead shot.

"First let me see my prize," Drake demanded.

Osei nodded, and escorted Drake to the holding pens. "Three hundred and thirty seven souls, counted and numbered as you requested," Osei said proudly.

"You promised me three fifty," Drake scowled.

"There is strong competition among the kingdoms now. It was only at great effort that I have provided you with what I have."

"I need three fifty," insisted Drake.

"When we get the guns we will be able to do better. I can make up the difference on your next visit," Osei suggested.

"There may be no next visit," Drake announced. "I have bought land and property in the New York Colony. With profits from this voyage I will be free from debts. But 350 souls I was promised, and 350 souls I shall have. I will give you two hours."

Drake pulled a watch from his vest and made a mental note of the time.

Osei looked at his brother. "Get me thirteen more bodies," he demanded.

Okomfu gave him a frantic look.

"Get them now," Osei repeated angrily.

Okomfu obediently turned away, and with a few Benin warriors began walking in the direction of the nearby Ashanti-controlled village of Quidah.

"My brother is strong as a lion, but meek as a lamb," Osei told Drake in a voice just loud enough for Okomfu to overhear. "A perfect slave," Osei thought.

Several hours later Drake's crew finished transferring their human cargo to the holds of their ship, and returned to shore with the guns and ammunition coveted by Osei. At that moment Okomfu reappeared with a dozen pathetic souls bound by strong ropes. Half were under the age of fourteen. Some appeared too old to survive the voyage.

Captain Drake immediately expressed his dissatisfaction. "One strong man will fetch over a thousand dollars at auction in Richmond.

This sorry lot will not fetch that much in total—even if they make it that far."

"This was the best I could do," Okomfu pleaded.

"Well it's not good enough," Drake said harshly.

Osei took Drake's anger out on his brother, berating him in the local language that the captain did not understand.

Okomfu was astonished that his brother would side with Drake on such a matter.

"I need the guns," Osei insisted, his face flushing with rage.

But Drake was intransigent. "I bargained for three fifty, and three fifty I must have," he insisted.

"I need the guns," Osei repeated with increasing fury. "Without guns I can provide no more slaves. Without guns the Ashanti will make slaves of the Benin."

"And I need 350 slaves," Drake demanded, unmoved by Osei's predicament or his passion.

It was in the course of this argument that Okomfu grasped the unmitigated evil that came from trafficking in human souls. Overcome by guilt, and furious at his brother for leading him astray, he picked up a piece of driftwood and swung it mightily at Osei, knocking him unconscious. Okomfu then looked hard into Drake's eyes and said in a calm, but defiant tone: "Now you have your three fifty. And that is the last slave you will ever take from the Kingdom of Benin. Leave your guns and go. But be forewarned: if you or any of your treacherous slave merchants ever set foot on this shore again, the Benin will slaughter you like the pigs that you are."

Drake was unmoved by Okomfu's threats. Instead he gave a subtle nod to one of his shipmates who was standing directly behind the Benin prince. An instant later the sailor's musket smashed across the side of Okomfu's head sending him crashing face first onto the beach.

The sailor looked approvingly at the two Kerekou brothers lying motionless in the sand. "Shall we take them both?" he asked Drake.

Drake shook his head. "Take only him," he said, pointing to Okomfu. "When Osei awakens, tell him what happened. He will be that much more compliant if we ever return."

When Okomfu regained consciousness, he was lying on his back, chained into a wooden stall deep inside the belly of Drake's schooner.

It took him several minutes to realize where he was. Amidst the cries and the moans, the prayers and supplications, the howls of pain and agony in dozens of different tongues, all he felt was fear. At first, he was terrified at the prospect of dying in this dark, horrible place with no one to offer even a word of praise or a tear of grief. Then he thought of something worse: "What if I survive?"

Okomfu did survive, but forty-three of his fellow passengers did not. Most perished in a slow, suffocating death.

Because he was young and strong, and could speak English, Okomfu was sold for over fifteen hundred dollars. He was brought to a plantation along the Potomac River in northern Virginia, and given the name Oko Robinson. Shortly after he arrived he learned firsthand of the fate to which men like Drake had condemned thousands of the Niger people.

Oko Robinson knew, of course, what slavery meant. But there were different forms of involuntary servitude, and the kind he experienced in Virginia was extreme in its cruelty. Not in his wildest imagination did he envision a master class that tried to delegitimize his heritage and dehumanize the holy spirit that dwelt inside him as a man. It was with this in mind that Oko found a purpose in life: "I will deny them the success of turning me into a brute," he resolved.

Some years after arriving in Virginia, Oko courted a slave woman who shared his Benin heritage. They sought nothing more than to live together as husband and wife without being separated by a chattel sale. Three generations later, their great granddaughter sought something more—her freedom. It was in her twenty-second year that Angela Robinson saw that dream come true. A man named Lincoln issued a Proclamation that abolished slavery in Virginia. Angela vowed that this blessing of freedom would not go to waste.

It wasn't until many months later, however, that soldiers in blue uniforms reached her plantation, burned down the three-story house with its whitewashed Doric columns, and liberated the people who toiled in its environs. Dozens of former slaves went off in different directions. Angela and her Uncle Calvin set out for Quaker territory in Pennsylvania. They had been traveling several days when they heard strange noises in the woods. They hid behind some rocks, and waited anxiously.

QUONCHOCK'S BOOK

In 1626, two years after contact between the Mana-hat-tan and the white people became frequent, and communication in words became common, Quonchock, Chief of the Mana-hat-tan, confided his dilemma to his wife. "These white people are host of everything that is evil," he began. "Their very breath causes us fever, trembling and death. Their guns are more powerful than our finest arrows. Their ways are incompatible with ours."

"Do you fear that our braves lack the courage to confront this evil?" she asked.

"They have the courage, but not the power," he replied. "I cannot ask them to die in a hopeless fight."

"What choice do we have?" she inquired.

"The white man has offered us cloth and kettles, axes, and hoes, in return for the tip of our land isolated in water," he replied.

"But the land is worth far more than that."

"If we don't sell it, they will take it from us; if we don't separate ourselves from them, we will die from the poison that they put in our air; if we don't make peace with them, they will enslave us," he concluded soberly.

"Then there is no choice at all," his wife consoled.

"We can move to our lands further north. We can trap animals and trade pelts for the goods of cloth and iron that we cannot make but desperately need for a better life. We can let the Delaware cross the water and raid the white man instead of us."

"Then it shall be done," she said.

"My bargain will be looked upon as naïve by my people," Quonchock said disconsolately. "And even worse, I will be looked upon as a fool by my only child."

"No you won't, father," interrupted his seventeen-year old daughter, Kentucken. "I will look upon you as a sage regardless what the others may say, and that should suffice."

Quonchock looked first at his daughter, and then at his wife who was nodding approvingly. "And so it will," he whispered.

Soon after this fateful decision, the Mana-hat-tan Chief and his daughter met with Peter Minuit and Charles Merkle of the Dutch West India Company, and sold the island that would be called Manhattan for goods worth sixty guilders in Dutch currency. It was the equivalent of twenty-four American dollars.

The first thing Minuit did after completing the transaction was rename the place New Amsterdam. The first thing Merkle did was talk to Kentucken, who had accompanied her father on several prior meetings with him and Minuit. With each successive meeting Merkle became more captivated by her beauty and grace.

"What does your name mean?" he asked with genuine interest.

Kentucken gave a quick glance at her father. He, in turn, gave a subtle nod, indicating that she was permitted to answer.

"It means 'Look to the Future,'" she answered shyly.

"It is a beautiful name—for a beautiful young lady."

"Thank you," she said with a trace of a smile. "You are very kind."

"Then I will look to the future with great hope," Merkle responded.

Quonchock listened to the conversation with suspicion, but was already aware of what the future would bring. Later that day he shared his thoughts with his wife. "Kentucken will marry the white man, and I will not object."

His wife raised an eyebrow, but said nothing.

"It is the only way that our blood will remain connected to the 'land isolated in water'—the land of our fathers."

That evening Quonchock's wife had an unnerving vision.

"The white man will come to our lands further north," she told her husband.

Quonchock looked at her in awe. "You are a wise woman," he said.

"What will happen to our people then?" she asked.

"What does your vision tell you," Quonchock responded.

The woman shook her head. "I see nothing further," she said sadly, "but my heart tells me that you know more, and what you know is something that will be painful for me to hear."

Quonchock looked at her pensively before responding. "Either our people will become yeoman farmers like the white man, or we will be herded into pastures and kept there—the same way that the white man now keeps his livestock."

Quonchock's explanation was more than his wife could bear. "If we become farmers, what will become of our revered spirits, our proud history and our venerated rituals?" she wailed.

Quonchock had a ready answer. "We will do what the white man does. Our wise men will write our legends and our beliefs onto papers and compile them into a book. It will be just like the white man's book with the cross on its cover."

"What will be on the cover of our book?" his wife wanted to know.

Quonchock took a stick and drew a horizontal line into the dry earth. At one end of the line he added an isocoles triangle with its apex pointed to the right.

"An arrowhead," his wife deduced.

Quonchock shook his head. Then with the same stick, he drew a second arrowhead at the other end of the horizontal line, pointing in the opposite direction. "It's a two-headed arrow," Quonchock explained. "Because with our own book, we will be able to preserve our heritage by looking back to the past, yet build a better life for our grandchildren by looking forward to the future."

His wife stared intently at the double triangle sign that her husband had drawn in the dirt. "You will be called a coward by the young braves who speak well, but rile up the people," she said at last.

"Those who follow me will, like Kentucken, look to the future with hope; those that follow the others will dwell on the past as victims."

A short time later, Charles Merkle married Kentucken. They waxed wealthy in the Dutch Colony. Among other things, they amassed vast properties along the Hudson including the entire finger of land jutting up from the west side of the island. The thirty-four square miles of woods and water that comprised Manhattan were, however, far more than the 200 Dutch settlers of New Amsterdam could possibly use or defend.

And so, one damp, bleak November morning, Merkle walked due north from the tip of the harbor for about a half mile into the wilderness that was then Manhattan. He stopped at a small clearing and ordered that a stockade wall be erected through that clearing across the entire width of the island. The foot path on the south side of the stockade therefore became known as Wall Street.

About twenty-five years later, when the Dutch surrendered control of Manhattan to the British, Merkle extended his holdings even further up the Hudson. Over the ensuing generations, Merkle's heirs intermarried with German, Swedish, Huguenot, and Scots-Irish stock. In the process, they established huge estates along the Hudson. One of these properties was called Maple Grove, in appreciation of the majestic trees that guarded the bluffs overlooking the river.

One afternoon early in the winter of 1863, the twenty-three year old heir to Maple Grove, Frederick Merkle, was sitting on a stump among the maple trees, chin in hands, contemplating his future.

"What's troubling you, son?" interrupted his father, James.

"It's the war," Frederick responded quickly. "I've been feeling that I was shirking my duty by not serving."

"The law does not require you to serve."

"But my heart does."

"And what is it that your heart tells you?"

"That I love the Union and I detest slavery," Frederick answered bluntly.

"Our newspapers have argued that freedom for the slaves is not worth the price that we must pay in treasure and blood."

"Such arguments only play into the hands of the rebels," Frederick responded. "They know that this is a war they cannot win. Their only hope is that we heed the voices of Lincoln's detractors and lose our resolve."

"They ridicule the president and call him an ape."

"The president shows his wisdom by ignoring such ridicule and praising those who serve."

"I can pay to have someone serve in your place," James offered.

"That will not be necessary, sir. I have already enlisted. I report to my unit tomorrow."

James paused for several seconds. "Then it is time for me to do what I should have done a few years ago," he said softly.

With that he reached under his shirt and withdrew two chains.

"This cross will keep and protect you," he said handing the silver icon to his son with genuine solemnity. "This medallion will give you the power to curse and to bless."

Frederick looked helplessly at his father. "Slavery shall be a curse upon our great nation for a hundred years," he said sadly.

"Then after that it shall be a blessing," James predicted.

"How so, sir?" Frederick asked plaintively.

"Because any nation in which different races can live peaceably together will be the glory of God, and see the coming of the Lord."

Frederick smiled for the first time. "Then so it shall be," he concluded.

James nodded. Then almost as an afterthought, admonished his son: "When you return home, you will give these pendants to your own son, as my father gave them to me. They have served our family well."

"As I will now serve my country," responded Frederick.

Father and son left the maple grove together. Neither noticed the remnants of colorful shells and a partially buried arrow with a flint tip at one end and the remnants of turkey feathers still glued into some hand carved slots at the other.

CALVIN'S RING

The Union sentry heard the crack of a dry twig along the wooded trail where he was posted and raised his Springfield rifle in the direction of the noise. An instant later, a Confederate soldier leaped onto him from behind and plunged a knife into his stomach.

"The road to Gettysburg is now clear, Sir," the sentry heard his attacker say in a soft Virginia drawl.

The two rebel soldiers left the Yankee for dead and disappeared into the woods. When they were out of sight, the sentry put his hands onto his abdomen with an expectation of fear and dread. He felt a warm, sticky fluid oozing from his blue, broadcloth shirt. Instinctively, he pressed his right palm firmly onto the wound in an effort to stanch the flow of blood that was pulsating from his body with each beat of his heart. With his other hand the sentry clutched for the silver cross and the family medallion that hung around his neck. Then he prayed that God would send him an angel.

From their hiding place in the woods, Angela Robinson and her Uncle Calvin saw the gray-clad soldiers rush off. Angela then raced in the direction of the deep moans emanating from a delirious man who lay in the undergrowth gasping for breath. She cradled the man's head in her arms and offered him words of hope and comfort.

"Let him die," Calvin growled unsympathetically.

"I shall do no such thing," Angela said defiantly. "This soldier has risked his life to set us free." Then looking at the handsome young man she held in her arms, she swore in the name of Jesus that she would keep him alive.

"Where is your home?" she asked him in a soothing voice.

The man opened his eyes and saw the angel that was the answer to his prayers. "Maple Grove...New York," he gasped before lapsing back into unconsciousness.

When Frederick Merkle opened his eyes again, he thought several hours had passed; in reality it had only been several seconds. The throbbing pain in his gut reminded him of his predicament. The kind, chestnut eyes peering down from above reminded him that there was still hope.

"Who are you?" he whispered.

Angela told him her name.

"You must take a message to General Doubleday," Frederick continued through the pain. "It is a matter of great urgency."

Angela called to Calvin, who was standing a few paces away examining Merkle's rifle. Reluctantly, her uncle came to her side. When she patted the ground impatiently, Calvin obligingly kneeled down on one knee so he, too, could hear Frederick Merkle's words.

"Go back over the hill," Frederick said, shifting his eyes in the direction behind him. "Go another mile or two and look for the smoke from our campfires. Find a bluecoat and tell him that the rebs will be grouping at Gettysburg."

"Gettysburg," Angela repeated. "Find the Yankees and tell them 'Gettysburg.'"

"I am a free man now," Calvin objected. "I don't have to take orders from anyone."

"Freedom does not come free, Uncle Calvin. Look at the price this man has paid."

Calvin Robinson looked down at the ugly gash in Frederick Merkle's gut, then up at his niece. He was almost thirty-years old, and had never made a single decision on his own. Now he would. Returning his eyes to Merkle, he tried to choose his words carefully. "I am a free man," he said again. "I will take your message to the Yankees, not because you told me to do so, but because I have decided to do so."

With that, he headed for the hill, not with the listless gait of a slave, but with the resolute stride of a soldier.

"I'm proud of you, Uncle Calvin," Angela called out as he disappeared into the woods.

After hiking for over an hour, Calvin thought he smelled the scent of campfire smoke emanating from somewhere in the distance. His pace quickened in anticipation of delivering his message. An instant later, he felt the butt of a rifle smash across the back of his head. One bluecoat quickly removed Merkle's rifle from Calvin's shoulder, while two others trained their guns at his head. Calvin's attempt to explain his mission was met with a rifle butt in the stomach.

Calvin quickly realized that the soldiers had erroneously concluded that he had killed one of their comrades and stolen his rifle. But he was a free man now. And since freedom did not come free, he would continue his attempt at explanation no matter what the price in pain and bruises.

Eventually the bluecoats stopped beating Calvin and allowed him to speak. Moments later, after a terse apology, the soldiers retrieved their horses. One of them then galloped off toward the Union camp to relay Merkle's warning, while Calvin and the others rode off in the opposite direction in search of their wounded comrade. They found Merkle soon enough. Somehow they hoisted him into the saddle of one of the horses. A soldier sat directly behind him, one hand around Merkle's waist and the other holding the reins. It was in this cumbersome manner that the group painstakingly made its way back to the Union camp.

At the camp, Frederick Merkle received medical treatment, such as it was, and miraculously began to recover. Calvin volunteered to assist in the Union war effort and was assigned the task of munitions handler. At the Battle of Gettysburg, he discharged his duties with dedication and valor. Angela served as a surgeon's assistant, aiding with dozens of amputations, many without benefit of anesthesia. Each day she worked from dawn to dusk, uncomplainingly treating both Union and Confederate soldiers with tenderness and compassion.

In the ensuing weeks, Merkle and the minority of soldiers who hadn't died from their wounds made steady progress toward recovery. But no sooner had the physical pain diminished than the mental and emotional damage became acute. Fear, loneliness, depression, despair and outright boredom spread like a contagious disease among the men. Fortunately, General Doubleday discovered a solution to the problem.

As a young man Doubleday was familiar with a game called "Baste Ball," that had become popular in New York several years earlier. The game was so named because the innards of the ball with which it was played were held in place by a two-piece covering that was basted together with strong thread. Doubleday recalled that the game engendered much enthusiasm and competition among the players, and thought it would be both a morale-booster and a form of physical therapy for his wounded soldiers.

Accordingly, Doubleday had a few balls made by winding twine around a cork core and stitching a two-piece horsehide cover over the rolled up string. He fashioned bats from barrel staves, and laid out the four-point diamond, thirty paces apart, as best he remembered. Then he stuffed four potato sacks with hay and had them staked into the ground at each of the four points of the diamond. When, however, pitched balls kept caroming off of the home point sack, repeatedly interrupting play, Doubleday ordered that it be replaced with a tin mess plate that was nailed into the ground, level with the surrounding earth. It was in this way that the home point became known as "home plate." And when the other three sacks, in accordance with military parlance, became known as "bases," both the name of the ball, and the name of the game itself, morphed from "basteball" to baseball.

Teams were chosen by battalion—the most athletic soldiers from each battalion being selected to represent their military unit. This had a wholly unexpected, unprecedented, and egalitarian result—officers and conscripts, Protestants and Catholics, English and Irish were treated as equals on the same team. As a result, scurrilous religious, ethnic, and geographical epithets were directed with far less venom at players on the same team, than they were at players on an opposing team. The worst abuse was directed at the Irish Catholics. And of all the slurs that were used—the most hateful and derisive pertained to their penchant for fisticuffs—from which evolved the ultimate Protestant insult: "the fighting Irish."

Frederick Merkle, forever unable to engage in any strenuous activity as a result of his near-mortal wound, was recruited by General Doubleday to serve as umpire. Merkle's infatuation with the game was instantaneous, and he repeatedly expressed his gratitude to the general for giving him the opportunity to participate in this way.

At the outset, Merkle was called upon to make an important ruling: could Calvin play for the regimental team to which he was attached even though he was a former slave. Since no one objected to non-uniformed adjuncts from other regiments participating on their regimental team, Merkle concluded that Calvin could play for his. As a result, Calvin's skin color and hair texture became the subject of greater verbal abuse by members of opposing teams than by members of his own.

In anticipation of the first game, many spectators began congregating in the territory outside of the diamond. Because of the excitement engendered by the occasion, Doubleday brought a military band onto the field for a pre-game song. His first choice was "The Battle Hymn of the Republic." At the last moment, however, the general realized that this would only instill even more hatred and resentment among the Confederate prisoners who had fought heroically, and suffered greatly, in the Gettysburg battle. "We are fighting to save the Union, not destroy it," he thought. "One day these boys must also go back to their homes and rebuild their lives as Americans." Accordingly, Doubleday ordered the band to play a song that was far less familiar, but far more appropriate: "The Star Spangled Banner."

The games were hard-fought, competitive and rough. Even the spectators grew fanatic in support of their chosen team. In due course, it was the spectators themselves who were referred to as "fanatics," which was soon shortened to "fans." Interestingly, the fans' cheers were reserved for excellent play rather than the rank or status of the player, and their jeers were made for poor play, even by an officer. Doubleday was pleased. "For better or worse, baseball embodies the meritocracy that differentiates America from every other country in the world," he thought. "It will become the national game."

Halfway through the first game, Frederick Merkle was called upon to make another important decision. Until then, a base runner could only be "put out" between the bases if an opposing player either touched him with the ball or threw the ball at him, and hit him with it. But a situation arose which required that this rule be reconsidered.

With runners on first and third, and two out, the striker batted a ball on the ground to the shortstop. The shortstop threw the ball to his second baseman, who was standing on the second base point waiting for the runner from first to get close enough so he could either touch him or hit him with the ball. The runner, however, deliberately stayed near first in order to give his teammate on third enough time to race home. The fielding team appealed this inherent unfairness to Merkle.

After due deliberation, Merkle ruled that, when first base is occupied, a base runner is "forced" to run to the next base when a teammate is directly behind him. If he doesn't run, he can be "forced out" by any fielder who merely touches that next base while in possession of the ball. Merkle further decided that it should make no difference if another base runner reached home before the "forced out" occurred that ended the inning. "The run does not count," he ruled.

Merkle's decision caused a furious dispute which could have erupted into a full-scale brawl had not General Doubleday personally intervened by unholstering his sidearm and firing several warning shots into the air.

As the summer waned, it became time for those soldiers who had fully recovered from their wounds to rejoin their units. Those, like Frederick Merkle, who were seriously and permanently disabled, were mustered out of the service. On the brisk, autumn day that he received his discharge papers, Merkle approached Calvin, and respectfully removed his blue cap. Angela watched anxiously from behind a supply wagon, but could not make out their words.

"I am in love with your niece," Frederick Merkle began rather bluntly, "and I want her to be my wife."

Calvin was nonplused.

"As best I know," Frederick continued, "you are her only relative, and therefore it is you from whom I seek permission to marry Angela. Though I am now a cripple, my family owns much land in New York. Please rest assured that your niece will never want for anything."

At first Calvin didn't know how to respond. "Three months ago I was a slave," he thought. "I was a piece of property owned by another man. Now, a wealthy landowner and heroic soldier is seeking my permission to marry my niece."

Merkle fidgeted nervously as he waited for Calvin's response.

"How does Angela feel about this?" Calvin finally asked.

"I haven't formally inquired," Frederick admitted.

"Well I have seen how she looks at you. From the first moment she saw you bleeding in the forest until today, you have brought a sparkle to her eye and a blush to her cheeks. I have no doubt how she will respond."

With that, Calvin reached under his shirt and removed a chain that hung around his neck. Attached to the chain was an ivory ring, meticulously carved with intricate geometrical designs. "I am Angela's uncle—not by blood, but by an oath I made to her parents when they were exchanged for a parcel of land. The day they were taken away, Angela's father gave me this." Calvin dangled the chain so Merkle could see the ring clearly.

"Angela's family once owned land as well," Calvin continued. "Her forebears were kings in a land called Benin. This is the only evidence that exists of her lost heritage. It would honor the memory of her dear parents if you consummated your marriage with this ring."

As Calvin gave the ring to Merkle, Merkle reached under his shirt and withdrew a chain from which hung a silver cross of the Latin style, and presented it to Calvin.

"My forebears also came from a strange and distant land. This cross was worn proudly by one of them."

Calvin accepted the cross and placed it around his neck. "I will wear it with pride," he said softly.

Frederick Merkle and Angela Robinson were married the next morning by an army chaplain. Arrangements were made for them to leave for New York that afternoon. Merkle asked Calvin to join them, but Calvin declined.

"I am going to stay with the army and see this wretched war to its end," he said firmly.

"And when it does end?" asked Angela.

"I've heard a lot of talk about California. I think it would be a good place to start a new life."

"May God keep you safe," Angela replied.

Calvin brought forth the silver cross that hung from his neck. "Rest assured, sweet niece, that with this by my heart, I will always be safe."

Now it was Merkle's turn to wax poetic. "I have been told that I have the power to bring both a blessing and a curse. It is by that power that I now bless the Robinson name, that it will be known throughout the land for its courage and strength."

"Amen," Angela responded. "And may a blessing also be for the safety of Mr. Lincoln, so that this nation may live out its creed of freedom and opportunity for all its citizens."

In the ensuing decades, millions of people in distant lands came to believe that their only hope for freedom and opportunity lay in America—a nation which Abraham Lincoln promised to a nearby crowd that very afternoon "would not perish from this earth." One of those people who held that belief was a Romanian orphan by the name of Benjamin Bar Kochba.

BENJAMIN'S PAYMENT

On a damp, dreary day in the fall of 1894, Benjamin Bar Kochba watched stoically as his father's casket was lowered into the black Gesher earth next to the grave of his mother. He removed the two chains that had been hanging around his neck since his father had given them to him at the onset of the old man's illness several month's earlier. Attached to one was a bronze medallion that had been handed down father-to-son for over 400 years. Attached to the other was an old coin that, according to family legend, had been in the family's possession since they left the Holy Land over 1750 years ago. He balled them both into his fist and threw them onto his father's coffin. Then he stalked away angrily, leaving the small group of people gathered at the gravesite to say the final amen after the Kaddish—a traditional Jewish prayer of mourning.

At seventeen, Benjamin now had no family, few friends, and little hope for the future. He had spent the better part of the past year caring for his mother and father, who were stricken with consumption. They died within a few months of each other, and now he was experiencing the same deep coughing spells that marked the onset of the disease that took their lives. There was nothing left for him in Gesher, and he had made up his mind to leave for America as soon as possible.

When the graveside service concluded, the rabbi, Mendel Levy, accompanied by his seven-year old daughter, Esther, left the mourners and approached Benjamin. The rabbi draped one arm on the young man's shoulder and offered words of consolation. When that had no discernable effect, he thrust his fist into Benjamin's palm and dropped the two chains into the young man's hand.

"Don't turn your back on your heritage," the rabbi admonished.

"I want no mementos from this wretched land," Benjamin scoffed.

"These are mementos of your family, not the land," the rabbi countered. "Turn away from your home, if you must, but give honor to your parents as our law requires."

This put the matter in a different light, and Benjamin knew it. He raised the chains in the air and stared at them for several moments. Grudgingly, he stuffed the medallion in his pocket. He took the Bar Kochba coin, however, and placed it over the auburn head of the rabbi's daughter. "You can remember the Bar Kochba family by this," he told her.

She gave him a happy smile in return.

"I'm still leaving this God-forsaken place," he said determinedly.

The rabbi accepted Benjamin's decision with a perfunctory nod. "I have a cousin in America who lives in a place called 'Shih Cawgo,'" he said, grimacing at the pronunciation. "His name is Avrom Levy, and he's also a rabbi. If you need assistance, I'm sure he will help you."

"I will need no help," the lad said defiantly.

"Rabbi Levy betrayed his displeasure in Benjamin's impertinence by slowly shaking his head.

Benjamin responded by jutting out his jaw.

"Then I request only one thing of you: go to America and make something of yourself."

"I will," Benjamin promised. And with a hint of contrition he thanked the rabbi for rescuing both his medallion and his coin pendant.

The next morning Benjamin sold the few possessions owned by the Bar Kochba family that could be paid for with hard cash. This included his father's treadle-operated sewing machine—the only means by which he could earn a living in his new country. "It will be too cumbersome to take with me," he thought. "I'll buy one after I arrive in America." He gave the rabbi everything that could not be sold, with instructions to distribute them to the Gesher poor as he saw fit. In return, the rabbi gave him a pamphlet that translated basic Romanian phrases into English, and vice versa.

After bidding a final farewell, the rabbi mounted his horse and rode off in the direction of an old Roman bridge. Benjamin watched the man disappear through a gap in the hilly landscape, then folded the pamphlet in half and tucked it into the back pocket of his trousers. On an impulse, he removed his left boot, and put a wad of folded money between the inside of his cotton sock and the sole of his foot. He put the remainder of his money and his bronze medallion in a draw-string pouch. Then he stuffed the pouch, a change of clothes, and a few personal items into a leather travel bag, saddled his horse and tied the bag to the back of his saddle.

Benjamin stared for a moment at the bare fields and naked trees that surrounded him. They looked cold and lonely against the leaden, autumnal sky. For reassurance, he patted his long cloth overcoat, and tugged at his tall fur cap. Then he gently rubbed his hand across the cheek of his mare, and looked the animal square in the eyes. "You've been a loyal friend," he said. "But when we arrive in Odessa, I must part with you and the saddle as well. With the money I get, and with what I already have, I'll arrive in America with enough to start my own tailor shop. I'll need help from no one." With that, he confidently mounted his horse, and left Gesher, thereby closing a two millennia chapter in the relationship between the Bar Kochba family and the land of Romania.

The Black Sea port of Odessa was in a land called Ukraine, birthplace of Benjamin's mother. He had been told by many that Odessa was a thriving port city where he could catch a steamer to Liverpool. From Liverpool he would transfer to an ocean-going vessel, and arrive in New York City, America, two weeks later. When he reached the main road, Benjamin gave a deep cough that summoned up a large glob of phlegm which he quickly spat into the weeds growing along the road side. "This is not a good omen," he thought.

On each of the first four nights of his journey Benjamin came upon an inn which provided a supper of bread and borscht, and a dormitory cot—all at a fair price. On the fifth evening, when he was less than thirty miles from his destination, neither inn nor hostelry could be found. With darkness approaching, he had no choice but to spend the night in a farmer's field adjacent the road. He tied his mare to a nearby fence, removed the saddle, and then made a "bed" for himself by gathering some of the tall, yellowed stems that remained in the ground after the harvest. Protected from the wind by the remaining rows of withered plant stalks, and kept warm by his heavy coat and fur hat, Benjamin spent the night in a sound sleep.

He awoke at dawn, only to discover that his horse, along with leather bag and saddle, were missing. A brief search near the fence to which the animal had been tied the night before revealed many boot prints, not his own. Benjamin quickly realized that his mare and his belongings had been stolen. Thus, with nothing but the clothes on his back and the money under his sock, he began the long walk to Odessa. He arrived mid-afternoon—coughing loudly.

Benjamin entered a tavern on Catherine Street, named for the Russian Tsarina who founded the city in 1794—exactly a hundred years earlier. A moment later, a group of militiamen rode up to the tavern, tethered their horses and burst through the door in a boisterous and contemptuous manner. They wore long gray overcoats cinched at the waist with a wide leather belt, rabbit fur hats and black, calf-length boots. A waitress immediately brought them several bottles of vodka without their asking.

Benjamin recognized the men as Cossacks—which meant "free men" in the Slavic language. "Free to steal and murder," Benjamin thought. Though ostensibly authorized by the Tsar to maintain order in the distant provinces, they were, in fact, rogue cavalry who periodically raided and pillaged defenseless communities, particularly Jewish settlements beyond the Russian pale. Word had spread all the way to Gesher of a particularly deadly pogrom that had occurred near Kiev only a year earlier.

"I will not sit in the presence of these murderers," Benjamin said to himself, rising from his table and leaving the building despite not having eaten anything but some apples and bread in the past twenty-four hours. At the hitching posts outside the tavern he saw the Cossacks' horses, still wet and lathered after a hard ride. Among them was his stolen mare, with his travel bag still strapped to the saddle. Unhesitatingly, and with a sense of poetic justice, Benjamin mounted the horse and rode quickly away in a direction that brought him close to the wharf. When he spied a blacksmith livery, he dismounted and walked his mare into an enclosed wooden structure that served as both a shop and a stable.

The smith was working bare-chested at a hot fire, hammering horseshoes on a steel anvil. When he saw the visitor, he stopped his work and wiped the filthy sweat from his face and hands with a cloth that had obviously been used previously for that purpose. The grime that remained between his wrist and elbow, however, hid a double triangle sign that was tattooed on his right forearm. The blacksmith gave Benjamin a friendly smile, and then turned to throw the soiled cloth onto a tool-laden table that stood directly behind him. Benjamin shuddered at the sight of numerous scars that criss-crossed the man's back.

"How can I help you?" the smith asked, returning his eyes in Benjamin's direction. He spoke in the Slavic tongue, but with a thick Romanian accent.

"Do you speak Romanian?" Benjamin inquired haltingly in the Ukrainian dialect that he learned from his mother.

"I do, I do," the man answered in his native language, his face brightening. "Where are you from?" he asked.

"Transylvania; near the Dracula Castle," Benjamin answered. "But I've left that miserable place for good. I'm here to find a steamer that can take me to America."

"There are no steamers in a blacksmith shop," the man chuckled.

Benjamin smiled. "I must first sell my horse and saddle so I can buy a steamer ticket."

"The only ship leaving here in the next week is the freighter *Aphrodite*. It leaves this evening for Marseilles with a cargo of grain. Once in Marseilles, you can easily catch a steamer to New York."

"Can the *Aphrodite* use another crewman?"

"Sometimes they take a strong man aboard and let him work in exchange for passage," but I am certain that it is too late for that now. The *Aphrodite* weighs anchor even as we speak."

"Then I must go. Keep the horse and saddle as payment for the information you've provided."

"I can give you one thing more," the smith said, quickly scribbling a few lines on a piece of foolscap. He folded the paper in half—then folded it in half again—before handing it to Benjamin.

"My son went to America several years ago. His name and address are on this paper. He's found success in New York as a worker in metal. He may be in a position to help you upon your arrival."

"I want no help," Benjamin thought, but said instead, "Thank you for your offer. I only wish there was a way in which I could repay you for your kindness."

"There is, my friend. Give my son my greetings when you see him in New York, and tell him that his mother and I are proud of him."

"I shall do that," Benjamin promised. And with that he stuffed the note into an interior pocket of his travel bag, left the stable and began running toward a circular promenade of stone steps that descended into the wharf.

As he neared the top of the stairway, he heard someone yell in the Slavic tongue, "There he is!"

HERMAN'S GIFT

Benjamin looked over his shoulder and saw a group of mounted Cossacks galloping his way. Then he heard a musket explode, and then another.

Benjamin was halfway down the steps, when the Cossacks reached the top, dismounted, and gave chase on foot. He made the mistake of taking another look over his shoulder and slipped on a broken stone. His travel bag tumbled in one direction and he in another. He contemplated abandoning the bag, but decided otherwise. By the time he recovered it, his pursuers had halved the distance that separated them.

When Benjamin reached the bottom of the stairs he saw the lamps of the *Aphrodite* glimmering at the end of a wooden pier. The ship's horns were bleating and her motors were grinding loudly. He was in a full sprint now. Several crew members gathered at the forecastle to watch the chase. Some were actually cheering him on.

As he neared the end of the pier, the vessel had already begun to separate itself from the dock. Benjamin summoned up all his strength and dived headfirst over a patch of water and landed in a disheveled heap on the main deck of the ship. A chorus of "hurrahs" erupted from the crew.

The Cossacks arrived moments later. They raised their fists in anger as the *Aphrodite* slowly made its way into the cold, choppy water. The mist gave the sea a dark, ink-like hue.

Benjamin laid spread eagled on the deck coughing uncontrollably. Some of the crew put him in a hammock below deck where he spent the night.

In the ensuing days, Benjamin proved to be a valuable addition to the *Aphrodite* crew. He was strong enough to shovel coal into the ship's boilers, and nimble enough to mend the sailors' garments. More importantly, the mild Mediterranean weather, warm breezes and spectacular scenery proved to be a panacea for his chronic cough.

The machinery below deck, however, is what most captivated Benjamin's interest. It was there, deep in the bowels of the ship where Benjamin spent his free time, mesmerized by the repetitive operation of the engine components. The fire in the boiler turned water into steam, the steam moved through synchronized valves to enter the man-sized cylinders, pistons reciprocated inside the cylinders like the arms of a trained, iron beast. "One day I'd like to work with such machines," Benjamin said to himself.

When the ship arrived in Marseilles, one of Benjamin's crew mates helped him book passage on a steamer to New York. He, and over 200 others from all over Europe, traveled in third class steerage. For eighteen days they learned to cope with only two toilets, maggot-laden food, no ventilation, lack of fresh water, and living space no greater than the size of their bunk bed. Sixteen of them died en route. Others just became seriously ill. Benjamin had a relapse of his coughing spasms. Aside from their prayers, the only thing that raised their spirits was the thought that they were going to a land of freedom and opportunity.

As the steamer plied its way through New York Harbor, Benjamin looked with delight at the Statue of Liberty, then stared in awe at the fifty-foot ceiling in the Great Hall on Ellis Island. After a multi-hour wait in agonizingly long lines, Benjamin found himself face-to-face with a husky immigration official who had thick, black hair, a ruddy complexion, a big head and a welcoming smile. The name on his desk sign said "Herman Ruth."

"What's your name," Ruth asked perfunctorily.

Benjamin paused. "My name?" he mumbled.

"Yes, your name."

Benjamin's face brightened with understanding. "Bar Kochba," he answered.

Now it was Ruth who lost something in the communication. "Bar, what?" he asked.

"Bar Kochba," Benjamin repeated.

"Let's just call you 'Barr,'" Ruth said, making a notation on Benjamin's immigration forms.

"Where are you from?" Ruth continued.

Benjamin's expression went blank.

After two more futile attempts to get a meaningful answer, Ruth called for a translator.

Benjamin had difficulty answering Ruth's questions even with the aid of the translator.

"Where are you from?" the translator inquired.

"America," Benjamin answered.

"No, no," corrected the translator. "Where was your home?"

"My home is America," Benjamin said proudly. "I am American." Benjamin pointed to the flag that hung in the Great Hall, pointed to himself, and said, "America."

Ruth laughed. "I'll take it from here," he told the translator. Then he made several check marks and a few notations on Benjamin's immigration documents, and stamped them "APPROVED."

Benjamin was already at the medical examining station when Herman Ruth impulsively pulled a medallion out from under his uniform and compared one of the names on the back with the name of the man whose documents he had just approved. He twitched nervously. "I'm taking a break," he told his supervisor.

"Five minutes," the supervisor responded.

By the time Ruth was able to locate Benjamin, the medical examiner had already taken a piece of chalk, written a large "T" on Benjamin's back, and directed him into a special holding room. Benjamin knew this was not good. Ruth knew that the "T" stood for tuberculosis, and meant that Benjamin would be sent back to Marseilles on the next steamer. Ruth found Benjamin sitting in the room—alone and forlorn.

Ruth looked around nervously, then quickly erased the "T" with the palm of his hand. He was about to inquire whether Benjamin was familiar with a family named "Mirceal," but was interrupted in mid-sentence when the door of the holding room opened abruptly.

An immigration clerk wearing a uniform similar to Ruth's entered the room, followed by an immigrant couple, each with the letter "S" written in chalk on their backs. It stood for "Scalp," which probably meant that they would need to be deloused before receiving their approval to enter the country.

"What are you doing in here, Herman?" the clerk asked.

Ruth cleared his throat nervously. "Correcting this man's paper work," Ruth said with a forced smile. Then turning to Benjamin, he said in an authoritative voice, "Follow me." Benjamin did as he was told, and followed Ruth out of the room, past a maze of iron railings, inspection stations and immigration personnel. The next thing Benjamin knew, he was outside, standing in line to board a ferry that would take him to Manhattan.

Uniformed police officers and federal agents were milling about. Ruth knew this was not the time or place for a discussion, even if he could converse with the young man in his new language. Accordingly, Ruth stuffed some documents into Benjamin's coat pocket, then quickly scribbled a name and address on the back of a postcard which had a picture of the newly-constructed Brooklyn Bridge on the front. "Contact this man as soon as you disembark," Ruth said with a sense of urgency. "He will find you a room to rent."

Benjamin gave him a blank stare.

Ruth pointed to the name he had written on the postcard. "He will get you a room. A room to live in."

Benjamin's expression brightened with understanding. "A room," he repeated, nodding his head at Ruth.

"I must go now" Ruth said, his eyes darting nervously. "I will find you when you get settled." With that Ruth rushed off in the direction of the side entrance of the building through which he and Benjamin had exited just a few moments before.

Benjamin looked at the monstrous bridge on the face of the postcard, and wondered how such a structure could have been built. It looked strong and indestructible, just like America. "I will treasure this gift for the rest of my life," he said to himself. Then he turned the card over and tried to pronounce the name that Ruth had printed in the language of his new country. "William Drake," he mumbled.

ISAAC'S STICK

William Drake owned many properties in New York City, including several rows of tenements on the Lower East Side. It was not his practice to interview any of his prospective tenants, but after receiving a personal request from Herman Ruth, he decided to make an exception. For some reason Ruth was desperately interested in keeping in touch with this particular fellow, and Drake owed him a favor. After all, it was Ruth who, for a few pennies each, had referred countless immigrants to Drake's Lower East Side apartments over the years. It was in this way that William Drake met Benjamin Barr at the corner of Bowery and Division Streets.

The young man wore a tattered cloth coat and a ridiculous looking fur hat. He carried a beat-up leather bag which, Drake was certain, contained all of the man's earthly possessions. In contrast, Drake was dressed in a long double-breasted frock coat, white shirt that buttoned up the front into a tight collar, silk cravat, black vest, and tall top hat.

The cobblestone street where Drake's carriage and driver waited was busy with the coming and going of horses and wagons. The curbs were cluttered with creaky pushcarts where everything from vegetables to rags was being bought and sold. On the sidewalk, impoverished women were haggling with venders, boys were hawking papers, and the clatter and clanging from men at work emanated from the surrounding storefronts. Amidst the din, Drake tried to converse with his prospective tenant.

"Do you have a job?" Drake asked.

The man spoke too fast for Benjamin to understand.

"Work. Work. What kind of work do you do?"

Benjamin pointed his index finger at himself.

"Yes you. What work do you do?" Drake repeated with growing impatience.

Benjamin's face brightened. "Tailor," he said, pointing to himself again. "Tailor," he repeated.

"Let me see your papers," Drake demanded.

Again, Benjamin could not understand.

"Papers. Papers," said Drake, reaching his hand into the young man's coat pocket and removing his immigration documents. Drake perused the papers quickly, and learned that the young man had been passed through Ellis Island only the day before. In the process his name was shortened from some unpronounceable consonant-clogged gibberish to the simple, poetic, one syllable name of Barr. "Ruth did him a big favor," Drake thought as he said the name to himself. It rolled easily off of his English-speaking tongue.

"Where did you come from?" Drake asked. "As if it matters," he mumbled. Then, without expecting, much less waiting for, an answer, Drake motioned with his hand and said, "Follow me."

Drake walked his prospective tenant up to the third floor of the four story building, proceeded down a narrow corridor to an apartment marked 3C, and unlocked the door. It opened into a single square-shaped room, about eight feet per side. It had no bathroom, no closet, no running water, no electricity and no windows. The only ventilation came from an open transom. There was a single kerosene lamp for light and a small coal stove for heat. A stained mattress supported on a flimsy frame was wedged into the far corner.

"It's two dollars a week or five dollars a month," Drake said with complete indifference. "You pay for the coal and the kerosene. The cot is extra, but as long as you're a friend of Herman's, you can have it for no charge." Drake paused for a response.

Benjamin had absolutely no idea what the man said. "Thank you," was all he could think to say.

"I need a month's rent in advance."

Benjamin made no reply.

"Money. Money," Drake said raising the fingers of his right hand and rubbing his thumb against them.

"Money," Benjamin repeated with a hint of comprehension. He reached into his pocket and pulled out the American money he had received in exchange for his foreign currency just that morning.

Drake counted out five singles, pointing to a different finger on his gloved hand as he did so. "Five dollars," he said pointing to the money he had taken from Benjamin

"Five dollars," Benjamin repeated.

"Five dollars every month," Drake said impatiently.

"Every month," Benjamin said. "Five dollars every month."

"Precisely. And if you don't pay when my superintendent comes by each month for collection, you will be evicted immediately."

"Thank you," Benjamin said uncomprehendingly.

"Here's your key," said the landlord, removing a key from a metal ring and handing it to his new tenant. "Welcome to America." And with that, he turned abruptly and walked out the door.

"America," Benjamin repeated. He put his hand into his pocket, withdrew all of his money, then sat on his cot and counted it with painstaking slowness. It totaled $11.27. He smiled happily. "One day I will be rich," he thought. "I am in America now." He withdrew a draw-string pouch from his travel bag and tried to stuff the currency inside, but a bronze medallion made it difficult. He removed the medallion and studied both sides carefully. "This is for you, Rabbi Levy," he thought as he dropped the medallion around his neck.

Benjamin's thoughts were interrupted by the sound of voices drifting over his transom. To his surprise, the people were speaking in the language of the Ukraine. He poked his head into the corridor and saw a woman with three young children, all under the age of ten.

"Excuse me," he said haltingly, in the language of his mother.

The woman and her two daughters turned his way; her little boy ran down the hall and disappeared into the family's apartment. The Ukrainian woman wore a threadbare dress and a kerchief over her head. The two girls wore plain, loose-fitting tunics that looked like nothing more than cloth sacks with openings for the head and arms. The woman gave a small paper bag, from which a loaf of bread protruded, to one of her daughters and motioned them to leave. Obediently, they scampered off toward their apartment. Then she and Benjamin exchanged greetings.

Her name was Frieda Mann, shortened from Manashevits when she and her husband Max arrived from Kiev almost a year earlier.

"And where are you from" Frieda asked.

"Gesher," Benjamin smiled. "It's a shtetl in Romania that no one's ever heard of."

Actually Frieda had heard of it. A fellow passenger on the boat from the old country—a rabbi named Avrom Levy—mentioned that he had a cousin who lived there. But Benjamin interrupted Frieda's train of thought before she could explain.

"Where does your husband work?" Ben asked.

"At a box factory near the wharf." Frieda went on to explain that Max labored twelve hours a day, six days a week. That, of course, didn't count the two hours it took him to walk back and forth to the factory each day. He earned less than ten cents an hour.

Frieda supplemented the family income by taking on piecework in her apartment. This involved sewing hems on unfinished dresses for a penny apiece. She could do four an hour, and she worked eight hours every day, four hours on Sunday. Her daughters also earned a few pennies a day sewing buttons onto unfinished garments. Her son Isaac, aged six, shined shoes after school and on weekends.

"We work harder here than in the old country," Frieda admitted. "But we are free, we are saving money, and we sacrifice now so our children will have a better life. And soon we can afford to move out of this place. I say *shehekianu* every single day," she added, referring to the Jewish prayer of thanksgiving.

Benjamin looked into her tired face, and then swallowed his pride. "Can your husband help me find work?" he asked plaintively.

"Jobs are plentiful for those who are not afraid of hard work." Frieda answered.

"I am not afraid," Benjamin responded, raising his jaw and gritting his teeth.

And so early the next morning Max Mann escorted Benjamin to the box factory where he helped Benjamin find a position as a "paster." The job paid seven cents an hour for seventy-two hours of work per week. To earn extra money, Benjamin accepted piecework from the Mann family. Among other things, he sewed the in-seams, cuffs, fly, waistband, and belt loops on to men's trousers. In his free time he studied English from the pamphlet he carried with him from Gesher—a place which seemed so distant, he could hardly remember living there.

After his first day of work Benjamin walked home in a downpour. While he was gone someone had slid an envelope under his door. Benjamin tore open the envelope and found a note written on thick stationary in a broad, bold hand. Max Mann helped him to decipher it. The note was from Herman Ruth, and inquired whether Benjamin was familiar with the names "Mirceal" or "Tover." If he was not, Ruth asked Benjamin to accept his apology for interrupting his evening. If those names were familiar, however, Ruth urged Benjamin to contact him immediately. He gave an address on Liberty Street, but Bejamin's damp hands had smeared the numers when he opened the envelope.

Benjamin removed the bronze medallion that hung around his neck. The names "Mirceal" and "Tover" could be no coincidence—especially in view of the name Ruth knew him by when they first met. "I will take a ferry to Ellis Island the moment I get a day off," he promised himself.

As Benjamin began to settle into his work routine, however, a day off was not soon in coming. Each morning Benjamin had a breakfast that consisted of a cup of coffee and a piece of bread with jam. He then walked to work with Max Mann, but they rarely spoke. For lunch he ate another piece of bread, an apple, and drank another cup of coffee. Each evening Benjamin ate dinner alone at the same diner. He had the identical meal every night: soup, beef stew, pickle, bread, a slice of apple pie and a schooner of beer. It cost 13¢.

After dinner he scavengered a newspaper from the diner and read it in his apartment from the light of a kerosene lamp. Except for little Isaac Mann, who poked his head through his door now and then with an impish smile, Benjamin had no visitors. On the boy's seventh birthday, Benjamin bought Isaac a small stick of the kind which boys on the street used to bat a ball in a popular game they called baseball. Benjamin taught Isaac how to swing the stick by pitching him a rolled-up rag. Ben also entertained Isaac with stories about how he came to America by eluding the Cossacks and shoveling coal on a tramp steamer. Once when his bronze medallion protruded through his shirt, he showed him the diagram on the front and the Star of David on the back. "This is our sign," Ben told him.

Every month Benjamin paid Drake five dollars, and every month he put a dollar bill into his draw-string bag. One day he would have enough to purchase his own sewing machine. With such a machine, he could quadruple his output, and thereby earn the astonishing sum of sixteen cents an hour on piecework alone.

One prickly problem stood in the way of Benjamin's long-term plans: paperwork. In order to get paid for each sewing job he completed, Benjamin was required to attach onto every garment a work slip which identified his name, date, and task performed. Each task required a separate slip of paper and would, in turn, result in a separate payment. Since he often performed as many as half a dozen tasks on the same garment, sometimes he had to attach six different work slips to the same piece of clothing.

The only practical way to do this was by sticking a straight pin through each slip of paper and into the fabric. Though essential household items for over 200 years, straight pins were nonetheless expensive. This is why frugal women still kept a glass jar in their kitchens to collect "pin money" for the time when these sewing and fastening necessities had to be purchased.

Because of the pins' cost, it would have been prohibitively expensive for Benjamin to attach each work slip to a completed garment with a separate pin. The only alternative was to align the six work slips edge-to-edge and attach them all to the fabric with a single pin. This was not entirely satisfactory because a solitary pin holding six work slips to the same garment easily worked free no matter how much Benjamin bent the pointed end of the pin back into the cloth. The result was many lost work slips and delayed payments, not to mention countless cuts and scratches on thumb and finger tips. Benjamin resolved that he would solve this problem one day when he found the time.

During the summer months, Benjamin often stopped at a public park where young men played the same game using bats and balls that the children played on the street in front of his apartment. Loud cheers greeted any striker who could drive the ball past one of the players on the opposing team. Benjamin was certain he could do that if given the opportunity. One day that opportunity came when Ben was literally pulled from amongst the by-standers to substitute for an injured player.

In his first at-bat, Benjamin hit a long, towering fly that produced audible gasps of awe from the onlookers at the game. Benjamin watched with joy as the ball soared into the air, and then appeared to stop in mid-flight as if the law of gravity had been momentarily suspended. When the ball completed its flight, it landed twenty-five feet beyond the center fielder's outstretched arms.

"Run! Run!" yelled the spectators. But Ben stood frozen in the batter's box until one of his fellow players gave him a push in the proper direction. When Ben still looked confused, others frantically waved and pointed where he should go. Belatedly, Benjamin began racing down the baseline as fast as he could. For a big, strong man, he moved swiftly. As he neared the first base, he heard his teammates exhorting him to keep running. And that's just what he did—for at least another twenty-five feet straight down the right field line. Only the collective moans from the onlookers caused him to realize that he had made a mistake.

It didn't matter. After the game he was approached by a distinguished gentleman who was clearly in a position of authority. The man was of medium height, had a muscular build and a pallid complexion. Despite the warm day, he wore a heavy starched shirt, buttoned at the collar, an expensive tie, three-piece hand-tailored black suit, and a tall stove-pipe hat. Though he walked with a conspicuous limp, he approached with an air of vitality, and exuded both confidence and humility. It was the first projection of graciousness that Benjamin had seen from a rich man since he had set foot in America.

"I've seen many players," he said with no hint of an accent. "You're a natural hitter."

Benjamin smiled. He could not remember the last time anyone had paid him a compliment.

"Would you like to try out for our team?" the man continued.

"That is an offer I cannot refuse," Benjamin responded without hesitation.

The man nodded and extended his right hand. "I am Frederick

Merkle," he said politely. "My son manages my baseball operations, but he could not be here today. If you would be kind enough to fill out this form, I will pass the information to him, and tell him to look for you here next Sunday."

The gentleman's comments sped past Benjamin like the blur of a pitcher's fast ball. But one of his words caused Benjamin to belatedly react. "Did he say his name was Mirceal?" Benjamin asked himself. For a fleeting moment Benjamin considered inquiring whether the gentlemen's family came from Romania, but quickly decided against doing so. He did not think it was his place to ask such a question to a person of such position and stature … at least not then.

Anson's Ultimatum

When Frederick Merkle returned to Maple Grove in the late fall of 1863, he and Angela began construction of a fine brick mansion on the bluffs overlooking the Hudson River. Two years after they moved in, Angela gave birth to a baby boy. They named him Lincoln, in memory of the martyred president.

Lincoln grew into a strong, athletic youngster. When he was about ten, Frederick began taking him to the fields north of Central Park between Fifth and Sixth Avenues. It was there that the upper crust of New York society enjoyed its favorite pastime—polo. Lincoln was a natural, and he waited with eager anticipation for those Saturday afternoons when he accompanied his dad to the polo grounds for lessons and play. By the time he was thirteen, he was competing against the best players in the club. By the time he was sixteen he had to compete against something else—the snubs, innuendoes and outright slurs of racial prejudice.

"Our son is strong," Frederick said, trying to console his wife. "He will persevere and so will we." Frederick reached for Angela's hand and drew her close.

"It is neither our strength nor his that is the cause of my concern," Angela responded. "My concern is for my country." Angela stared for a moment at the contrast between her hand of color, and the pale hand

155

of her husband that was clasped around it. "Maybe it is too much to hope that people of different races can live together peaceably in the same country?" she asked herself. Though she radiated a quiet charm and grace, her chestnut eyes burned, and her mouth grew tight and determined.

"If our nation survived the Great War, it will survive this as well," Frederick replied.

"I thought the war would change the way the races viewed each other," she said sadly. "But in some ways things are worse. There is no less racial hatred—either in the north or the south."

"Races do not hate each other, people do," Frederick said philosophically.

"So if the people who play polo hate our son and, I daresay his mother as well, just what is it that you intend to do?"

"I will show you soon enough," he said, closing his eyes and templing his fingers in front of his chin. Almost immediately, a satisfied smile appeared on his round, white face.

Angela reached for her husband's hand, squeezed it tightly and thanked God for bringing him to her. "As long as America produces men like Frederick Merkle, we have hope," she said to herself.

The next day Frederick Merkle contacted his attorney and put into motion a plan to purchase large tracts of the polo grounds, and convert them into a baseball field. Angela was delighted with the decision. By the following year, baseball had entirely replaced polo play on those fields, the polo players had abandoned Manhattan for the more distant precincts of Long Island, and Lincoln had left Maple Grove for Harvard College.

Early in the semester, Lincoln Merkle sent his parents an encouraging letter. He had been selected to represent his school on a team that played an entirely new sport—football. Frederick and Angela looked at each other with the same expression of bewilderment.

"I just want my son to be happy," Angela said with a feeling of apprehension familiar to every other mother who sends a child off to college for the first time. As it turned out, Lincoln was very happy at Harvard. In his third year he met a beautiful woman of Swedish extraction, whose father had become a wealthy merchant during the War Between the States. Carole Lindstrom was studying literature at the Harvard Annex—a course of study for women offered by the University faculty. When the administration refused to allow co-educational instruction at Harvard, however, the Annex evolved into a separate college, named Radcliffe. Lincoln married the Swedish woman shortly after his graduation. A few years later Frederick and Angela became grandparents when Lincoln and Carole had a baby boy. They named him Grant, in memory of the president whose tomb was erected not far from the Merkle estate.

About a year after Lincoln matriculated at Harvard, Frederick Merkle invested in a Major League Baseball Club called the New York Gothams. He and his partners decided to use Merkle's field at the old polo grounds as the Gothams' home park. When the City of New York confiscated that property to build a subway, Merkle purchased a tract of land thirty blocks further north called Coogan's Hollow, and built a contemporary stadium on that site.

Merkle officially named the stadium "Brotherhood Park," though the New York fans insisted on referring to it as the new Polo Grounds. Within a short period of time, the New York Gothams changed their name to the New York Giants when a newspaper writer reported that the manager congratulated his team after a hard-fought victory because they played like, well, giants. About the same time the name of the new stadium in Coogan's Hollow was formally changed to the fans' choice: "The Polo Grounds."

The Giants were associated with an organization of teams formally known as the National League of Professional Baseball Clubs. And as both the rules of the game and the by-laws of the League congealed into a more orderly system of retaining players and maintaining schedules, paying spectators began attending games in droves. Within a short time, loyalties to local teams reached the same fervor as national patriotism, and opposing teams became hated rivals.

The Giants' chief competitor in those days was a charter member of the National League, then known as the Chicago White Stockings. In the first season of the new League's existence, the team from Chicago had the best record in baseball, and was given a pennant flag to fly over their ballpark for their efforts.

Chicago's success was due to the remarkable pitching of a decorated Civil War veteran by the name of A.G. Spalding. Spalding won forty-seven games that season, but soon discovered it was more profitable to manufacture baseballs rather than pitch them. As a former pitcher, he deliberately made "dead" baseballs, and for that reason the first forty years of Major League baseball were known as the "dead ball" era.

In those days, the best hitter in all of Major League baseball was a strapping Iowa farm boy who played first base for the Chicago team. His name was Adrian Anson, though his teammates called him "Cap," short for Captain. Anson was an astute tactician, a fierce competitor and a gifted athlete. Throughout the long, storied history of the Chicago National League Baseball Club, no player in a Chicago uniform would ever get more hits, hit for a higher average, or drive in more runs—not Chance, Kuyler, Wilson, Hornsby, Hartnett, Caveretta, Pafko, Sauer, Banks, Santo, Williams, Sandberg, or Sosa. And in the entire history of Major League baseball, from its origins in 1876 until the present day, no one from any team would ever bat over .300 in more seasons than Cap Anson.

In 1876 Anson was so eager to get an edge on the opposition that he called his team together for exercise and practice two months before opening day. When the weather in Chicago proved to be too cold and inclement to conduct the intended training sessions, he decreed that his pre-season regimen would be moved to a warmer venue—Hot Springs, Arkansas. Other teams quickly followed Anson's lead, thus beginning a vernal rite now known to the baseball-loving world as spring training.

When Anson left the Chicago White Stockings after almost twenty years of service, the team was so bereft of leadership, that it was renamed, "the Orphans." A decade or so later, a New York sports writer would refer to three scrappy, young infielders on the Chicago team as "bear cubs." The name stuck, and as a result, the Chicago National League Baseball Club formally changed its name to the "Cubs."

Despite his greatness as a baseball player, Cap Anson was an out-spoken racist. So when the Chicago National League team came to New York in 1884, Anson announced that he would not play because the local team had several Negro players. This created a major uproar among the fans who had bought advance tickets to see Anson play. As a result, several members of the syndicate that owned the New York team voted to temporarily remove the Negro players from their team's roster in order to appease Anson. Frederick Merkle persuaded them to change their minds, and when they did, Anson backed down from his one man boycott.

A few years later, when Anson's fame and influence grew even stronger, he informed the scions of Major League baseball that he would not play against any team that had a Negro player. This infuriated Frederick Merkle, who saw baseball as a vehicle for healing the nation's geographical, religious, and racial divisions, rather than aggravating them. Indeed, he already knew that many of the immigrant families took great pride in watching their sons participate in America's game, and thereby felt closer to their adopted country as a result. Nonetheless, despite Merkle's strenuous arguments to the contrary, the baseball owners capitulated to Anson's ultimatum. It was in this way that Major League baseball adopted an informal ban on Negro ball players that lasted sixty years.

In the aftermath of the baseball owners' capitulation to Anson's ultimatum, Frederick Merkle indignantly sold his stake in his beloved Giants. Shortly thereafter he was asked to join a syndicate intent on buying the Chicago Cubs. His adamant refusal was motivated entirely by an undisguised antipathy at the Cubs for Anson's role in initiating "the ban."

Some years later, Frederick Merkle decided that the only way to change the business of baseball was to get back into the baseball business. Because shares in his beloved Giants were unavailable, he accepted an opportunity to invest in a more recently organized New York team called the Brooklyn Bridegrooms. A year later, the Bridegrooms built a park on the site of George Washington's Long Island encampment during the Revolutionary War. Washington Park, as it was called, became surrounded by a maze of trolley tracks which both players and fans had to avoid, at their peril, in order to get into the park. It was in this way that the Brooklyn team changed its name from the Bridegrooms to the "Trolley Dodgers," which it soon shortened to the "Dodgers."

Frederick Merkle tried to use his position as a baseball insider to make the game as accessible as possible to all Americans. In some ways he succeeded and in some ways he failed. Thus, over the years baseball not only became the national pastime but, for better and for worse, became a mirror of the American culture.

159

Merkle also decided to sponsor several semi-professional teams in New York City. So, when Lincoln returned from Harvard, his father asked him to not only help manage his investments and supervise his businesses, but oversee his baseball teams. Among other things, Merkle insisted that his semi-pro rosters be based solely on merit, and in this way he believed that they would include young men from both Negro and immigrant backgrounds.

Lincoln was therefore disappointed when the player that his father recruited from the Lower East Side failed to show up for his first Sunday practice. Later that afternoon, Lincoln asked his driver to take him to the young man's apartment on Division Street. He found Benjamin in his room, fingertips so red with blood that he could not shake hands after introducing himself. Dozens of hat pins, twisted and bent into every conceivable shape were lying on a cot in the corner of the room. Benjamin gave a sheepish "hello" and invited the visitor into his apartment.

Lincoln had heard about the deplorable state of immigrant housing, but naively thought it could not be as bad as it actually was. "Maple Grove has twelve bathrooms, each considerably larger than this apartment," Lincoln said to himself. He thought of saying something aloud, but could think of nothing that would not be embarrassing to Benjamin. Instead, motioning to the pins on Benjamin's cot, he simply asked, "What on earth are you doing?"

Benjamin held a bent pin between the teeth of a needle nose pliers and thrust it in front of Lincoln's eyes. "Look at that," Benjamin said.

"At what?" Lincoln said, squinting at the twisted strand of metal.

Benjamin turned his wrist so Lincoln could see the pin from different angles. "Do you see the two triangles? One inside the other?"

"What of it?"

"Watch carefully," Benjamin said with enthusiasm. He then took several slips of paper, aligned their edges, and carefully slid them between the top points of the two nested triangles. "See how the bended wire holds the papers together."

"It's a paper fastener?" Lincoln deduced.

"Of course," said Benjamin proudly. "But it holds the papers together without making holes in them. It works just like the hair clips used by the two little girls who live down the hall."

"So instead of a hair clip, it's a paper clip," Lincoln said with a smile.

"Call it what you wish," Benjamin conceded. "But there is a great need for this in the garment industry. Take it from me." He held up his pin-pricked hands as proof.

"There is a need for this in many other industries," Lincoln added, "including those owned by my own family." Lincoln was already doing some mental calculations. "With the right machines you could probably make a pound of these fasteners for twenty-five cents and sell them for forty cents," he thought. "The market for these is in the thousands of pounds, maybe more." Then he was struck by an obvious problem, which he did not confide to Benjamin. "The moment anyone sees this, it will be copied and sold to the public at lower and lower prices, until there is insufficient profit to warrant the investment," he thought.

Benjamin would not have understood Lincoln's explanation, but even if he did, he would not have been discouraged. "What do you recommend I do next?" he asked.

Lincoln looked at the pins more carefully. "First, you need to use heavier gauge wire, and you must cut them into somewhat longer pieces. Then you need to find a machinist," he advised. "Preferably before you lose all your fingers and can't play baseball anymore."

"A machinist?" Benjamin asked.

"A machinist is an artisan," Lincoln answered. "Someone who knows how to work in metal."

"Work in metal," Benjamin repeated, recalling his brief encounter with a blacksmith in Odessa. "I think that I have a note in my travel bag that contains the name of someone who does just that," he said to himself. Lincoln, meanwhile, was looking curiously at the dozens of pins, twisted into every imaginable configuration, that were strewn on Benjamin's cot. Then he picked up the fastener that Benjamin had successfully demonstrated, and studied it carefully.

"What made you decide on this double triangle design?" Lincoln asked.

"It is a version of my family's sign," Benjamin beamed.

When Lincoln gave a blank stare, Benjamin withdrew a bronze medallion out from under his shirt. On one side was a strange diagram. On the other side was an even stranger imprecation that was sworn to in the Bar Kochba name. Below it was a Star of David. Benjamin pointed to the star. "This was my inspiration," he confided.

Lincoln broke into a cold sweat. He put his hand under his own shirt and pulled out a bronze medallion that was identical to the one that Benjamin had just shown him.

Benjamin gawked at it in disbelief. He and Lincoln traced their fingers over the sign of the comet on the front, and the strangely worded imprecation on the back.

"Do you know what this means?" Lincoln asked.

"I can translate the words," Benjamin answered. "But I do not know where they came from."

"Neither do I," Lincoln whispered.

MARVIN'S CONFESSION

The Civil War ended for Calvin Robinson near a burned-out planta-tion in southern Georgia. He had marched to the sea with General Sherman, and then moved back inland for what the army politely called "mop-up duty." In the process he had a firsthand glimpse at hell—a fifty mile-wide swath of death and destruction that extended all the way from Atlanta to Savannah.

Towns that had no military value were burned to the ground. Homes were plundered and torched, livestock was destroyed, men were murdered, women were raped, children were left to starve in the fields. Fertile farmland, once verdant with bountiful plant life, was seeded with salt to prevent growth of even a subsistence crop.

Calvin often shuddered at the needless destruction, and the result-ing misery and privation, that the Union Army had wrought upon the people who once farmed the rich red earth of Georgia. And the irony of the situation was not lost upon him. Only such wanton cruelty could make him take pity on these wretched landowners who had held his family in bondage all these years.

Unfortunately, in the decade following the Great War many of those Southerners who managed to survive only found distraction from their miserable existence with thoughts of vengeance and hate. Their hate was directed first at the Yankee soldiers, then at the Yankee carpetbaggers, and ultimately, at all Yankees, no matter what their station in life. The hate was, unfortunately returned in manner and kind. "What happened to Mr. Lincoln's wish of 'malice toward none and charity for all'?" Calvin wondered.

In time Calvin grew to resent the Yankees as well. Among other things, he deeply objected to the vindictiveness of radical Reconstructionists who sought to deny former Confederate soldiers the right to vote. He had no desire to deprive the white man of any rights; he just wanted to ensure the same rights for the Negro. He knew, however, that Yankee pandering to receptive Negroes and guilt-ridden whites would produce a horrible backlash—an emotional reaction against people of color that would retard Lincoln's vision for a hundred years. It was under these circumstances that Calvin tried to convince his wife, Willa Mae, that they should move to California—where some of his relatives had migrated immediately after the war.

"White people blame us for their misery," Calvin argued, "yet it is our misery that grows worse every day. And it will never end as long as white babies are taught to hate us with their mother's milk and white fathers extract an oath of revenge from their children with their dying breath."

"What makes you think the white folk will be any better in California than they are in Georgia?" Willa Mae countered. "I am not going all the way to the ends of the earth just to find the same troubles that we have here."

Calvin knew that arguing with Willa Mae was fruitless. She simply was not going to leave her Georgia roots, or the remnant of her family, no matter what praises Calvin sang about California. And so, with the money he saved from his military service, in addition to that which he earned after several years of work as a free man, Calvin purchased a three-room cabin and a small patch of dirt. Together with Willa Mae, they grew vegetables in their garden and caught fish from the nearby stream. To supplement their income, Calvin earned a few dollars a week chopping cotton and Willa Mae earned a dollar a week taking in laundry.

In 1875 the event that both Calvin and Willa Mae had prayed for daily finally occurred. Willa Mae gave birth to a baby boy—the first Robinson in Calvin's line to be born in freedom in over a hundred years. Though Calvin wanted to name the boy Frederick, in honor of a Union soldier who paid a steep price for his son's freedom, such as it was, he succumbed to Willa Mae's preference—Jerry. In 1896, on Jerry Robinson's twenty-first birthday, Calvin gave the young man a silver cross of the Latin style, and retold the story of how it came into his possession.

"Let this be a reminder," he lectured him. "At one time or another we all need help; and the help we get may come from the unlikeliest of places."

At that very moment, Benjamin Barr was searching for the name of a machinist whose help he'd need if he wanted to manufacture his triangular-shaped paper fastener. He thought he would find the name of such a person on a piece of paper that was inside his old leather travel bag. He dumped the bag's contents onto the floor and frantically pawed through the items that had spilled out, but no note could be found. Benjamin then loosened the cords of a draw-string pouch, removed a wad of bills, and thrust his hand inside. Again he found nothing.

Desperate, he looked inside the travel bag one more time. When he glimpsed an interior pocket, his lips parted into a happy smile. He reached in and withdrew a folded piece of foolscap.

Benjamin tried to recollect the words of the Odessa blacksmith who gave him the note. "He said something about having a son who was a worker in metal," Benjamin recalled as he unfolded the paper and pressed it flat against the bare wooden floor. A faded message revealed a name and an address. The address was on First Avenue, not too far from Benjamin's apartment. The name on the paper caused the blood to immediately drain from Benjamin's face. It said, "Mariv Tover."

Benjamin pulled the bronze medallion out from under his shirt, and checked the words on the back just to be certain. "Tover" was the name that appeared just above the name that was formerly his own. He quickly stuffed the foolscap note, along with a straight pin painstakingly bent into a double triangular shape, into the front pocket of his trousers. Then he left his apartment.

Benjamin was not sure whether the palpable excitement he felt in his breast was the result of his hope that Tover was a machinist who could manufacture his paper fastener, or his hunch that Tover could explain the writing on the medallions which he and Lincoln Merkle wore around their necks. "And what about that immigration clerk?" he thought. "I wonder what he knows about this."

Benjamin found the Tover address with little difficulty. He rapped his knuckles against the door and waited impatiently for someone to answer his knock. A thin, haggard woman, who he assumed looked older than her years, opened the door just wide enough to reveal her high-necked dress and long work apron. She eyed Benjamin suspiciously, but said nothing.

"I am looking for Mariv Tover," Benjamin said haltingly.

The woman frowned. A baby's cry could be heard from inside the apartment. The woman gave a quick look behind her. When she heard a male voice respond to the child's cries with the comment, "I've got him, Roma," followed by some muffled words that sounded like "Hush, John," she turned her attention back toward her visitor.

"I'm looking for Mariv Tover," Benjamin repeated.

The woman started to close the door, but Benjamin put his hand against the frame. "Please," he pleaded.

The woman bit her lip, then pushed her shoulder against the door.

"I have a message from his father," Benjamin said loudly, just as the door slammed shut in his face.

Benjamin stood at the threshold for a moment in the false hope that the door would re-open. When it did not, he turned and disconsolately walked away in the direction of Division Street. He was uncertain what to make of his encounter with the grim-faced, inhospitable woman. "Perhaps she didn't understand my English," Benjamin rationalized. "Or maybe the address I was given by the blacksmith is now out of date."

His thoughts were interrupted by a gentle tap on his shoulder. "How do you know my father?" he heard a strange voice inquire.

When Benjamin wheeled around he came face-to-face with a small, wiry man with dark hair and an olive complexion. The two strangers studied each other in silence.

"I met him briefly at his shop in Odessa," Benjamin explained.

As he spoke, Benjamin extended his hand and introduced himself.

Tover grabbed it firmly, revealing a double triangle tattoo on his right forearm. Benjamin recognized it immediately as the honored sign of the Tover that was etched onto the back of his medallion. "My name is now Marvin," Tover said a bit sheepishly. "It sounds more American."

"Can I buy you a drink?" Benjamin suggested, trying unsuccessfully to avoid staring at the tattoo.

"I will buy the drinks," Marvin said raising his hand. "In return, you will tell me about my father."

Benjamin nodded. "Your father told me to tell you that he and your mother are proud of you," Benjamin said, as he followed Marvin into a nearby tavern.

Marvin Tover insisted on hearing the entire story about Benjamin's chance meeting with his father. And so, suppressing his eagerness to inquire about the Tover name and the familiar tattoo sign, Benjamin recounted the story, sparing no detail.

"And now I must ask you a question," Benjamin said, after he had given the foolscap note to Marvin as a memento.

Marvin Tover nodded.

"Are you familiar with the name 'Bar Kochba?'" Benjamin began.

"So you call the name 'Bar Kochba?'" Tover asked, pronouncing the 'ch' as Benjamin did—with the same guttural sound that a German would pronounce the surname of Johann Sebastian Bach.

Benjamin's excitement grew as he sensed recognition of the Bar Kachba name in Marvin's manner and expression. "I do," he said tersely.

"I have heard the name," Marvin said. "But why do you ask?"

Benjamin could no longer restrain his excitement. "Like you, my name was changed when I came to this country. Though it's now Barr, my family name is Bar Kochba," Benjamin continued. "More importantly, I think you're familiar with my name for the same reason I am familiar with yours." Benjamin pulled his bronze medallion out from under his shirt and showed it to Marvin.

Marvin, almost trance-like, reached his hand under his shirt and withdrew an identical medallion.

"Do you know what any of this means?" Benjamin asked, repeatedly turning his medallion from one side to the other.

Marvin's expression betrayed a feeling of disappointment. "I do not. And you don't either?"

Benjamin shook his head.

Then suddenly Marvin threw his forearm in front of his eyes and winced in pain. In his mind's eye he saw a terrible explosion that left a small crater in the earth.

"Are you all right?" Benjamin asked.

Marvin took a deep breath and opened his eyes. "I'm sorry," he apologized. But then he winced again. Next to the crater he saw his son, John.

FREDERICK'S PROMISE

Herman Ruth helped his wife Margaret into the hansom. They gave a last, longing look at their white frame home on Liberty Street before the driver released the brake and cracked his whip. The carriage lurched forward. A moment later the horse began a steady clip-clopping down the cobblestone street in the direction of the river.

By 1896 the Pennsylvania Railroad still had not yet completed its bridge across the Hudson. Until it was finished, passengers traveling from New York City, down the coast to Philadelphia, Wilmington, Baltimore and Washington, had to take a ferry across the river, and then board their train at a depot in Jersey. Herman checked his inside coat pocket to confirm that he had not forgotten the tickets. Then he contemplated the circumstances that gave rise to their trip.

"Our son is a ne'er-do-well," Herman grumbled, just loud enough for his wife to hear,

"He is still our son," she said defensively.

"George is no longer a child; he is a grown man who has spent his life running away from his troubles."

"He is a grown man who is down on his luck," Margaret corrected him. "We should thank the Lord that we are in a position to be of help." Margaret made a quick sign of the cross for emphasis.

Herman turned away with an audible, "Harrumph."

The ferry hadn't passed halfway across the Hudson, before Herman was regretting his decision to move to Baltimore. He had a good job with the Immigration Office at Ellis Island, qualified for a small pension, owned his own home, and was finally beginning to partake in the excitement and gaiety of his native city. He wasn't sure why, in middle age, he was first starting to enjoy life. But now, for the first time, he and Margaret—the usually stuffy Margaret—had begun going out with friends on Saturday nights to hear the music that was all the rage. It had a ragged, off-beat melody originally written for banjos by Negro slaves. Now it was played on the piano for white tavern patrons who called it "ragtime." The rest of the world would soon call it jazz.

Herman had given his son some money to start a tavern in the hope that such an establishment would attract the same enthusiastic patrons in Baltimore that similar clubs were attracting in New York. But, through a combination of too much drinking and too little attention to business, George's tavern went belly-up. Even worse, George's wife Kate had become seriously ill after giving birth to her eighth child. The baby boy had been christened George Herman Ruth.

Herman fixed his eyes on the Jersey shore, wondering where this uncertain journey would lead. Had he turned his eyes back toward the city, followed the shoreline of the Hudson upstream for a few miles, and then looked up the steep embankment, he would have seen an unlikely trio of men marveling at the scenery below. Herman would have been shocked to know that each of these men, as they sat around a table on the verandah of the Frederick Merkle estate, wore the identical medallion around their necks that he wore around his. He would have been even more surprised to learn that he was the only one who knew the history of those medallions, and the origin of the curse that was etched therein.

Frederick Merkle emerged from the rear entrance of his magnificent mansion to greet his guests. He limped noticeably. Lincoln introduced his father to Marvin and reintroduced him to Benjamin. Frederick had asked his son to invite them to his home in the hope that, together, they could solve the mystery of Mirceal's curse. He beckoned Benjamin to explain what he knew about his medallion.

"I don't have much to say," Benjamin apologized. "I was born on a small farm in the Transylvania Province of Romania. I never left the farm until the day I set out for America. I was orphaned at seventeen, and shortly before my father died he gave me a medallion. He made me swear an oath on my mother's grave that I would pass it on to my son. I was shocked to learn, only recently, that there was a second, then a third, medallion of the same kind.

"Did your father tell you anything else?" Frederick asked.

Benjamin shook his head. Then suddenly his eyes widened. "He also gave me a pendant with an old coin," Benjamin remembered. "He said it was taken from the Holy Land when my people left there for Romania. It bore the same six pointed star that is on our medallions."

Frederick Merkle then turned his eyes toward Marvin.

"My father was also born in Transylvania," he began, "so I assume that our possession of these medallions can only be explained by our common origin from that place."

Before he could continue, however, Angela Merkle walked onto the verandah followed by two servants. One carried an elegant tea service; the other carried a sterling silver basket containing morsels of pastry. Angela was still a beautiful woman. Despite the passage of time, her copper skin remained smooth; the corners of her eyes betrayed no wrinkle. Nonetheless, both Benjamin and Marvin were unable to suppress their surprise when Lincoln introduced this Negress as his mother.

"Please continue," Frederick said, after the tea had been poured.

Marvin gave a furtive look at Angela, then returned his attention to his host. "My father was a slave," Marvin explained. "He was freed in 1863, and I was born two years later—the first Tover born in freedom in over a hundred years."

"There were slaves in Europe?" Angela asked incredulously.

"Yes ma'am," Marvin assured her. "My father's back still bears the scars of his bondage."

"I have seen them myself," Benjamin assured her.

"Pardon my asking," Angela interrupted, "but how common was this European slavery that you mentioned. Little is ever spoken about it."

"I am quite certain that there were slaves in every country of Europe," Marvin responded. "We talk about it in America because we acknowledge our sins and our shame."

"But the sins continue," Angela observed.

"And so does the shame," Marvin added quickly. "The Europeans, however, have no shame. And they admit to sins of the past only as an excuse to commit worse sins in the future."

"Do you harbor anger over your father's past slavery?" Angela wanted to know.

"Of course," Marvin admitted. "But when I left for America, my father warned me to focus on the future, lest my anger make me a victim of our past."

"And how do you feel about the people of your native land?" Angela asked Benjamin.

Benjamin looked at her incredulously. "They are beasts," he said tersely.

"About the medallions," Frederick interrupted before the conversation drifted too far off course.

"Yes, sir," said Marvin. "My father served his master as a blacksmith. After he became a free man, he moved to Odessa where freedom was somewhat more accepted, especially for people of our complexion. He opened a shop which he still owns and operates."

Marvin looked toward Benjamin to corroborate his words.

"I have seen that, too," Benjamin confirmed.

"What do you know of the Tover sign?" Lincoln asked.

Marvin exposed the tattoo on his right forearm. "The two triangles with their points touching each other are a symbol for a two-headed axe. That is what the name 'Tover' means in our ancient language."

"And the tattoo?" Frederick inquired.

"It is the mark we give our sons when they are young."

"Did you also get your medallion from your father?" Frederick continued.

Marvin took a deep breath. "I received my medallion from my father in much the same way Benjamin got his—with an oath that I must pass it on to my son. My father also gave me this," he said, withdrawing a two-headed axe from beneath his waistcoat. Marvin held the axe aloft for all to admire, then passed it around for each to examine. As they did, Benjamin took a sip of tea, and let its soothing warmth trickle down his cough-reddened throat.

"My story is not without irony," Marvin continued. "One of the reasons I came to America is because I wanted the freedom to do something different from my father. And yet here I am, a worker in metal, just like him. I wrote him a letter some years ago to tell him that."

"Maybe that is why he is so proud of you," Benjamin smiled.

"What work in metal do you do?" Lincoln asked.

"I have machines that make braided wire," Marvin said proudly.

"Braided wire?" Frederick inquired.

"I notice that your beautiful home has been retrofitted for the Edison lamps and the Bell talking device," Marvin explained. "It is my braided wire, twisted from thin filaments of copper and steel, that safely carries the electricity to and from your switches and handsets."

"I am hoping to work with Marvin to adapt one of his machines to draw and bend wire for me," Benjamin added.

"So you prefer bending wires to hitting baseballs?" Lincoln asked.

"I think my future is in Marvin's machines," Benjamin said politely.

"I am still interested in our past," Frederick interrupted. "As you surmised, I too have a family connection to this place you call Transylvania. An ancestor moved from there to Holland, and from Holland to America. He was among the founders of this great city. My father gave me the medallion for good luck when I went off to war. He told me that I was given the power to bless and to curse, just as the medallion suggests. I passed the medallion on to Lincoln when he went off to college. Our surname is a virtual homonym of the name on the medallion, so I assume the latter is merely an Anglicized version of the former. But I have no further information on the origin of the curse or its meaning. Apparently, neither do any of you."

"Excuse me, sir," Benjamin said nervously. "I do have one further piece of information." He removed the note he received from Herman Ruth two days after he arrived in America, and laid it on the table for all to read.

"This morning, in advance of our meeting, I took a ferry out to Ellis Island in the hope of ascertaining what Mr. Ruth may know about the very questions you have asked. Unfortunately, his supervisor informed me that Mr. Ruth had recently resigned his position, and left no information as to his future whereabouts."

Frederick Merkle read, and re-read Mr. Ruth's note. "I will find him," he said with the resolve of a man who usually got what he wanted.

Frederick rang a bell that rested on the table, and a servant instantly appeared. "Get a man from Pinkerton's here as soon as possible," he ordered. Then he turned to Marvin and Benjamin. "You have graced me by coming here this afternoon, and I intend to compensate you both for your time and trouble. I confess that I am obsessed with the mystery of Mirceal's curse, and the possible role that my family may have played in this intrigue. For this reason, I solicit your cooperation in keeping my son, Lincoln, informed of your whereabouts. I am willing to pay you for that as well."

"It would be payment enough for me to learn the secret of this medallion myself," Marvin answered.

Benjamin nodded his head in agreement.

"Your generosity is appreciated," Frederick continued. "Nonetheless, a promise of compensation I made, and a promise of compensation I will keep. Lincoln, please give each of these gentlemen a hundred dollars for their time in meeting with us today, and for their trouble in keeping you apprised of their whereabouts until we locate this mysterious Mr. Ruth."

Lincoln opened his billfold and gave both Marvin and Benjamin a crisp, one hundred dollar bill. "The carriage that brought you here will now take you home. I hope we will be in touch soon."

Benjamin was so stunned that his "thank you" got stuck somewhere between his throat and his lips. He held in his hand the equivalent of almost six months' work at the box factory. He decided immediately that he would give part of his windfall to his neighbors, Max and Frieda Mann.

Pinkerton's Ticket

About twenty-five miles northwest of the southern tip of Lake Michigan there exists a slight wrinkle in the flat Midwestern prairie. Being only about three feet high, and having the subtlest of slopes, the town that now sits on this modest ridge is nonetheless referred to, rather pretentiously, as "Summit." On a rainy day, water flowing off of the east side of the Summit ridge gathers into rivulets that form the south branch of a river that connects with Lake Michigan. The Pottawatomie Indians named this river the Checagou, for the wild onions that grew along its banks. The white men who arrived centuries later called it Chicago.

Rain water falling off of the west side of the Summit ridge forms into a stream which flows into the Des Plaines River. The Des Plaines empties into the Illinois River which, in turn, empties into the Mississippi. The distance across the Summit ridge varies according to the season. During the rainy season it is only a short walk.

For generations the Pottawatomie knew that the Summit ridge was all that blocked an uninterrupted water route between the Mississippi River and the Great Lakes. The short portage across that ridge gave them a decided advantage in trade, travel, and warfare. Centuries later this route would also become of vital importance to white men, be they explorers, fur trappers, or settlers. Through the ages, a natural resting and

175

reprovisioning spot for both red man and white man was where the river highway ended, and the lake began. It is for this reason that the City of Chicago exists where it does.

Only after the ferocious Indian Wars had ended, the chronic lawlessness had been curtailed, and a reliable fiscal organization had taken root, was the City of Chicago finally able to take advantage of the inland waterway that flowed past its doorstep. By then, however, this waterway had been rendered obsolete by a more versatile transportation system—the railroads. Even before the peace at Appomattox, railroad tracks extended from Chicago in all directions, like spokes from the hub of a gigantic wheel. By the turn of the century this tough, brawling town had become the second largest city in the nation. It was also at that time that a New York newspaperman would refer to Chicago as the "Windy City," not because of the prevailing winds that would one day blow out toward the Wrigley Field scoreboard, but the blow-hard politicians who so shamelessly promoted their city.

After the great fire, the City of Chicago evolved into a patchwork of ethnic neighborhoods, each internally clannish and each outwardly hostile. The names of the storefront proprietors made it perfectly clear which ethnic neighborhood a person was in. There were, for example, so many storefronts on North Clark Street that bore the name Anderson, that the entire Swedish enclave became known, simply, as "Andersonville."

These storefront names also served as a warning to outsiders: enter this neighborhood at your own risk. It was for this reason that, unless someone was looking for a fight, a Pole would not enter a German beer garden, a German would not enter an English pub, an Englishman would not enter an Irish tavern, and an Irishman would not enter an Italian bar. If he was smart, a Jew would not enter any of these saloons.

In those days, Chicago's Jewish neighborhood was located on the near west side, not far from the "West Side Grounds," as the field where the Chicago Cubs played was commonly called. Down the left field line, just beyond the stands, stood an imposing red brick building that housed the Cook County Mental Hospital. On a hot summer day, when the institution's windows were open, many a wacky comment could be heard from the hospital inmates, giving rise to the expression: "That came out of left field."

Next door to the hospital on West Polk Street was a Western Union Office. It was from that office that a rabbi by the name of Avrom Levy telegraphed an urgent request to his fellow Ukrainian émigré who now owned his own frame home in Manhattan. The wire was dated September 21, 1908. Max Mann read it to his wife, Frieda, the moment it arrived. "Please meet my cousin Mendel Levy & family when they arrive in NY on steamer *Mauretania*."

"It's from Avrom Levy—the rabbi who we met on the boat," Max informed Frieda. "Avrom and his wife, Ida, took the train to Chicago the very day that we docked in New York," Max reminded her.

"I have no time for telegrams right now," Frieda told her husband. "Benjamin is joining us for dinner tonight, and I still have much to do."

In the dozen years that had passed since Benjamin Barr's windfall, he and Max Mann had become good friends and business partners. With the hundred dollars he received from Frederick Merkle, Benjamin bought a sewing machine. He and Max then took a great risk: they quit their jobs at the box factory and opened a small shop on Fifth Avenue which they called "Max-a-Min Tailors." Though the name was originally derived from separate syllables in the partners' first names, it quickly evolved into a shorthand for their company's slogan: "Maximum Quality at Minimum Cost."

Max originally worked fourteen-hour days at the tailor shop, but even at the outset he was able to take home twice as much money, after expenses, as he did at the box factory. Ben worked about ten hours a day at the tailor shop, but also put in a few hours every evening at Marvin's wire factory, trying to develop a machine that could automatically draw, cut and bend wire into paper clips. He and Marvin had a "handshake" agreement: if anything came out of the enterprise that used Marvin's machines and Benjamin's labor, they would share equally in the profits.

After a short time in business, Max-a-Min Tailors was able to buy a second sewing machine, and then a third. Both of the Mann girls worked there part-time as teenagers, and then full-time after they left public school. During breaks from work, the girls sometimes walked down Fifth Avenue, admiring the fashionable clothing stores and the wealthy women who patronized them. One day the youngest Mann daughter made the mistake of spontaneously complimenting an upper class young lady on the dress she was wearing, and asked where it had been purchased. The young lady looked at the immigrant girl and sneered, "What possible difference could that make? You could never afford it anyway."

The girls walked back to the store angry and hurt. By the time they had resumed their work, however, they had made a handshake agreement of their own. "One day we will design clothes that are so expensive that even arrogant people like her will be unable to afford them."

As it turned out, the girls did have a talent for fashion, but not in the area that they had originally envisioned. Recognizing that, in the new century, wealthy women wanted the freedom to engage in outdoor activities such as bicycle riding, tennis and golf, the girls designed a line of clothing that paired shorter, looser fitting skirts with blouses that did not need to be tucked into the waistband. A dozen years later the girls designed something even more audacious—they eliminated the skirt altogether and lengthened the blouse until it flapped just above the knee. The women who wore these provocative outfits were called "flappers."

Unlike the Mann girls, their brother was shy and reserved. He did, however, have a penchant for science. After finishing high school, he matriculated at nearby Columbia University to study medicine. Throughout high school and college he, too, spent countless hours at the tailor store. Among other things, he handled Max-a-Min's accounts and ledgers, and along with Benjamin, kept the machines in good repair.

It was during that time that Benjamin's paper clip enterprise took an unexpected turn. After years of work, Benjamin and Marvin developed a machine that could produce the fasteners in a profitable manner. The market for these clips was not in the garment industry as Benjamin had originally thought. Instead, as Lincoln Merkle had predicted, the clips would find widespread use in the countless stores, offices and government buildings where papers needed to be temporarily fastened, unfastened, and refastened without destroying their integrity by repeated piercing and punching.

Just as their business began to grow, the entrepreneurs received papers of a different kind: a formal letter from the president of a competing company demanding that they cease their operations or be sued for patent infringement. Neither Marvin nor Benjamin was familiar with such words, so the next morning they decided to personally meet with the letter-writer and inquire. That afternoon, the company president, along with some of his engineering and financial advisers, reconvened at Marvin's factory where they could review Benjamin's books and inspect his equipment. By the meeting's end, Marvin and Benjamin agreed to sell their paper clip company, including their fastener-making machinery, for a handsome sum of money. The two partners split the sum in half, exactly as they had agreed years earlier.

Before leaving, the president of the purchasing company shook hands with both Marvin and Benjamin.

"I think you gave us a jewel of a deal," Marvin told him.

"I think you make a jewel of a product," he said with a smile. Apparently he did, for sometime thereafter, he changed the brand name of all of his paper-fastening products to "Jewel."

In the years since he had left his home, Benjamin had distanced himself from the faith of his fathers. The Mann family had not. This, of course, made for interesting dinner table discussion.

"So," Ben began, looking directly at Max, "Are we Jewish Americans, or are we American Jews?"

The three Mann children looked immediately at their father for an answer, but their mother interrupted before he could respond, "What's the difference?" she inquired.

"Are we Americans who happen to be of the Jewish faith, or are we Jews who happen to be living in America?" Ben explained.

"I still fail to see the difference," Frieda insisted.

Benjamin tried again. "To whom do we owe our loyalty, our country or our faith?"

This time Max's son, Isaac, interrupted, "It is one thing to ask an Irishman if his loyalties reside with his former country or his adopted country. And he would surely say his adopted country, just as I would surely answer America instead of the Ukraine." Despite his passion, young Isaac spoke in a soft, measured tone.

Frieda pretended to spit out loud at the very mention of the wretched country she left for America. "And that goes double for the Tsar," she said, pretending to spit twice.

"But," young Isaac continued, "if you asked an Irishman to choose between his adopted country and his faith, here in America he could properly choose both, as can we."

Max cleared his throat, and everyone at the table turned their attention to him. "We owe our loyalty to America," he said with strong conviction. "We will abide by her laws, pay our taxes and defend her with our lives. America is the best hope for the world. Now, let us say the prayers for bread and for wine, and enjoy the meal that God has given us."

This time it was Frieda who cleared her throat.

"With Frieda's help," Max quickly added.

Max recited the customary prayers in the ancient Hebrew language. No one present knew exactly what the words meant. Nonetheless, when Max was finished everyone said, "Amen."

After dinner Isaac excused himself to pursue his studies, but the conversation resumed with a question from the eldest Mann daughter. "Immigrants work in sweat shops for pennies a day; the colored are treated like dogs. What hope does America hold for them?"

"The same hope it held for us," Max said.

"Is it not a false hope?" she insisted.

Now Benjamin was emboldened to speak. "It is a distant hope, not a false hope," he said, carefully measuring his words. Then recalling his conversation on the Frederick Merkle verandah in the presence of a former slave woman several years earlier, he added, "America is becoming a strong, powerful nation. In time I suspect it will be measured, not in comparison with other countries, but by her distance from absolute perfection. The rest of the world will then be measured by its distance from America."

"Perhaps we should all be measured by the distance we have traveled, rather than the mile posts we are at," Max added. Then he turned abruptly in the direction of his wife, as he was prone to do when suddenly reminded of an unrelated thought. "And now it is our turn to help some people who have traveled a long distance themselves."

"And who might that be?" asked his youngest daughter.

"Cousins of a friend," said Max, handing her the telegram that had been delivered to their house earlier that afternoon.

The young lady read the message out loud.

"I know those people," Benjamin blurted out spontaneously. "It was the same Rabbi Mendel Levy who recited the Kaddish at the graveside of my parents."

There followed an audible buzz of astonishment. After it subsided, Benjamin volunteered to meet the Levy family at Ellis Island on Max's behalf. "I believe I can recognize Rabbi Levy even after all of these years," he said. "And I'll make sure that all of us get together before they board their train for Chicago."

After dinner Benjamin took his leave, and walked to his own frame house which was located a little further uptown from his partner's. He arrived tired and drowsy. At first he didn't even notice the uniformed man from the Pinkerton Agency who was waiting outside his door. "I have a message from Frederick Merkle," the detective intoned.

"How long have you been waiting here?" Benjamin asked.

The Pinkerton man ignored Ben's question, but continued with his message in the same dull monotone in which he had begun. "You are to meet Mr. Merkle, his son and Mr. Tover in Mr. Merkle's box at The Polo Grounds tomorrow afternoon. Here is a ticket that will gain you admittance to the ballgame."

Benjamin looked at the ticket, and then gave the Pinkerton man a quizzical look.

"We have finally found the elusive Mr. Ruth," the Pinkerton man said. "He will be at the game as well."

Benjamin looked at the ticket again, but before he could ask the detective another question, the Pinkerton man had disappeared.

"Who are the Giants playing?" Ben yelled into the darkness.

"The Cubs," came the detective's distant reply.

MATTY'S KNUCKLER

By 1908, electricity and telephone lines were no longer uncommon in the homes and apartments of American cities, automobiles were competing with horse drawn carriages for space on American streets, and baseball had taken a tenacious hold on the American culture. Baseball's incomparable popularity was, perhaps, best exemplified by the pretty young woman who, when asked by her fiancé where she wanted to go for her twenty-first birthday, told him not to take her to dinner or to a fancy night club. Instead, she implored him to, "take me out to the ball game." A creative songwriter turned her plaintive request into a popular song that seemed to sum up where all of America then wanted to be.

In those days, the best Major League team in America was, by far, the Chicago Cubs. They had already won eight National League championships, one in each of the last two years. They finished the 1906 season twenty games ahead of the second place Pirates, but suffered a shocking loss to the cross-town White Sox in the World Series. The team redeemed itself the next year by winning the National League pennant by seventeen games, amassing 107 regular-season wins, and then defeating the Ty Cobb-led Detroit Tigers in four straight games to win their first World Series.

In 1908, the Cubs were odds-on favorites to win the world championship again. The influential New York journalists had already proclaimed the Cubs to be a baseball dynasty. At the outset of the season they collectively announced that the 1908 Cubs were far better than the Giants and probably the best Major League team ever assembled. The Chicago papers had a different explanation of why the Cubs were better than the Giants. The Cub players had nice-sounding English and German names, whereas many of the Giants' players—including their fiery manager, John McGraw—were Irish.

The only two challengers to the Cubs' third successive National League pennant were the Pittsburgh Pirates and the New York Giants. The Pirates were led by the best position player in the National League, Honus Wagner. The Giants were led by the best pitcher in baseball, Christy Mathewson. Twenty-eight years later, when the Baseball Hall of Fame was established with the induction of the five best players in baseball history, Wagner and Mathewson would join Babe Ruth, Ty Cobb and Walter Johnson as the initial inductees.

During the 1908 season both Wagner and Mathewson would lead their teams in inspirational ways on and off the field. Unlike many of the ballplayers who spent their time drinking and carousing, Wagner and Mathewson instinctively understood that they were role models to the countless men and boys who patronized the game. And they conducted themselves accordingly.

In 1908 Wagner hit .354, scored a hundred runs, collected over 200 hits, had 109 RBIs and stole fifty-three bases. As a shortstop, he was a graceful, near-flawless fielder, on diamonds that were bumpy, lumpy and dumpy. As the game's best pitcher, Mathewson would win thirty-seven games that season, and compile an ERA of 1.43. In the process he struck out 259 batters, walked only forty-two and completed an astonishing thirty-four games.

But the Cubs were better. Their infield of Joe Tinker, Johnny Evers and Frank Chance became the most renowned double-play combination in baseball history. As a New York sports columnist would one day write, their names alone struck fear and sadness into the psyche of the opposing fans. So entwined in baseball history did their names become that, when the time came, all three were inducted into the Hall of Fame—simultaneously.

And though Mathewson was the game's best pitcher, the Cubs had a better staff—maybe the best pitching staff ever assembled in any baseball season. The leader of the Cubs' pitching corps was Mordecai "Three-Finger" Brown. Raised on a farm, Brown got his pitching arm caught in a mechanical corn chopper when he was a boy, and lost a finger before his hand could be extricated. Nonetheless, in 1908 Brown compiled a record of 29–9, and a 1.47 ERA. Pitcher Ed Ruelbach added twenty-four wins and a 2.03 ERA, Orvall Overall won fifteen games and had a 1.92 ERA, and Jack Pfiester added twelve more wins and compiled a 2.00 ERA.

Frank Chance, who served as the Cubs' manager as well as their first baseman typified the Cubs' toughness, personified the Cubs' dominance, and embodied the Cubs' arrogance. A former boxer, he was as mean and fearless as anyone who had ever played the game. Nicknamed "Husk" by the sportswriters for his rough, ornery nature, he was reverently referred to by his teammates as their "Peerless Leader."

Husk Chance thought that baseball success at any level could be achieved with four key ingredients: dominant pitching, superb defense, speed on the base paths, and alert, aggressive play with each and every pitch. If you could mix in timely hitting, teamwork, and a confident air of invincibility, you would have a decisive advantage over your opponents before they even took the field. And the Cubs did.

Just as the pundits predicted, the Cubs started the 1908 season at a torrid pace. By May 25th they were in first place with a record of 18–8. At that clip they could easily equal or exceed their previous year's mark of 107 wins. And best of all, the struggling, fifth place Giants were coming into town for a four game series at Chicago's West Side Grounds.

To the disappointment of the Cubs, and their boisterous fans, the Giants won three of those four games. They would have swept the Cubs on their home field if the Giants' manager realized that, in the second inning of Game Two, Joe Tinker batted out of turn. Had McGraw made a timely appeal, the three runs that the Cubs scored in their half of the second would not have counted, the game would not have gone into extra innings, and Tinker's game-winning single in the bottom of the tenth would never have occurred. The Giants' fans thought the game was stolen from them anyway, and were beside themselves with anger at their hated rivals. Nonetheless, the visitors' success on

Chicago's home field took a little swagger out of the Cubs' walk, and revitalized the confidence of both the Giants and the Pirates.

In July the standings tightened considerably. So when the Giants again visited Chicago's West Side Grounds, the Pirates had clawed their way into first, the Cubs were in second, and the Giants were but a half game behind the Cubs. The New Yorkers won the first game of the four-game series to move ahead of Chicago. In the second game, the Cubs fell behind 4–1, but loaded the bases with nobody out in the bottom of the seventh. McGraw called for Mathewson to come on in relief, but the Giants' ace was in the clubhouse, soaking an aching body in a hot bath.

On the very next play, the Giants' second baseman, "Laughing" Larry Doyle, proceeded to get into a prolonged argument with the umpire. Eventually, Doyle was ejected from the game, but not without getting the last laugh. The argument gave Mathewson time to get dressed and run onto the field—in street shoes. He then proceeded to snuff out the Cubs' rally, and save the game for New York.

The Cubs bounced back from their inauspicious beginning of the series by winning the final two games. When the Giants left town, the Pirates were still in first place. And the Cubs remained in second, a half game ahead of New York.

Throughout the summer, the three contenders traded places atop the National League standings. During one six-week span, Pittsburgh won twenty out of thirty games and again climbed into first place. But on August 24th the Giants completed a sweep of the Pirates and took over the lead. The Cubs, meanwhile, had just won nine straight games to claw their way to within a half game of New York. By the first week of September, only a single game separated the first place Giants from the third place Pirates.

It was in the midst of this heated chase for the pennant flag that the Cubs played a crucial game in Pittsburgh on September 4th. The Cubs threw their ace, Three-Finger Brown, at the Bucs, and Brown obliged with nine scoreless innings. Unbelievably, Pittsburgh's Vic Willis matched Brown pitch for pitch, and then held the Cubs scoreless in the top of the tenth. In the bottom of the inning, the Pirates loaded the bases, and a two out single to center brought the winning run across the plate.

As was common in those days, the security people allowed ecstatic fans to run out onto the field and celebrate the home team's victory. It was up to the players still on the base paths, and their opponents in the field, to make a mad dash to the clubhouse in order to avoid being trampled by the exuberant crowd. That's exactly what Pittsburgh base runner Warren Gill tried to do.

But, as was also common in those days, Gill headed for the clubhouse without first touching the base ahead of him to avoid being forced out, and thereby nullifying the winning run. Amidst the chaos and the din, Cub second baseman Johnny Evers alertly yelled for the ball. And when center fielder Jimmy Slagle threw it to him, Evers immediately stepped on second to force Gill, who had since disappeared through a door in the outfield wall that led into the Pirates' clubhouse. Evers then corralled umpire Hank O'Day, who was himself trying to avoid the melee, and demanded that he call Gill "out" for failing to touch second base. O'Day refused on the grounds that he hadn't seen the play.

Later that afternoon the Cubs filed an appeal to the league president, Harry Pulliam. Pulliam denied the Cubs' appeal, not because Evers was incorrect, but because umpire O'Day could not confirm that Gill failed to touch second. The next morning the *Pittsburgh Post* reported the accounts of the game as well as the results of the Cubs' appeal. In a concluding comment, the paper presciently observed that "... it is safe to predict that no one who took part in the game will overlook the importance of touching second base."

When Benjamin Barr arrived at the Polo Grounds on September 23rd, Pinkerton ticket in hand, the Cubs and the Giants were in a virtual tie for first place, with the Pirates just a half game behind. Though he got there well over an hour before game time, the streets were thick with people. Some were desperately seeking tickets at ten times their face value; others were searching for some high ground from which to catch a firsthand glimpse of the action. Ben stopped at a street vendor who was selling something advertised as a "hot dachshund sausage on a bun," and asked for directions to the main gate.

"You better have a ticket," he said in a thick German accent, pointing to a swelling crowd in Coogan's Hollow. "They started lining up early this morning and just kept coming."

Ben pulled his ticket out of his pocket, and held it up for the man to see. "What's a 'datshes hund' sausage?" Ben asked.

The vendor winced at the mispronunciation. "A dachshund is a German hound dog with a torso that looks like a sausage," he said, taking a pair of tongs and removing a sausage from a steam -filled metal box. "Try one."

Benjamin shook his head. "Maybe later."

With an usher's help, Benjamin worked his way through the stadium crowd, and into the Merkle family box. It was in the first row, next to the Giants' dugout. Marvin Tover was already there when he arrived. The two friends greeted each other warmly.

"Have you ever seen a Giants' game?" Marvin asked.

"This is my first." Benjamin confessed.

"Then we'll enjoy our first game together," Marvin said, "but not on an empty stomach. I'm going to get a sandwich; you want anything?"

Benjamin thought for a moment, unsuccessfully trying to remember the name of the steaming sausage that looked like a German hound. "I'd like one of those German dog sandwiches," he finally blurted.

Marvin squinted.

"The German hound dog sausage," Ben explained. "They put it on a bun."

"The hot dachshund sausage?"

"Yes, yes," said Ben. "The hot dog."

Just as Marvin was about to depart for the concession stand, many of the spectators started to clap and cheer. Their applause was apparently directed at a tall, handsome man who emerged from the Giants' dugout. He and a teammate walked toward a patch of grass between the playing field and the low brick wall behind which Marvin and Ben were seated. At first the two men just lobbed the ball back and forth like children. The cheers, however, grew louder with each throw.

After a couple of minutes, the handsome man's throwing motion became more exaggerated. This, in turn, allowed the man to propel the ball with greater and greater speed. Pretty soon Ben could actually hear the ball hiss as it sped through the air, and then crash into the teammate's mitt with a loud "pop." When the man's throwing motion became even more fluid and rhythmic, Benjamin noticed something extraordinary. The catcher held his mitt out as if it were a target for the pitcher. And despite the great speed at which the ball was thrown, it unerringly found its way into the mitt without the catcher having to move it so much as an inch in any direction.

Frederick Merkle and his son Lincoln arrived while Marvin and Ben were watching the Giants' pitcher warm up. "That's Christy Mathewson," Lincoln told them. "He's the best there is." As if on cue, the pitcher waved his mitt at his catcher. "Now watch this," Lincoln said with a look of awe.

The great pitcher wound up as he did before, but instead of throwing the ball directly at his teammate, he gave his wrist a noticeable snap as he released the ball. The ball sped toward the catcher, but an instant before reaching his mitt, it swerved sharply to the left and abruptly dropped six inches.

"That," said Lincoln, "is a Major League curve ball."

Benjamin recalled how he had once batted a ball thrown by a sand-lot pitcher, but pitches like this seemed impossible to hit.

After throwing several curve balls, Mathewson waved his mitt at the catcher again. Lincoln and Frederick Merkle leaned over the brick wall toward the field with anticipation.

Again the pitcher wound up, but instead of releasing the ball with a snap of the wrist, he held it deep in his palm and pushed it gently toward the catcher. The ball moved comparatively slowly through the air, but with no spin. Like Munsee's original arrows, the ball fluttered and darted in an unpredictable manner.

"And that," said Lincoln, "is Matty's knuckler."

While Christy Matthewson was warming up on the sidelines, Marvin Tover was mesmerized by the warm-up routine that was taking place on the infield. A coach, standing at home plate, would deliberately hit a ball into the ground toward one of the fielders. The fielder would throw the ball to the first baseman who, in turn, threw it to the catcher. The players would then send the ball from base to base with strong, accurate throws. All the while, the players were engaging in enthusiastic chatter and yelling, sometimes to each other, and sometimes to no one in particular. Marvin was about to inquire about the purpose of these exercises when he was interrupted by a uniformed

Pinkerton detective. The detective escorted a husky, middle-aged man into the Merkle box. "Good afternoon, gentlemen, the Pinkerton man said. "I'd like you to meet Mr. Herman Ruth."

McGraw's Protest

Ruth recognized Benjamin immediately. "I knew it was you the minute I read your name on the ship's manifest," he said. "But when you didn't answer my note, I began to have doubts. Drake told me you got my message, but I never heard from you?"

Ben hastily explained why. "And then," he concluded, "when I was finally able to get a day off from work, and take the ferry out to Ellis Island, I was told by your co-workers that you had left town. But then Mr. Merkle took over and tracked you down."

"And for that I will be forever grateful," Ruth said humbly. "Now forgive my impertinence, but I can't control my curiosity any longer. I must know by what miracle of Jesus the three honored names on my medallion came to find each other in the City of New York?"

Frederick, Lincoln and Marvin all looked at Ben, who was the logical person to provide the explanation. Benjamin did so in as few words as possible, and then looked at Ruth.

"It's truly a miracle," Ruth whispered, hastily making the sign of the cross. With that, he withdrew his bronze medallion from under his shirt and showed it to the others. Lincoln, Marvin and Benjamin did the same. "To miracles," he said touching the edge of his medallion against the others as if he were offering a toast with a glass of wine.

"To miracles," the men repeated.

As the gentlemen in Frederick Merkle's box were celebrating the miracle that bought them together, the Polo Grounds' field announcer was informing the crowd, with the aid of a megaphone, of the starting line-ups for the afternoon's game. He began with the visiting Cubs, and each name he mentioned was followed by a loud chorus of jeers. When the Giants' line-up was announced, the crowd responded to each name with an enthusiastic cheer.

No one in the Merkle box paid much attention to these introductions. And certainly, none of them noticed that the Giants' regular first baseman, Fred Tenney, had been scratched from the home team's line-up. Apparently, Tenney had an awkward night's sleep, and when he awoke in the morning, he couldn't straighten his back. It would be the one and only game he missed all season. Starting at first base in Tenney's place was a nineteen-year old apple-cheeked rookie from a little town in central Wisconsin. His name, coincidentally, was Fred Merkle. Young Merkle had never before started in a Major League baseball game.

"And now, Mr. Ruth," Frederick Merkle said without trying to hide his own eagerness, "would you please be so kind as to explain the last time these four medallions were all in the same place."

Herman Ruth looked around with noticeable discomfort. He believed that the story he was about to recount warranted telling in the quiet of a cathedral rather than the boisterous environment of a baseball stadium. Nonetheless, he was even more certain that it was an Act of Providence that brought him to this place and time, and so it would be there and then that the story would be told.

"What I am about to reveal is the Gospel truth," he began. "The words I speak have been handed down from generation to generation for almost 500 years. Only now, that I have seen your medallions and heard your names, will this story be told to someone outside the House of Ruth."

Ruth then turned to Frederick. "You and I are descendants of Mircea the Old and Georges the Wise, the revered kings who unified the Romanian Principalities of Wallachia, Transylvania, and Moldavia. And though we are of royal blood, we owe our lives to the courage and righteousness of the families Tover and Bar Kochba. Frederick put a grateful arm on the shoulder of each man.

"The story begins in the middle of the fifteenth century when

King Georges sired three children: Vlad, Mirceal and Anna. By virtue of your name and your possession of the medallion you showed me, I am quite certain that you, Frederick, as well as your son Lincoln, are direct descendants of Mirceal, and through him, the revered kings of Romania.

"Vlad was prone to violence and cruelty. One evening, marked by the appearance of a comet in the northern sky, Vlad murdered his parents in a manifestation of jealousy, paranoia, and rage. He then tried to kill both his brother and his sister. The sister was sent to Germany, where she was given protection by the House of the Ruth, a brotherhood of Bavarian Knights which trained King Georges when he was a boy. It was there that Anna married a member of that Ruthian brotherhood, and I am the issue, many generations removed, from that marriage."

The game had quickly turned into a classic pitchers' duel between Mathewson and Jack Pfiester. The previous day the Cubs had expended their ace, Three-Finger Brown, who saved the first game of a double-header by pitching two scoreless innings in relief of Orvall Overall. Brown then came back in the night-cap to defeat the Giants 3–1 with a complete game victory. Now the Giants were desperate for payback. But when Joe Tinker lined a homerun over the left field wall in the top of the fourth, the Giants' fans feared the worst.

In the course of the next few innings, Ruth explained the details regarding the rise of Dracula, the sacrifices of the families Tover and Bar Kochba, the origin of the bronze medallions, the martyrdom of Alexandru, the heroism of Mathieu and the curse of Mirceal. He also explained the circumstances and purposes by which the progeny of Mirceal could effect a curse, and how such a curse could be undone. "All of the events which I have recounted were either experienced by Anna firsthand, or were revealed to her by her brother Mirceal in letters she received from him while in Germany. These ancient letters have been in the continuous possession of the Ruth family until this day."

The Giants got an RBI single from "Turkey" Mike Donlin in the bottom of the fifth to tie the score. But when New York stranded two runners in the bottom of the ninth, the game was destined for extra innings. "At least Brown will not be around to save them today," Lincoln said to no one in particular.

————————

"Do you not have a son to whom you will bequeath your medallion?" Frederick asked Herman after he had completed his story.

Herman's expression turned grim. "I have but one child—a prodigal son who lives in Baltimore. But I have a grandson who was committed to the St. Mary's Industrial School when my wife passed, and I became ill."

"St. Mary's?" Tover asked.

"It's an orphanage," Herman continued. "The boy is now in his thirteenth year, and it is to him that I plan to pass on both the talisman and its legend."

Ruth was interrupted by a deafening cheer from the New York fans. The five gentlemen turned their eyes from each other to the field in time to see the Giants' right fielder, Turkey Donlin, line a one-out single into center field. The game, now in the bottom of the tenth inning, remained tied at one run apiece. Mathewson had pitched another masterpiece, and the Giants' fans sensed that the valiant effort by Pfiester was about to end.

Hard-hitting left fielder Harry "Moose" McCormick was the next batter for the Giants. He promptly smashed a hot grounder to the right side. When Johnny Evers glided to his right and deftly flipped the ball to his shortstop, Giants' fans feared an Evers-to-Tinker-to-Chance double play. But Donlin nearly tackled Tinker as the Cub shortstop made his pivot, thereby allowing McCormick to beat the relay.

Rookie Merkle now advanced to the bat, and it was only then that Lincoln realized that the young man had the same name as his father. "Get a hit, Fred," he yelled, giving his father a playful elbow in the ribs.

"I think I will," Frederick answered.

Merkle obliged by lining a single down the right field line, sending McCormick lumbering into third. Lincoln and Frederick sprang to their feet and spontaneously hugged. "Way to go, Dad," Lincoln laughed.

By now the New York crowd had whipped itself into a frenzy.

When their pesky shortstop, Al Bridwell, came to the plate with two out and the winning run just ninety feet away, all 25,000 of them urged him on with unprecedented exuberance. Apparently the cheering did some good, because on the very first pitch Bridwell stroked a clean single into right-center field. McCormick romped home with the winning run.

Pandemonium ensued. Even before Moose McCormick crossed the plate, the New York fans rushed onto the field like a herd of buffalo. No effort was made by the police or the security people to stop them. Fearful of the mob, all the Cub players still on the field made a furious dash for the sanctuary of their clubhouse—all except second baseman Johnny Evers.

Evers noticed that rookie Merkle had not touched second base, but was making a bee-line straight toward the Giants' clubhouse—for exactly the same reason the Cub fielders had been rushing toward theirs. Evers immediately began screaming for the ball, just as he did in Pittsburgh two weeks earlier. Somehow, amidst the chaos, Evers caught outfielder Circus Solly Hofman's attention. Hofman quickly ran over to retrieve the ball that had, by then, come to rest on the outfield grass.

Mathewson fearing something was amiss when he saw Hofman about to pick up the ball and throw it to a frantic Evers, caught up to Merkle, grabbed him by the arm, and started walking him back to second. As they neared the bag they were rushed by a crazed mob of fans. "Let's go, Rookie," Mathewson yelled, and the two players immediately made haste toward the Giants' clubhouse.

Giants' pitcher, Joe "Iron Man" McGinnity had been coaching third when McCormick scored. Somehow McGinnity realized what Evers was up to, so when Hofman finally retrieved Bridwell's single and threw it toward the infield, McGinnity intercepted it. Evers came at McGinnity like a raging bull, and McGinnity reacted quickly. He flung the ball into the first row of seats near the Giants' dugout.

The ball landed in the lap of Benjamin Barr. Ben immediately put it into his pocket to keep as a souvenir. A moment later he was confronted by a furious Evers who was demanding the ball back. Ben felt it was rightly his, and was not going to give it up without a fight. The two were about to come to blows when Evers had a better idea.

Spotting a bag of practice balls lying on the ground near the dugout, Evers grabbed one of those, and ran back onto the field to get umpire O'Day's attention.

Unlike the situation in Pittsburgh, O'Day had clearly seen that Merkle failed to touch second base. So when Evers, with a dramatic flourish, put his right foot on second with a ball, albeit the wrong one, in hand, O'Day knew what he had to do. "You're out," he yelled into the din, raising his right thumb over his right shoulder.

Few of the ecstatic fans swarming the field or celebrating in the grandstand saw O'Day's call. The few who did were oblivious to its effect. The bedlam on the field continued with exuberant Giant partisans celebrating what they thought was a glorious extra-inning victory.

Umpire O'Day knew it would be impossible to clear the field so the game could resume. He also knew that he'd be taking his life in his hands if he actually tried to do so. The circumstances demanded a creative decision and O'Day made one: he declared the game "over on account of darkness," and ruled that the contest had ended in a tie.

The Giants' manager was irate when he was informed of O'Day's ruling. Ironically, neither he nor the Giants' players were angry at Merkle for the simple reason that the rookie had only done what baseball custom and common sense dictated under the circumstances. It was therefore on this basis that McGraw formally protested O'Day's decision to National League president, Harry Pulliam.

Pulliam had seen the game himself. For this reason he called no witnesses to his suite at the New York Athletic Club when he considered the matter. Nonetheless, he reviewed McGraw's protest and the Cubs' response with great anguish. In the end, Pulliam knew that Section 59 of the Official Baseball Rulebook was unforgiving on this issue and that O'Day had therefore made the legally correct call. He also knew the consequences: if the Cubs and the Giants tied for first place at the end of the regular season, there would have to be a one-game play-off to determine the winner of the National League pennant. In reluctantly denying the Giants' protest, Pulliam hoped and prayed that it would not come to that.

CHANCE'S GIANT-KILLER

The next morning, newspapers across the country printed stories of the Cubs-Giants game under headlines of a size and boldness usually reserved for reports of wars and natural disasters. One particularly ostentatious headline read "BONEHEAD." Frederick, sitting on his verandah, folded his newspaper and angrily slammed it onto the table.

"They blame the young man Merkle when they should be blaming the old man Pulliam," he complained to his wife. "In the process those despicable Cubs gain an undeserved victory and our good name is shamefully dishonored."

"No one is dishonoring our name," Angela reassured him.

"Then how do you explain this?" he challenged, unfolding the paper and holding the headline in front of her with both hands, as if it were a legal proclamation.

"This has nothing to do with us," she answered indifferently. "And for the life of me I don't know why all of you men become so emotional over the outcome of a silly game."

"The game is not silly and its outcome is not without importance," Frederick countered.

Angela's jaw went agape.

"The New York Giants represent the city founded, built, and defended by my ancestors. They share the same Manhattan soil that the Merkle family has called home for almost 300 years. The team instills as much pride and passion in my breast as does the country of my birth."

When Angela challenged her husband to explain why thousands of grown men ran onto the field and behaved like children, Frederick had a ready answer. "Baseball players have become a substitute for the soldiers of valor that men and boys used to admire. Fans get a vicarious thrill from running on the same grass, racing across the same infield, and touching the same bases as their heroes."

"Have they forgotten that it is men like you who are the real heroes?"

"Perhaps they have," Merkle conceded, "but I don't see what harm it causes."

Angela disagreed but decided to try a different tack. "That doesn't explain why people cheer for their home team with such fervor. Look at men like Mr. Barr, who have been in this country only a short time. How can a game that was unknown to him when he arrived on these shores arouse such passion?"

"Mr. Barr feels a familial bond with his home team, just as I do," Frederick explained. "And it will grow stronger the longer he lives in New York."

"And the same can be said for Mr. Tover and Mr. Ruth?"

"The same can be said for Mr. Tover and Mr. Ruth," Frederick repeated. "All of us, in our own way, are experiencing something that resides deep in the human race—a primordial identification to a group, a tribe, a clan. The home team is like our family. And Messrs. Ruth, Tover and Barr are like cousins."

"Cousins?"

"Cousins," Frederick echoed. "And therefore, I have invited all three here for lunch the day after the season ends. We have resolved to formulate a plan by which the Merkles, the Ruths, the Tovers and the Barrs will never again lose track of one another."

"What day?" Angela inquired, withdrawing a small pocket calendar from her purse.

Frederick did a quick mental calculation. "Thursday the eighth," he answered.

Angela grimaced. "Then you will have to meet with these gentlemen somewhere else," she said with the authority of the person in charge of the Merkle household. "I am holding a luncheon meeting here that day with many people, including the gentleman from Mr. Roosevelt's office to whom you introduced me last month."

Frederick's face brightened. "I told you Teddy would be sympathetic to your idea."

Angela's jaw stiffened and her expression became serious. "It's strictly off the record," she cautioned. "I've been told that the government simply cannot be involved in the formation of a private political association—even one having the laudable purpose of advancing the rights of colored people."

"I seem to recall the government fighting an entire war to advance the rights of colored people—and it wasn't exactly 'off the record,'" Frederick said somewhat sarcastically.

Angela gave her husband an unsympathetic look. "You fought your war, honey. Now I must fight mine."

"Just tell Teddy's aide to remind the president that the Merkles came to New Amsterdam long before the Van Roosevelts."

Angela embraced her husband and gave him a kiss.

"And one more thing," Frederick added. "Make sure the president knows that I am tired of those ridiculous 'Teddy Bear Cubs' that carry his name. Has he forgotten that he and I are Giants fans?"

In the ensuing days, few Giants fans had forgotten the so-called "Merkle" game. If anything, public discussion and printed speculation regarding Merkle's boner became more spirited, and more widespread. Some newspapers suggested that Pulliam had been paid off by Chicago gamblers. New Yorkers were actually insulted that the Second City could be more audaciously dishonest than they. The New York crime syndicate took that as a challenge, brazenly vowing that one day they would retaliate against Chicago for such an effrontery to their own city's well-deserved reputation for corruption.

Incited by a constant stream of inflammatory newspaper editorials, and an intensely close competition for the pennant flag, cries of "Bonehead Merkle" became common on the streets of New York. Frederick was, of course, indignant that his proud family name had somehow entered the vernacular as a synonym for a "numbskull." And for that he blamed neither the Giants nor their fans, but the hated Chicago Cubs.

As September rolled into October, another new term had entered the American lexicon: "pennant race." And it was safe to say that more Americans were concerned about the pennant race than they were about the presidential race that would be decided a month later. As of Friday October 3rd, the race for the National League pennant could hardly have been closer. The Cubs had just won seven of their last eight games, while the Pirates had actually done them one better by winning eight in a row. So, going into the final week-end of the season, the Pirates found themselves in first place with a record of 97–55. The Giants and the Cubs were each a half game back with records of 95–54 and 96–55, respectively. Ironically, the race in the American League was just as close, with Ty Cobb's Detroit Tigers clinging to a slim lead over the Chicago White Sox and the Cleveland Indians.

On Saturday, the Giants lost and the Cubs and the Pirates won. This put Pittsburgh ahead of the Giants by one and a half games, with New York having only three games to play—all against the lowly Boston Braves. Meanwhile the Cubs and the Pirates were preparing to square off in Chicago for their last game of the regular season. If the Pirates won, they would win the National League championship outright; if the Cubs won, Chicago would be the National League champions unless the Giants won all three of their remaining games against Boston. In that event, the "Merkle" game would have to be replayed as a one game play-off.

Sunday, October 4, 1908, would prove to be the most frenetic day in Chicago baseball history. At White Sox Park on Chicago's South Side, the second place Sox would play the first place Tigers; in Cubs Park on Chicago's West Side, the second place Cubs would play the first place Pirates. Thousands of fans who couldn't get tickets tried to storm the gates at White Sox Park. They had to be beaten back with night sticks and fire hoses. The situation was even worse on the West Side where unruly Cub fans rushed police lines, resulting in multiple injuries, many of them serious.

Inside the Cubs' West Side Grounds, over 30,000 fans, the largest crowd to ever watch a baseball game, spilled out of the grandstand and stood over ten deep along the baselines, all the way from home plate to the outfield wall. The same phenomenon occurred on the South Side. Thousands more gathered downtown, where workmen from the *Chicago Tribune* erected a makeshift scoreboard to display an inning-by-inning account of the games. The city literally came to a standstill as desperate fans sifted facts from rumors regarding each game's progress.

In Pittsburgh, thousands of Pirate partisans gathered in the stands and on the playing field to hear a megaphone announcer describe each pitch, as the information was telegraphed to the stadium from the press box in Chicago. In New York, the Polo Grounds was filled just to watch the stadium scoreboard recreate the game that was being played in Cubs Park. Similar events were occurring in Detroit and Cleveland, as well as other cities and towns across the country.

The Cubs sent their ace, Three-Finger Brown, against the Pirates. Brown was his masterful self until, halfway through the game, he faced Pittsburgh's weak-hitting second baseman Ed Abbaticchio. Abbaticchio had managed but a single home run throughout the entire season, but with the score tied at two runs apiece he pulled a long fly down the left field line. Though the ball cleared the fence, Umpire Hank O'Day called it "foul," and it was that call which enabled Brown to get out of the inning without further damage and go on to a 5-2 victory.

In the mad scramble for Abbatacchio's ball, a woman was severely injured. And in an ensuing lawsuit, her ticket stub was received into evidence at trial. It showed she was sitting in "fair" territory and poor Ed Abbaticchio had been deprived of his second home run of the year by umpire O'Day's blown call. Had the proper call been made, the victory might well have gone to the Pirates.

By then, of course, it was too late. At day's end on October 4th, both the Cubs and Sox had won their games. The city celebrated in expectation of another cross-town World Series. For that to occur, however, the Sox would have to win their remaining two games against the Tigers, and the Giants would have to lose at least one of their three games with the Braves (or lose their play-off game with the Cubs, if it came to that.)

The next day the Sox defeated the Tigers 6–1. That victory, combined with Cleveland's loss, eliminated the Indians from contention.

Thus, the winner of the game between Chicago and Detroit on the following afternoon would decide the championship of the American League. Unfortunately for the White Sox, Bill Donovan of the Tigers threw a two-hitter, leading Detroit to a 7–0 victory, and the American League pennant.

The Giants, however, took three successive games from the Braves. At the end of the day on October 7, 1908, the Cubs and the Giants had identical records of 98–55. Had the "Merkle" game not been declared a tie, the Giants would have finished the season one game ahead of the Cubs, and won the National League pennant outright. Rookie Merkle's failure to touch second, second baseman Evers's force play, umpire O'Day's "out" call, President Pulliam's protest denial, Chicago's victory against Pittsburgh, and the Giants' sweep of the Braves completed a bizarre chain of events that led to the unprecedented one-game playoff. It was scheduled to take place the very next day on the Giants' home turf—the Polo Grounds. Harry Pulliam's worst nightmare had come true.

If the scene in Chicago on October 4th was frenetic, the scene in Manhattan on October 8th was many times worse. As many as 250,000 fans showed up in the environs of Coogan's Hollow. As in Chicago, thousands had to be chased from the stadium gates with truncheons and water hoses. Mounted police ringed the stadium. Though the official capacity of the Polo Grounds was 16,000, over 30,000 maniacal fans somehow managed to gain admittance. Among them were Frederick Merkle, Herman Ruth, Marvin Tover and Benjamin Barr. As Frederick explained, "If we can't meet at my house, we can meet at my ballpark."

Outside the park, the crowd turned angry. Some tried to knock down the center field fence with a make-shift battering ram in a desperate attempt to witness the game by removing the outfield wall as a visual obstruction. Others tried to burn down the fence in right field as a means of gaining entrance to the park itself. Forty thousand of the less unruly fans climbed the bluffs overlooking the stadium in faint hopes of seeing some of the action on the field firsthand. Others climbed on top of the city's elevated tracks. Still others made their way onto housetops, climbed trees, and shinnied up telegraph poles. One fan fell from his perch, and broke his neck in the fall. As an ambulance carried him to the morgue, another fan immediately climbed the pole to take his place.

The Cubs had to enter the Polo Grounds under police protection. But even inside the park they were far from safe. Giants' manager McGraw decided that he would deliberately curtail the Cubs' allotted time for batting practice, and enlisted three goons to enforce his arbitrary deadline. In doing so, McGraw hoped to provoke the feisty Cubs into fisticuffs, blame the ensuing riot on the visitors and demand that the umpires forfeit the game to the Giants. Although only twenty-seven years of age, Cubs' player-manager Husk Chance foresaw what McGraw was up to. Even though he would have thoroughly enjoyed pummeling McGraw's stooges into oblivion, he warned his players not to be goaded into doing anything stupid. It was only in this way that McGraw's scheme was foiled.

Although Mathewson didn't pitch in the Boston series, he was pretty much enervated by the long season in which he had appeared in fifty-six games and pitched over 390 innings. Nonetheless, he was the Giants' horse, and McGraw was going to ride him. Chance took a different approach. Though his ace Brown had not pitched since he defeated Pittsburgh in the regular season climax three days earlier, the Cubs' manager decided to go with Jack Pfiester—who had pitched superbly against the Giants all season long.

Brown urged Chance to reconsider. He had been receiving vicious death threats from crazed New York fans all week and wanted to prove to them and the Giants that he could not be intimidated. But Chance would not be deterred. "I'm going with my 'Giant-Killer,'" he insisted. It would prove to be a terrible mistake.

PULLIAM'S REVOLVER

Mathewson started strong by striking out the side in the top of the first. With each successive out, the crowd noise reverberated through Coogan's Hollow like rolling thunder. It grew even louder when Mathewson slowly walked off the mound, touched the stubby bill of his ill-fitting cap as a sign of appreciation to the New York faithful, and disappeared into the Giants' dugout.

The lead-off hitter for the Giants was their first baseman, Fred Tenney—the same Fred Tenney who strained his back the night before the infamous "Merkle" game a few weeks earlier. On this particular day, however, Tenney was healthy, and rookie Merkle had the good sense to sit inconspicuously within the sanctuary of the home team dugout. Had the young man dared to show his face on the field, he'd have been greeted by a hailstorm of epithets and beer bottles from the angry, unrestrainable New York fans.

Pfiester's first pitch to Tenney plunked the first baseman right in the ribs. And when "Bucky" Herzog walked, the Giants had a rally going. This, in turn, served as a signal for the New York partisans to direct a furious chorus of insults, slurs and maniacal threats at the Cubs' players, in general, and Pfiester, in particular.

But then Pfiester bore down. He struck out the Giants' catcher, Roger Bresnahan, who had been courageously playing with a broken wrist for most of the season. And when Cub catcher, John Kling, picked Herzog off of first on the same play, it looked like Pfiester might squirm out of the inning unscathed.

Turkey Donlin had other ideas: he scorched a double into center field chasing home Tenney with the first run of the ballgame. After Pfiester walked the next batter, Cub manager Chance had seen enough. He walked to the mound, took the ball from Pfiester, patted the south-paw on the shoulder, and motioned to the bullpen out in right-center field. Chance was calling for his ace, Three-Finger Brown.

Brown had to push and shove his way past a throng of belligerent Giants fans, whose standing- room-only admission allowed them to congregate on the outfield grass in the field of play. The fans responded with a fusillade of curses and oaths. Brown recalled the many death threats he had received during the week, but showed no fear.

The first batter Brown faced was the Giants' third baseman, Art Devlin. Devlin was a feisty hitter, but in this at-bat he was no match for the adrenaline-pumped Cubs' pitcher. Brown struck him out swing-ing, ending the Giants' rally with minimal damage.

Chance, the Cubs' "clean-up" hitter, led off the visitors' half of the second. A big, strong man, Chance could not only hit, field, and throw, but was the Cubs' leading base stealer; to this day, no Cub has ever stolen more bases. In addition, he intimidated more opponents and got hit by more pitches—most of them deliberately—than any other player in baseball. To his teammates, Frank Chance was an inspira-tional leader. To opposing fans, he was the object of visceral hatred.

As the husky first baseman emerged from the Cubs' dugout, the New York partisans vented their single-minded rage with a ferocity never before heard within the confines of a baseball stadium. Chance was unintimidated; he lined a Mathewson fastball into left field for the Cubs' first hit of the day. The "crack" of the ball off of Chance's bat was so loud it temporarily silenced the crazed fans. More importantly, at least for the Cubs, their Peerless Leader made a strong statement that Mathewson was vulnerable.

Mathewson, however, kept his poise. And when he noticed out of the corner of his eye that Chance was taking an overly-aggressive lead off first, he quickly wheeled and fired a strike to Tenney who slapped a hard tag on Chicago's player-manager. To the delight of the Giants' fans, umpire Bill Klem threw his thumb in the air in dramatic fashion and called Husk "out." Chance was furious, and went after Klem jaw-to-jaw. He was saved from ejection by the quick-thinking of Circus Solly Hofman, who flew out of the Cubs' first base dugout like he was shot out of a gun, pushed Chance out of the way, and called Klem every curse word he could imagine until the ump tossed Hofman out of the game instead. The New York spectators then whipped themselves into a frenzy when Matthewson proceeded to strike out Cubs' third baseman Harry Steinfeldt and outfielder Del Howard, who was brought in to replace Hofman.

The brouhaha in the top of the second had no adverse effect on Three-Finger Brown. He put the Giants down in order with little effort. Even worse, as far as the Giants were concerned, Brown seemed to be settling into a calm, focused rhythm despite the barrage of jeers and threats emanating from the crowd.

Joe Tinker was the first Cub batter in the third. Mathewson looked in at Tinker, then out at his center fielder, Cy Seymour. Tinker was not a long ball hitter, but for some reason, Matthewson motioned Seymour to move back toward the fence. Inexplicably, Seymour stayed put. A moment later, Tinker hit a ball directly over the center fielder's head—a ball which Seymour might have caught had he been positioned where Matthewson wanted him to be. The next batter, Kling, then singled home Tinker with the tying run. Brown sacrificed Kling to second, and one out later, Evers drew a walk. Right fielder, Frank "Wildfire" Schulte then doubled home Kling with the go-ahead run. When the dust settled, the Cubs had runners on second and third with two out, and Husk Chance advancing to the bat.

The game was on the bases now, and everyone in the Polo Grounds knew it. Absolute bedlam reigned in the stands and spread through Coogan's Hollow like a rushing creek after a spring thaw. "Give 'em what for, Matty," Frederick Merkle yelled into the din, but the noise was so powerfully loud that Marvin Tover, seated in the adjacent seat, couldn't hear a single word.

Chance saw that Mathewson had been laboring hard against both Schulte and Evers. Indeed, the wiley first baseman noticed a tell-tale grimace on the big right-hander's normally stoic countenance when he didn't get a strike call he wanted against Schulte, a moment before the Cub outfielder's clutch double. Chance figured that Matthewson might be losing something off his fastball, and decided to pounce on the first one he saw. He did. And at that particular emotion-filled moment, the Cubs' Peerless Leader proved to be, well, peerless. He drilled a double into right, sliding into second amidst a huge cloud of dust, just ahead of Donlin's strong throw to Bridwell who was covering second. The raucous enthusiasm of the Giants' fans sunk like a rock in a pond. Chance's two-run double gave the Cubs a 4–1 lead. And the way Brown was pitching, it looked as if that lead would be insurmountable.

But the Giants mounted a threat in the bottom of the seventh. Art Devlin and Moose McCormick both singled to start the inning, and when Bridwell followed with a base on balls, the Giants had the bags loaded with nobody out. McGraw pulled Mathewson for a pinch hitter—Laughing Larry Doyle. Doyle was greeted by a re-energized New York crowd. The screams and yells of adulation and encouragement for Doyle, exceeded by several decibels the jeers and hisses of derision and hate that had greeted Frank Chance only a few innings before.

Doyle took a mighty swing at Brown's first offering and hit a high foul that drifted near the stands behind the plate. John Kling sprung out of his crouch and raced back for the ball. As he looked up, pounding his mitt in anticipation of the catch, Giants' fans tried to distract him—interfering with him would be a more accurate description—by throwing beer bottles, debris and even their own derby hats into the air over the Cub catcher's head. Kling hung in there, however, and caught the ball for the first out of the inning. Tenney hit a sacrifice fly to bring Devlin home from third, but Brown got Herzog on a vicious grounder to short to end the inning.

"Oh what might have been," groaned Frederick Merkle to no one in particular. But now the crowd was uncomfortably silent, and everyone in his box could hear him. "A pop foul near the stands that easily could have been dropped and a play at shortstop that easily could have been an error," he lamented.

As the Cubs came to bat, however, the pallor of gloom that quieted the crowd turned into an ugly storm of anger. Fistfights spontaneously broke out in many different places throughout the grandstand. Garbage and debris was thrown onto the playing field. Several fans went so stark raving mad that they had to be carted away from the stadium by white-coats, and driven to an asylum by ambulance. Though Chance got his third hit of the game, the Cubs did no further damage. It didn't matter. Brown methodically retired the last six Giants in order. The coveted National League pennant belonged to Chicago for the third straight year.

In their collective despair, "Bonehead" Merkle became New York's scapegoat, and the Cubs became an object of uncontrollable loathing. As the last out of the game was made, the Giants' fans descended onto the field looking for blood. Chicago blood.

During the ensuing riot, the Cubs literally fought their way to the clubhouse door. In the process, Tinker and Howard were cut by flying beer bottles, Pfiester suffered a knife wound on the shoulder, and some incensed fan blind-sided Frank Chance with a fist to the Adam's apple. The blow rendered the big first baseman unable to speak above a whisper for almost a week.

Once inside the locker room, the Cubs' players celebrated their victory and voiced their admiration for Brown's gutsy performance. Brown said it was the best game he ever pitched, but deflected credit for the victory to an even gutsier performance by Chance. For the first time in his life, Husk Chance couldn't say a word.

Outside the Cubs' locker room, the New Yorkers were literally trying to break down the clubhouse door. It took a cordon of police, handguns drawn, to deter them. Hours later, the team still needed a police escort to ride from the Polo Grounds to the train station.

That night the Cubs caught a train to Detroit where they would take on the American League champs in the first game of the World Series. Already, however, the 1908 Major League Baseball season had been hailed as the most exciting in baseball history. Never before—or since—would both the American and National league pennants be decided on the final day of the season, with the winning team defeating their closest rival to claim the league championship. And never, in the long, glorious history of professional baseball, would there be a game as climactic and controversial as the "Merkle" game.

The following morning, the New York papers would blame the Giants' disastrous season on "Bonehead" Merkle. National League President, Harry Pulliam, would blame only himself. During the off-season, Pulliam remained deeply depressed over his role in the outcome of both the pennant race and the "Merkle" game. It was for this reason that one evening he sat down on his sofa clad only in his underwear, placed the barrel of a five-chambered revolver to his right temple, and put a bullet through his head.

ESTHER'S SMILE

Herman Ruth, Marvin Tover and Benjamin Barr left the Polo Grounds dejected. Frederick Merkle left the ballpark seething with frustration. It was Herman Ruth who was the first to try to console him.

"I beg you not to take the loss so hard," Herman began.

Frederick turned abruptly. "It's not the loss of the game that causes such strong emotions to well up inside of me; it's the loss of my good name."

Marvin and Benjamin looked at Merkle in disbelief.

"It's been three weeks now," Frederick continued. "The references to 'Bonehead' Merkle come from the lips of trusted colleagues and total strangers. I have read it in pedestrian newspapers and reputable magazines. It is the subject of endless gossip on the streets of New York and in my own office."

"But the words are directed at another," Herman insisted.

Frederick's jaw hardened. "The words make a mockery of my name no matter who is the subject of the slander. And I can assure you that they cause me more pain than the wound in my gut that I have carried with me for over forty years."

Now it was Benjamin's turn to offer words of consolation. "Perhaps it would ease your pain if you met personally with Manager McGraw," he suggested. "I have read that Mr. McGraw has absolved the young man from any wrongdoing. And so have his teammates."

"It is not the young man who is the object of my derision," Frederick responded. "It is that contemptible team from Chicago; it is that group of louts that disingenuously holds itself out as professionals."

"The Cubs?" Benjamin asked rhetorically.

"The Cubs," Frederick asserted with uncharacteristic bitterness. "They conjure up rules when none exist, they transgress on rules that do exist, and they interpret rules in unprecedented ways that suit their own mischievous purposes."

"That is not law," Herman interjected. "It is anarchy."

"It is tyranny," Frederick corrected him. "And it is for this reason that I have come to believe that the Chicago team has been a blot on our league since the day their captain refused to play with Negroes."

Now it was Herman's turn to speak. "Perhaps it would give you peace if you placed a curse upon the team that is understandably the object of your passion."

Benjamin and Marvin both believed Ruth was joking. But when they saw his expression remain serious and Frederick Merkle's anxiety visibly ebb, they knew otherwise. "You don't mean..." Frederick began, pausing in mid-sentence.

"That is precisely what I mean," Herman said quietly. "You should impose on the Chicago team the curse of your ancestor Mirceal."

Marvin and Benjamin gave each other an incredulous look, but said nothing.

"Can this be done? I mean can it really be done?" Frederick asked, looking longingly at Marvin, then at Benjamin and then at Herman.

It was Herman Ruth who spoke next. "It most decidedly can be done, sir. The families Tover and Bar Kochba are present; the medallions they wear under their shirts carry the honored signs of their patriarchs; and the words etched into the medallions are written in their native tongue which both of them can formally recite."

Frederick tugged nervously at his collar, still buttoned at the top with necktie in place despite the tumultuous afternoon at the ball park.

"The curse must, of course, be offered to repair the damage to your good name," Herman continued, "but that's precisely what you hope to accomplish."

"And you know the ritual needed to validate the imprecation?" Frederick asked, looking at Herman.

"I do," Herman said with conviction, "Yes, Mr. Merkle, I am quite certain that it can be done exactly as you would wish."

Frederick Merkle smiled for the first time in weeks. "Then it shall be done," he decided, extending his hand in Herman's direction. Herman clasped it instinctively. So did Marvin and Benjamin. Then the four men spontaneously placed their opposite hands onto the knot of fingers and shook their arms together in one deliberate up-and-down motion.

"It shall be done," repeated Herman.

"It shall be done," the four companions repeated, this time in unison.

Frederick's cheerful expression suddenly turned serious. "What formal preparations must be made?" he asked Herman.

Herman closed his eyes as if in meditation. "A silver pitcher and matching basin are all that are needed," he said after a moment of thought. "But the Ruth family has in its possession precisely the silver service that would be required. I can personally bring it to the ceremony as early as tomorrow morning."

Frederick templed his fingers together in thought as he was wont to do. "I have matters to attend to tomorrow and Saturday," he said. "But I am available on Sunday."

Herman stroked his chin in a pensive manner. "With all due respect, sir, I suggest that it be done on a day other than the Sabbath."

"I am free all next week," Frederick volunteered quickly.

Now it was Benjamin who hesitated. "I must meet the *Mauretania* when it docks in New York on Monday," he explained. "An immigrant family is coming here from the very same community that I left when I was seventeen years old. I'm afraid that I may be occupied with them the following day as well."

"Then the matter is decided," Frederick concluded, "we will formalize the imprecation on Wednesday, at say 4 p.m."

Marvin, then, offered an idea of his own. "At the risk of being presumptuous, I would like to suggest a venue for this solemn occasion." Marvin waited for an objection, but on hearing none, he continued with enthusiasm. "An Eastern Orthodox church, founded by immigrants from Greece, just opened its doors on East 79th Street, a block from the park. The Eastern Church has served my family for over 500 years."

"It was in an Orthodox Church where the imprecation of Mirceal was first intoned," Herman interrupted.

"Then it will be there that the second imprecation shall be intoned as well," Frederick said decisively.

"Agreed," said Herman.

"Agreed," said Benjamin and Marvin.

The four companions clasped their eight hands together again, shook them up and down, and repeated the word, "agreed." Marvin promised to meet Frederick and Herman at the church fifteen minutes before the appointed hour so that they could make all the arrangements needed for the imprecation.

Benjamin and Marvin watched their two companions head off in different directions. When they were well out of earshot, it was Benjamin who spoke. "They take this rather seriously," he observed.

"At first I thought it was just a joke," Marvin confessed. "I had no idea a man so distinguished as Frederick Merkle would treat this … this curse, so seriously."

"But if it raises his spirits?"

"Then we must help him, as he has helped us."

"Agreed," said Benjamin, grabbing Marvin's hand and shaking it firmly.

———

The *Mauretania* arrived in New York City as scheduled. Benjamin stood in the greeting area with a handwritten sign that said, in his native tongue, "Looking for Rabbi Levy." Friends and relatives of the new arrivals held up similar signs written in German, Italian, Yiddish, Polish, Swedish and Greek.

"They will be tired, scared, and disoriented—just as I was thirteen years earlier," Ben thought. Then it occurred to him how long ago it had been since he had first set his boots upon the very pavement that now stood beneath his feet. "Has it really been thirteen years?" he asked himself. Then a happy thought crossed his mind. "This will be a special day for me," he smiled, "for it is on this day that I celebrate the 'bar mitzvah' of my arrival in America. Now I am a man." He looked appreciatively out at the Statute of Liberty guarding the harbor of New York. "An American man," he added proudly.

Suddenly passengers began emerging from the inner sanctum of the red brick building at Ellis Island, each weighted down by an assortment of bundles, packages and suitcases. Almost subconsciously, Ben found himself trying to guess their ethnicity by studying their native dress. The Germans wore dark wool coats over high-necked, brass-buttoned vests; the Scandinavians wore leather breeches and waistcoats. The Irish could be identified by their corduroy trousers, threadbare overcoats, and woolen caps; the Jews wore fur hats and black frock coats which, when opened, sometimes exposed fringes hanging from their waist in a manner commanded by their Torah. Though they spoke in a confused babble of languages, the immigrants that Ben knew had at least one thing in common: they were buoyed by the fervent hope of freedom and opportunity that awaited them in their new country. He also knew that America would be all the better for admitting them to her shores.

Benjamin's thoughts were interrupted by a gentle tug at the sleeve of his coat. He saw a short, middle-aged man with a salt and pepper beard standing before him. "I am Mendel Levy," the rabbi said in the Romanian tongue.

Benjamin would not have recognized this gentleman as the same person who officiated at the funeral of his father. He was now thin and frail, and looked far older than his years. Nor did the rabbi recognize Ben as the young, impetuous youth whom he had tried to console at his father's graveside.

"My name is Benjamin Barr," Ben responded. "You knew me in Romania as Benjamin Bar Kochba." The rabbi gave Ben a quizzical look, but said nothing, so Ben continued. "I am close friends with the Mann family, whose name in the old country was Manashevits. The Mann family came to America on the same boat as your cousin Avrom, who now lives in Chicago. Your cousin sent a telegram to Mr. Mann here in New York, asking him to meet the *Mauretania* upon its arrival in this city. Mr. Mann showed me the telegram, and when I recognized your name, I volunteered to come in his place."

Rabbi Levy touched Benjamin's hand, as if trying to read something in Ben's wrist and palm by the Braille method used by the blind. Slowly his face brightened with recognition. "You were so young and vulnerable," he said in a soft voice that was barely audible above the noise on the wharf. "But look at you now—so tall, so handsome, and so successful."

"I was also very stubborn," Benjamin admitted. "But I took your parting advice to heart. I have tried to make something of myself."

"It looks as if you have," the rabbi said admiring Ben's clean white shirt, black tie hanging neatly from a stiff collar, black vest, long dark overcoat and derby hat.

"This is America," Ben answered. Then he switched the subject to the rabbi's family.

"My wife passed away a year ago," the rabbi answered sadly. "I decided to come to this country upon the invitation of my cousin, Avrom, and at the urging of my daughter, Esther."

"I'm sorry. I … I … didn't know."

Before Rabbi Levy could respond, he was distracted by a young woman at his side who cleared her throat loudly, then bowed her head with embarrassment. The rabbi looked at the young woman, and his face reddened. "I apologize for not introducing my daughter," he said. "Surely you remember Esther?"

Esther looked up at Benjamin and gave him a shy smile.

Benjamin remembered Esther as a playful seven year old girl. Now he saw a beautiful twenty-year old woman. His legs immediately went limp, but the rest of his body tingled with excitement. Ben tried to turn his gaze back in the direction of the rabbi, but felt powerless to do so. He wanted to burn into his memory every feature of Esther's exotic face: the curly auburn hair and hazel green eyes, the high cheekbones blossoming with natural color, the button nose, the creamy complexion, and most of all, that magnetic, provocative smile.

"I remember a little girl, but what I see is a beautiful woman," Benjamin blurted out.

Esther bowed her head again, but this time it was not due to embarrassment. She was smiling.

Rabbi Levy's face betrayed no emotion, but he knew exactly what was happening between Benjamin and his daughter. "So this is America," he said to himself.

MENDEL'S BLESSING

The 1908 World Series began on Saturday in Detroit, two days after the Cubs' tumultuous play-off victory against the Giants. The National League champs took the first game by scoring five runs in the top of the ninth to overcome a 6–5 Tigers' lead. Three-Finger Brown was credited with the win in relief of starter, Ed Ruelbach. In Game Two of the series, which was played at Chicago's West Side Grounds on the following afternoon, Orvall Overall held the Tigers to four hits as the Cubs won a convincing 6–1 victory.

Detroit's bats finally came to life on Monday in Game Three. Ty Cobb's four hits led the assault on lefty Jack Pfiester, and the Tigers coasted to an easy 8–3 win. The only highlight for the hometown fans occurred when Circus Solly Hoffman threw Cobb out at the plate after Detroit's speedy outfielder tried to tag up from third on a shallow fly to center. In his next at-bat in the top of the ninth, Cobb was determined to "show-up" the Cubs. After reaching first, he promptly stole second and third despite his team's five run lead. He then tried to put John Kling out of the game by stealing home with his familiar "spikes high" slide. Kling, however, would not be intimidated, and nailed the "Georgia Peach" with a hard tag. At game's end, both teams went straight to Chicago's Union Station to catch a seven o'clock train to Detroit, where the series was scheduled to resume the next day.

While the Cubs and the Tigers were boarding their train to Detroit, Benjamin Barr, Mendel Levy and his daughter Esther were boarding the Ellis Island Ferry to Manhattan. Ben remembered well his first trip from Ellis Island as a naïve teenager. "If I knew then, what I know now, I would have been much more afraid," he said to himself with a shake of the head.

As the ferry glided into the Manhattan wharf, and was secured to the dock by several cigar-chomping longshoremen, Ben also recalled how, years earlier, he and his fellow immigrants were greeted at the same spot by a multitude of charlatans and swindlers. Each had a different scheme for cheating the new arrivals: some sold phony train tickets; some gouged the immigrants when exchanging foreign currency for dollars; others simply stole their belongings on the pretense of delivering them to a transit carriage. Wizened by his travails en route to Odessa, Ben had managed to avoid the thieves, con-artists and muggers by spending his first night in America sleeping on the pavement in front of a police station.

In the intervening years, the city had made genuine efforts to purge the waterfront of these shameless predators. Nonetheless, the wharf and its immediate environs remained a dangerous place for the vulnerable immigrants. It therefore gave Ben great joy to know that he could offer the rabbi and his daughter a chance to spend their first evening in America in far better circumstances.

"I have a modest home uptown," Benjamin began in the old language. "I am sure you are weary and hungry after your difficult voyage. I would be honored if you would allow me to be your host until you get yourself settled in New York. I can offer you food to eat, fresh water to drink, and a comfortable place for your rest and repose."

The rabbi listened politely, but was unmoved by Ben's offer. "We will not be settling in New York," he said perfunctorily. "Our plan is to catch a train to Chicago as soon as possible. I have cousins in that city, and they have already made living arrangements for Esther and me."

"A red brick building with cousin Avrom's apartment on the second floor, and ours on top of it," Esther volunteered enthusiastically.

Benjamin tried to hide his disappointment. "The time is getting late," he noted looking at his pocket watch. "It will not be feasible to make train reservations at this hour."

"Your help is very much appreciated," the rabbi continued, "but I am sure we would be better served by spending the evening in a hotel, and making our travel arrangements first thing in the morning."

Benjamin was quick to reply. "When I left my home for this country many years ago, I rejected a helpful hand whenever it was offered. In the end, however, I learned that I could not have survived without help from many people. I beg you not to deprive me of the opportunity of repaying those who helped me by assisting you in your moment of need. Please accept my hospitality, at least until proper arrangements for your trip to Chicago can be made."

Mendel Levy stroked his beard as if it would bring to his lips the precise turn of words that he was seeking. When he finally spoke, he found those words from the Book of Genesis. "Our patriarch Abraham, upon seeing strangers approach his tent after a long, difficult journey, implored them, as you now do me: 'My lord…pass not away, I pray thee…Let now a little water be fetched…And recline yourselves under the tree. And I will fetch a morsel of bread, and stay ye your heart; after that ye shall pass on.' I therefore accept your offer, and ask you to forgive my rudeness in not immediately acknowledging your graciousness. One who so naturally emulates the conduct of our patriarch, Abraham, must truly be a righteous man."

It was in this way that Esther Levy spent the evening behind the locked door of Benjamin's spare bedroom, Rabbi Levy slept in Benjamin's bed, and Ben slept on the sofa in his living room. Not unexpectedly, the Levys slept late. After a leisurely breakfast, Benjamin took the rabbi and his daughter to his tailor shop where he introduced them to Max Mann, and his family. By then it was almost noon.

The Mann daughters insisted on taking Esther on a complimentary shopping spree for the purpose of buying her some "American" clothes.

Rabbi Levy demurred. But Esther put her hand on her father's arm. "I want to be American," she said in broken English.

Max's expression betrayed his surprise that the young lady was already familiar with the language of her adopted country.

"If you passed through Ellis Island and can speak English, your desire is already a reality," Max's son, Isaac, assured her in a calm, soothing tone.

Mendel Levy thanked the young man for making them feel

accepted in their new home. "We have been studying for almost a year," the rabbi explained. He then withdrew from his pocket a copy of the same soft-cover, English/Romanian dictionary that he had given to Benjamin many years earlier. Its pages were well-worn and splattered with stains.

Esther gave an impatient look at her father.

"Go," he said in English.

Esther and the Mann girls rushed out the door before the rabbi could reconsider. Max, meanwhile, insisted on personally taking Rabbi Levy to New York's Union Station. There he could purchase the necessary train tickets, and wire the rabbi's Chicago cousins with the particulars regarding the Levy's scheduled arrival in the Windy City. It was almost four by the time they returned. "We leave the day after tomorrow at ten a.m.," the rabbi announced.

Esther and the Mann girls returned a couple of hours later. They had numerous packages in tow, and urged Esther to try on her American clothes for her father's approval. Esther was too bashful to do so, though with each purchase she had wondered whether they would engender approval, not from her father, but from the handsome Mr. Barr.

By then the evening newspapers were already on the streets. The sports page announced that the Cubs, behind the four hit pitching of Three-Finger Brown, had shut out the Tigers 3–0. Brown extended his string of World Series innings without an earned run to twenty, and the Cubs were now one game from their second successive world championship. Game Five of the Series would begin in Detroit at three p.m. the next day.

The Levys spent their second night in America at Benjamin's home, using the same sleeping arrangements that they had the evening before. In the morning, Esther emerged from her room wearing one of the outfits the Mann girls had purchased for her the previous day—a blue and white striped, long-sleeved dress that stopped a breath-taking two inches above her ankles. It was cinched at the waist with a matching blue sash. She also wore opaque cotton socks, black in color, and black pumps with a high tongue and a thin one-inch heel. From a large cardboard box, she removed a black cloth hat that had a bulbous crown and a wide, downward-pitched brim. It gave her a decidedly mysterious look. Benjamin drew in his breath.

Esther enjoyed being the object of Benjamin's awkward stares, but simultaneously felt a need to deflect his attention elsewhere. "What is this?" she asked in English, reaching for the ball that Ben had caught during the Merkle game, and that now rested obtrusively in a glass bowl otherwise filled with apples.

Benjamin laughed. "It's a baseball," he explained. "And if you are going to become an American, it is one of the many things with which you must become familiar."

"Baseball," Esther repeated.

Benjamin took the ball from Esther and stuffed it into the pocket of his trousers. "I will explain it to you later." Then he turned in the direction of Rabbi Levy. "With your permission, I would like to show your daughter some of the other sites in America."

Esther looked pleadingly at her father.

"You have my permission," he said impassively.

Mendel Levy watched the couple bounce out the door with grave concern. His worry, however, was not about the blossoming relationship between Benjamin and Esther. He had already judged Benjamin to be a good man, and if that is where his daughter's heart led her, he would give her his blessing. Instead his concern was the challenge that this busy, bustling place called America would present to traditional Judaism. "A religion that is incompatible with modernity, will become irrelevant," he thought. "A country that is incompatible with religion will become decadent."

MERKLE'S CURSE

Benjamin and Esther spent the day exploring both the traditional and the modern. They had brunch at the Waldorf Hotel, admired the huge stone mansions that lined Fifth Avenue, took a ride, for a fare of five cents each on New York's new subway, and by mid-afternoon found themselves walking through the fall foliage of Central Park.

The couple stopped to rest on a wooden bench. Benjamin began explaining some of the park attractions, including a new musical carousel, but Esther was not listening. Instead she removed a chain from her pocketbook and dangled it in front of Ben's eyes.

"Remember this?" she asked.

Benjamin recognized the Bar Kochba coin immediately.

"I promised myself I would return it if I ever saw you again." Esther put the coin around Ben's neck. "Every night since I was seven-years old, I prayed to God that I would."

Benjamin held both of her hands in his, stared into her hazel eyes and leaned toward her. Esther leaned toward him.

Suddenly Benjamin pulled out his pocket watch and cried out with genuine concern, "I am late!"

Esther gave him a puzzled look.

"It's three forty-five, and I must be at the church by four," he stammered. But his terse explanation created only more confusion.

"What Jew goes to church?" Esther asked in the old language.

"It's not for prayers, but for friendship," Ben offered illogically. "Please," he said, "we must quicken our pace."

The couple exited the park on the east side, just below the reservoir, walked briskly down Fifth Avenue to 79th Street, and then turned left. The small stone Church of St. Athanasius was on the corner. It was almost 4:15 when Benjamin and Esther entered the modest chapel. Benjamin grabbed Esther by the arm, took a deep breath, and walked slowly down the center aisle.

Esther was bewildered by the smell of frankincense and the plethora of candles. Benjamin could feel the young woman trembling.

"There is nothing to fear," he whispered. "Please sit down and make yourself comfortable. I will explain everything upon the conclusion of the ceremony."

Standing in front of the altar was a small oak table on which rested a two-handled silver pitcher with an unusual seal. The pitcher sat inside an ornate silver basin. Frederick and his son Lincoln stood behind the table facing the church entrance. Standing next to the Merkles was Marvin Tover. Herman Ruth stood on the opposite side of the table with his back facing the pews. Seated in the front pew was Angela Merkle, and her daughter-in-law Carole. Sitting next to Carole Merkle was Marvin's thirteen-year old son, John, flanked by Marvin's wife, Roma.

Benjamin seated Esther in the aisle seat of the unoccupied second pew. "I apologize for being late," he said, taking his place on the far side of the oak table, next to Lincoln.

Herman looked at his pocket watch without acknowledging Benjamin's apology. "Almost 500 years ago, the families of Mirceal, Tover and Bar Kochba were joined together by common acts of courage, justice, unselfishness and reverence. As a result of their heroic deeds, the Mirceal family was given the power to avenge the defamation of its good name for twenty-five generations with a hundred year curse." Herman then explained how the curse could be made and undone. "The families of Mirceal, Tover and Bar Kochba are gathered here today to again redeem the good name of the Mirceal family," Herman continued. He looked at the men gathered around the oak table and asked if they were ready to proceed.

"We are ready," they said.

Ruth turned his attention to Marvin. "Mr. Tover, do you have a personal item which you swear to be a family icon?"

Marvin removed the bronze medallion that hung around his neck and withdrew the axe that hung from his belt. "This is the medallion etched by the hand of my patriarch, Guruv Tover. It embodies the double triangle sign of my family, as does my father's axe. With that he pulled up the right sleeve of his shirt and showed off the sign of the Tover tattooed on his forearm, and raised the axe above his head. "In the name of my family, I so swear."

Herman poured water from the pitcher onto both the medallion and the axe, and let it spill into the basin. He returned the medallion and the axe to Marvin, and turned his eyes toward Benjamin.

Benjamin withdrew the bronze medallion and the Bar Kochba coin that Esther had placed around his neck less than an hour earlier. "This is the medallion etched by the hand of Guruv Tover. It also bears the double triangle sign of my family. The same sign appears on this ancient coin which had its origins in the Holy Land almost 2,000 years ago. In the name of my family, I so swear."

Herman again poured water from the pitcher onto both the coin and the medallion, and let it drip into the basin. He then returned both pendants to Benjamin.

Herman then turned toward Frederick. "And by what personal item do you swear?"

Lincoln removed the bronze medallion that had been placed around his neck by Frederick on the day that his own son, Grant, was born. Though it seemed illogical to Lincoln that everyone was taking this "curse" so seriously, he handed the pendant to his father with the air of solemnity that he knew his father expected.

Frederick accepted the medallion with reverence. "This medallion was also etched by the hand of Guruv Tover, he said. It bears the sign of the Latin Cross that was given to our family patriarch upon completion of his training in the land of the Ruth."

Herman then removed a silver Latin cross from around his neck and showed it to Frederick. "It's a match," Frederick exclaimed.

Herman poured water from the pitcher over both the medallion and the cross, and let it fall into the basin. He then returned the medallion to Frederick and placed the cross back around his neck.

Herman continued with the ceremony. "Now Mr. Merkle, do you have an additional item that is evidence of the reason for the curse that you are about to make?"

It was at that point that Frederick stammered. "What kind of evidence?" he asked plaintively.

"Any physical evidence will do," Herman said matter-of-factly.

"I thought my medallion would be sufficient," Frederick tried to explain.

Herman Ruth lowered his eyes and shook his head adamantly; then he turned back toward Frederick. "Without such evidence, the imprecation cannot proceed," he admonished.

Frederick searched his pockets frantically, but could find nothing that could qualify as physical evidence of the type Herman required. The rustling in the first pew became audible; the fidgeting in front of the oak table became uncomfortably embarrassing.

It was Benjamin who saved the day. "Will this do?" he asked, reaching into his pocket and producing the ball from the Merkle game.

"A baseball?" Herman questioned.

"Not just any baseball," Ben responded. "This is the ball that landed in my lap at the very game when the young Merkle's lapse occurred."

"This is the only ball with which the disputed 'out' could have been made," Frederick interrupted. "Its very existence is compelling evidence of the injustice that the Chicago team has caused to fall upon my name."

Herman's face brightened. "So it is," he acknowledged. "Then let us conclude."

Herman poured water from the pitcher onto the ball and let it fall into the basin. He then returned the ball to Benjamin with a satisfied smile. Benjamin, in turn, discreetly handed it to Lincoln Merkle. "Give it to your grandson one day," he whispered. "He'll appreciate this a lot more than me."

Lincoln whispered his thanks. Then he deftly withdrew an ink pen from his inside coat pocket and wrote "Cubs Cursed 10/14/08" in a strong, purposeful hand. Underneath the date he put the double-triangle signs of Tover's axe and Bar Kochba's coin.

Lincoln then transferred his gaze from Ben to Marvin. He contemplated the hardship that the two men—a Jew and a man of color—had endured in the old country and contrasted that with the consideration and kindness that they now offered his father. Although he was half Negro, he had endured no such hardship himself. Caught up in the moment, and flush with emotion, he offered an oath of his own. "May the curse of my ancestors fall upon the nations of the world that mistreat such people," he whispered. Lincoln rolled the ball around in his hand, then impulsively returned it to Ben. "It belongs to your grandson, not mine," he said under his breath.

Herman Ruth frowned at the interruption, then cleared his throat. "What say ye, Frederick Merkle?"

Frederick was quick to respond. "I hereby curse the Chicago Cubs National League baseball team, whereby that team shall not win a Major League championship for a hundred years. I also bless the Merkle name which has been so unjustly defamed by the team now cursed. Henceforth the name of Frederick Merkle will enjoy the same honor and respect that it had experienced before all these slanders and libels occurred."

As Frederick uttered the curse, Herman poured the contents of the basin back into the pitcher. He then held Frederick's head over the basin and, as in a baptism, washed the contents of the pitcher onto Frederick's head and face.

"The curse now lives," Herman announced.

"Amen," said all in attendance.

Benjamin removed his pocket watch from his vest and flipped open the cover. It was now 4:36 p.m. Unbeknownst to him and everyone else in the ceremony at the church, the fifth game of the World Series started seven minutes late, but was completed in a record time of one hour and twenty-five minutes. The Tigers managed only three hits against Orvall Overall, and succumbed to the Cubs 2–0. Frank Chance singled home Johnny Evers with what proved to be the winning run in the game's very first inning. Overall made short work of the vaunted Detroit offense after that.

It was in this way that the Chicago Cubs won their second straight world championship in the City of Detroit—a mere four minutes before Merkle's curse had been uttered in the City of New York.

During the imprecation ceremony, a twelve year old Greek-American boy, serving as a church acolyte, was polishing candlesticks behind the altar curtain. Though not entirely fluent in English, he fully appreciated the fact that a curse of some kind was being placed upon the Chicago Cubs baseball team. As a Giants' fan, that suited him just fine.

Lost in the translation was how the curse could be done or undone. Though the boy understood this required the presence of certain families, the names of those families were unfamiliar to his immigrant tongue. It was for this reason that when he heard the word "Kochba," he thought he heard the word "tragos," which meant "goat" in his native language.

That evening, when he told an uncle of the strange ceremony he had overheard at church, the boy mistakenly explained that the curse could be done or undone only in the presence of a family goat. His uncle took this information to Chicago when he moved there the following year.

After the ceremony, Herman Ruth quietly took Marvin and Roma Tover aside, and explained the origin of Constantine's pitcher. "This was given to the Bund of the Ruth for safe-keeping by a member of the Eastern Church when our matriarch Anna was delivered in our care almost 500 years ago. It was accepted only to keep it out of the hands of the infidels who were advancing from the East. We promised to return these icons of your faith when their security could be assured. Now that your church has taken root in America, I am fulfilling the obligation of my Holy Order by consigning these treasures, along with our original correspondence written in the hand of Mirceal and Anna, to this holy place. I can now rest comfortably, knowing that they will be safe in America."

Marvin and Roma Tover accepted the treasures with trembling hands. "We will deliver them to the priest immediately," Marvin whispered. "And I will tell him that I have never met a more honorable man." From that moment on, the little church on 79th Street became the most important thing in the lives of the Tovers.

Herman Ruth watched with satisfaction as the Tovers made their way toward the priest's study. "I have removed one of the great burdens of my life," he said to himself. "Now if I can only find a way to remove the other."

PART III
CHICAGO

MURPHY'S LAW

Frederick Merkle was greatly disappointed to read in the evening paper that the Cubs had won the World Series despite his curse. It never occurred to him or any of his companions that Chicago's victory against Detroit actually preceded the end of the imprecation ceremony that took place at Marvin's church earlier that day. Accordingly, Frederick reluctantly concluded that the Cubs' success in Detroit was a refutation of both his curse and its underlying history. So did Angela.

"I'm glad you've finally realized that the Merkle family curse is more superstition than substance," she said.

"I am not going to be baited into an argument on that subject," Frederick answered somewhat defensively. "I must, however, admit that the Cubs' victory is inconsistent with this afternoon's ceremony."

Angela relented. "Perhaps the curse needs time to take effect," she suggested.

Frederick's face brightened immediately. "It is a wise woman who comforts her husband, even when he is wrong."

"Right or wrong, you will always be my hero." She smiled.

He smiled back. "And you, my angel."

A year later, at the conclusion of the 1909 season, Angela's theory about the curse echoed in Frederick's ears. Indeed, he could not help but notice that the Cubs failed to overtake Pittsburgh for the National League pennant despite amassing 104 victories and a .680 winning percentage. No team had performed better in either category without winning the league championship before. Perhaps the curse was having a belated effect.

But the following year the Cubs bounced back—winning their fourth National League pennant in five years. This time, however, luck did not continue to go Chicago's way. Johnny Evers broke his leg in a freak accident and missed the entire World Series. Even more peculiar, three-fourths of the Cubs' vaunted pitching staff—Overall, Ruelback and Pfiester—suffered from debilitating post-pennant injuries. As a result, the Cubs lost the Series to the vastly inferior and over-matched Philadelphia Athletics, four games to one. Even more ominous for Chicago's future, Overall quit the Cubs, and retired from baseball after a bitter salary dispute that could have been easily resolved had Chicago's miserly owner Charlie Murphy not been so intransigent in dealing with his legendary pitcher.

By the following year, deep fissures appeared in the very foundation of Chicago's once invincible Cubs. Frank Chance, their Peerless Leader, suffered blood clots in the brain from repeated beanings by opposing pitchers. The neurological damage was not only making him deaf, but precipitated unbearably painful headaches, even for a man as tough as he. As a result, Husk Chance had only eighty-seven at-bats in the 1911 season, and the Cubs finished the year seven and a half games out of first place. By the following year, Chance's playing days were over.

Chance, nonetheless, was still a young man, and wanted to remain on as the Cubs' manager. Though his teammates supported him, Charlie Murphy didn't. Ultimately, he fired Chance outright even as Husk lay in the hospital recovering from brain surgery following the 1912 season. When reporters demanded to know how Murphy could treat Chance in such a shabby manner, Murphy responded with characteristic arrogance: "When it comes to the Cubs, I am the law."

On the other side of the coin, the young man once vilified as "Bonehead" Merkle became a fixture in the Giants' starting line-up.

The first baseman led the New Yorkers to three successive pennants between 1911 and 1913. In that span he was the team's leading home run hitter, while rarely making an error in the field. He was cheered enthusiastically by the New York fans.

It was because of this turn of events that Frederick Merkle became convinced that the curse he uttered five and a half years earlier had actually taken effect. He offered three irrefutable facts as proof: his good name, as well as that of Fred "Bonehead" Merkle, had been restored, the Giants had replaced the Cubs as the best team in the National League, and most convincingly, in the season just past, Chicago had fallen on hard times—finishing a distant third, thirteen and a half games behind New York. Thus, when the scion of Maple Grove, New York, passed away early in the spring of 1914, his last words to his wife and son were, "The curse lives."

His funeral was attended by prominent members of New York City's business, political, and blueblood communities. Dignitaries from professional baseball, charitable institutions, and civil rights organizations also paid their respects. So did Civil War veterans, baseball players, and countless ordinary folks who were the beneficiaries of his munificence over the years.

Marvin Tover, Benjamin Barr and Herman Ruth attended the funeral as well. By then, Marvin and Roma had abandoned their First Avenue flat for a modern uptown apartment. They had not, however, forgotten their modest origins, and strong work ethic. The same could be said of their son, John, who had received a scholarship from the University of Chicago to pursue a course of study in an exciting new field—atomic physics.

Benjamin, on the other hand, had left New York shortly after the 1908 baseball season had concluded. He followed the love of his life, Esther Levy, to the City of Chicago. As Frederick Merkle and his comrades previously agreed, Benjamin left a forwarding address with the Pinkerton Agency before leaving town. That address was on the west side of the city where Esther's father had been offered a pulpit in the rapidly expanding Jewish community that had taken root there. With the money he received from his share of "Max-A-Min" Tailors, Benjamin was able to establish his own tailor shop in the shadow of the Cubs' West Side Grounds. He and Esther were married shortly before the new year. That very evening Ben moved into the third floor apartment that Esther shared with her father, Mendel.

Ben and Marvin had kept in touch over the intervening years. So when Marvin informed Ben that his son, John, would be attending school in Chicago, it was Ben who met John at the train station and helped him get situated in the tony Hyde Park neighborhood of Chicago where the university was located. And when Marvin wired Ben that Frederick Merkle had passed away, Ben immediately boarded the Twentieth Century Limited so he could pay his respects to the man who had given him his big break in America—a crisp one hundred dollar bill. Esther wanted to make the trip as well, but was admonished not to go because she was seven months pregnant with the Barr's first child. It would be a boy whom they named Teddy in honor of the former president.

Upon arriving in New York, Benjamin noticed that Herman Ruth had aged considerably. The once-strapping man had lost much weight, and now walked hunched over on a bone-handled cane. His thick head of black hair had become thin and gray, and his big round face drooped under its own weight, deeply creviced with wrinkles.

After the funeral, Herman cornered Benjamin and made an unusual request—he wanted Ben to accompany him to Baltimore to meet his grandson, George Herman. "I am an old man," Herman began, "and don't have long to live."

"Nonsense," Ben replied not very convincingly.

"I have one last mission in life, and can procrastinate no longer," Herman continued, ignoring Ben's comment.

Benjamin furrowed his brow.

Herman looked left and right, then lowered his voice as if he were about to reveal a secret. "I am convinced, as was our comrade Frederick—God rest his soul—that the curse lives."

"So it does," Benjamin said, not because he believed it, but because he felt good manners required that he humor his aging companion.

"It is for this reason that I have made arrangements to have private papers explaining the secrets of the curse transferred to my grandson upon my death. But he is a headstrong and incorrigible youth who would give no credence to the rantings of an old man like me. I need to personally give him my medallion while you are there to verify my words by showing him your matching pendant and the corroborating Bar Kochba coin."

Herman, his hands shaking from palsy, unbuttoned his collar, reached under his shirt and held up his medallion so that it reflected the sunlight like a mirror. Instinctively, Benjamin did the same. Then they touched their medallions together as if confirming a fraternal bond of friendship. As they did so, Herman looked pleadingly into Ben's eyes. "It would be my honor to meet your grandson and confirm the Mirceal legend," Ben told him.

"You are a blessing to your family," Herman said, choking back tears.

That evening Herman and Benjamin caught a train to Baltimore where they met a big, strong nineteen-year old lad who the country would soon come to know as "Babe" Ruth.

TEDDY'S INHERITANCE

Jack Dunn was the owner and manager of the Baltimore Orioles which, in 1914, was a minor league baseball team in the Boston Red Sox organization. Dunn had been informed of George Herman Ruth's talents as a baseball player by the Prefect of Discipline at St. Mary's Industrial School for Boys, Father Matthias. Dunn had gone to see Ruth play as both a pitcher and a position player on many occasions.

Jack Dunn prided himself on having an eye for baseball talent and frequently gave local youths an opportunity to try out for his Orioles' team. Thus, when one of the veteran Oriole players asked the name of a big-boned, barrel-chested nineteen-year old who was wandering cluelessly through the locker room one April afternoon, his teammate told him that the young man was one of "Jack's new babes." It was in this way that George Herman Ruth became known in the clubhouse as "Jack's Babe," and ultimately immortalized throughout the world as Babe Ruth.

Shortly after Ruth signed his first contract with the Baltimore team, he met with his grandfather and Benjamin Barr at a diner located on South Calvert Street near the City's historic inner harbor. Herman Ruth attempted to steer the dinner conversation in the direction of Mirceal's curse, and the Ruthian family history associated therewith, but his grandson expressed no interest whatsoever. Instead, the brash young man was entirely preoccupied with the young lady who was waiting on their table—an attractive dishwater blonde who could not have been older than seventeen.

"I'm going to marry you one day," he told the girl matter-of-factly, as she delivered three steak dinners to the booth where the men were seated.

The girl gave him a quick "once over," and apparently liked what she saw. "Not if I marry you first," she responded dryly.

"Then I'll need to know your name," Ruth answered without hesitation. But the waitress had already turned her back on the impulsive young man, and walked briskly in the direction of another table.

She returned a few moments later with a bottle of ketchup. "Helen Woodruff," she said, emphatically placing the glass bottle onto the table as if it were a stack of poker chips that she was using to call her opponent's bluff. "I get off at nine."

Ruth smiled with satisfaction. His grandfather grimaced in pain, which Benjamin mistook as a sign of disappointment in his grandson's juvenile behavior. After dinner, the three men left the diner and headed toward the harbor without further comment. They had walked only a short distance when Herman grimaced again, grabbed his chest and teetered into Benjamin's arms.

"Give the boy my medallion," Herman implored in a hoarse whisper a moment before he lost consciousness.

"Oh, God," the lad cried. He quickly gathered up his grandfather's limp body and carried it over to a nearby bench. By then Herman Ruth had died.

The young man held his grandfather's head in his cupped hands. Then he poured out his guilt between deep, uncontrollable sobs. "He wanted me to be the son my father never was," Ruth cried out in anguish, "but I ignored him as cruelly as my father ignored me."

Benjamin decided to let the young man exhaust his grief. When the tears began to subside, Benjamin removed both the bronze medallion and the silver Latin cross from under Herman's shirt and placed them around Ruth's neck.

"This medallion was the object of your grandfather's overtures," Benjamin said softly. "He wanted you to know that you come from

235

a proud family steeped in courage, knighted by Bavarian kings, and nourished with royal blood."

George Herman Ruth gave Benjamin a bewildered look, but Benjamin believed that this was not the time for further explanation.

The next day Herman Ruth was laid to rest beside his wife Margaret in a small Roman Catholic cemetery not far from the harbor. The brief service was officiated by Father Matthias and was attended only by Benjamin Barr and George Herman Ruth. Benjamin's eyes darted back and forth between the freshly interred earth that marked the final resting place of his friend Herman, and the grave site of Herman's beloved wife. His thoughts immediately went back to a moment almost twenty years earlier when he stood at the graves of his own father and mother. Then he looked at the young man standing next to him, stooped of shoulder, bereft of family and friends, and saw a distant echo of his former self. "What on earth will ever become of him?" Benjamin thought.

When the final prayer was invoked, and a brief eulogy intoned, Benjamin thanked Father Matthias and gave him a ten dollar gold piece. "It's a donation to the orphanage in memory of Herman Ruth," Benjamin said, hoping he hadn't embarrassed himself or the priest with an offer of money. "Mr. Ruth was the first person I met when I came to these shores, and was the first of many to offer me help," he continued. "This is the least I can do for an old friend."

Father Matthias accepted the generous donation with a grateful smile. "It will buy six months of breakfasts for one of our children," he said.

Benjamin then turned his attention toward the young man, standing at his side. He appeared far too lonely and depressed to be left alone. "C'mon," Ben began in an effort to raise his spirits. "Let me buy you some lunch, and I will explain the ancient legends that surround your remarkable family—just as your grandfather told them to me."

Ruth looked blankly at Ben. "Remarkable?"

Ben nodded. "C'mon. I know a diner where we can get a nice, thick steak."

Ruth's big face brightened.

It was in the course of his lunch with Mr. Barr that Babe Ruth learned of his family history, came to understand the meaning of the bronze medallion that he now wore around his neck, and acquired a visceral loathing for the Chicago Cubs. It was during the same lunch that Babe Ruth vowed to one day repay the kindness of a modest tailor from Chicago who comforted him in his bereavement, gave him hope when he was discouraged, and persuaded him, during the height of his despondency, not to quit playing the game that he loved. And largely because of Benjamin Barr's choice of diner, a seventeen-year old waitress became Mrs. Babe Ruth a few months later. She made her husband a steak dinner for their first meal.

By the following season, Babe Ruth's prowess as a baseball player had begun to flower. As a young pitcher with the Boston Red Sox, he would appear in thirty-two games, compiling a record of 18–8, and a respectable 2.45 ERA. Even more remarkable, in ninety-two at-bats he batted .315 with more than half of his hits going for extra bases. The Red Sox didn't know whether Babe Ruth was a good pitcher who could hit, or a good hitter who could pitch.

One summer evening in the middle of the 1915 season, after a successful outing against the White Sox in Chicago, Ruth impulsively decided to pay a personal visit on his friend Benjamin Barr. When the taxi dropped him off in front of a red brick three-flat on Chicago's West Side, Ruth was bursting with anticipation at seeing the man who had helped him so much at such a vulnerable time in his young life.

After giving the cab driver twice the required fare, Ruth removed a dog-eared piece of paper from his billfold, double-checked the address, then climbed up to the third floor and knocked on the door.

An attractive woman with auburn hair and hazel eyes responded to his knock. A one-year old toddler was clinging to her dress.

Ruth awkwardly removed his woolen cap and twisted it nervously in his hands. "Is Mr. Barr at home?" he asked in a quiet voice that seemed inconsistent with his larger-than-life appearance.

The woman briefly turned her eyes away from the visitor, caught her breath, and then returned her gaze to the imposing man that stood in her doorway. "My husband died from consumption over the winter," she said softly.

Tears welled in the big man's eyes. "I am very sorry," he apologized. "Your husband was a dear friend of my grandfather, and was kind and generous to me as well."

Esther Barr hesitated uneasily.

"My name is George Herman Ruth," he continued. "I am very sorry," he repeated. Then he started to turn, but Esther interrupted him.

"I am Esther Barr," she volunteered. "Can I offer you a you a cup of tea, Mr. Ruth?"

The toddler at her side pulled on her dress and said, "Mama."

"Teddy, shah," Esther chided.

"I don't want to impose," Ruth responded. He loomed over her like an oak tree that hovers above a child who plays in its shadow. Through his sport coat, she could see enormous strength in the stranger's arms and brute power in his chest. Yet she was not afraid.

"It would give me great comfort to hear stories of my husband's kindness," she said.

Now it was Ruth who hesitated.

"I also knew your grandfather," she continued. "I was present at the imprecation made by Mr. Merkle over which your grandfather presided."

Ruth's eyes widened with astonishment.

"Please come in, Mr. Ruth."

Ruth followed Esther into the modest apartment and seated himself on an overstuffed arm chair. Teddy climbed onto his lap and began playing with his necktie.

Esther disappeared into the kitchen, and returned a few minutes later with some tea and crackers. After serving her guest, she sat down on an upholstered sofa and signaled her son to join her by patting the cushion next to her. Teddy crawled off Ruth's lap, and snuggled close to his mother.

It was then that Esther removed two chains that she wore around her neck. "My husband explained the meaning of these pendants the week I arrived in this country," she said proudly. "I will give them to Teddy when he comes of age. They will be his inheritance."

Babe Ruth withdrew a baseball from his pocket which he had purposely brought to the Barr household. Using a black grease pencil, he inscribed the ball as follows: "To Teddy - Babe Ruth." Ruth wasn't sure of the date, so he just wrote, "Aug. '15" under his signature. It was the first ball he ever autographed with his clubhouse name.

"Your son can add this to his inheritance," Ruth said with a grin. "Maybe it will be worth something someday."

"I only wish he had a father to throw it to him," Esther thought.

Ruth seemed to have read her mind. "One day, when you least expect it, I'll come back here to tell your son what a great father he had. And if for some reason you don't hear from me, just send a note to my hotel, and I'll come immediately."

Esther held her talisman in front of the ballplayer's eyes. "With this medallion as my witness, I know you will keep your promise."

Ruth withdrew his own medallion from underneath his shirt, and touched it to Esther's. " Til we meet again," he said with a smile.

Rabbi Mendel Levy poked his head out of his bedroom door, rubbed his beard skeptically, and wondered what could ever become of such a meeting. The answer, of course, would be the most storied moment in baseball history.

WEEGHAM'S SALE

Almost ten million soldiers were killed during the "war to end all wars." One was a recent physics graduate from the University of Chicago who wanted to make the world safe for democracy. He was felled by an artillery shell on May 31, 1918, while trying to stop a German advance through the Belleau Woods near the road to Paris.

John Tover left behind a wife, Serena, and twins he had never seen—a son, Peter, and a daughter, Patrice. They were conceived over a year earlier. As Tover lay on the cold, damp earth, mortally wounded, his greatest regret was that he had never even held his own children.

The medic assigned to John Tover's unit was a young physician from New York City by the name of Isaac Mann. Dr. Mann reached Tover's side shortly before he succumbed. When the medic saw a torrent of blood rushing from his comrade's chest, he knew immediately that the wound was fatal.

"Rest easy, John," Isaac whispered in a soft, comforting voice.

"Remove my medallion," Tover gasped through his agony.

Isaac Mann gave him a puzzled look.

"My medallion," Tover repeated, pointing a limp finger toward his chest.

Isaac opened Tover's shirt and saw the object of his friend's request. He held the talisman up for the soldier to see.

240

"Give it to my son," Tover pleaded. His voice was now reduced to a hoarse whisper.

"I will," Isaac promised, raising his friend's hand so that his cold fingers could close around the medallion one last time.

"Have my father ... " Tover gagged on his own blood.

Isaac cradled the dying man's head in his arms.

"Have my father explain it to him," he pleaded through heavy, labored breathing.

Isaac Mann looked down at his friend helplessly.

"Tell my father ... " Tover stopped in mid-sentence, grimacing in pain.

"Tell my father ... " Tover tried again. But then his voice trailed off and his eyes closed.

Isaac Mann removed his comrade's bronze medallion and pushed it into his pocket. Then he picked up the fallen soldier's body and ran back through the woods in the opposite direction of the advancing American troops. Isaac did not know John Tover's parents, but could imagine their grief. "God's biggest mistake when He created the world," Isaac thought, "was that He sometimes allowed parents to live long enough to bury their own children."

Marvin and Roma Tover were inconsolable upon learning of the death of their only child. The pain was aggravated by the fact that John's wife, Serena, rejected the Tovers' offer to move to New York with her children and share their spacious uptown apartment. Instead, Serena moved in with her own parents—who rented a modest three-bedroom flat on Chicago's North Side. The Tovers mistakenly interpreted Serena's decision as both a personal insult, and a selfish refusal to give Peter and Patrice the better life that the Tovers offered them in the City of New York.

The Tovers were still estranged from Serena when they, along with almost a million other Americans, perished from a pernicious strain of influenza that same year. It was for this reason that New York City's St. Athanasius church on 79th Street was the only beneficiary named in their will. And despite sincere efforts to keep in touch, no one from the families of Merkle, Barr or Ruth was even aware of the Tovers' passing.

Isaac Mann was not discharged from service until well after the Armistice had been declared. Upon his return to the States, he obtained Serena Tover's Chicago address from the War Department. Coincidentally it was not too far from the prestigious Chicago hospital that was recruiting him to become the founding physician for a burn treatment center that it had created to serve all of the city.

Immediately following his hospital interview, Isaac dutifully visited Serena Tover in order to keep his promise to her deceased husband. But to his surprise, Serena knew nothing about John's medallion, other than that it was an old family heirloom that he intended to pass on to his son. She did, however, show Isaac an old, two-headed axe which she found among her husband's belongings.

"Did John mention anything about an axe?" she asked.

Isaac briefly examined the relic, then shook his head.

Somehow I feel the axe and the medallion are connected," she mused. "But with my in-laws' death, there is no Tover left on earth to explain either one." Serena looked at Isaac and begged him to help her fulfill her husband's dying wish that such an explanation be provided.

It was only then that Isaac looked carefully at the medallion for the first time.

"I have seen this before," he told Serena, trying not to sound too hopeful. Then he shook his head. "I just don't know where."

Isaac held the medallion between his thumb and forefinger, and turned it from one side to another as he spoke. His eyes focused on the Star of David. Then suddenly his expression brightened. He recalled the tenement house where his family lived when they first came to America. He recalled a strong, young man who moved in shortly after they arrived. The man taught him how to swing a baseball bat when he was a little boy. A medallion had protruded from beneath his shirt and the man had showed it to him. "This is our sign," the man had said, pointing to the Star of David.

Serena could tell that Isaac had thought of something. "Well?" she said impatiently.

"I know a man who has a similar medallion," he responded. "He and my father were partners in business before he moved to Chicago."

"He lives here now? Do you know his name?"

"Benjamin Barr," Isaac said, his voice fading as he forced his memory to re-create an image of the man's face in his mind's eye. "I am certain that Mr. Barr can explain the meaning of the medallion."

"It was my husband's last request," Serena said.

"It is a request that I am bound to honor," Isaac told her.

Though the year 1918 proved to be heart-breaking for the thousands of American families whose sons died for democracy, it was a good year for the Boston Red Sox. They won the American League pennant in a season shortened twenty-five games by the war. The team had won the World Series four times since the turn of the century, and they were now bidding for their third world championship in four years. If successful, it would be a feat accomplished by no other team, including the Chicago Cubs in the heyday of their dynasty ten years earlier. Ironically, it would be that hated team from Chicago that stood in Boston's way when the Series opened in Chicago on September 5th.

The Cubs team had changed drastically since its historic playoff game against the Giants in Coogan's Hollow a decade earlier. Not a single player from that legendary team would even be listed on their 1918 World Series roster against the Red Sox. Ironically, there was one player in the Cubs starting line-up who did remember that playoff game very well. He was now a veteran first baseman traded to the Cubs a year earlier. His name was Fred "Bonehead" Merkle.

The Cubs ownership had also changed. Charles Murphy, the Cubs previous owner, was not only despised by his players, he was disliked even more by his fellow National League owners. When, at the end of the 1914 season he deliberately humiliated Three Finger Brown by spitefully optioning his contract to a minor league team because Brown refused to accept a massive pay cut, loyal Cub fans were ready to revolt. This was more than Murphy's fellow owners, not known for their patience to begin with, were willing to tolerate. They forced Murphy to sell his stake in the Cubs to his business partner, Charles Taft, half brother of the former President, William Howard Taft. Ironically, it was not Charles, but his half brother, the President, who started a memorable baseball tradition of his own when he threw out a ceremonial "first ball" to open the 1910 season.

In the meantime, a rival Federal League had placed a team in Chicago that became known as the Chicago Whales. The owner of this team was a shrewd businessman by the name of Charles Weegham. In

1914, Weegham purchased a vacant, four acre parcel of land from the Lutheran Church at the intersection of Clark and Addison Streets on the north side of town, and built a 14,000 seat stadium for his Federal League Whales. He named the new ballpark Weegham Field. The team was managed by Joe Tinker who immediately picked up the minor league contract of his friend and former teammate, Three-Finger Brown. By 1915, the North Side Whales became a threat to out-draw both the South Side White Sox and the West Side Cubs.

The National League owners recognized a threat when they saw one, so they arranged for Weegham to acquire the Cubs from Charles Taft. Thus, in one fell swoop they got rid of the rival Whales, and replaced an inept owner of an anchor National League franchise with one who knew how to sell his product to the masses. That business acumen was probably more attributable to Weegham's silent partner, a chewing gum company executive by the name of William Wrigley.

Upon acquiring the Cubs, Weegham moved the team from the West Side Grounds, which they had occupied since 1893, to Weegham Field. Due to the small capacity of that stadium, however, the Cubs arranged to play their home games of the 1918 World Series in the more spacious Comiskey Park. The first game of that Series therefore took place on the south side of Chicago rather than the north side. It featured a duel between two huge left-handed pitchers: a 300 pound flamethrower for the Cubs by the name of "Hippo" Vaughn, and a six-foot two-inch, 215 pound fireballer for the Red Sox by the name of Babe Ruth.

Ruth's previous pitching performance in a World Series occurred when the Red Sox defeated Brooklyn in 1916. In Game Four of that Series, after giving up a solo run in the first inning, Ruth went on to pitch thirteen consecutive innings of scoreless ball, leading Boston to a 2–1, marathon victory. It would be hailed as the best pitching performance in World Series history until—forty years later—Don Larson pitched a perfect game against the same Brooklyn team in the World Series of 1956. Ruth looked at the medallion that hung around his neck, recalled the curse of Merkle as explained by his grandfather's friend at a Baltimore diner a few years earlier, and vowed that he would not allow the Cubs to defeat the Red Sox for the World Championship.

Vaughan held Boston to five hits in nine innings, allowing only a solo run in the fourth on a "seeing eye" single that barely eluded the Cubs' shortstop. Ruth, however, did the Cubs' southpaw one better—he threw a complete game shut-out. Combined with his thirteen innings of shut-out ball in the fourth game of the 1916 World Series, Ruth had achieved the memorable feat of pitching twenty-two consecutive innings of scoreless ball in World Series play. It surpassed the record held by the Cubs' Three-Finger Brown.

Game One of the 1918 series was memorable for one other reason: to honor the thousands of American soldiers who had fallen in battle during the Great War, a band was supposed to march onto the field before the start of the game and play the National Anthem. The band was late in arriving, however, so instead of performing when scheduled, it performed in the middle of the seventh inning. During this brief intermission, all the spectators rose to their feet out of respect for the dead, many of them stretching their arms and legs as they did so. It was in this way that the "seventh-inning stretch" formally entered the baseball tradition; and the performance of "The Star Spangled Banner" became a commonplace occurrence at the beginning of every Major League baseball game.

The Cubs won the second game of the Series and then, in a show of confidence, sent Hippo Vaughan against Boston in Game Three after only a day's rest. Vaughn pitched brilliantly, but the Cubs' bats were again silent. Chicago fell 2-1. The Series then shifted to Boston's Fenway Park, a recently-constructed stadium built by the owners of the *Boston Globe*. The newspaper owners leased Fenway to the team's current owner, Harry Frazee.

Ruth started Game Four, and hurled seven shut-out innings, before being touched for two runs in the top of the eighth. Those runs ended Ruth's string of consecutive scoreless innings in World Series play at 29 2/3—a record which stands to this day. Ruth also drove in two of Boston's three runs with a triple in the bottom of the fourth to lead his team to a 3-2 victory. And though the Cubs managed to win Game Five, Boston squeaked out another 2-1 victory in Game Six, giving them their fifth World Series of the young century.

The next year Boston sold Babe Ruth to the woeful New York Yankees for $125,000 in cash. When the New York press asked the brash newcomer whether he could help the Yankees surpass the Red Sox and defeat the Cubs in a future World Series, Ruth nodded emphatically. Then, thinking of the Cubs rather than the Red Sox, he told the reporters one more thing: "We are destined to win because my opponents are cursed."

With Ruth's help, the Yankees went on to become the winningest team in baseball history. And because of his prodigious feats of strength and skill, Ruth became acclaimed throughout the world as the "Great Bambino." The Red Sox, however, would not win another world championship for eighty-six years. Their fans erroneously attributed this long drought to Ruth's earlier quip to reporters which came to be known as "the curse of the Bambino."

Looking for a scapegoat, and mistakenly thinking that Frazee was a Jew, Bostonians attributed the Ruth transaction to Frazee's greed. In reality, Frazee was a Christian, and the Ruth deal was made, not to selfishly finance a Broadway play, as Bostonians argued, but to obtain sufficient cash to purchase Fenway Park. Frazee lost Ruth but insured for the people of Boston that the local team would be associated with its gem of a ball park for the foreseeable future.

Ironically, in the aftermath of the 1918 World Series, Charles Weegham was experiencing similar financial problems in holding onto both his team and his ballpark. His solution, however, was much less controversial than Frazee's. Weegham simply offered to sell both his team and his field to his silent partner, William Wrigley. Wrigley immediately renamed the stadium "Cubs Park."

As baseball owners such as those in Chicago and Boston wrestled with numerous financial and personnel issues, they ignored a widespread problem that threatened to destroy the game itself—gamblers. One of the most ubiquitous of these underworld figures was a transplanted New Yorker who, by the 1919 season, operated out of Chicago. He parted his dark hair down the middle, and slicked it back with so much grease that his head shone brighter than the fenders of the his black Packard motor car. The gambler's name was Blackie Drake.

LANDIS'S DECREE

Blackie Drake made a habit of hanging around ballparks in the hope of gleaning information from players and coaches. He knew that the best marks were lonely players from visiting teams who had time on their hands and no one to talk to. So when Babe Ruth emerged from the Comiskey Park clubhouse near the end of the 1919 season, Drake decided to pounce.

The Boston pitcher was alone, nattily dressed and, inexplicably, carrying a baseball bat which rested on his left shoulder as he walked through the stadium concourse.

"You need that for protection, Babe?" Drake began.

Babe Ruth looked up and down at Drake's tall but scrawny frame. "I don't need a bat to take out pencil-necks like you," he said, not entirely in jest.

Drake tried a different approach. "My father was good friends with your grandfather," Drake began again.

Ruth's jaw tightened. "Talk," he said tersely.

Drake could tell that Ruth had sized him up as a phony, but Drake didn't mind. In Drake's business, information meant money—sometimes big money; and no one had more information than Babe Ruth.

"Why don't we talk across the street," Drake suggested, referring to an Irish pub that was a popular watering hole for visiting and home team players alike. Soon Blackie was nursing a martini and Babe was chugging a brown-bottled Schlitz in a dark corner booth of the South Side tavern. "My father and your grandfather were business partners," Drake exaggerated. Ruth gave a skeptical frown, which prompted Drake to cut his explanation short. After an uneasy pause, Drake directed the conversation to a different subject. "So who's going to win the Series?" he asked, probing for information.

"I don't know about anyone, but Boston," Ruth answered. "And this ain't our year."

"Why don't you tell me something I don't know?" Drake suggested.

Ruth poked his head outside the booth, then lowered his voice so as not to be overheard. "Chicago is cursed," he whispered.

"Cursed?" Drake asked incredulously.

"Cursed," Ruth repeated. They will not win a world championship for a hundred years. No matter what the odds, always bet against them."

Drake put his fist into a bowl of peanuts and threw some into his mouth. Then he raised his martini glass to his lips and took a prolonged swallow. "How can you be so sure?"

Ruth removed a bronze medallion from under his shirt, and held it within an inch of Drake's beak-like nose. "With God as my witness, I swear that the curse exists."

Ruth finished his drink, returned the baseball bat to his shoulder, and left Drake in the booth to pick up the tab. Drake watched him go, convinced that, if nothing else, Ruth believed with all his heart and soul that such a curse existed. Drake, however, thought the curse applied to the Chicago White Sox, not the Cubs, and it was for this reason that he decided to place a wager that the Reds would defeat the Sox in the upcoming World Series.

The odds were heavy against the Reds; in fact they were too heavy. And that convinced some two-bit Chicago gamblers that they should lay big money on Cincinnati—especially if they could convince enough of the White Sox players to take a "dive" during the Series. The key player in this intrigue was the ace of the Chicago pitching staff, Eddie Cicotte.

Cicotte was vulnerable. Two years earlier, he had a clause in his contract that promised him a $10,000 bonus if he won thirty games. This bonus far exceeded Cicotte's entire annual salary which, as it was, fell well below the salaries being paid to lesser players on other teams. After his twenty-eighth victory of the 1917 season, however, White Sox owner Charles Comiskey deliberately had Cicotte benched so that the bonus could never be earned. It was because of this, and similar acts of miserliness and mean-spiritedness, that Comiskey was deeply disliked by Cicotte and his teammates.

In 1919 gamblers were as ubiquitous as sports reporters in the hotel lobbies, bars, and restaurants frequented by the ballplayers. Sox first baseman "Chick" Gandil became acquainted with this sordid under-world crowd, and ultimately served as the conduit between Cicotte and those who would later be called the "Black Sox" gamblers. Cicotte initially rejected Gandil's overtures, but the bitterness of being cheated out of his 1917 bonus helped change his mind. On reconsideration, Cicotte told Gandil he'd do it for $10,000—the exact amount he believed Comiskey cheated him out of two years earlier.

Once Cicotte was "in," it became relatively easy to recruit the other players that Gandil believed would be needed to ensure that the "fix" would be successful. After a game against the Yankees in the waning days of the 1919 season, eight White Sox players met in Gandil's room at the Astoria Hotel in New York City where they agreed to "throw" the World Series for $10,000 apiece. In addition to Gandil and Cicotte, those players were starting pitcher "Lefty" Williams, infielder Fred McMullin, hard-hitting third baseman "Buck" Weaver, outfielder "Happy" Felsch, and superstar left-fielder Joseph Jefferson Wofford "Shoeless Joe" Jackson. Shoeless Joe earned his nickname because, due to severe blisters that developed after "breaking-in" a new pair of spikes, he actually played a game in his stocking feet for a minor league team near his hometown of Greenville, South Carolina.

Shoeless Joe soon had second thoughts about the fix. So when the conspirators met with the Black Sox gamblers at the Sinton Hotel in Cincinnati the day before the Series began, Jackson was a no-show. Instead, he met personally with Charles Comiskey himself, informed the Sox owner that there was a move afoot to "throw" the World Series, and asked Comiskey to remove him from the lineup so there would be no question regarding his intentions. Comiskey's response was to ignore Jackson's warnings and order him to play.

The Black Sox gamblers who conceived this "half-baked" scheme had a problem of their own. They had to raise $80,000 on short notice, and didn't have anywhere near that kind of money on hand. They went to a much bigger fish in the gambling sea, Arnold "Big Bankroll" Rothstein. Rothstein rejected the idea, at least initially. As a result, the gamblers had to search elsewhere for their sugar daddy. Eventually they went to Blackie Drake.

When the Black Sox gamblers approached Drake, he was already convinced that there was some truth to Ruth's testament that the White Sox were destined to lose the World Series. He therefore increased his wager dramatically. Drake also knew, however, that it couldn't hurt to minimize his risk. It was for this reason that he put up half of the $80,000 requested by the Black Sox gamblers. And though he had no intention of doing so, he promised them that the other half would be paid when the outcome of the Series went according to plan.

Halfway through the Series, Chick Gandil threw an envelope containing $5,000 in cash onto the bed in Jackson's hotel room. Jackson's wife, Katie, implored her husband to return it; instead Shoeless Joe stuffed the envelope into his pocket. Despite keeping the money, Jackson never "tanked" a single play of the World Series. On the contrary, Jackson played hard in every game, led both teams in batting with a .375 average, ran aggressively on the base paths, and made no physical or mental errors whatsoever. His record-setting twelve hits in a World Series has yet to be exceeded.

The 1919 World Series "fix" wasn't publicly exposed until three days before the end of the 1920 season. Like countless other fans, Grant Merkle cursed the name of the White Sox for besmirching the game that he loved so well. Baseball Commissioner Kenesaw Mountain Landis went further. He immediately suspended the eight White Sox players for the remainder of the year. He promised to re-instate them if they were acquitted at their upcoming trial, but vowed to ban them for life if they were found guilty. Though Jackson was acquitted, Landis nonetheless banned him from the game forever. At the time of the ban, Jackson had played thirteen years in the majors, and had a lifetime batting average of .356—still third best in baseball history.

Joe and Katie Jackson, who got married when she was fifteen-years old and he was nineteen, went back home to South Carolina immediately after Landis's decree. But Jackson did not brood about the ban, never sought reinstatement, and did not spend the rest of his life secretly trying to play ball under an assumed name. What he did do was earn an adequate living from his liquor store on East Wilborn Street in Greenville.

Nor was Jackson the illiterate mill-boy that the Eastern press made him out to be. This yarn was made up out of whole cloth in order to win sympathy for *their* crusade to gain his reinstatement, not Jackson's. In addition, no one ever implored Shoeless Joe to "say it ain't so." That story was concocted by a Chicago sportswriter. Together, these stories helped sell a lot of newspapers.

Joe and Kate Jackson lived out their days as a happily married couple until Joe died of a heart attack thirty years later. Even though his career was cut short, Joe believed he had pretty much accomplished everything he could as a Major League player. His biggest regret in life was that he and Katie had no children. When he passed away in 1951, Shoeless Joe was comforted by the belief that the most important umpire in his life—the one in the sky not on the base paths—was not going to deal too harshly with him.

Unlike many of the other great hitters of the dead ball era, Shoeless Joe Jackson did not merely slap at the pitch. He took a mighty swing that nonetheless brought the head of his bat quickly into the hitting zone. As a result, Jackson could not only hit for average, but hit for power. And though he threw right-handed, he batted lefty.

It was for these reasons that Babe Ruth had studied Jackson's batting style at every opportunity, including Jackson's four at-bats during the game preceding Ruth's meeting with Blackie Drake. By then Ruth had become convinced that his future lay as a position player rather than a pitcher. He also became convinced that it was Jackson's swing that he should emulate. "People want to see homers, not singles," Ruth concluded.

And it was homers that the people were beginning to see. Ruth swatted a record-breaking twenty-nine homers during the 1919 season. This was a remarkable feat considering that the previous American League record was twelve, held by a man who, at the time, hit so many homers he was called "Home Run" Baker.

The bat which Babe Ruth used to hit one of his twenty-nine homers that season was a massive thirty-six inch, forty-six-ounce "Louisville Slugger." It was intended to be a present for a five-year old boy by the name of Teddy Barr. So after leaving Blackie Drake in the tavern, Ruth took a cab to the west side of town and climbed up the stairs to a familiar third floor apartment where he intended to keep a promise he had made five years earlier.

A prim, but plain-looking lady with sandy hair and sky-blue eyes answered Ruth's knock.

"Can I help you?" she asked.

Ruth gawked. The young lady was a complete stranger. "I was looking for a different woman," he finally stammered. Then he realized that his words didn't come out right.

The blue-eyed, sandy-haired lady looked at Ruth suspiciously, but made no response.

"She has a little boy," Ruth continued somewhat awkwardly.

The young lady glared at the baseball bat in the stranger's hand, and could not imagine the purpose of his visit.

Ruth's thoughts, meanwhile, were interrupted by a soft-spoken male voice coming from inside the apartment: "Rosie, is that someone from the hospital?"

The lady named Rosie did not answer.

"I'm expecting someone from the hospital," the man repeated, raising his voice a little louder.

"It's not for you, honey," Rosie called back. Then she returned her eyes toward the visitor and began to lean on the door.

Ruth fidgeted nervously. "Sorry to bother you," he said uneasily. Then he retreated disconsolately down the stairs.

Once outside, Ruth removed a yellowed piece of paper from his billfold and compared the number with the address of the building. They were the same. Then he returned to the vestibule of the three-flat and read the name on the mailbox for the third floor apartment he had just visited. It said, "Isaac Mann, M.D."

WESLEY'S SERMON

Several months after Babe Ruth walked disconsolately out of Dr. Mann's apartment in the middle of the summer, Mallie Robinson's husband, Jerry, walked defiantly out of his Georgia home in the middle of the night. Suddenly, he stopped in his tracks, stealthily re-entered the cabin and peered into the room where his five children, aged one to eleven, were sound asleep. Robinson looked at them one by one, then quietly removed a silver cross from around his neck, and placed it over the head of his youngest son, Jack. "Help will come from the unlikeliest of places," he whispered. He took one last, anxious look at his sleeping children, then left Georgia forever.

When Jerry's wife, Mallie, awoke the next morning, and discovered that her husband had left her, she decided to leave Georgia as well. After selling the cabin, she and her children boarded a train for a faraway place where she had some distant relatives. A few days later the Robinsons arrived in Pasadena, California. Other than the pittance she received from the sale of the cabin of her father-in-law, Calvin, the only material possession of any value which the family owned was Jack's cross. Mallie decided to wear it openly around her neck until Jack became an adult.

Shortly after Mallie Robinson arrived in Pasadena, she saw a "help-wanted—female" ad in the local newspaper. She tore the ad from the

253

page and boarded a city bus that took her within a half mile of the residence of her hoped-for employer. Fifteen minutes later she found herself at the foot of a long gravel driveway guarded on each side by a pair of stone obelisks that stood strong and rigid—like sentinels. Embedded in one of the obelisks was a brass plate that bore the address that Mallie was looking for; embedded in the other was a matching plate that bore the name of the family that lived there—Castillo.

In the seventy years since California had joined the Union, the large rancheros that once quilted the landscape, including the Castillo estate, were divided up and sold off to developers. By 1920, all that remained of Miguel Castillo's holdings were the rustic hacienda and twenty acres of citrus orchards. They were now owned by his great-grandson, Alejandro, and Alejandro's wife, Evita.

Alejandro was standing on the patio of his hacienda, proudly surveying his groves of oranges, lemons and grapefruit. A moment later he was joined by his winsome, nineteen-year old daughter, Maria, who looked longingly at the orderly rows of fruit trees. Alejandro could read Maria's mind. The handsome man put a strong arm around his daughter and smiled. "I will never sell my orchards," he promised her. His hug, however, was interrupted by the door chimes.

"I'll get it, Padre," she said, before giving her father a peck on the cheek.

When Maria pulled open the heavy, oaken door of the Castillo hacienda she saw a bedraggled Negro woman standing at the threshold. The Negress was wearing a bell-shaped hat and a thread-bare dress adorned with a shiny silver cross that glimmered in the sunlight. She looked down at a wrinkled want ad that she held in her hand, then turned her eyes hopefully up at Maria.

"I am responding to your advertisement for a laundress," she said nervously.

It was in this way that Mallie Robinson became employed by the Castillo family. In the process, she raised five children and took care of her own home on Pepper Street in a neighborhood that included whites, blacks, Mexicans, and Japanese. On the best of days, the neighbors got along with grudging tolerance.

It was Mallie's daughter, Willa Mae, who watched over Jack. Each morning, when Willa Mae went to elementary school, she put Jack in the schoolyard sandbox to play. And each afternoon, after school let out, she took her little brother by the hand and walked him home. On the rare days that it rained, Jack was allowed to sit quietly in the school's modest library and look at picture books.

By the time he was twelve, Jack started running with a street gang. They engaged mostly in acts of juvenile bravado. When one of the older gang members challenged Jack to take a joy ride in a Chevy that was parked in the lot of a used car dealer, Jack had the good fortune of getting caught by a mechanic instead of a cop. Wesley Wright also served as a part-time pastor at Jack's church. He gave a sermon the following week which Jack and his family attended.

"I'd like to talk briefly about being different," Pastor Wesley began, rubbing a thumb and forefinger across his thick black mustache.

Somehow Jack knew that the pastor was speaking to him, but didn't yet know why.

"Does anyone here know what it's like to be different?" the pastor continued innocently enough.

"We all do," came a deep male voice from one of the pews. "We're black."

Several parishioners murmured their agreement.

"So does it take more courage to be different or the same?"

"That's like asking whether it takes more courage to be black or white," the same deep voice answered.

This time everyone in the church voiced their agreement.

"So if it takes more courage to be different, why do all of us behave the same? Is it because all of us lack courage?"

The murmuring among the congregation immediately ceased, and the church became eerily silent.

"Let me give you an example," the pastor continued.

"Suppose I have a group of friends who break the law. Now I want my friends to think I'm cool, I want my friends to like me, I want my friends to think I've got the guts to break the law as well."

Jack now knew where the Pastor Wesley was headed, and why his words were intended for him.

"Does it take more courage to be the same as my friends, or does it take more courage to be different?"

Jack could feel the pastor's eyes glaring down at him from the pulpit and quickly looked away. But the pastor did not relent. "When

God asked his servant Noah to build an ark, did Noah give up after his friends and neighbors ridiculed him?"

A few of the congregants answered, "No."

When God told Abraham to leave his home for the Promised Land, did Abraham refuse because his kith and kin mocked him for following the dictates of an invisible deity?"

This time, most of the worshippers responded, "No!"

"When God ordered his prophet, Moses, to challenge the evil of slavery, did Moses decline because no one else had the guts to confront the pharaoh and tell him to 'let my people go'?"

Now the entire congregation raised its voice in unison and clamored, "No!"

"Sameness is for the cowards and the weak. Differentness is for the brave and the strong."

The congregants now fidgeted nervously in the pews.

"Look at your neighbor," the pastor ordered.

The worshippers did as he asked.

"What do you see?"

There was a buzz of different answers.

"You don't see sameness; you see differentness. "Our skin is of different hues—not because we have mixed with whites—but because that is how God made us before we were taken out of Africa." The pastor paused momentarily to mop his brow with a monogrammed handkerchief. "God made us different for a reason," he resumed, halting for a second after each word for emphasis. "It's from our differentness that we get our strength."

The pastor continued for another ten minutes, his voice growing louder and more emotional with each sentence. Then he reached a crescendo. "And just one more thing," he said, staring directly at young Jack with eyes of fire, "Jesus was not afraid to be different, and neither should you."

Mallie Robinson was the only other person in the church who knew that the pastor was talking to Jack. On their way home she told him so.

"Don't think I don't know what you're doing when you go out at night with those hoodlum friends of yours," she added.

Jack tried to look surprised, but she wasn't buying.

"You promise me right here and now that you'll have the courage to be different," she demanded.

Jack hesitated.

"You promise me," Mallie demanded again.

Jack looked admiringly at his mother, whose face brimmed with dignity and strength despite having toiled twelve hours a day since the family moved to California.

"Okay," he said. "I promise."

MALLIE'S BASKET

Lincoln Merkle had been concerned about his mother for several weeks. Now approaching her eightieth year, Angela was not doing well. Her energy had begun to fade, her enthusiasm for life had begun to wane, and she had grown testy. The cold dark winter months were particularly bad for both her health and her disposition. Particularly disturbing was the fact that she had little memory or cognizance of recent events. This in spite of her ability to recall with great clarity even the most minor details that occurred in her life immediately before and after the War Between the States.

One evening in March of 1920 Lincoln met with his son Grant in the parlor of the Merkle's Maple Grove mansion to discuss the problem. After his father's death, Lincoln had assumed full responsibility for managing the Merkle family's businesses as well as their considerable investments. In recent years he had delegated management of the family's real estate holdings to his son. Though not yet thirty, Grant had worked hard and done an admirable job. As a result, Lincoln also appointed his son to represent the family's interests in the Brooklyn baseball team—an investment which had appreciated considerably since Frederick Merkle's purchase before the turn of the century. It was after a recent meeting with the team board of directors that Grant was struck with an idea that might successfully address the problem of his grandmother's health.

"I recommended to the board that we consider investing in one of the minor league teams that play out on the Pacific Coast," Grant began. He paused momentarily, noticing his father had become pre-occupied with pushing a pipe cleaner into the stem of a shiny, cherrywood pipe. When Lincoln was satisfied that the air passage was clear, he removed some tobacco from a humidor and pressed it into the hand-carved pipe bowl. Then he struck a match off the bottom of his shoe, lit the tobacco, and took several satisfying puffs before turning to his son.

"I understand the talent out there is superb," Grant continued.

"If the talent is so good, why would the better players not want to test their mettle in the Majors?" Lincoln inquired as he exhaled a plume of smoke in his son's direction.

"In some cases the Pacific Coast League salaries actually exceed those in the Majors," Grant explained. "And some of the players prefer not to play so far from home."

Lincoln removed his pipe from his lips and stared intently at his son. "Is spectator support and paid attendance sufficient to maintain such salaries?"

"That is one of the questions I have been asked to investigate," Grant explained. "And because of its importance, the board has asked me to investigate in person. My train to Los Angeles leaves next week." Lincoln said nothing, so Grant continued. "I've been told that the weather in Los Angeles is warm and sunny, so I thought it might be a good idea if Gramma Angela joined me. A few weeks in the sun may be a panacea for what ails her."

Lincoln leaned back in his easy chair, and drew a deep breath of smoke. The tobacco in the pipe bowl glowed bright orange. Lincoln then nodded his head approvingly. "You will be taking Miss Meade, I assume," he said, referring to Angela's fulltime nurse.

"That was my plan," Grant replied.

Lincoln reached under his shirt and removed a bronze medallion that his own father had given him years earlier. "Your grandfather believed that this brought him good luck," he said as he placed the family heirloom over his son's head. Lincoln succumbed to his own skepticism regarding medieval curses and superstitions, so he only told Grant one more thing: "Give this to your own son when comes of age."

Grant started to ask about the inscription on the medallion, but his father had already turned away and began striding with purpose toward an ornate two-tiered cabinet that served as a small parlor bar. Lincoln opened the doors in the upper section, selected his favorite cognac and poured some into a glass snifter with a script "M" etched into the bowl. He handed the snifter to his son, then poured some of the brandy into a snifter of his own. "Here's to a safe journey," he said, raising his glass.

Grant, Angela and Nurse Meade arrived in Los Angeles after a scenic train ride that took them past wide rivers, great plains, rocky mountains, and painted deserts. Also scenic was their limousine ride from the train station to their hotel. The art deco buildings, tall palm trees, and wide flower-lined boulevards were a sharp contrast to the dull, drab Manhattan landscape. Indeed, the Los Angeles culture seemed to have been deliberately created as a mirror image of New York City's. This became apparent when Angela screamed loudly after the limousine driver went through a red light.

"We are allowed to make a right turn even though the traffic signal is red," he explained.

"Yet you wait for dawdling pedestrians even when the light is green" she observed.

"We are in no rush here," the driver answered.

"In New York the pedestrians would be honked at and worse," she responded with uncharacteristic impatience.

A few screams later, the Merkle entourage checked into a three-bedroom suite at The Ambassador Hotel—an expansive six-story Mediterranean style building with a red-tiled roof and a matching cupola. The luxury hotel had opened its doors only that year, but already it had become the stop-over of choice for the rich and famous.

The next morning the clouds became so dark that they blotted out both the sun and the surrounding hills. Then it began to rain—not as a fierce thunderstorm as happens in the East, but as a thick, steady drizzle. Angela's disposition remained as dreary as the weather.

Three days later the skies cleared and the temperatures rose into the upper seventies. Grant was, however, disappointed to see that neither the change in scenery nor the change in weather had the salutary effects on his grandmother's spirits that he had hoped for. Nor did her morning walks with Miss Meade or their afternoon dips in the swimming pool, which was heated to bath-like temperatures.

One Friday afternoon, Grant concluded his business earlier than expected, and rushed back to the hotel with information that he hoped would perk up his grandmother. He bounded onto the deck surrounding the swimming pool, found the chaises occupied by Angela and her nurse, and gave them the news.

"Tomorrow we have a luncheon invitation at the estate of a very distinguished gentleman," he began enthusiastically.

"Go on," Angela said, her voice sounding somewhat raspier than usual.

"He is of Mexican extraction," Grant continued. "And is in the process of organizing a professional baseball league in Mexico. If everything works out as we have tentatively discussed, he will advise the Dodgers of the best prospects that his new league produces."

"This is a cause for celebration?" Angela challenged.

"It will give us entree into the best Latin talent," Grant explained.

Now Angela's face tightened, and her chestnut eyes burned with emotion. "When will you pursue an entree into the best Negro talent?" she demanded.

Grant looked sheepishly at his feet. "You know I am helpless to oppose the ban," he pleaded.

"You are helpless only because you allow yourself to be," Angela insisted.

Grant's expression became pained, but his grandmother was in no mood to hold back. "My fondest wish was for Lincoln to pursue a career in professional baseball," Angela scolded. Then she gasped for a breath before continuing. "I would have loved to have seen the cowards who control our nation's pastime try to tell Frederick Merkle that his own son could not play Major League baseball because of the color of his skin."

Grant looked away from his grandmother but her words brought him back.

"It would have changed everything," she insisted, now speaking so rapidly that she slurred her words. "It would have shown the entire country that we are just like everybody else. Instead it gave everyone a justification for their pernicious prejudices and insulting stereotypes." Suddenly Angela's cheeks grew pale and her forehead became damp. For a moment Grant feared that his grandmother would faint. Then, just as suddenly, the color returned, and her eyes focused like a pair of Buick headlamps onto her grandson.

"Now there is nothing left to wish for except that you promise me that you will end the ban."

Grant turned his eyes from his grandmother, to Miss Meade, then back to his grandmother. "I promise," he said.

Angela gave her grandson a skeptical stare.

Grant knew that his own grandmother doubted his capacity to make good on his promise, and his face flushed. Then he summoned up the courage to answer his grandmother in the most convincing way he could. "I promise on the grave of my grandfather, Frederick Merkle," he said decisively.

It was only then that Angela gave a satisfied smile. "In that event, Miss Meade and I will look forward to joining your luncheon tomorrow at the home of … of … " Angela groped for a name.

"Alejandro Castillo," Grant said.

"Mr. Castillo," Angela repeated.

The next morning Grant rented a six passenger black sedan—one of the first automobiles with balloon tires—and headed toward Pasadena with his mother and her nurse. They traveled east, through the center of town, then turned north onto Mission Road. Halfway through the beautiful hills, their left front tire blew out. As Grant was struggling with the jack, a black coupe pulled off the road and parked behind Grant's sedan. Two muscular teen-age boys jumped out of the car. The taller boy asked if Grant needed any help. Grant accepted the offer, and soon the sedan was returned to running condition. The boys refused Grant's offer of payment, but were quick to identify the place where the flat tire occurred. "Chavez Ravine," one of them said. Grant looked at the acres of bean fields, surrounded on all four sides by scenic mountain views, and thought, "This would be a beautiful place for a ballpark."

Eventually Grant found his way to the residential community of Pasadena. It had taken him over two hours to travel less than fifteen miles from The Ambassador Hotel on Wilshire Boulevard to the Castillo hacienda off Colorado Avenue. Alejandro, or "Alex" as he insisted on being called among Anglos, greeted him warmly. It was, however, Alex's daughter, Maria, who caught Grant's eye. And when Maria offered to take Angela and Miss Meade on a tour of the hacienda grounds, Grant knew that the young lady had a kind heart to go with her beautiful face.

Grant, in the meantime chatted at length with Alex Castillo about the business of baseball on the West Coast. He was surprised to learn that there was a wealth of talent in California, particularly in the Mexican-American community. Alex was surprised at Grant's surprise. "Our boys love the game like any other American boys," he said.

"I suspect the same also applies to Negro boys," Grant mumbled, searching the room for his grandmother. "Or boys of mixed blood, like me," he said to himself. It was then that he spotted his grandmother on the other side of the room, staring intently at a faded fresco of the Archangel Gabriel.

The angel summoned up in Angela's memory the very first moment she saw her husband-to-be, and the warmth she felt in her heart when she cradled that handsome Union soldier in her arms. Every aspect of that moment—the sights, the sounds, the smells, the fears—was frozen in her mind. As was the time when, after he recovered from his wounds, her husband told her that, as he lay bleeding on the forest floor, he prayed for an angel, and that she was the answer to his prayers. Angela looked up at the visage of Angel Gabriel and for the first time in months felt at peace with the world. "I'm thankful to my grandson for bringing me here," she said to herself.

The Castillos proved to be gracious hosts for the two dozen people who congregated at their home. A wooden table accented with hand painted tiles held an assortment of hors d'ouvres presented in an elegant fashion. These included guacamole salads, a variety of cheeses, purple grapes, an elaborate spread of sliced melons, citrus fresh from the Castillo orchards, tortilla chips and several fancy breads. The hors d'ouvres were followed with bowls of hot food that included beans, rice, peppers, mixed vegetables, sliced chicken, and chopped beef. A

Latin band featuring a guitarist, stand-up bass, violinist, three horns and a percussionist performed non-stop.

Grant could tell that his grandmother was having an enjoyable day, and complimented himself on his idea to bring her along. Nonetheless, by mid-afternoon, he and Miss Meade both observed that Angela was becoming tired and disoriented. They decided to take their leave.

The three of them approached Maria's mother, Evita, to offer their appreciative good-byes. They found their hostess in an animated discussion with one of her female servants. Evita was insisting that the woman accept a basket of food to take home to her children. The servant was balking, apparently because the basket was so heavy that she was unable to carry it back to her small stucco house on Pepper Street.

"I will divide this in two," Evita suggested. "You can take half now, and the remainder tomorrow."

It was at this moment that Angela interceded.

"At the risk of being presumptuous," she said turning to Evita, "we have a large sedan parked outside, and it would be no inconvenience for us to drive this young lady home."

Angela then turned and introduced herself to the young woman. "What's your name, child?"

The young woman turned to Evita with a puzzled look. Only after Evita gave her an encouraging smile did she respond. "Mallie Robinson," she said in a slow drawl that betrayed her South Georgia roots.

It was then that Angela saw the silver cross that Mallie wore around her neck. "Robinson," Angela said to herself.

Instantly, Angela's memories rewound to an event that took place in Pennsylvania almost sixty years earlier. With perfect clarity she could see Frederick Merkle hand that same silver cross to her Uncle Calvin. And she could see her Uncle Calvin remove an ivory ring that he wore on a chain around his neck, and give it to that young Union soldier. The next day she and that Union soldier had stood solemnly before an Army chaplain. With her Uncle Calvin as a witness, she had extended her left hand and watched Frederick Merkle slide that ring onto her finger. The stark realism of that recollection and the enormous excitement of the moment caused the old women's heart to go into spontaneous fibulation.

With the blood in her arteries buzzing out of control, Angela pulled the ivory wedding band off of her ring finger for the first time since her husband had placed it there. Then she thrust it into Mallie Robinson's hand. It caused Mallie to drop her food basket with an embarrassing thud.

"This ring belonged to your ancestors," Angela whispered a moment before she died. No one, including Mallie Robinson, ever understood what prompted Angela's last words.

MARIA'S BETROTHAL

When Isaac Mann came to Chicago after his discharge from the Army in the Spring of 1919, he accepted the position that West Park Children's Hospital offered him. It wasn't the compensation that attracted Dr. Mann. It was his future colleagues' commitment to burn treatment as a recognized medical specialty, their resources to pay nurses and staff, and their understanding that compassionate healing involved both physical and psychological attention. "This is a payment on the debt we owe to the victims of the Great Chicago Fire," one doctor told him.

Only after Isaac accepted West Park's offer, did he visit Serena Tover, deliver her late husband's bronze medallion as he had promised, and remember that a similar medallion was in possession of his father's partner, Benjamin Barr. And it was only after he left Serena's apartment that he began his search for both Mr. Barr and an apartment of his own that was close to the hospital where he'd soon be working.

Isaac knew that Benjamin Barr had married a young woman named Esther Levy, daughter of an immigrant rabbi who had a pulpit on the near west side of the city. "Find the rabbi, and I will find Mr. Barr," he thought. After making only a few telephone calls, Dr. Mann spoke with a synagogue receptionist who informed him that the spiritual leader of her congregation was indeed, "Rabbi Levy." When he walked into the rabbi's study at the appointed hour, Isaac was sure that the location of Mr. Barr was at hand, and his promise to Serena Tover that he would solve the mystery of her husband's medallion was about to be fulfilled.

The rabbi and the doctor exchanged brief pleasantries. Then Isaac explained that he was searching for the married daughter of Rabbi Levy in order to keep a promise to the widow of a comrade who died in his arms during the Great War. "I met with his widow only this morning," Isaac continued.

The rabbi's response gave Isaac a jolt. "I have a daughter named Rosie," the rabbi said matter-of-factly, "but she is not yet married.

Isaac could not hide his look of disappointment.

But then the rabbi's next comment gave him hope. "I am Avrom Levy; you are undoubtedly looking for my cousin, Mendel."

"Mendel? Where can I find him?"

"He is dead," Avrom answered. "May he rest in peace," the rabbi mumbled in a foreign language.

"Amen," Isaac responded in the Hebrew pronunciation.

The rabbi nodded in appreciation. "But Mendel had a married daughter," the rabbi added.

"Do you know the name of the man she married?"

The rabbi nodded.

"And his name is …" Isaac prompted.

"Benjamin Barr."

Isaac's face brightened.

"But he is also dead," the rabbi continued.

Isaac hesitated, unsure how to respond. "Is his widow named Esther?" he asked.

"It is," answered the rabbi.

"And …"

"And she is not dead," the rabbi smiled, certain that he had finally given his visitor some useful information.

"Do you know where she can be found?"

"She has an apartment in the same building as mine—one floor above. But she will be vacating it soon. Esther is remarrying—a man named Sam Rosen who has a haberdashery further north. She and her son will be moving in with him."

"I must see her immediately," Isaac said, maintaining his composure despite his excitement.

The rabbi looked at the young doctor, and made a quick decision. "Esther will be having dinner at our apartment tonight. It will be no trouble for us to set another plate for you." He scribbled an address on a piece of note paper. "We will expect you at seven."

"You are very kind," Isaac said before taking his leave.

Rabbi Avrom Levy closed the door of his study and sat contemplatively at his desk. Only after several seconds had passed did he finally realize that he had met Dr. Mann many years earlier. That memory prompted him to call his wife immediately.

"Ida," he said impatiently. "Use the good dishes for dinner tonight." His wife tried to interrupt, but the rabbi spoke with a strong sense of purpose. "Make sure Esther and Rosie are there at seven. And set an extra place, because we'll be entertaining a guest."

"A guest?"

"Remember the Manashevits family that we befriended on the boat?" he began. "They had a little boy? His name is Isaac?" Avrom waited for some acknowledgement from his wife, but she said nothing. "That little boy is now a doctor in Chicago?"

Ida started to respond, but her husband interrupted. "Make sure Rosie wears a nice dress."

Avrom Levy looked at the black and white framed photograph of his son and daughter that sat on his desk. His son, Reuben, had followed him into the rabbinate, and had already given him a grandson, Aaron. His daughter, though twenty-seven years of age, was not yet married. "My little rosebud has become a lonely woman," he thought sadly. In his mind's eye, Rosie's sky-blue eyes, framed by tresses of sandy brown curls, stared back at him with a Mona Lisa smile that betrayed an unfulfilled expectation. "I had hoped she would marry a rabbi," he thought, "but a doctor will have to do."

It was in this way that Dr. Isaac Mann found a job, an apartment and a fiancée, all on the same day. In the process, he confirmed that Esther Levy was possessed of an identical medallion as Serena Tover. And to his surprise, Esther had firsthand information about its history and its meaning. He couldn't wait for the two women to meet.

Isaac introduced them the following day when he escorted Esther and her five-year old son, Teddy to the three-bedroom apartment that Serena Tover shared with her toddler twins, Peter and Patrice.

After the widows confirmed that the medallions in their possession were identical, Serena begged Esther to explain what she knew about them.

"I met my husband the day I arrived in America," she began tentatively. "To my surprise, two days later my father—of blessed memory—allowed me to spend an afternoon with him unescorted. Would you believe he took me to a church?"

Serena gave Esther a dubious look.

"Well, of course, I had never set foot in a church before," Esther continued somewhat defensively.

Serena's face turned pale, and she took a step backward.

"We are Jews," Isaac explained in a calm tone. "Our house of worship is called a synagogue, not a church."

"Jews," Serena repeated.

Isaac demonstratively moved the palms of his hands across the crown of his head. "You see, Mrs. Tover, we do not have horns."

"I am sorry," she said, regaining her composure. "I have never known a Jew before."

"Your husband's father certainly did," Isaac assured her. "He and Mr. Barr were apparently close friends and business partners."

"So they were," Esther interceded. "Did you know they invented the wire fastener that attaches papers together?"

"They invented the staple machine?" Serena asked incredulously.

Esther was unfamiliar with those words, but nodded her head anyway. "And they sold their business for a considerable sum of money," she added.

The conversation was momentarily interrupted by children's laughter. Teddy had brought a toy top from home and was spinning it on the hardwood floor to the delight of Peter and Patrice.

"So what happened in the church?" Serena asked with a combination of curiosity and impatience.

Esther cleared her throat nervously. "Ten years ago there was a ceremony for the benefit of a wealthy gentleman by the name of Merkle," she explained. "It was my understanding, that some time prior to that, the families of Tover and Barr agreed to assist the Merkle family, and now Mr. Merkle had formally solicited their help."

"Help to do what?" Serena wanted to know.

Esther's memory flashed back to St. Athanasus church a decade earlier, and Benjamin's subsequent explanation. She remembered the events clearly, but had no understanding of what they meant.

"Don't be bashful," Isaac prodded

Esther gave Isaac a troubled look. "It had something to do with a brood of baby bears," she began self-consciously. "You have a name for such animals in America, but I forget the word."

"Cubs?" Serena suggested.

"Yes, Cubs," Esther continued gaining confidence. "I think these Cubs were causing Mr. Merkle a great deal of stress, so he solicited the assistance of Mr. Tover and Mr. Barr to relieve his anxiety. They did so with some elixir that was poured from a magnificent silver pitcher."

Serena's jaw dropped open and her forehead creased. "What else?" she asked.

Esther hesitated for a moment, but then continued. "There were also some strange rituals and incantations said over our medallions and ... "

"And" Serena prodded.

"And a baseball," Esther stammered.

Now it was Serena who stammered. "Are you sure it was a baseball?" she asked.

Esther nodded

"It was all very mysterious, but I think the entire ceremony was simply a confirmation that each could depend on the other—a bond of friendship."

"I have heard of such things," Serena said. Then she abruptly excused herself, disappeared into her bedroom, and returned a few moments later with an old, two-headed axe. "Did the ceremony that you witnessed involve this?" she asked.

Esther needed to examine the axe only briefly before acknowledging that it did. "I thought so," Serena concluded. Then she excused herself again and this time headed for the kitchen. She returned momentarily with three glasses of wine resting on a simple metal tray. "I'd like to propose a toast," she began.

Esther and Isaac each removed a glass from the tray.

"To friends," Serena said.

"To friends," repeated Esther and Isaac.

The "toast" convinced Isaac that his obligation to his fallen comrade had been fulfilled in every respect. That John Tover's dying wish involved some mysterious rite of friendship between his family and the Barrs was none of his business. He was far more interested in pursuing his friendship with Rosie Levy. The moment he had set eyes on her at dinner the night before, he believed she was his intended.

The families of Avrom Levy and Max Mann were delighted with their children's engagement. As Ida Levy told her husband, Avrom: "They are a perfect match." Evita Castillo, on the other hand, felt quite different when her daughter, Maria, announced her betrothal to Grant Merkle.

WILSON'S BLUNDER

"It is one thing to live amongst Anglos, but quite another for my daughter to marry one," Evita thought. "Where will they get married? Who will be their priest? What will become of their children?" she worried.

"I am not leaving the church," Maria assured her mother.

Evita put her hand into the pocket of her dress and gripped her rosary as tightly as she could. "It's not that your father and I don't like Grant," she began awkwardly, "but why don't you marry a nice Spanish boy, a good Catholic who we can go with to church."

"I will attend mass as I always have."

"But not with your husband and children," Evita argued.

"Grant will retain his affiliation. But each week we will alternate churches, and take communion together."

"And your children?"

"Our children will do the same. But ... " Maria paused.

"But what?"

Maria's eyes began to water. "They will be raised in the Presbyterian tradition of their father," she blurted out.

Evita Castillo's lips moved rapidly, but all of her "Hail Mary's" were uttered with an indistinct mumble.

"No priest will perform a marriage ceremony under such conditions," Alejandro interjected.

"Grant and I decided that we will be married in a civil ceremony." The prayers of her mother now became audible.

Alejandro looked deep into Maria's dark brown eyes. He could tell that her decision had already been made and there was nothing he could do to change her mind. Maria stared back at her father. Alejandro remembered that stare from when he had consoled his little girl after she had fallen from an orange tree in the family's orchard. Now it was she who was, in effect, consoling him. The only question left for Alejandro and his wife was whether to accept Maria's decision, or risk losing both their daughter and her husband. "Do you love this man?" he asked.

"I do, Mi Padre."

"What does she know about love?" Evita interjected. "She's just a child."

Maria glared at her mother but said nothing.

"And just how do the Merkles feel about their son marrying a Spanish woman?" Alejandro continued. "Especially a Spanish woman whose complexion is darker than theirs."

"They are probably threatening to disinherit him," Evita interrupted. "I know the Anglos. They are all very polite to us as long as we stay with our own kind."

"You don't understand," Maria began, trying to hold back her tears. She contemplated telling her mother that Grant had Negro blood himself, but thought better of it. "The Merkles are good people," she said instead. "They have no reservations about our family." Maria's voice tailed off noticeably.

"Just wait until you and Grant have your first argument. Then you will hear what these people really think about us," Evita continued, one word flowing off of her tongue after the other in rapid succession.

"Listen to what you are saying," Maria said, her voice breaking. "Padre," she pleaded, "tell her to stop."

"You don't think the Merkles have concerns about this marriage?" her father asked in a serious tone.

"They have the same concerns about our religious differences that you have," she confessed. "But Grant and I will work them out." Maria paused for a breath of air. "Just like you, the Merkles only want us to be happy."

"They will accept you as their daughter?" Alejandro persisted.

"They have offered to host a wedding celebration for us following the ceremony," Maria continued, her eyes turning moist and red.

Alejandro Castillo put his arm around Maria's shoulder and pulled her chin into the crook of his neck. "The honor of hosting such a celebration falls upon the father of the bride," he said decisively. "Do the Merkles think that we cannot afford to give our only daughter the wedding that she deserves?"

Maria looked up and gave her father a cautious smile.

"We will show the Merkles how to throw a fiesta," he concluded.

"Do I have your blessing, as well, Madre?"

Evita thought of the red hereditarial sign that she bore on her back, a sign in the flesh that she was of Mayan—not Spanish—blood. She thought how difficult it must have been for her criollos in-laws to have initially accepted her. Then she closed her eyes, took a deep breath and squeezed her rosaries one last time. "Your father sees more clearly than I. When it comes to the wedding of our only daughter we will spare no expense." Evita then welcomed Maria into her arms. The two women embraced, half-laughing and half-crying.

And so the Castillos agreed to the marriage of their daughter, Maria, to Mr. Grant Merkle of New York City. By the time the Merkles and the Castillos were celebrating the birth of their first grandchild, Theo, the Cubs had hit rock bottom. Chicago finished the 1925 season in last place—the first time that had happened since they joined the original National League of Professional Baseball Clubs almost fifty years earlier. "My grandfather would have been delighted," Grant told Maria.

But the Cubs' eighth place finish gave Chicago the first pick in the minor league draft. When, through a clerical error, the New York Giants left a five foot, six inch, 190 pound center fielder off of their roster, the Cubs used that pick to obtain Lewis "Hack" Wilson. In that same draft they plucked left fielder Riggs Stephenson out of the Cleveland organization. A year later they traded an over-the-hill second baseman for a graceful future hall-of-fame right fielder by the name of Kiki Cuyler. This trio became one of the hardest hitting and most colorfully-named outfields in the annals of baseball.

Despite the Cubs' miserable performance on the field, William Wrigley began pouring money into Cubs Park. Among other things, the playing field was reoriented, which is why the furthest point from home plate is a few degrees to the right of straight-away center field. In addition, a second deck was constructed above the grandstand and modern concession stands were built for the fans' convenience. It was only after all of this was completed in 1926 that the stadium's name was changed to Wrigley Field.

The Cubs' mediocrity continued into 1927. But though the team finished eight and a half games out of first place, the Cubs drew well over a million fans—the first Major League baseball team in history to reach that attendance milestone. It marked the beginning of a strange phenomenon—a genuine love affair between the Chicago Cubs, and their north side fans. It would be an affair that would retain its passion regardless how poorly the team played on the field.

In 1928 the Cubs plugged the hole at second base with Rogers Hornsby, once the best right-handed hitter in the Major Leagues. With "Gabby" Hartnett behind the plate, "Woody" English at short, and "Jolly" Charlie Grimm at first, the 1929 Chicago Cubs would bat .303 as a team, scoring over six runs a game in the process. And with Charlie Root, Guy Bush, and Pat Malone on the mound, they had a formidable pitching staff as well. They won the National League pennant by ten and a half games, and met the Philadelphia Athletics in the World Series.

The 1929 World Series would be memorable for one thing—the Cubs took an eight run lead into the bottom of the seventh of a pivotal game and blew it. It is the largest blown lead in World Series history. In the course of the A's ten-run seventh inning, the usually reliable Hack Wilson inexplicably lost two balls in the sun. "We were jinxed," was all Wilson could offer as an excuse for his costly blunder. The stock market crashed two weeks later.

The following year Hack Wilson atoned for his blunder with one of the best season performances in baseball history—a .356 batting average, fifty-six homeruns, and 190 runs batted in. His record for RBI's stands to this day. But luck seemed to be working against the Cubs when Rogers Hornsby retired as a player and Wrigley installed him as manager. A maniacal perfectionist and disciplinarian, Hornsby drove the heavy drinking Wilson off the team and out of baseball. Referring to himself as a gambler on horses, a slave driver, and a disgrace, Hornsby effectively drove himself out of the game halfway through the 1932 season.

With Hornsby gone, a more relaxed Cubs team went on to win the National League pennant. Their opponent in the 1932 World Series was the New York Yankees, led by the most formidable duo in baseball history—Babe Ruth and Lou Gehrig. The once hapless Yankees had become the favorite team of countless baseball fans, including a seven-year old New York City native by the name of Theo Merkle.

THEO'S DELIRIUM

Lou Gehrig hit a game-winning homer to give the Yankees a 5–2 victory over the Cubs in the first game of the 1932 World Series. In Game Two, "Lefty" Gomez allowed only one earned run as New York took a 2–0 Series lead. After the game, Grant, Maria and Theo Merkle left Yankee Stadium in high spirits.

"Remind your Daddy who pitched for the Yankees," Maria urged her son.

"Gomez!" he yelled gleefully.

"I didn't hear you," Maria teased.

"Gomez!" Theo hollered even louder.

"You don't have to rub it in," Grant protested, raising his hands in a sign of surrender.

Maria playfully removed Theo's New York Yankee cap and rubbed her palm back and forth over the top of her son's head. "Yes, we do," she insisted. "And if Daddy had listened to Grandpa Alex, and signed some Latin players, Lefty Gomez would have been on the Dodgers—not the Yankees."

"I'm glad he didn't listen," Theo laughed.

Maria gave her husband a satisfied stare. "It looks like you're outnumbered by Yankee fans in your own family, honey."

But Grant was no longer listening. A Curtis biplane was buzzing overhead, and it gave him an idea. "Let's go to Chicago," he suggested.

"Chicago?" Maria questioned.

"The League gave us tickets on the third base line," Grant explained, "but no one from the front office wanted them." Then he turned to his son and said, "Theo, how'd you and Mom like to go to Game Three?"

The boy's face lit up like a beacon.

Maria reacted immediately. "Now don't start putting wild ideas into his head," she cautioned. "You know we have plans tonight, and even if we didn't, how do you know whether we can even get a berth on such short notice?"

"We're not going by train, honey. Theo, my boy, how would you like to fly?"

Maria interceded before her son could respond. "Oh no," she insisted. "I get scared enough every time you fly off somewhere on business, but I am not allowing our seven-year old son to go up in the air on one of those corrugated apple crates. I'd feel safer going over Niagara Falls in a barrel."

Theo looked squarely into his mother's eyes. "I'm not scared, Mama" he insisted.

Grant turned and looked into Maria's eyes as well. "Now you can tell me how it feels to be outnumbered in your own family," he chided.

"My vote should count twice," Maria grumbled with obvious resignation.

At 8 a.m. the next morning the Merkles boarded a thirteen-passenger Ford Tri-Motor. A uniformed young lady, well-groomed and well-dressed, loaded their luggage into the fuselage and handed out chewing gum to each passenger as they boarded the aircraft. There was no seat for Theo, so he sat on his father's lap. Then, to Maria's surprise, the young lady boarded the plane herself. The air stewardess warned everyone not to be alarmed by any loud noises emanating from the engines, or flames that were visible from their rear. "There may be some turbulence during takeoff," she added, "but after that, we should have a smooth flight."

There was no seat for the stewardess either, so she remained on her feet throughout the flight. When a gentleman passenger became nauseated, she gave him an airsickness bag. When engine exhausts made his wife queasy, she opened some of the windows and let the outside air circulate through the stuffy cabin. And when the flight became calm, she served all of the passengers sandwiches and water.

The plane refueled in Cleveland, then took off for Chicago. Within a few hours, Grant was showing Theo the outline of Lake Michigan which protruded into the flat midwestern landscape like an inverted thumb. Soon he was pointing out the steel mills, the railroad tracks and the stockyards. Moments later the plane bounced through an air pocket and veered into a tight arc before straightening out for its final approach. The next thing they knew, the Tri-Motor had touched down at Chicago's Municipal Airport.

Some of the passengers were already queued up in front of the cabin door even as the aircraft began taxiing toward the terminal. The Merkles disembarked quickly, recovered their luggage, and had it loaded into a cab. Before long they were on their way toward the center of the city.

Grant was contemplating Game Three of the series, and his first visit to Wrigley Field, when he heard loud, unfamiliar staccato popping sounds coming from the car in front of his taxi. He looked in the direction of the noise, and was shocked to see a man in a sharkskin suit and felt hat, standing on the running board of an automobile, firing a Tommy gun toward a trailing car. A man in that car was firing back.

Reflexively, Grant swept Theo and Maria to the floor of the cab. They felt the taxi swerve hard to the left. The cab's windshield cracked, and the driver shrieked in pain. Grant threw himself on top of Theo and Maria to protect them, as the taxi careened into a lamppost, and burst into flames. Maria spilled out of the cab's curb-side door, pulling Theo out after her.

Grant, who was unhurt by the crash, managed to extricate himself from the opposite door of the burning taxi. He spotted Maria and Theo sprawled along the curb. He was about to run to them when, through a jagged hole in the driver's-side window he saw the operator of the cab slumped against the steering wheel, bleeding profusely. Grant tugged at the driver's door but it didn't open. He tugged again with the same result. By then the flames had engulfed the cab. Desperately, Grant thrust his arm through the hole in the driver's-side window, groped his hand along the interior of the door and yanked on the door handle. When the door flew open, Grant reached his hand into the inferno, grabbed the driver by the collar and dragged him to safety. In the process, Grant's hands and clothes became soaked with blood.

Grant set the driver on the curb and turned to Theo. His son was screaming in pain. The boy had been lying directly over the gas tank when it ruptured. Maria was trying unsuccessfully to use her coat to smother the burning gasoline that blazed from her son's legs and abdomen.

Theo writhed in agony on the curb amidst the twisted steel and broken glass. Grant lunged on top of his son, pressing his own body onto the flames that were already eating at Theo's flesh. After the fire was extinguished, he prayed for God to help his son.

Sirens began to wail, and lights began to flash. By the time an ambulance arrived ugly, bubbly blisters had appeared on the boy's stomach and thighs. Maria felt faint; Grant became nauseated. Together, however, they remained calm and whispered comfort to their son all the way to the hospital.

The doctor who met the ambulance at West Park Children's Hospital was Isaac Mann. With the help of his nurse, Dr. Mann quickly stabilized his patient and administered some morphine to ease the pain. But by then Theo had lost a lot of blood. "If he doesn't get blood immediately, he will go into shock," Isaac Mann said to himself.

"Should I make arrangements for a transfusion?" asked the nurse, as if reading the doctor's thoughts.

Dr. Mann nodded, then he turned to Grant and Maria. "Do you know the boy's blood type?" he asked. Despite the emergency, the doctor remained calm and focused. His soft, measured tone of voice had a soothing effect on Grant and Maria.

Each looked at the other and shook their head.

"No matter," he said. "We'll transfuse with type O."

"It's a universal donor," the nurse reassured them.

"Start with a pint," the doctor instructed.

The nurse hurried from the room and returned a few moments later, perspiring and ashen-faced. "There was an emergency at Methodist General this afternoon; the brass upstairs authorized us to give them every unit of O that we had, just like they did for us last year," she explained. "We've been promised some emergency units from Northeastern within the hour."

Isaac Mann surveyed the situation, then spoke decisively. "We can't afford to wait," he said.

Maria Merkle fidgeted nervously, alternately dabbing her son's forehead with a damp wash cloth, and then looking up searchingly at her husband. Grant, no longer calm and in charge, was frustrated by his helplessness, and guilt-ridden for suggesting the ill-fated trip in the first place.

Dr. Mann turned to his nurse. "I am type O," he said tersely. "Bring me a pair of hundred milliliter flasks each fitted with a two-hole rubber stopper. I'll also need two sterile syringes and several lengths of tubing."

"Dr. Mann," the nurse exclaimed, immediately grasping the dangerous procedure that he was about to undertake.

The doctor gave his nurse a stern look, but made no comment. She rushed out of the room to do his bidding.

The doctor looked down at Theo. "You're a brave boy," he said. Then noticing a baseball cap on top of the family's belongings piled on a guest chair, he asked if he was a Yankee fan.

Theo nodded. The morphine had taken hold and he lay quietly.

"Who's your favorite player?" the doctor continued.

Theo looked up at his parents who were hovering above him. "Babe Ruth," he whispered.

"Well, the Babe's a friend of mine," the doctor went on in an exaggerated drawl. "Maybe we'll just have to get him in here to help us out." Isaac Mann believed in little white lies to raise a patient's spirits, and this patient needed all the help he could get. "Would you like that?" Mann asked

Theo smiled for the first time since the accident.

Then the doctor spoke quietly to Grant and Maria. "Your son is a tough little boy," he whispered. "But this will be awkward and difficult. Why don't you let him hold the baseball cap while we perform this procedure? It will have the dual effect of giving him comfort and distracting his attention from what will be happening,"

"I've got a better idea," Grant suggested. Without waiting for a response, he removed a medallion from under his shirt. "It's just an old family heirloom," he said. "But it meant a lot to Theo's great grand dad."

Isaac Mann didn't need to take a closer look at the medallion to know that he had seen such a pendant before. He was about to ask about it when the nurse walked briskly into the room with the paraphernalia he had requested. "If anyone's a little squeamish, now is the time to leave," she said looking pointedly at Maria.

"I will be fine," Maria answered bravely. Then she looked fondly at Grant. "And my husband's like the Rock of Gibraltor."

By then, however, Grant Merkle had pulled a chair alongside his son's cot, and was showing him a dulled diagram on a bronze medallion. "Your Grandpa Lincoln received this from his father, just as you will receive it from me, Grant began. "Grandpa Lincoln told me that this medallion would bring us good luck."

Dr. Mann fitted the rubber tube extending from each syringe into a different flask. Then he connected the different flasks together with a separate piece of tubing, the ends of which descended into each flask. In the meantime, the nurse had affixed one syringe into an artery in Theo's forearm. The doctor then carefully pushed the other syringe into his own forearm.

With the aid of a small rubber bulb in one of the tubes that served as a pump, Dr. Mann's type O blood began to flow from his arm, into one of the flasks. When the blood level in the flask reached the height of the descending tube, it began to flow from that tube into the second flask. When the level of the blood in the second flask reached the bottom of the tube connected to Theo's syringe, Dr. Mann's blood began to flow into his patient.

"I learned this in the army," Dr. Mann explained as he watched blood pulse out of his arm and into Theo's. In due course, the transfusion was completed, and the syringes removed. By then Theo had fallen asleep.

Grant Merkle rose from his chair and extended his hand. "We can never repay you, doctor," he began.

But Isaac interrupted. "Your son's recovery will be my reward." The doctor's expression then turned serious. "I must warn you, however, that your son will sleep for awhile, but the most difficult time still lies ahead. When he awakens he'll be in extreme discomfort. It'll be absolutely imperative for us to keep his spirits up."

"We'll do whatever it takes," Maria vowed.

Dr. Mann nodded. "Then there's nothing for us to do at the moment," he said softly.

Maria exhaled a deep sigh. So did her husband. It was then that Dr. Mann turned back toward Grant. "At the risk of being intrusive, may I ask you a question?"

"Anything," Grant responded.

"I couldn't help but notice the medallion you were showing your son during the transfusion. Would it surprise you to learn that I know of two other people who are in possession of an identical pendant?"

"I would be shocked," Grant confessed. "But if such people exist, I'd pay for a chance to meet them."

"I'll accept nothing of value," the doctor continued. "But I'm eager to make a few calls if for no other reason than to clear up this enigma that has now touched my professional life on two continents."

Within an hour, four people came to visit Theo Merkle at the West Park Children's Hospital. The first to arrive was Serena Tover, accompanied by her fifteen-year old daughter Patrice. A few minutes later, Esther Barr Rosen arrived with her eighteen-year old son Teddy. Dr. Mann escorted Serena and Esther into Theo's private room to meet the Merkles, but insisted that the teenagers remain in the lobby. After comparing medallions and exchanging hypotheses, the best anyone could conclude was that a New York ancestor from each of their families had some shared experience that created a bond of friendship.

Their discussion was interrupted by Theo, who awakened from his slumber in severe pain.

"Where's Babe Ruth?" Theo asked through his anguish.

The room became uneasily silent. When it became apparent to Theo that the Yankee slugger was nowhere to be found, the combination of pain, blood loss and despondency caused the boy to lapse into delirium. Dr. Mann rushed into the room and administered another dose of morphine, but Theo kept calling for Babe Ruth.

It was then that Esther Barr Rosen made a fateful inquiry. "Would it help if I asked Mr. Ruth to join us?"

BABE'S SHOT

The attempt to bring the legendary Yankee outfielder to the bed-side of Theo Merkle ultimately became a joint effort. Esther Barr Rosen provided the information that Dr. Mann would use in composing his note to Mr. Ruth; Grant Merkle provided the name of the hotel where the Yankees would be staying while they were in Chicago; Serena Tover provided the Ford motor car that Teddy would drive to the hotel; Patrice Tover provided the charm needed to get Teddy's note delivered to Mr. Ruth's room; and Maria Merkle provided the twenty dollar bill in the event charm alone was insufficient to ensure the delivery.

Later in the evening a uniformed bellboy walked down a wide carpeted corridor toward Babe Ruth's room with a sealed envelope in one hand and a twenty dollar bill in his pocket. The envelope was addressed to Mr. George Herman Ruth and bore the hand-printed word "Urgent" in the lower right corner. The bellboy could feel something heavy and bulky concealed inside the envelope, but the pretty, dark-haired girl who gave it to him, along with his twenty dollar "tip," did not disclose what it was.

Ruth was about to leave when the bellboy rapped on his hotel room door. He accepted the delivery with a barely audible, "thanks," and gave the lad a few coins. Then, without even looking at the envelope, he threw it in the direction of the small Chippendale table that stood near his bed. The envelope slammed into the front of the night stand, ripped open and fell to the floor. Ruth, however, was already on his way out the door.

He paused for a moment to adjust his necktie—a wide four-in-hand whose ends extended barely below his rib cage. Then he walked down the hotel corridor to an adjacent room, knocked on Lou Gehrig's door, and waited impatiently for his teammate to answer. It was Gehrig's wife, Eleanor, who responded to his knock.

"Hi, Babe," she said pleasantly.

Ruth removed his fedora, and acknowledged Ellie's greeting. "Is the college boy still up for a drink?" he asked, peeking into the room.

"He's on long distance with his mother," Ellie explained. "She's probably reminding him to eat all his vegetables," she continued, deliberately speaking loud enough for her husband to hear.

Babe and Ellie waited for a comment from Lou, but none was forthcoming.

Ruth broke the silence. "I may have to belt a couple of homers tomorrow," he told Ellie. Then he, too, raised his voice for his teammate's benefit. "I'm tired of the college boy getting all the headlines in this Series."

Gehrig clasped his hand over the mouthpiece of the phone and yelled toward the door: "I'll match you homer for homer."

Ellie shook her head. "You two are such children," she scolded.

Ruth glanced nervously at his watch. "I've got to get going," he said.

Ellie saw through Ruth's uneasiness immediately. "C'mon, Babe," she protested. "Lou will be off the phone in a minute. Then we'll all go downstairs and have a drink together—like old times."

"No," Ruth insisted, running the side of his hand through the crease in his felt hat. "You're a great kid, Ellie. Just tell the college boy that he's the luckiest guy on the face of the earth." Ruth then turned abruptly, put on his hat, and headed back toward his room.

"I'll tell him, Babe," Ellie called out.

Ruth sat on the edge of his bed deep in thought. "Lou had doting parents, and mine dumped me in an orphanage," he said to himself. "Lou is a refined, educated man, and people think I'm just a dumb buffoon who can hit a baseball." Then he thought about his first wife,

Helen, who had died in a house fire shortly after they had separated; and his present wife, Claire, an aspiring actress whose alleged "commitments" in New York prevented her from even making the trip to Chicago. "Does Claire love me like Ellie loves Lou, or is she just using me?" he wondered. The big man bent down to untie his shoes, and it was then that he saw the torn envelope that was lying on the floor.

A length of chain was visible through the tear. On closer inspection, Ruth discovered that the chain was attached to a bronze medallion. He recognized the medallion immediately. Then he ripped open the envelope and read the note that was inside. When finished, he put both the note and the medallion into his pocket and mumbled to himself, "The curse lives." Forty-five minutes later he arrived at West Park Children's Hospital, and poked his big head into the room of Theo Merkle.

Esther spotted him first. "I knew you would come," she said smiling.

"I tried to visit you years ago," Ruth apologized, "but you must have moved.

Esther nodded. Her curly auburn hair was now streaked with gray, but her smile remained captivating and her hazel eyes shone clear and bright.

"Anyhow," Ruth continued, "I always keep my promises, no matter how long it takes." Then he took the medallion that he found in the envelope and placed it around Esther's neck. "I thought I'd better return this or people will start to talk," he joked.

Esther felt her face redden with embarrassment. But then Maria approached the ballplayer and introduced herself. "My husband and I cannot thank you enough," she said extending her hand. "Your reputation as a good man may last even longer than your home run records as a baseball player."

Now it was Ruth who blushed. "How's your son doing?" he asked.

Maria took his hand and walked him over to Theo's cot. The boy lay on his back covered with three blankets, but was shivering nonetheless.

"Theo," Maria began in a calm, reassuring tone.

The boy looked up at his mother. His eyes were deep and bloodshot.

"Theo," she repeated. "I'd like you to meet Mr. Babe Ruth."

Ruth bent over his bed, but Theo gave no response.

"Hi, Theo," Ruth began somewhat hesitantly.

"Are you really Babe Ruth?" Theo asked in a hoarse whisper.

Ruth nodded, lowering his big head closer to the boy. He pushed a lock of black hair from his forehead with a paw-sized hand and smiled. "Do you know anyone else with a mug like this?"

Theo remained unconvinced. "Where's your uniform?"

Maria and Grant were shocked at their son's skepticism, but Ruth restrained their inclination to explain by raising his hand.

"I will be wearing my uniform tomorrow," Ruth promised. "And when I do, I'm going to hit a homer just for you."

Theo looked up at the man in silence.

"Maybe I'll even hit two," Ruth told the boy.

Theo turned his eyes toward his dad.

"Can you imagine Babe Ruth hitting a home run just for you?" Grant said, smiling.

"Just for me?" Theo responded, pulling his blankets up under his chin in an unsuccessful effort to keep warm.

"Just for you," Maria reassured him.

"Tomorrow, I'll bring a radio into your room, and we'll all listen to the game together," Grant said. "How does that sound, Theo?"

Theo nodded, his eyes closing.

"Do you understand, Theo?" Maria asked.

The boy nodded again, then wrapped himself in the blankets and rolled over on his side. He had stopped shivering.

Over 50,000 fans showed up at Wrigley Field for Game Three of the 1932 World Series. The Cubs sent right-hander Charlie Root to the mound. No pitcher in history, including Hall of Famers Three Finger Brown and Fergie Jenkins, would ever win more games in a Cub uniform than Charlie Root. Unfortunately, for the Cubs, Game Three would not be one of them.

The game started inauspiciously for Root when Yankee center fielder Earle Combs reached base on an error, and second baseman Joe Sewell drew a walk. The enormous crowd then roared in anticipation of Babe Ruth coming to the plate.

Ruth waited for Gehrig to join him in the on-deck circle.

For a brief moment, the two baseball legends stood side-by-side. A photographer on the field aimed his huge flash camera at their backs and pushed the shutter. The resulting photo caught Ruth's number three and Gehrig's number four—chosen for their respective spots in the Yankee batting order—on the back of their gray traveling uniforms. "He's got nothing, college boy," Ruth said. "Better get ready to meet me at the plate to shake my hand." Gehrig could only shake his head at his teammate's bravado. Ruth grinned. "I've got a promise to keep."

As he approached the plate, Ruth put his right hand over his chest, fingered the medallion through his heavy wool uniform, and squeezed it for good luck. Then he dug his left foot into the back of the batter's box and stared down at the Cub pitcher. A moment later he sent a Root fastball deep into the right-center field bleachers. "That's for you, Theo," he said to himself as he began his home run trot. "That's for Merkle's Curse," he yelled into the Cub dugout as he rounded third.

But the Cubs fought back, so when Ruth came up in the Yankee half of the fifth, the score was tied at four runs apiece. As Ruth approached the batter's box, the crowd noise became so loud it shook the stadium, threatening to tear the entire grandstand loose from its foundation. The vilest language, however, came not from the hometown fans, but from the Cub dugout. The Chicago players spewed epithets at the Yankee star with a hatred not seen since the Cubs faced the Giants in their historic playoff game in 1908. When Ruth let two strikes go by to even the count at two and two, the noise reached a crescendo.

Ruth stepped out of the box and waved an angry fist at the Cubs' dugout. Then he did so again with a long-sweeping motion culminating with him pointing his left index finger toward the right-center field bleachers—the same spot where his home run landed after his first-inning at-bat. The crowd hushed momentarily, but resumed its feverish roar when Ruth returned to the batter's box.

Root glared in at the Yankee slugger. He thought Ruth's gesture was intended to remind him that Ruth's at-bat wasn't over yet; that Ruth still had one more strike left; and that Ruth was not going to let a third strike go by with the bat on his shoulder. But now Root became confused. Ruth had just taken two fastballs for strikes. As a result, his catcher, Gabby Hartnett, was calling for a curve. But after Ruth's gesture Root was certain that a curve was exactly what the Yankee slugger was expecting. At the last moment Root shook off Hartnett's sign, and decided to come back with another fastball.

Ruth was thinking differently. "I just showed Root that I'm going to put this pitch in the same spot I put his first-inning fastball. Nothing he can do can stop me because he and his team are cursed."

Ruth took a ferocious swing at Root's next pitch. The crack of the bat hitting the ball sounded like a gunshot. The sheer force of the swing left Ruth momentarily frozen in his tracks—his right leg straight as a lever, his left leg bent at the knee with his toe twisted into the ground. His eyes followed the ball as it traced a high, towering arc through the clear October sky. It landed deep into the right-center field bleachers, almost precisely where he had pointed.

Ruth's shot completely humiliated the Chicago faithful. Even worse, they had to endure the Yankee slugger's triumphal strut around the bases. As Ruth rounded third, he shook his fist at the entire Cub dugout. Then he yelled into the din: "The curse lives!" It would be a fitting climax to the last World Series home run that Babe Ruth would ever hit.

Gehrig followed Ruth's momentous blast with a homer of his own. Then he added a solo home run in the top of the ninth for good measure. The Yankees won Game Three 7–5. Despite the relative closeness of the score, the Cubs were devastated. The next day they succumbed to the Yankees 13–6, giving the New Yorkers their third World Series sweep in a row. Psychologically the Cubs would never be the same.

Gabby's Gallop

When William Wrigley passed away in 1932, his son Philip inherited both the Cubs, and the stadium that bore his name. As it turned out, Phil Wrigley was more interested in the beautification of his field than the success of the team that played on it. Thus, one of the new owner's first decisions was to plant a stand of Chinese elm trees just beyond the center field wall.

When leaves from Wrigley's elms rained onto the outfield grass, interfering with play, he reluctantly had the trees pulled out. In their stead, Wrigley ordered that sprigs of ivy be planted at the base of the outfield wall, along its entire length from foul pole to foul pole. Heartened by the success of this experiment, he next decreed that a gigantic, hand-operated scoreboard be constructed in the airspace above the center field bleachers. A few years later he added a ten foot clock on top of the scoreboard. A few years after that, Wrigley Field became the first ball park to have a permanent organ installed within what would later be referred to as its "friendly confines."

Though Phil Wrigley spared no expense in beautifying his ballpark, he refused to invest $25,000 to purchase the contract of a promising center fielder from the San Francisco Seals of the Pacific Coast League. Wrigley spurned the opportunity even after the Seals' owner promised Wrigley a full refund if the outfielder failed to live up to expectations during spring training. As a result, shortly before the 1935 baseball season began, Joe DiMaggio became a New York Yankee instead of a Chicago Cub.

Despite Wrigley's stinginess when it came to acquiring and paying ballplayers, the Cubs won the pennant in 1935. Their hundred victory season was accomplished by a remarkable September surge that included a twenty-one game winning streak. It was during that streak that Cub fan Teddy Barr wore the same socks and Cub fan Patrice Tover sprayed on the same perfume for over three straight weeks. Similarly, countless other never-before- superstitious Chicagoans ate the same dessert, drank at the same bar room table, sat in the same bus seat, applied the same shade of lipstick and said the same prayers. The same prayers were repeated when the Cubs met the Detroit Tigers, led by future hall-of-famer, first baseman Hank Greenberg, in the 1935 World Series.

The Cubs and Tigers split their first two games in Detroit. Many Chicagoans thought it was a good omen, however, when Greenberg broke his wrist after colliding with Cub catcher Gabby Hartnett in Game Two. Cub manager Jolly Charlie Grimm thought it was destiny.

Despite Greenberg's broken wrist, and timely hitting by Cubs' infielders Stan Hack, Billy Jurges, and Billy Herman, the Tigers won the next two games to take a commanding 3–1 Series lead. All of a sudden Jolly Charlie Grimm wasn't feeling too jolly. But the Cubs eked out a 2–1 win in Game Five—their first World Series victory in Wrigley Field—to send the Series back to Detroit.

Ironically, it would be Hank Greenberg's weak hitting replacement, Marv Owen, who tied the game in the bottom of the sixth by poking a soft single to center. It would be his only hit of the Series. And it would be an even more dramatic bloop single, with two outs in the bottom of the ninth, that would send the winning run home from second, and send the dispirited Cubs home from Detroit with their third World Series defeat in six years. "Destiny will just have to wait until next year," Grimm muttered to a reporter as he left the ballpark.

Three years later—on an unseasonably warm day in early September of 1938—twenty-year old Patrice Tover walked into Rosen's Haberdashery on the north side of Chicago. Behind the counter was twenty-four-year old Teddy Barr. No other customers were in the store, so the two childhood acquaintances and neighborhood friends spent a moment exchanging small talk and sharing reminiscences.

"I'll never forget how you flirted the pants off of that bellboy," Teddy laughed.

Patrice was not listening. Her eyes darted around the empty, lifeless store and, without thinking, blurted out a question that she immediately regretted. "How's business?" she asked.

Teddy forced a smile. "Every time I think business can't get worse, it does," he said.

Patrice looked awkwardly down at her shoes—white pumps with an open toe and a two-inch heel—then tried to salvage the conversation. "It's my brother's birthday," she began somewhat tentatively. "I came to buy him a new hat. I want a nice felt one with a little red feather in the headband."

Teddy reached under his coat and tugged nervously on his suspenders. "They're not cheap, Patty," he said as he walked her over to some shelves stacked with straw hats, derbies and fedoras. The prices were as high as $5.00.

Patrice was wearing a short-sleeved yellow dress whose hem stopped at mid-calf. She also had on white silk stockings, white wrist length gloves and a white bonnet with a flared brim. The bonnet had a yellow flower attached to a ribbon that was sewn into the base of the crown. She looked so good that Teddy wanted to reach out and hug her.

"I've managed to save a few dollars," she answered. "For the past few months I've been working as a chorus girl during stage shows at The Chicago."

Teddy gave her a suspicious look, then tugged again at his suspenders.

"I also do a lot of waitressing," she confessed.

Patrice and Teddy stopped in front of the hat-filled shelves. "He's a seven and an eighth," she volunteered, anticipating Teddy's question. "Bet you didn't think I knew that."

Teddy was thinking of something else. He looked at Patrice's rosebud lips and rouged cheeks, and wanted to say something meaningful. "Is Pete still working at the Texaco?" was all he could think of.

Patrice nodded. "He's overhauling engines, rebuilding transmissions, and Lord knows what else. They say he's a genius when it comes to working with metal."

"And where, do they say, is the genius of his twin sister?"

Patrice removed her bonnet, took a gray felt hat off the shelf and placed it delicately on her head. Then she admired it in the mirror. "Though people think we look alike," she said, tilting her neck from side to side in order to get different views of the fedora, "we are really quite different." She removed the hat from her head and handed it to Teddy. "I'll take it," she said decisively.

"Quite different?" Teddy asked.

Patrice looked in the mirror, put on her bonnet, and carefully adjusted it by moving it slightly one way, then another. Then she looked at Teddy through the mirror. "He was an altar boy, and I am an atheist; he is a dreamer, and I am a realist; he makes his living with his hands…" Patrice paused to do a graceful pirouette, as if the store were a stage. "…and I intend to make a living with my feet." She held her hands in a circle above her head for a moment before letting them fall to her sides. "And most importantly, Peter likes the Sox, and I—well, I love the Cubs more than…" Patrice stopped abruptly in mid-sentence, concerned that she was sounding too self-absorbed. "And what about you, Teddy?" she asked.

The familiarity with which she said his name made Teddy feel warm inside; but the brief moment of happiness quickly ebbed. He looked nervously to his left, then his right; then he looked straight at Patrice. "I'm trapped," he said with deep resignation.

"Trapped?"

"Trapped in my job, trapped in my apartment, trapped in Chicago." Then he hesitated, embarrassed that he had already bared too much of his soul. He needed to change the subject, but wasn't sure how. "Trapped into being a Cub fan," he said with a grin, catching her eyes at the same moment she caught his. For a fleeting moment that feeling of attraction returned; Teddy was certain that Patrice had the same feeling, but she said nothing.

Teddy broke the uneasy silence. "So what does Peter's sister want for her twenty-first birthday?" he asked.

Patrice gave Teddy an inviting smile. "I want you to take me out to the ball game," she pleaded.

Three weeks later, on a gray, overcast afternoon late in September, Teddy Barr and Patrice Tover boarded the Howard El, exited at Addison Street, walked a block and a half to the Wrigley Field ticket office, and purchased two fifty-cent tickets that gained them admission to the left field bleachers. They found a pair of seats in the second row.

With six games left in the season, the Cubs had put on a furious charge, including a seven game winning streak, and now trailed the visiting Pirates by only half a game. After seven innings, the game was tied 3–3. Despite two pitching changes by the Cubs' player-manager, Gabby Hartnett, the Pirates pushed two runs across the plate on a lead-off walk and three successive singles. In the bottom of the eighth, however, the Cubs strung together three hits and a pair of walks to tie the score at five runs apiece.

Before the start of the ninth inning, the umpires met at home plate. One pointed demonstratively at the dark, overcast sky. A twenty mile-an-hour wind, blowing in over the right field wall, was pushing big black clouds from the lake directly toward the ballpark.

"Do you think they're going to call the game?" Patrice asked.

Teddy looked up at the threatening sky, but shook his head. "They've got to try to get it in," he said. "Otherwise they'll have to play two tomorrow."

"Wouldn't that be better for us?"

Teddy shook his head again. "Gabby just burned out two starters trying to put out the fire in the eighth. We don't have much pitching left in the tank for tomorrow."

The umps decided to play one more inning. To the Cub fans' delight, Pittsburgh went down quickly in the top of the ninth. A huge roar erupted when teenage outfielder, Phil Cavaretta led off the bottom of the inning with a deep drive to center. Unfortunately, it was not deep enough. Pirate center fielder Lloyd Waner speared the ball on the run, brushing Phil Wrigley's ivy after the catch. When Waner's opposite number on the Cubs bounced out, Gabby Hartnett advanced to the plate, representing Chicago's last hope.

Hartnett had been the Cubs catcher since 1922. Of the dozen catchers that would enter the hall-of-fame, only Bench, Berra, Dickey and Fisk would drive in more runs or get more hits. Only Bench, Berra, Campanella and Fisk would hit more homers; and Hartnett's .297 lifetime batting average was the highest of all five. But when he swung and missed the first two pitches, it appeared that it was too much to ask, even of Hartnett, that he get his bat on the ball in the dim twilight of the day.

Hartnett stepped out of the box and rubbed some dirt on his hands. By the time he resumed his stance, yet another layer of shadows had spread itself over the infield. Hartnett could barely see the pitcher, and vice versa. "He wants to get this game over with right now," Hartnett thought. "He's not going to waste one."

And so, when Hartnett saw a white blur coming toward him, he swung from the heels. Hartnett knew from the absence of any vibration when his bat struck the ball that it was "gone." Few spectators at Wrigley Field, however, actually saw the flight of Gabby's blast until it bounced off the outstretched hands of Teddy Barr, and into the grasp of a spectator in the row behind him.

Cub fans were overcome with joy. They poured out of the stands and surrounded Hartnett as he galloped from third to home. Other Chicagoans, listening on their radios as they were about to sit down for their evening meal, raced out of their bungalows and apartments, and danced in the streets.

Patrice literally jumped into Teddy's arms and gave him a kiss, and then another and another. Along with 40,000 other gleeful fans, they remained in the stadium and cheered at the dark, empty field. Neither remembered leaving the park, waiting in line to get on the El, or walking home. When they reached Patrice's apartment, Teddy handed her the scorecard. "One day it will be worth something," Teddy assured her.

Patrice tried to give it back.

"If it wasn't for you, we wouldn't have even been there," Teddy insisted.

Patrice looked down at the scorecard, then up at Teddy. "I'm dancing Saturday evening," she began hesitantly. "I can get you in free, and we can watch the double-feature after the stage show."

"I'm sorry," Teddy shrugged, "but I can't go."

Patrice's eyes looked hurt.

"It's not what you think," he said quickly.

"What am I to think?" she asked.

Teddy put his thumb under her chin and pushed her head up gently until their eyes met. "I joined the Army, Patty. My train leaves for Fort Riley tomorrow morning."

"Oh, no!"

"My father came to this country with nothing but the shirt on his back," Teddy tried to explain. "He learned English, started a business, and made something of himself all on his own. I can't even make a success out of the job that's been handed to me."

"You're a success in my book," Patrice insisted.

Teddy shook his head disconsolately. "But not in mine. Our forefather Jacob wrestled with an angel; since then it's been our fate to leave our home, wander the earth, and struggle with God and man. Unfortunately, my struggles end only in disappointment."

"Struggle with God and man?"

"That's what it says," Teddy answered. Then, impulsively, he pulled her into a tight embrace until he could feel her heart beating against his own chest. She responded by thrusting her arms around his shoulders and pressing her mouth onto his lips for a long passionate kiss. They kissed again, but not a third time. It was Teddy, not Patrice, who turned away. "The world is on the verge of war and I'm leaving tomorrow for—God knows where," he thought. "I cannot hurt this girl any more than I already have." Teddy relaxed his arms from around Patrice's waist, and took a deep breath. "I'm sorry, Patty," he said hiding his emotion. "I've got to go."

"Teddy," she cried.

But Teddy had already begun walking toward the sidewalk that extended in front of Patrice's apartment building. He forced himself not to look back. He could not bear to see the pain on Patrice's face.

Patrice, however, was transfixed by Teddy. "There is a mystery about the Jews that seems impenetrable," she thought. Then she gritted her teeth and raised her jaw. "A mystery that I am going to solve." She watched Teddy walking briskly into the damp, overcast night, and began to weep. In the midst of her tears a thought came: "I will study their book and figure it out." By the time Teddy had disappeared into the darkness, her crying had ceased.

PEEWEE'S GESTURE

The Cubs went on to win the 1938 National League pennant, but lost the World Series to the Yankees in four straight games. By then Teddy Barr had become a soldier. After basic training he was attached to the Army Air Corps. Eventually he was assigned to an elite group of airmen trained to fly America's biggest and best bomber—the B-29 Superfortress. Late in the war, he hurt his ear during a bombing run, and was grounded by his commanding officer. Otherwise Teddy Barr would have been the bombardier on the *Enola Gay* during its fateful mission over Hiroshima.

Peter Tover joined the Army the day after Pearl Harbor. He was assigned to the motor pool and kept American tanks rumbling through Europe right up until VE Day. When he returned home, his mother, Serena, put a family heirloom around his neck. It complemented the three sergeants' stripes on his shoulder and two purple hearts on his chest. The same day that Serena Tover gave Peter her husband's medallion, she gave Peter's twin sister, Patrice, her husband's axe.

Theo Merkle suffered through ten years of painful rehabilitation before fully recovering from his near-fatal burns. In the process, he learned the value of hard work and the uselessness of self-pity. He thought he could put that knowledge to good use when he joined the Marines the day after he finished high school.

Theo was wounded in the battle for Okinawa, but nursed back to health by a devoutly religious, second generation Christian woman of Chinese extraction. Chen Wong had suffered greatly. During their occupation of Nanking, the Japanese invaders had murdered her parents along with over 100,000 other innocent civilians. She was enslaved and sexually abused. "It was only my faith that kept me alive," she confided to Theo in between sobs.

For the second time in his life, Theo suffered through a difficult and painful rehab. It was only after he regained his strength that he offered his nurse a proposal of marriage. "It was your kindness and compassion that brought me to this day," he told her through tears of happiness. "Maybe together we can begin to heal the world."

Chen removed a hanky from her pocket and dabbed at the tears that traced a crooked path down Theo's full, round cheeks. She noticed the lack of contrast between his bamboo-colored skin and her own slender fingers.

"What does it take to be an American?" she asked suddenly.

Theo paused, unsure how to answer so simple a question. Then a thought occurred to him. "Our nation's motto is *e pluribus unum*," he explained. "It means: from many, one."

Chen gave Theo a skeptical look.

"Imagine a pot of tea," Theo continued. "To be an American we each add a measure of our own individuality into the common pot, while accepting a swallow of the English language and the Protestant ethic from the resulting brew."

Chen tried to imagine how the hue of the tea would be altered ever so slightly by the color of her skin, and how its temperature would be raised by a fraction of a degree from the heat of her passion. In return, she would enthusiastically swallow the values of honest hard work, self-reliance, humility—and a national pledge of liberty and justice for all.

"I wish my parents had had the opportunity to become Americans," she said to herself. Chen repeated her wish to her father-in-law, Grant Merkle, after she and Theo arrived in New York at the end of the war. Grant looked at the compassionate young woman who had nursed his son back to health. She reminded him of his grandmother, Angela, who saved the life of Merkle patriarch Frederick during the War Between the States. The memory caused Grant to gulp in shame because it echoed back to an unfulfilled promise he had made to his grandmother twenty-five years earlier.

The very next day, Grant Merkle marched into the Ebbets Field office of the Brooklyn Dodgers' General Manager, Branch Rickey. Though it was a sunny afternoon, the Venetian blinds in Mr. Rickey's office were tightly drawn, and his desk lamp was toggled off. The only light came from a single incandescent bulb that hung from a dust-laden ceiling fixture.

Rickey was puffing on a long slender cigar. A mound of ashes and several stogie butts littered two large ashtrays that rested on his dark walnut desk. The writing surface was otherwise blanketed with several layers of documents, manila folders, and newspapers. Many of them were stained with coffee.

Rickey welcomed his visitor with a firm handshake and a friendly "hello" that betrayed his Midwestern roots. Then he pushed an upholstered armchair closer to his desk, swiped a monogrammed hankie across the cushion, and beckoned Grant to take a seat. "Care for a cigar," Rickey asked, moving toward a glass humidor that was perched on an adjacent end table.

Grant waved his hand, partially to decline Rickey's offer and partially to clear the air of smoke.

The Dodgers' General Manager retreated from the end table, returned to his desk chair, and peered intently at his guest through wire-rimmed spectacles. Then he exhaled deeply. "What can I do for you, Mr. Merkle?"

Grant Merkle peered back at his host, initially uncertain what to say. "My grandmother was born into slavery," Merkle began hesitantly. Then to his surprise, the words came quickly and easily. Ten minutes later the two men rose to their feet and shook each other's hand. Two years after that, Jack Robinson made his Major League debut.

Robinson's entrance into Major League baseball in 1947 was met with a torrent of hate mail, threats, insults and slurs that had the potential to undermine all that was good and decent about the great American pastime. The most contemptible behavior came from the big cities in the Northeast. It reached a climax during a game against the Boston Braves when the epithets were so vile, and the abuse so vitriolic, that a physical attack on the Dodger infielder seemed imminent.

It was at the height of this frenzy that Pee Wee Reese—a small-town boy from Kentucky—called "time-out" from his shortstop position and jogged over to talk to Robinson. Reese put his arm around his teammate, then pointed hither and yon as if discussing how to play the next Boston batter. In reality Reese was making a statement to America that Robinson was just another ballplayer and should be treated as such.

Jack nodded his appreciation. Then Peewee gave his teammate a piece of advice that Jack would never forget. "Remember the hatred you see here today, and then forget it."

Jack gave Peewee a bewildered look, but an umpire was already approaching to break-up their conversation. "Okay," Jack said, unsure how he could remember and forget at the same time.

Though Reese's gesture didn't end Robinson's ordeal, Jack viewed it as a turning point. Eventually he won the admiration of his teammates and the grudging respect of his opponents. In the end, he couldn't have persevered without the comfort of his wife, support from Mr. Rickey, and the knowledge that he was single-handedly changing the course of history by having the courage to be different. And whenever times got particularly bad, he would grasp—through the front of his Dodger uniform—a silver cross of the Latin style that his mother had placed around his neck before he left home. "Help will come from the unlikeliest of places," she had said before kissing him good-bye.

Patrice's Conversion

At 11:55 p.m. on July 17, 1945—five minutes before the trading deadline expired—the New York Yankees sold the winningest pitcher in the American League to the Chicago Cubs for a mere $97,000 in cash. Though the circumstances and timing of the Cubs' acquisition of Hank Bowery smelled of big city corruption, the St. Louis Cardinals' protest to the Commissioner of Baseball was rejected. Cardinal fans deeply resented this "corrupt bargain," which is why it is said, they detest the Cubs even now.

Bowery went on to compile an 11–2 record for the Cubs, including four victories against the rival Cardinals. Then, on September 29th, he defeated Pittsburgh to clinch the pennant for Chicago. That very evening, on a bench in a near-northwest side park, Teddy Barr made a proposal of marriage to Patrice Tover. It was almost seven years to the day that Teddy and Patrice had witnessed Gabby Hartnett's now-famous "homer in the gloamin.'" No sooner had Patrice accepted the proposal, then Teddy tried to convince her to reconsider.

"I have little to offer you," he confessed.

"There is little that I need."

"You don't understand," Teddy continued. "I am not the man I was before the war."

Patrice's expression grew pained. She looked down. "Are you trying to tell me that you are incapable of having..."

"No, no, no," Teddy interrupted. "The only thing I am incapable of..." He paused momentarily for a labored breath, "...is getting through the day without being..." He paused again to reconsider what he was about to say, "...without being haunted by life."

Patricia met his gaze.

"Six million Jews were murdered during the war," he began. "Countless gypsies as well," he said recalling Patrice's heritage. "How could God let that happen? It makes me doubt there is a God."

"And that's what haunts you?"

Teddy shook his head. "At first I felt guilty for being alive when so many perished," he explained. "But now I spend my day haunted, receiving retribution for the life that I have lived." Teddy stopped abruptly, and looked anxiously at Patrice.

"Retribution for what?"

Teddy weighed the consequences of what he wanted to say, then summoned up the courage to speak. "Because I am a coward," he blurted out.

Patrice didn't know where to begin. "You flew dangerous missions over the Pacific," she reminded him.

Teddy looked Patrice in the eye, and held her hands tightly to give him strength. "It wasn't the missions I flew," he said, his voice creaking with emotion, "but the mission I didn't fly."

Teddy's eyes sunk deep and dark into his face; his cheeks were hollowed out; his lips were parched and white. Patrice put one arm around his shoulder and pulled his head into her bosom. Then she patted his hair with her free hand, as if he were a child.

"I was grounded after the concussion from a bombing run damaged my ear," Teddy continued, his forehead dampening and his face flushing. "A young lieutenant fresh off an Iowa farm took my place. It was his first mission—a bombing run over Yokohama. He never came back, and neither did my crew."

Patrice again tried to comfort Teddy, this time by squeezing him tightly. "It's okay," she whispered.

"I stood at the tarmac with my binoculars raised and watched our planes return to base, one-by-one. Some had lost an engine, some trailed a plume of black smoke, some were shot up pretty bad." The more Teddy spoke, the more pained he became. "I waited all afternoon, and into the night, but that one never came home."

"It's okay, honey," Patrice repeated. "If you could have flown you would have."

"You don't understand," he stammered." I had a bad feeling about that mission. I knew our plane wouldn't come home. I wasn't disappointed to have been grounded—I was relieved."

Never before had Patrice seen such raw guilt.

"I now see that boy's face materialize on strangers that I pass in the street, on photographs I see in newspapers, and in my sleep every time I close my eyes. If I had flown one more mission, I would have died in peace."

"God kept you alive for a purpose," she said softly.

Teddy straightened abruptly. "God?" he asked in a skeptical tone.

"The war has made me a believer," she answered without hesitation.

"A believer in what?"

"A believer in the God that you now question, a believer in the God of Abraham, Isaac and Jacob, a believer in the God of the chosen people."

"I wish God had chosen someone else," Teddy muttered with more than a trace of bitterness.

"How odd of God to choose the Jews?" She asked, repeating the old doggerel she heard parishioners chant in her churchyard when she was a child. "Not only did God choose the Jews," she continued, "but it was the Jews who chose God."

Teddy wanted to speak, but held back.

"And now I have, too," Patrice continued.

"And just where do you think this choice will take you?" Teddy asked, now more composed.

"Where thou goest, I goest; your people shall be my people; your God shall be my God," Patrice quoted from the Book of Ruth.

"What about your dreams of becoming a dancer?" Teddy asked.

"A youthful passion, tempered by the Depression and war," she said matter-of-factly. "Now my passion is for the commandments."

Teddy looked at her without speaking. He sensed that Patrice needed to talk of her past just as he had done.

"Do you know what my first memory is?" she asked. Teddy's expression didn't change, but she wasn't going to wait for his response even if it had. "I wasn't much more than a baby. A little boy came over to our apartment with his mother. And while his mother talked to mine, the boy showed me a spinning toy. He made me happy. It was the first time in my young life that I had known what it was to be happy."

She paused.

"Do you know who that boy was?" she asked.

Teddy slowly shook his head.

"It was you."

Her answer brought no response from Teddy.

"And do you remember when you drove me to the hotel to deliver your mother's message to Babe Ruth?"

This time Teddy nodded.

"You thought I was flirting with the bellboy?"

Teddy nodded again.

"Well, all the while I was making believe that I was flirting with you. That was the second time in my life that I felt happy."

Teddy didn't know what to say.

"And do you remember when I came to your store to buy a hat for my brother?"

Teddy nodded again.

"I came, not because my brother needed a hat, but because I needed to see you. And you made me happy once again. And one of the happiest times in my entire life was when you took me to the ballgame a few weeks later."

"It was?" Teddy managed to mumble.

Patrice opened her purse, removed a seven year old scorecard, and showed it to Teddy. "You told me this would be worth something some day."

Teddy recognized the scorecard and smiled.

"It was worth more than anything money could buy," Patrice explained. "For seven years it reminded me of that wonderful day that we shared together."

"I had no idea," Teddy said in amazement.

"And the saddest time in my life came that same day—when you told me you had enlisted."

Teddy looked down at his feet, too embarrassed to face Patrice, much less attempt an explanation.

"When I went to bed that night I humbled myself in prayer for the first time in my life. I prayed to your God, the God of Abraham, Isaac and Jacob. I prayed that He bring you home. I said the same prayer every night for the next seven years. And in the course of those prayers I made a bargain with God that I would become a child of the covenant if He delivered you safely home."

Teddy saw Patrice's face radiate with a combination of sincerity and goodness. Nonetheless, he felt compelled to challenge her. "What can Judaism offer you?" he asked. "We are few in numbers, the remnant of our people is scattered throughout the world, we live at the mercy of others, we have no home, we have no protection, we have no peace."

Patrice opened her purse and this time removed a small, soft-covered Bible. Its edges were darkened from use. She raised her eyes from the book and smiled at her betrothed. "I have studied with Rabbi Levy," she said softly. Then she turned to a dog-eared page from Deuteronomy and began to read in a slow, steady voice. "And these are the words that Moses said unto the children of Israel." She gave a quick glance at Teddy, then returned her eyes to the holy book.

"'And ye shall be left few in number ... And the Lord shall scatter thee among all peoples ... And among the nations shall thou have no repose, and there shall be no rest ... and thou shalt have no assurance of thy life.'" Patrice turned the page and began to read again. "And the Lord thy God will curse thine enemies, and on them that hate thee, that persecuted thee ... And the Lord thy God will make thee over-abundant in all the works of thy hand.'"

What does it mean?" Teddy entreated.

"Rabbi Levy taught me that it is a blessing and curse, for us and the world."

Teddy gave Patrice a blank stare, so she went on.

"It is our mission to pursue God's commandments with all our heart, and thereby become a light unto the nations. We are to carry God's law out of Zion so that the rest of the world may know that there are alternatives to violence and hatred, immorality and injustice, vulgarity and blasphemy. If we fulfill our mission our people will be blessed; if not we will be cursed."

"And what of the rest of the world?" Teddy asked. "Are they to become Jews?"

Patrice shook her head. "They are to pursue these alternatives to wickedness, each in their own way. But they are to shine their face kindly onto our people. Their efforts will determine their fate as well."

"How will this be done?" Teddy asked.

"Rabbi Levy believes that God gave the power of the blessing and the power of the curse to someone of his choosing long ago. But how that was done will remain a mystery forever."

"And you believe all this?"

Patrice nodded.

"Why?" he asked.

She looked directly into his eyes and he saw that she was weeping. "Because you are here," she said. "Because you are back."

Teddy began thumbing through the pages of Patrice's Bible until his eye caught a poignant passage, which he hoped would provide her with comfort. He read it aloud. "I have set before thee life and death, the blessing and the curse; therefore choose life..."

"So it is written," said Patrice.

"Then only one further question remains," Teddy observed.

Patrice gave him a hopeful look.

"I have no education; I have no trade; I have no money. For what purpose, then, do you believe God kept me alive?"

"To be fruitful and multiply," she answered with a smile.

"Be fruitful and multiply?"

"It's God's first commandment to man," she grinned.

In his mind's eye Teddy could see a little boy at play. When the child's face morphed into that of an Iowa farm boy, Teddy realized he had discovered his calling. "Though I may not be a success in business, at least I can be successful as a husband and a father," he said to Patrice. "And that will have to be enough."

Patrice immediately began rifling through the pages of the holy book one more time. When she found the passage she had been searching for, she looked hard into Teddy's eyes. Then she began to read:

"After Jacob wrestled with the angel he was told: 'thou hast struggled with God and with man, and hast prevailed.'"

Teddy embraced his betrothed. "Perhaps I have," he whispered in her ear.

PART IV
WRIGLEY FIELD

SHEILA'S KEY

As he did every morning throughout the summer of 1953, seven-year old Shelly Barr sprang out of bed before 7 a.m. By then his father had already left for the store and his mother was in the basement washing clothes on a corrugated scrub board. Shelly threw on a pair of blue jeans with iron-on knee patches, white tee shirt, white cotton socks and black gym shoes whose laces he could now tie. Then he ran to the front door of the family's five-room, brick bungalow and peered out the glass to see if the newspaper had arrived, so he could read about the Cubs. "Phooey," he grumbled, when he did not see the *Sun-Times* lying on the front walk.

Shelly opened the front door anyway, walked out on to the small cement porch, and took a deep breath. The air was already warm and humid, but he felt a refreshing southwesterly breeze. "The wind's blowing out at Wrigley," he smiled. "There'll be some homers today."

Shelly retraced his steps through the living room, whose main furnishings consisted of a red, three-cushioned sofa in front of the bay windows and a cabinet-sized RCA radio that sat flush against the opposite wall. He grabbed his mitt—a Pee Wee Reese model—which was resting on top of the radio, and absent-mindedly began throwing a baseball into the pocket as he walked through the tiny dining room and into the kitchen. He emptied some Cheerios into a glass bowl, and added a tablespoon of sugar. Then he took a quart of milk out of the ice box—really a gas refrigerator—and carefully removed the cardboard cap from the bottle's mouth. Mindful of his mother's admonishment not to waste milk, he poured a small amount into the bowl, and watched with curiosity as the grains of sugar mysteriously disappeared into the liquid. Then he ran back to the front door.

"Ah," he smiled happily when he saw the rolled up, rubber-banded paper sitting on the walk.

He was already aware that the Cubs had won the day before, so reading the paper would be particularly enjoyable. Shelly didn't actually read the paper—he memorized the sports page. He knew the starting line-ups of all sixteen major league teams; he knew the league leaders in home runs, RBI's and batting average; and he knew the stats of every Cub player.

Shelly also had some vague notion that there were things going on in the world other than baseball. He knew, for example, that Cincinnati had changed its name from the Reds to the Redlegs because red was emblematic of a mortal enemy known as the Communists. They were bad people, sort of like those traitors growing up on the north side of Chicago who rooted for the White Sox.

Despite their victory of the day before, the Cubs were mired in seventh place, thirty-three and one half games behind the league-leading Dodgers. The only sliver of a hope was that maybe—just maybe—the Cubs could catch the Redlegs and finish the season in sixth. But that was not meant to be. The Cubs would finish seventh, forty games behind Brooklyn. They had no player who was even in contention for leading the league in any category of hitting, fielding or pitching. The Cubs led the league in only one stat—errors. They committed an astonishing 193 errors—thirty more than the last place Pirates. In Shelly's neighborhood, their double-play combination was called, "Miksis-to-Smalley-to-grandstand."

Before Shelly finished breakfast, his twin sister Sheila wandered into the kitchen, still in her pajamas, rubbing the sleep out of her eyes with her knuckles. She got her box of Rice Krispies, poured some into a bowl, and inched her way into the breakfast nook next to her brother. Shelia was about to dip her spoon into her cereal bowl when she was interrupted by her brother.

"You're using a 'meat' spoon," he warned.

Jewish dietary laws required separate utensils for meat and dairy—a sweeping interpretation of the simple biblical commandment that "Thou shalt not seethe a kid in its mother's milk." It was Patrice—the convert—who insisted on keeping a kosher home in accordance with the ancient laws of her adopted people.

Sheila returned to the breakfast nook with the proper spoon and sidled next to her brother. "Did Fondy get any hits?" she asked looking over Shelly's shoulder.

"Two," Shelly answered quickly. "And Jackson had a single and a homer," he added. Then he pointed to a newspaper photograph of Cub third baseman "Handsome" Ransom Jackson crossing home plate.

Sheila looked at the grainy black and white photo. "He's dreamy," she sighed.

Shelly, of course, also liked Fondy and Jackson, but his favorite player by far was the Cubs' tobacco-chewing left fielder, big number nine, Henry "Hank" Sauer. "Sauer hit one onto Waveland," he beamed. The mere thought of Waveland Avenue made Shelly shiver with joy. "It's my favorite street in Chicago," he said to himself. "But they ought to change the name to Hank Sauer Street."

By then Sheila was bouncing a red rubber ball on the linoleum floor while singing a rhythmic refrain that Shelly had heard countless times before. "'A,' my name is Alice and my husband's name is Alan and we come from Atlanta with a ship load of apples." Each time Sheila said a name that began with the letter "A" she deftly raised her leg over the bouncing ball without hitting it. "'B,' my name is Betty and my husband's name is Bob …" she continued, but by then Shelly had turned his attention back to the newspaper. He was studying a chart bearing the caption "Major's Top Ten." It listed the hits, at-bats, and batting averages of the best players in each league. "Does not include yesterday's games," the chart informed its readers in barely visible print.

Shelly knew—but did not know why—that if a batter got one hit in three at-bats, his average was .333. He also knew that if a batter got two hits in six at-bats then he was still hitting .333. These morsels of knowledge prompted Shelly to remove a pencil from a drawer beneath the telephone, sharpen the point with a kitchen knife, and try to figure out how close Stan Musial's average would be to .333 after going four for four the previous day. After a few minutes, he dropped the pencil in frustration. Sheila, meanwhile, was still bouncing her ball.

"'R,' my name is Ruth and my husband's name is Ralph and we come from … Rhode Island," Sheila blurted at the last second so as not to miss a beat, " … with a shipload of … rats."

"Rats," Shelly interrupted, causing Sheila to lose her concentration, and hit the ball with her leg just as she began the Esses. "You should have said 'rice.'"

Sheila picked up the ball and threw it at her brother. It missed Shelly, but hit the milk bottle, knocking it over and spilling most of its contents.

"You better not tell," Sheila threatened as she ran to the sink to get a rag so she could begin sopping up the mess.

"I won't tell," Shelly promised. "At least you don't throw like a girl."

Sheila smiled. She knew that was the highest compliment her brother could give her.

By the time Sheila had rinsed out the rag and put it in the sink, Shelly had grabbed his mitt and a sponge rubber ball and flown out the door. A moment later he was imitating the wind -up of the Cubs best pitcher, Bob Rush, by throwing his ball against the common brick wall of the six-flat apartment building that was next door. After a few other boys had joined him, they ceased taking turns pitching Shelly's ball against the wall, and started a game of line ball in the alley. After a few innings, several other boys—many as old as nine or ten—had congregated in the alley. En masse they adjourned to the schoolyard, which was two blocks away. There they met with other neighborhood kids to do what they did every morning—play baseball.

The two boys whom everyone acknowledged to be the best players immediately became team captains. One threw a bat in the air, which the second boy caught one-handed with the nub of the bat facing up. The captains alternated putting a hand, then a finger, up the bat handle until the second boy called "crow's feet." He then gripped the handle nub, talon-like, with the tips of his fingers. When his counterpart failed to kick the bat out of the second boy's hand, the second boy had first pick in selecting his team. The captains alternated picks until every one was chosen. Even though he was the youngest in the group, Shelly was not chosen as quickly as he thought he should have been.

"They'll regret it," he mumbled under his breath.

The game was tied going into the bottom of the seventh—and last—inning. Though Shelly had cleanly fielded all the balls that came his way, he had failed to reach base in three at-bats.

When he came up with two outs and nobody on, the opposing catcher—who was two years his senior—was quick to remind Shelly of his ineptitude at the plate. "No hits today, Jew boy?" Swede Torberg taunted.

Swede Torberg was big, but had hands like rocks. The pitcher, Dummy Dumant, was even bigger, and just as clumsy. Dummy's nickname was not derived from his last name or his stupidity, but because he had difficulty speaking. Shelly knew that Swede and Dummy had something else in common besides their size and lack of coordination; they were bullies and Jew-haters.

Shelly squeezed the handle of his bat as if he were trying to wring water from a damp rag, but otherwise ignored Swede's slur. Then he surveyed the field. The infielders played in front of the base paths, and the outfielders were disrespectfully shallow. Out of the corner of his eye Shelly also noticed that the first baseman—in his arrogance—was positioned well off the bag, and the right fielder was playing too far toward center.

Shelly took his stance in the batter's box two inches further from the plate than usual. On the first pitch, he put his right foot in the bucket, and took a smooth, level swing. He saw the ball jump off his bat and scoot down the first base line, just inside the bag. When the ball reached the dry, sun-hardened outfield grass, it seemed to accelerate—separating itself rapidly from the mis-positioned right fielder. By then, Shelly was sprinting toward second.

As he rounded second and sped toward third, Shelly could hear nothing but incoherent screams and vulgarities. He looked for a third base coach, but saw only a group of teammates who still had their eyes trained toward right field. The third baseman was well off the bag, not expecting a throw. Shelly knew it wasn't a decoy, so he made a split-second decision. He tilted his body toward the infield, touched the inside corner of the bag with his outside foot, and ran with all his might for home.

Pitcher Dummy Dumont was standing in the base path, grunting audibly. His arms were extended like a linebacker readying himself for a tackle. Shelly feinted left but Dummy didn't move. A collision was imminent. A moment before impact, however, one of Shelly's teammates lunged at the opposing pitcher and knocked him down; punches immediately began flying. Shelly leaped over the combatants only to see Swede Torberg blocking the plate and awaiting the relay throw home.

Shelly saw the approaching ball out of the corner of his eye. It was going to reach Torberg a moment before he did. He lowered his shoulder and rammed into the catcher. For a fleeting second Shelly saw the ball in Torberg's hands. Then, just as quickly, he saw it fall to the ground. Shelly fell to the ground as well, dazed. Instinctively, however, he extended his left hand and slapped it on to home plate in one glorious moment of exultation.

Shelly's joy was short-lived. Torberg leaped at him, cursing gutter profanities. Shelly scooped up a handful of gravel, and was about to fling it at his assailant, when several of the bigger guys from both teams held Torberg back. Within a few minutes the brouhaha came to an end, and the game's participants began melting away. As a parting shot, Swede Torberg shook an angry fist at Shelly. "You haven't seen the last of this," he threatened.

Shelly was scared but not intimidated. He left the playground happy and upbeat after his game-winning homer. Then reality set in. "I'd trade it all for a Cub pennant," he said wistfully.

Halfway home, Shelly saw his sister on a street corner jumping rope with a group of girls. A pile of clamp-on roller skates lay on a tiny plot of grass near where they were playing. Hopscotch diagrams were drawn on the adjacent sidewalk with colored chalk.

Shelly tried to conceal amazement as each girl took her turn jumping between oppositely spinning ropes in a game the girls called "Double Dutch." At that moment, Sheila's best friend, Lillian Greenberg was jumping gracefully as the others chanted one of their rhythmic "girl" songs. Lillian's pigtails were flying madly and her round cheeks were beet red from the eighty-five degree heat and ninety percent humidity.

Shelly secretly liked Lillian and wondered whether his sister knew. On the other hand, he had figured out that Sheila had a crush on his friend Howard Weiss, so he resigned himself to the fact that Sheila somehow knew that he liked Lillian. He would have been shocked, however, if he knew that Sheila and Lillian had secretly talked about Shelly's infatuation on numerous occasions, and had already decided that they would one day become sisters-in-law.

When Sheila caught her brother's eye, Shelly immediately looked away. Then, just as quickly, he looked back. "Time for lunch," he called out, walking past the girls without looking at any of them.

Sheila caught up with her brother in an instant.

The "key" Sheila used to tighten and loosen her roller skates dangled from a shoelace which she, like all the other girls, wore around her neck like a necklace. It bounced against her chest when she ran. As the twins neared their bungalow, Sheila nervously fingered her key. Then, suddenly, her expression became pained. "My skates," she blurted.

Shelly and Sheila looked back at the street corner from which they came. All the girls were gone, and the pile of skates had disappeared. Immediately Shelly took off for the corner in a full sprint. Like her twin brother, Sheila had a limber, athletic body. She followed close at his heels. "Mom's gonna kill me," she wailed.

Luckily the skates were still there, camouflaged by the weeds. Shelly picked them up and gave them to his sister. Then, despite the heavy heat, they raced each other back to their bungalow.

Plotkin's Number

Patrice was toasting American cheese sandwiches on a frying pan when Shelly and Sheila raced in, their faces shiny with perspiration. She put the sandwiches on a plate, along with some potato chips taken from an enormous cylindrical tin that bore the name "Jays" in blue script. Then she poured each of them a tall, cold glass of milk. "I thought I told you not to waste the milk," she scolded, looking directly at Shelly.

Sheila shot her brother a glance, but it was unnecessary. "Sorry," Shelly apologized.

But Patrice wasn't listening. She had something more important on her mind. "I don't want either of you running out after lunch," she warned. "You've got to rest until ... " she looked up at the kitchen clock which said 12:20. "Until one thirty," she ordered.

"It's polio season," Sheila mouthed to her brother, anticipating her mother's next words.

"I borrowed some books from the library, and I put them on your bed," Patrice continued. "I want both of you reading for at least an hour. It's polio season."

Shelly dutifully went into the bedroom and found a book entitled "Chicago Cubs-From Depression to World War" resting against his pillow. It was in those pages that he learned of the exploits of such Cub standouts as Stan Hack, Phil Cavaretta, Bill "Swish" Nicholson, and Andy Pafko. "The last pennant that they won was the year before I was born," he thought. Then he made a wish that he would repeat daily throughout his childhood. "I hope they win one before I die."

On the bed next to her brother's, Patrice had placed a book about two young girls called "The Bobsey Twins." Sheila left the room before reading the first page, and walked into the living room where her mother was listening to a soap opera while darning socks.

"I don't want to read," she groaned.

"Sit with me and I'll teach you how to sew," Patrice suggested.

Sheila's face brightened.

An hour later, Shelly emerged from the room, and scowled when he saw his mother and sister eagerly awaiting the next soap opera.

"The Cub game starts in a couple of minutes," he complained.

Sheila looked at her Mom, wondering whose side she'd take in this potential disagreement.

"I need some white bread," Patrice said without hesitation. Why don't you listen to the game at Howard's house, and pick up a loaf of bread for me on the way home."

She removed some coins from her purse, and handed them to her son. Shelly was out the door in a flash. "There's an extra nickel in there for you," she yelled a moment before the front door slammed.

Shelly purchased the bread first. Then he went to "Plotkin's" candy store and bought a "six pack" of baseball cards. He placed a nickel on Mr. Plotkin's glass counter. "Hope you get a Hank Sauer," Plotkin said with a distinctly European accent as he reached for the coin.

Shelly looked over the glass counter and smiled as Mr. Plotkin handed him the pack of baseball cards.

Plotkin had a faded tattoo on his forearm. It wasn't a design, but a number. Shelly knew how the number got there and it made him shudder. A moment later he smiled with pride. "Now the Nazis are dead, Germany is cut in half, and the Jews have a country of their own," he said to himself. "Serves 'em right." Then he turned his eyes toward his six-pack of cards. Slowly and carefully he removed the colorful waxy wrapper. On top of the pile of cards was a slab of pink bubble gum which Shelly immediately popped into his mouth. Then he looked with great anticipation at the treasure that awaited him.

The first card was Eddie Mathews of the Braves. "Got him,"

Shelly mumbled. Then came Ralph Kiner of the Pirates. "Got him," he repeated to himself. Kiner was followed by—the name at first gave him a start—Hank Bauer of the Yankees.

Mr. Plotkin thought his young customer had struck gold. "It's Hank *Bauer*, not Sauer," Shelly grimaced. Shelly grimaced again when he saw the next card: "Nellie Fox of the Smelly Sox," he groaned. Then came Jackie Robinson and a young outfielder from the New York Yankees by the name of Mickey Mantle.

"Anything good," Plotkin asked?

"Jackie Robinson," Shelly answered, but I already got two of him. With that he stuffed the six cards into his pocket, indifferent to the fact that five of them were future Hall of Famers, and if his mother hadn't thrown his entire card collection away when he went off to college, they could have paid for the first year of his own son's college tuition thirty years later.

Shelly had two pennies left in his pocket. "I'll have a red licorice and a bulls-eye," he told Mr. Plotkin. He threw the penny candies into the sack containing the bread. An instant later he was off to his friend's house. A familiar voice came over the radio. "We don't care who wins as long as it's the Cubs," Burt Wilson began.

As they listened to the game, the boys thumbed through Howard's baseball card collection and played dice baseball. In the process, Shelly traded his triplicate Jackie Robinson and his Mickey Mantle for a nickel and a Phil Cavaretta. When the Cubs fell far behind, they went outside and began playing "pinners"—a made-up variation of baseball requiring one boy to throw a rubber ball against the front steps in an effort to have it rebound over the head of the other for a home run. Within minutes two other boys materialized on the sidewalk and the "pinners" game expanded into a team game of two-on-two.

After the game ended, Shelly and Howard went back inside and shared a Coca-Cola—wiping the top of the bottle with their palms as they alternated sips. Shelly pulled his red licorice apart and gave the larger half to his friend. He saved the bulls-eye for himself, to eat on the way home. An electric fan in the living-room stirred up a sufficient breeze to keep them from sweating in the Weiss' hot, humid apartment.

Somewhere about the seventh inning Shelly suggested that maybe the Cubs would win the game if they both took a blood oath of loyalty. Howard immediately disappeared into his parents' bedroom, emerging a few moments later with a needle taken from his mother's sewing box.

"This should work," he said, handing the needle to Shelly.

Shelly tapped the point of the needle against his finger tip and nodded his agreement. Then each pricked his left index finger, touched their bleeding fingers together, and simultaneously swore everlasting allegiance to their Chicago team.

It didn't help. The Cubs lost to the Phillies ten to six, four of the Philly runs being unearned. Smalley and Miksis each made a costly error, and Hank Sauer went hitless. Shelly knew that the story of the game in the morning paper would be no fun to read.

After the game, Shelly left his friend's apartment, popped a bulls-eye in his mouth and walked home dejectedly. When he fingered Howard's nickel in the pocket of his blue jeans, however, he detoured to Plotkin's to buy another six-pack of baseball cards. He didn't notice Swede Torberg and Dummy Dumont loitering outside the entrance of the store until it was too late.

"Hey, Jew boy," Torberg taunted.

Dummy grunted something in an attempt to echo his friend's words. Then he snaked behind Shelly and put the younger boy in a full-nelson. Shelly's arms dangled helplessly in the air.

"This is what we do to Christ-killers," Torberg growled. "Christ-killers," he repeated. Then he reached back and thrust an angry fist hard into Shelly's gut. Shelly felt the remnant of his lunch pushed out of his stomach and up into this throat until he almost vomited. Swede reached back to hit Shelly again, but suddenly a forearm with a faded tattoo wrapped tightly around Swede's jugular and stopped him in mid-swing.

Torberg gagged, but Plotkin did not loosen his hold on the boy's neck. Instead, Plotkin glared at the bigger boy who was restraining Shelly. "Let him go," Plotkin ordered in heavily accented English. Dummy immediately released his grip.

With his free hand, Plotkin motioned Shelly to step aside. Then he seized Dummy by the throat as well. "I know where you live," Plotkin threatened. "If any Jewish child in this neighborhood is ever bullied again, I will assume you did it. I will come into your house at night. I will strangle you to death with my bare hands."

The two boys shuddered.

"Strangle you to death!" Plotkin repeated.

The boys shuddered again, certain that Plotkin was not bluffing.

Plotkin spat on the ground. "You are filth," he said through pursed lips and grinding teeth. Then he waived his fist at them. "Filth," he repeated. "Now get out of my sight."

The boys ran off without looking back.

Shelly looked up at the shopkeeper and began to sob. "You could go to jail, Mr. Plotkin; you could lose everything," he sniffed.

Plotkin patted Shelly gently on the head. "I already have," he said to himself. Then he patted the boy on the head once more and told him, "Go home now, and don't worry about me. You're only a boy. Worry about your Cubs instead."

Swede Torberg and Dummy Dumont never bothered Shelly again. And by month's end, Shelly's worries had indeed returned to his beloved Cubs.

Two weeks later a short, inconspicuous blurb in the sport's section gave Shelly genuine cause for optimism. The Cubs were bringing a promising second baseman named Gene Baker up from the minors. What the article didn't say was that, because he was a Negro, the Cubs were desperately looking for a roommate for Baker. It was for this reason that the team later obtained the rights to a lanky shortstop from the Negro League by the name of Ernie Banks.

PIEPER'S ANNOUNCEMENT

On the last school day of March in 1957, eleven-year old Greg Tover peeled out the door the moment the dismissal bell rang. A heavy morning rain cleaned away all the dirt that the harsh winter had left behind, leaving a distinct aroma of spring in the crisp Chicago air. Greg tied the sleeves of his jacket around his waist and ran for home. Halfway there he heard the "smack" of a ball, followed immediately by the sonorous sound of a wooden bat dropping onto the street. "Someone's already playing," he beamed. He quickened his pace to the intersection where the first pick-up game of the spring had already begun.

As far as Greg was concerned, there were only three seasons in Chicago: baseball season, football season, and the dead time between Christmas and Easter. Though Greg's family followed the Orthodox tradition of celebrating Christmas in January according to the old calendar, the dead time seemed interminable. Greg tried to accelerate winter's end by stomping on the ice after the first thaw, and then shoveling the slush into the sewer at the street corner near his house. Now that sewer was serving as "home plate" for the neighborhood's first game of the new season.

Greg turned glum, however, when he reached the corner. Three or four boys who were a couple of years older than he were waiting for their turn at bat; an equal number of older boys were out in the "field," which, in Greg's neighborhood, meant the street. "The big guys will never let me play," he groaned to himself. But then yet another older boy showed up, and joined the team that was out in the field. "Red" Collins, the captain of the team that was then at bat, turned toward Greg and gave him an authoritative look. "You're up next," he ordered.

On the first pitch, Greg singled off the fender of an Oldsmobile that had the misfortune of being parked on the field. "This is a good sign," Greg thought as he took his lead off of the first base sewer. "The Cubs are going to win the pennant."

Unfortunately, 1957 would not be a good year for the Cubs. They finished in last place, a pathetic thirty games below .500. The only bright spot was Ernie Banks. He hit forty-three home runs, one behind league leader Hank Aaron, and finished third in RBI's with 102. Every kid on the north side was aware of Ernie's upright bat position, and nervous fingers which twitched on the bat handle as he waited for a pitch.

Once the season began, Greg would race home from school to watch the last few innings of the Cub game on the family's twelve inch Admiral television set. Even before the picture tube warmed up, Greg could tell instantly from the tone of Jack Brickhouse's voice, or the background noise of the crowd, whether the Cubs were ahead or behind. Invariably they were behind. Nonetheless, Greg refused to give up hope that somehow, some way, the Cubs might salvage a victory. For that reason, he never turned off the game until the final out was made, and Jack Brickhouse reported "the unhappy totals" to his die-hard audience.

In the evenings, Greg would listen to the "away" games on the Motorola that rested on his nightstand. The announcer, Jack Quinlan, seemed like part of the family. Quinlan described balls bouncing onto the pavilion at St. Louis' Sportsman's Park, the laundry at Cincinnati's Crosley Field, and the light towers at Pittsburgh's Forbes Field. Greg often fell asleep wondering what those ballpark landmarks actually looked like.

Greg had only one worry in life. It was not death; it was not taxes; it was not the Russians. It was an obsessive fear that the Cubs might move out of Chicago. Despite the incomparable loyalty of its north side fan base, attendance at Wrigley Field had dipped below 700,000—second worst in the league. This dip in attendance was attributed, at least in part, to the fact that Wrigley Field was the only Major League baseball park without lights. Greg knew, however, that throughout the '30's and '40's, during war and the Depression, attendance was far higher than it was now.

Unfortunately, many Cub games during the late summer of the year had a paid attendance of fewer than 3,000 people. Even worse, the crosstown White Sox were playing good ball and drawing large crowds. People were asking whether Chicago was big enough to support two Major League teams. It made Greg hate the rival White Sox more than ever.

Most disconcerting were the persistent rumors throughout the summer that the Dodgers might abandon Brooklyn. "If the Dodgers could leave Brooklyn, the Cubs could leave Chicago," Greg worried. In his mind, there was only one solution: "Cub fans just need to go to more games."

It was partly for this reason that Greg was elated when Red Collins told him it would be okay for him to tag along that afternoon when a group of the "big guys" were taking the El to Wrigley Field. Grace Tover was skeptical about giving Greg permission. The trip to the ballpark was complicated and non-intuitive—requiring the boys to take the Ravenswood El southeast, then transfer to the Howard El which went due north; going home they'd have to take the Howard El south, then transfer to the Ravenswood El going northwest.

Eventually, Grace succumbed to her son's pleas and packed him a bologna sandwich, some chips and a few home-made cookies. Then she reached into her purse and gave Greg a crumpled dollar bill: ten cents for each trip on the El, sixty cents for a bleacher seat ticket, ten cents for a Coke, and ten cents for a bag of peanuts. Greg grabbed his mitt—a Mickey Mantle model—and raced out the door. "Don't let Red out of your sight," Grace hollered as the screen door slammed.

When the boys got off the El at Addison Street, they were greeted by a billboard which pictured a huge bar of orange soap above a tag line which read "The Cubs use Lifebouy." Underneath the tag line were four words of graffiti: "And they still stink."

"Must have been a Sox fan," Greg concluded as he followed the boys down the steps and out of the station.

They got to the game in time for batting practice. Red Collins, the unelected leader of the group, promptly caught a batting practice homer off the bat of Cub utility infielder Jerry Kindall. Kindall was hitting about .150 and led the team in errors. "Throw it back, throw it back," one of the other boys began to chant. All of the others immediately joined in the chorus.

Red Collins looked at the ball, looked at his buddies, and mumbled, "What the hell." Then he wound up and threw the ball back onto the field. It rolled almost all the way to third base. The fans who had congregated in the left field bleachers roared their approval.

That was the most exciting play of the day. Cub starter Dick Drott, the league leader in yielding bases on balls, walked six batters in four and two-thirds innings, giving up eight runs in the process. The Cubs eventually lost twelve to three.

After the game, the boys remained in the bleachers, turning empty cardboard beer cups upside down, and stomping on them until they "popped," like a bursting balloon. It took Greg several tries to get the hang of it, but soon enough he was gleefully "popping" away. When he next looked up, he was shocked to find that Red and the guys were gone.

Greg raced out of the ballpark and ran toward the El station looking in vain for his neighborhood friends. Through the crowd, he saw a big red head that was standing on the platform several layers of people ahead of him. Greg knifed his way onto the same car, only to discover that the red head was not Collins. When he saw the Lifebouy billboard through the window of the moving train, he knew he was going north instead of south.

Greg did not panic. Knowing that his apartment building was on the 5200 block of North Sherman, he decided to take the northbound train as far north as he lived. He'd then have to walk west until he got home—how far that would be, he did not know.

When the train stopped at a station that said "Foster Avenue—5200 North," Greg got off. He found himself in a strange, unfamiliar neighborhood. A squad car was parked at the curb in front of the station. An officer was sitting at the wheel smoking a cigarette.

"I think I'm lost," Greg told the policeman.

"Where do you live?" the officer asked unsympathetically.

Greg told him his address.

"It's three miles that way," the officer said, pointing in the direction of the sun. "Now you're not lost," he snickered.

Greg saw a telephone handset in the squad car. "Can I make a call?" he asked.

The policeman turned the ignition key, and the car's engine sprang to life. "Do I look like a phone booth?" the officer laughed. Then he put the vehicle into gear and roared off without looking back.

Greg watched the squad car screech around a corner. When it disappeared, he resigned himself to the long, lonely walk that lay ahead, and the paddling he would certainly receive the minute he arrived home. Immediately he began thinking up excuses. About a half hour into his hike, and lost in thought, he failed to notice four ruffians sitting on a pile of dirt near a home construction site whose basement excavation had filled with rainwater during the fierce thunderstorm of the night before. One of those ruffians was a tall, angular kid with dark hair and a pale complexion named Bucky Drake.

Moments earlier, Drake had captured a stray kitten that he found in the alley, threw the terrified creature into a potato sack, and was threatening to drown it in the water-filled excavation. Drake looked up and spotted a thin, swarthy kid walking forlornly down his street. "There's an easy mark," he said, prodding his buddies into action. A moment later they surrounded Greg Tover, and began taunting him. The boy's fear only emboldened them further.

Bucky grabbed Greg's baseball mitt and raised it high over his head.

"What are you doing with my glove," Bucky challenged.

"It's mine," Greg whined.

"Not anymore," Bucky sneered.

Bucky's sycophants sneered as well.

"Give it back," Greg pleaded.

One of the ruffians put Greg in a hammer-lock. "What should we do with him?" he asked.

"Let's see if he can swim," suggested another. Two of the bullies then began pushing Greg in the direction of the water-filled excavation.

Greg was now on the verge of tears. "Let me go," he screamed.

Despite Greg's screams and struggles, the bigger boys wrestled him toward the edge of the water. But then they the heard the familiar bells of a Good Humor "man" approaching their street. The Good Humor man was actually a teenager trying to earn a few bucks during the summer by selling ice cream. He rode a bicycle-like contraption, the front end of which contained a dry-ice freezer filled with ice-cream bars, and other treats known as Popsicles, Creamsicles and Dreamsicles.

"See if he has any money," Bucky ordered.

Greg was quickly frisked, but nothing was found.

One of the ruffians glanced longingly in the direction of the bells. "We're gonna miss him," he moaned as the jingling became louder. The others gave Drake a desperate look that begged him to let them run off and buy ice cream.

"I'll take it from here," Drake responded.

The others pushed Greg to the ground, and ran in the direction of the jingling bells.

Drake looked down at the dirty, whimpering boy. "Are you a Cub fan or a Sox fan?" he growled.

Greg and his gang of friends had asked that same question to every new kid who appeared in their schoolyard. Now he knew what it felt like to be on the receiving end of such naked intimidation.

"A Cub fan," Greg answered, certain that his tormentor was one of those north side traitors who rooted for the Sox, and that he was about to pay a heavy price for his Wrigley loyalty.

"Prove it," Drake snarled.

"The Cubs lost twelve to three; Drott gave up eight runs, seven of them earned. Banks went for the collar."

"What's Banks' average?" Drake barked.

".288," Greg responded quickly. "He's got thirty-six homers and ninety-one RBI's so far," Greg added for good measure.

Drake wasn't impressed. "Everyone knows that," he sneered. "Tell me something everybody doesn't know."

Greg didn't hesitate. "In order to 'pop' an empty beer cup, you've got to stomp on it with your heel, not the middle of your foot." Greg looked anxiously at his tormentor.

"What else?" Drake demanded, but his voice didn't sound as threatening.

"The fans in left field are called bleacher bums. When a foul tip lands on the screen behind home plate, everyone yells, 'whoooooop' when it starts to roll back down." Greg could see a hint of a smile on Drake's face, so he just kept talking. "And 'boom' when the batboy catches it. There's a beer man in the left field boxes named 'Gravel Gurdy,' who yells 'Cooooold Beer.' Before the game, a guy named Pat Pieper announces the line-ups."

"What does he say?" challenged Drake.

Greg knew the answer: "'tention, tention, please.'"

"What else?"

"'Have your pencils and scorecards ready, and I'll give you the correct line-up for today's game.'"

Drake was convinced. "Get out of here," he ordered gruffly, curling his lip for emphasis.

Greg dusted himself off and nervously started walking away.

"Hey kid," Drake yelled after Greg had left the excavation site and reached the sidewalk.

Greg turned around, stricken with fear. A second later his Mickey Mantle mitt came flying through the air in his direction. Greg grabbed it with both hands. "Nice catch," Drake muttered.

RON'S LEAP

Ernie Banks took his place in the pantheon of baseball superstars that emerged during the 1950's. Unlike Mays, Aaron, Clemente and Mantle, however, Banks did not play on a pennant winner, much less win a world championship. Nonetheless, a genuine love affair blossomed between Banks and the baby boom generation of Cub fans that now extended from the north side of Chicago, far into the suburbs that were gobbling up the Midwestern prairie.

Unfortunately, the decade embracing 1957 to 1966 would prove to be a particularly miserable one for the Chicago Cubs. No team ever played worse in a ten year span except, of course, the Cubs of the previous ten years. This led one baseball insider to conclude that Cub fans are the best in baseball. "They gotta be," added another.

Greg Tover, Shelly Barr, and the hundreds of thousands of other post-war Cub fans took this quip, not as a slight, but as a badge of honor. "Today's misery will only make our World Series victory that much sweeter," they commiserated. It seemed, however, that no spike of joy would ever interrupt the misery that these loyal Cub fans were destined to endure.

Of the 154 games they played in 1957, the Cubs managed to lose ninety-two of them. One of those was a 4–3 loss to the Dodgers on August 28th. It was the last game the Cubs would play at venerable

Ebbets Field. By then the Dodger ownership had decided to move the franchise to Los Angeles, and began acquiring land for a new ballpark in a place just east of downtown called Chavez Ravine.

In 1958 Banks hit .313, pounding out forty-seven homers and driving in 129 runs. He was the National League's Most Valuable Player. And for the first time in decades the Cubs actually led the league in an important offensive category: they walloped a team record 182 home runs. Nonetheless, they finished in fifth place, a hopeless twenty games behind the league-leading Milwaukee Braves.

The Cubs did no better in the standings the following year. Even worse, the Sox won the pennant and played the Los Angeles Dodgers in the World Series. This presented Cub fans with a dilemma. Although they had a genetic loathing for the White Sox, they hated Los Angeles even more. After all, these were the interlopers who stole a team out of Brooklyn. And what right did they have to host a World Series after only two years of existence, when Cub fans had rooted so hard, and waited so long, but had nothing to show for their efforts except misery?

In the aftermath of the 1959 debacle, Phil Wrigley told the press that there should be relief managers just like relief pitchers. For this reason he called Jolly Charlie Grimm out of retirement and appointed him manager for the 1960 season. Grimm lasted seventeen games before Wrigley abruptly had him switch places with the Cubs' radio announcer, and former All-Star, Lou Boudreau.

It became an interesting topic of conversation in Chicago's north side bars who was worse at the other's job. Though Grimm couldn't speak an intelligible sentence from the broadcast booth, Boudreau guided the Cubs to a seventh place finish, a whopping thirty-five games behind the formerly hapless Pirates. It was a dreadful realization for the Wrigley faithful that every team could make a full circle from futility to success except the Cubs. By season's end, fans began asking themselves whether the team was cursed.

One snowy evening in 1960, shortly before Christmas, Shelly Barr and his twin sister Sheila were throwing snowballs at trees outside their red brick bungalow. Shelly pointed to a huge elm that stood naked and forlorn against the overcast sky.

"If I hit that tree ten times in a row, the Cubs will win the pennant next year," Shelly told Sheila.

Shelly hit the tree with six straight snow balls before missing.

"Try again," Sheila urged.

On his second effort Shelly missed the tree on his fourth throw, but decided to try one more time. It was at that moment that Patrice stuck her head out the door and yelled to the twins that dinner was ready. Shelly ignored his mom. He got up to seven in a row, but missed on his eighth attempt. "My turn," Sheila told Shelly, just at Patrice again opened the front door and yelled, "Dinner!"

Sheila never hit the tree after several throws, so Shelly took over. When Shelly reached nine in a row he felt he was on the threshold of making Cub history. Shelly packed the tenth snowball carefully, took steady aim and wound up for the decisive pitch.

"Dinner!" Patrice yelled impatiently, a split-second before Shelly released the snowball. The snowball flew a foot to the left of its mark.

"That one doesn't count," Sheila rationalized.

Shelly nodded and quickly made another snowball.

"Come in this second, or there's no dinner!" Patrice threatened.

For the first time Shelly looked in the direction of his mom. "If I come in now, the Cubs won't win the pennant," he answered curtly. He then threw another snowball at the elm, but it missed its target by a wide margin.

At the start of the 1961 season, Phil Wrigley astonished the baseball world when he announced that, henceforth, the Cubs would not have a manager, but would be led by a so-called "College of Coaches." This resulted in a revolving door leadership which, in turn, after turn, produced a seventh place finish. When, in 1962, the league expanded to ten teams with the addition of the Houston Colt 45's and the New York Mets, the Cubs amassed 103 losses, good for ninth place—and an incredible forty-two and one-half games out of first. The next year Phil Wrigley, apparently thinking he was provost of some kind of baseball college, hired an athletic director and a head coach to run the Cubs. The team responded with another seventh place finish.

By 1964, however, the Cubs had the core of a competitive team.

Revered Ernie Banks was now at first base, fan-favorite Ron Santo was at third, sweet-swinging Billy Williams had become a fixture in left field, and two potential stars appeared on the Wrigley firmament. One was second baseman Ken Hubbs, who had earned rookie of the year honors the year before, and the other was a speedy right fielder by the name of Lou Brock.

Less than six months into the year, two events prompted Cub fans to openly discuss the possibility that the team was cursed. The first event occurred just before spring training when Hubbs tragically died in a plane crash while flying his Cessna through a Utah snowstorm. The second occurred on June 15th, when the Cubs traded Lou Brock to the St. Louis Cardinals for Ernie Broglio—a transaction which Cub fans regard as the worst player trade in the history of Major League baseball. Brock would play fifteen more years, accumulating over 3000 hits and 938 stolen bases in his Hall of Fame career. Broglio would go 7–19 over three seasons for the Cubs, while compiling a dreadful 5.40 ERA.

The Cubs followed their eighth place finish in 1964 with another eighth place finish in 1965. By then, Phil Wrigley had enough— he hired a tough, abrasive manager by the name of Leo "the Lip" Durocher. Upon looking at his 1966 roster, which included long-time Cub stalwarts Banks, Santo and Williams, a talented double-play duo of Don Kessinger and Glenn Beckert, catcher Randy Hundley, and pitchers Fergie Jenkins, Ken Holtzman and Bill Hands, Durocher remarked that this was no eighth place club. The Lip proved to be correct. The Cubs finished the season in tenth place.

Despite the last place finish, Cub fans continued to support their team. For the first time in over twenty years, their loyalty was rewarded. The Cubs soared to third place in 1967, and finished third again in 1968. By the following spring, the Wrigley loyalists accepted on faith Ernie Banks' optimistic prediction that the Cubs would shine in '69.

True to Ernie's prediction, the Cubs started strong. By June 25th they were in first place with a record of 46–25. That was a sufficient reason for Shelly Barr and his cousin, Greg Tover, to play hooky from work on the very next day. Their decision was rewarded when, in the bottom of the tenth, Cub right fielder, Jim Hickman, hit a walk-off homer to defeat the Pittsburgh Pirates. As the Cub players trotted playfully down the left field foul line toward their clubhouse door, Ron

Santo got caught up in the emotional "high" that gripped the capacity crowd of deliriously happy Cub fans. When he reached the bullpen, Santo impulsively leaped into the air and clicked his heels. Then he did so again. And then again. The fans acknowledged each leap with enthusiastic cheers. Such unrestrained joy was a rare experience for both Cub players and their long-suffering fans.

Two weeks later, Theo Merkle took his wife, Chen, and their 21-one year old son, Franklin, to a Cubs-Mets game at Shea Stadium. The Cubs took a 3–1 lead when Hickman homered in the Cubs' half of the eighth. Meanwhile Fergie Jenkins was breezing into the ninth with a one-hitter when Don Clendenon pinch hit with one on and one out. He lofted a routine fly to center which Cub center fielder, Don Young, misjudged for a tainted double.

Mets fans instantly sprung to life. When Tommy Agee doubled home two runs to tie the game, the noise became so loud it seemed that the stadium would collapse. One out later, the Merkles thought the game was headed into extra innings when Ed Kranepool popped a short fly to center. Inexplicably Don Young was nowhere to be seen, and the ball dropped softly onto the outfield grass for the game-winning hit.

"Ya gotta believe," yelled Theo.

"Ya gotta believe," Frank echoed.

But the Cubs regained their equilibrium. On the evening of July 20th, when Major League baseball took its annual All Star break, and Neil Armstrong took man's first walk on the moon, the Cubs were back on top of the world. They had just swept the Phillies in a doubleheader, giving them a record of 61–37—best in the National League. They had won seven of their last ten games. They were a full five games ahead of the Mets in the National League-East standings. To the delight of Cub fans everywhere, long-time favorites Banks, Beckert, Hundley, Kessinger and Santo were selected to the 1969 All Star team. And none of those fans could have ever been convinced that Williams and Jenkins didn't deserve to be All Stars as well.

When the regular season resumed, the Cubs went on a tear, winning fourteen of their next twenty games. By August 13th they stood atop the National League standings, eight and one-half games in front of the Cardinals and nine and one-half games ahead of the Mets.

Santo was back to clicking his heels after each Cub victory and relief pitcher Dick Selma could be found coordinating cheers by the left field bleacher bums during the game. Even hometown announcers Jack Brickhouse and Vince Lloyd had taken up singing a newly composed pennant chant entitled "Hey, Hey, Holy Mackerel," based on their respective, on-the-air exclamations following Cub homers.

Then disaster struck. Over the next month and a half, the Mets would win an amazing thirty-eight of their remaining forty-nine ball games. In the same period the Cubs won nineteen and lost twenty-seven. Each day brought such heartache that by season's end, the entire North Side of Chicago was in a state of shock. Never, since their founding in 1876, had a season ended on such a sad, gut-wrenching, heart-breaking, tear-shedding, emotion-draining "low."

GREG'S THEORY

Shelly Barr had been working as an engineer for a medical products company ever since he graduated from college in 1967. Four years later the job had brought him into contact with physicians, attorneys, and businessmen, many of whom carried mobile pagers. All of these pager subscribers had the same complaint: the batteries died out too quickly. Though the pager industry was trying to remedy this problem by developing extended-life batteries, Shelly believed that a more promising solution lay in a pager design that used less energy.

Shelly was thinking about the problem one night while driving home from the office. As usual, he had been working late—so late that the streets were empty and the traffic lights were set to blink red instead of cycle through their familiar tri-color sequence. After proceeding through an intersection, Shelly was transfixed by the blinking red light that was flashing in his rear view mirror. It was then that the idea for an electronic battery-saving circuit hit him.

"The circuits inside the pager don't have to remain 'on' all the time," he said to himself. "They only have to be 'on' long enough to recognize the paging signal transmitted from the mobile base station." Shelly glanced at the flashing traffic signal in his rear view mirror for reassurance. "If the circuits blinked 'on' for only a small fraction of each second, the pager could recognize the incoming signal just as if it had been continuously 'on.' But battery life could be extended by ten, maybe even a hundred times," he concluded.

No sooner had the blinking red light faded from view, then Shelly's optimism faded as well. "How can I ever get the battery-saving circuit inside an existing pager?" he thought. "No subscriber is going to open up his pager and solder an after-market circuit in place." Shelly struggled with the problem the rest of the way home, but could not devise a solution. As he pulled into his driveway, he decided to talk over his idea with his cousin, Greg Tover. "Greg will know what to do," Shelly thought. "He's a genius when it comes to working with metal."

Greg Tover devised an answer almost immediately: put Shelly's battery-saving circuit onto a customized semiconductor chip, embed the chip into an extension device, fit one end of the extension device with terminals that would mate with the ordinary nine volt battery used in conventional pagers, and fit the other end of the extension device with terminals that would mate with the pager's existing wire harness configured to snap directly onto the battery. "If we can make the extension flat enough, it will easily fit inside any pager," Greg explained. "And you won't need the hands of a surgeon or the expertise of an electrical engineer to snap it into place."

"That's a jewel of an idea," Shelly beamed, after listening to his cousin's explanation for a second time to make certain that he understood it. But then his optimism faded once again. "Customized chips are expensive," he moaned. "Where are we going to get the money to pay for them? And even if we could make the chips, how would we ever get financing for the business as a whole?"

Greg had no immediate answer. Instead he nervously fingered a bronze medallion that had been hanging around his neck since the day he married. It had a peculiar design on one side and a foreign language inscription on the other. "I wonder how much this is worth," he mused to himself. Then he pulled the medallion out from under his shirt and asked Shelly the same question.

Shelly responded by removing two chains that hung from his neck. Attached to one was an identical bronze medallion; attached to the other was an old coin. He studied them carefully. "I think we ought to find out," he suggested.

Two weeks later they learned that their pendants weren't worth very much. And though the numismatist who appraised both the coin and the medallions translated the inscriptions and informed the cousins that the objects were far older than either of them had originally thought, this information provoked more questions than they answered. The cousins left the appraiser's shop confused.

"What revolt occurred in Transylvania and what role did our ancestors play in it?" Shelly asked. "What's the meaning of the comet and the spear? Who was Mirceal, and who did he curse?"

"Maybe your folks can shed some light on this?" Greg suggested.

Thirty minutes later the two cousins pulled up to the curb in front of Patrice and Teddy Barr's red-brick bungalow on the north side of Chicago. When Shelly explained the reason for their visit, Teddy lowered the volume of the Cub game he was watching on his new color TV and looked apologetically, first at Greg, then at his son.

"My father died when I was a baby," Teddy began. "My mother, may she rest in peace, remembered a ceremony involving the Tovers, the Barrs, and a very wealthy family from New York. She thought it occurred on the day she arrived in America. Mother was certain that it had something to do with baseball, not a revolt in Europe. She was also certain that the ceremony not only involved a curse, but a bond of friendship that the three families shared." Teddy then gave a subtle glance in the direction of his wife. "I think that's what our little adventure to the hospital burn unit was all about."

Patrice nodded.

Shelly looked hopefully at his mother for elaboration. "My brother, Peter, and I never knew our father," she said stoically. He was killed in France during the First World War. My mother knew nothing of the medallions or this bond of friendship except for what she learned from Esther Barr. And I know nothing more than what your father just told you."

Patrice retreated into the kitchen and returned with four bottles of Old Style. Then her eyes brightened with one further memory. "My mother was absolutely certain that the Tover sign on your medallions was derived from a two-headed axe." Patrice then turned her eyes toward Greg. "She believed the axe was some kind of family relic. So when your Gramma Serena passed the medallion on to Peter, she gave me the axe. She thought the Tover women should have the axe to hand down to their daughters just as the Tover men have the medallion to hand down to their sons." Patrice took a sip of beer without taking her eyes off of Greg. "I gave the axe to Shelly's sister, Sheila, when Teddy gave Shelly both his medallion and his coin."

Teddy finished his beer, then looked at the two cousins. "What brings on this sudden interest in family history?" he asked.

Shelly and Greg explained their planned business venture and the need for a loan.

"We are so close, I can taste it," Greg moaned as Patrice put a bowl of chips and some dip onto the coffee table in front of the TV.

Hank Aaron had just lined a homer into the left field bleachers. A teenager in a Cub hat put the ball in his pocket instead of throwing it back onto the field in accordance with Wrigley Field custom. The bleacher bums jeered, but Jack Brickhouse exonerated the fan. "That ball will be worth a small fortune one day," Brickhouse opined into his microphone. "Especially after Hank passes Ruth."

The comment piqued Teddy's interest.

"Imagine what a Babe Ruth homer would be worth today," Brickhouse added as an afterthought.

Brickhouse's innocuous comment struck a nerve in Teddy Barr that propelled him off the couch like a rocket. He looked excitedly at his son, and yelled, "That's it." Then he ran up to the attic and began rummaging feverishly through a stack of cardboard boxes that was thick with dust. After a brief search he found something he wasn't looking for. It was an old baseball with a faintly-visible notation that Teddy couldn't read without his glasses. It said, "Cubs Cursed." Teddy tossed the ball back in the box and continued his search. Ten minutes later he returned to the living room in triumph.

"This will get you your financing," he beamed through an ear-to-ear grin. Then he held aloft a yellowed baseball that, in black grease pencil, carried the brief message: "To Teddy–Babe Ruth." It was dated August, 1915.

Teddy handed the ball to his son. "This is your inheritance," he announced proudly.

The "Ruth" ball was appraised at over $50,000. It got Greg and Shelly their business loan.

With financing in place, Jewel Electronics Corporation was born in Greg's garage. After six months of working nights and weekends, the cousins finally saw the orders begin to trickle in. It was then that the two entrepreneurs decided to take an enormous risk: they quit their jobs, and devoted their full time energies to their infant enterprise. Their wives, both of whom were pregnant, thought they were crazy.

Less than five years later, during the nation's bicentennial, their business was on the rise. The fortune of the Cubs, however, went into a precipitous decline. The team had failed to finish above .500 for the last seven years of the 1970's, and by 1980 it had again hit rock bottom. The Cubs lost 98 games, tops in the National League, and finished a whopping twenty-seven games out of first place. In the course of this free-fall back to futility, Phil Wrigley passed away. It was widely believed that he bequeathed the Cubs to his son, William, on the condition that the team never be sold to anyone outside the Wrigley family. Less than a year later William Wrigley sold the Cubs to the Tribune Company, owner of Chicago's largest newspaper.

There were but two bright spots in the otherwise dismal season of 1980. The first was that Cub first baseman, Bill Buckner, won the National League batting title with a .324 average. The second was that relief pitcher, Bruce Sutter, who threw an unhittable pitch called a "split-finger fastball," saved twenty-eight games. For a team that managed to win only sixty-four games all year, this was a remarkable achievement. Nonetheless, the Cubs traded Sutter to the Cardinals after the season ended because management thought he was being paid too much money. In return they got Leon "Bull" Durham. Durham played first base—the one and only position where the Cubs already had an adequate player. The Cubs therefore traded Bill Buckner to the Boston Red Sox.

As bad as 1980 was, 1981 was considerably worse. The Cubs lost an astonishing thirty-six of their first forty-six games. If the players hadn't gone on strike for two months at the start of the summer, the team would have surely exceeded its record-setting 103-loss season of 1966.

Before season's end, Jack Brickhouse announced that he would retire. Though his public persona was corporate, Brickhouse was a decent, unpretentious gentleman. He appeared frequently and inconspicuously at countless charity events, supporting a diversity of causes. Despite thirty-three years of service, during which he cheerfully promoted the most poorly run organization in the history of professional sports, his last broadcast on September 27th ended without fanfare by the Tribune Company. A month later the Trib hired Harry Caray as Brickhouse's replacement.

Unlike Brickhouse, Caray was an entertainer. He didn't simply report what was happening, he became a part of what was happening. This fit perfectly with the Tribune Company's plans to broadcast Cub games, not just on local television to a fervently devoted Chicago fan base, but via cable to tens of millions of viewers all over the country. As a result, Harry Caray achieved greater popularity than any of the Cub players, including the talented, but bland, Cub second baseman, Ryne Sandberg. By 1982 attendance was up, viewership was increasing, and the Cubs' financial future was looking good.

So was that of the Barrs and the Tovers. Despite their success, however, the two families lived well below their means. They did so for the same reason. Greg wanted his eight-year old son, Peter John—he called him P.J.—and Shelly wanted his eight-year old son, Henry, to have an unspoiled childhood. It wasn't easy, however, to avoid the temptations presented by a new-age culture steeped in superficiality, self-centeredness, and brazen consumption.

One June afternoon, when the two families had gotten together for a Sunday barbeque, Greg asked Shelly an unusual question. "How do you deal with Henry when it comes to Christmas?"

The two partners had been sitting in the Tovers' den, watching the Cubs-Expos game on TV. Greg's question jolted Shelly's attention away from the broadcast, but resulted in no response. So Greg started over. "Do you think Henry feels, well, left out, when he knows that all the other kids in the neighborhood are getting presents on Christmas morning."

Shelly rubbed his chin once, then twice, before answering. "I don't think Henry feels any different than I did," Shelly explained. "We have plenty of our own holidays; it never troubled me that Christmas wasn't one of them."

"Yet you don't spread the good news of your holidays as we do ours?"

Shelly gave his friend a pensive stare. "Ours is a long, complicated, and demanding tradition," he began. "It can never become a religion of the masses. To spread the word of God throughout the world, we have relied on others—like the Christians."

Now it was Greg who looked thoughtfully at Shelly. "And for everything else it is the Christians who have relied on the Jews," he said.

Shelly acknowledged Greg's observation with a bob of the head and a tightening of his lips. "Yet something's troubling you about Christmas?" Shelly asked, returning to his friend's earlier question.

"The Orthodox Christmas doesn't come until January," Greg answered. Aside from being able to buy all of our gifts 'on sale,' Greg momentarily paused for a forced chuckle. "I think P.J. feels a little awkward about not celebrating the holiday when everyone else does. Grace and I were thinking of ... well ... maybe having two Christmases."

Shelly unsuccessfully tried to restrain a surprised smile.

"Bad idea?" Greg asked.

Shelly nodded. "We all have to make compromises with the popular culture. But if you don't draw the line at your most fundamental religious beliefs, where do you draw the line?"

Greg grimaced.

"I've got it all figured out," Shelly continued. "If you can stand firm with your values until your kids are eighteen, your job will be done."

"So we've got only ten more years?"

"I think they're going to be the hardest—like a Catch-22."

"How do you figure?" Greg asked.

Shelly's expression turned serious. "We're in a position to give our kids all the things we wanted, but never had. But the moment we do, we'll be depriving them of the thing we want to give them most."

"So you're saying adversity tests our character, but success tests our values."

"Something like that," Shelly grinned.

Just then Henry and P.J. came running into the den, followed by their mothers.

"We need ten dollars," Henry announced to his father.

Shelly gave his son a defiant stare. "What for?" he demanded with unconvincing authoritativeness.

"I promised the boys they could get a video game if they helped with the dishes and took out the trash," Lillian explained. "Grace and I are taking them to Babbages."

Shelly rolled his eyes. Then he reached into his wallet and gave Henry a twenty dollar bill. "I expect change," he said.

An instant later, Greg and Shelly were left alone in the den.

"Catch-22?" Greg chided.

Shelly's face turned beet red. "It's a new generation," he grumbled.

Shelly's words triggered an unexpected response from his partner. "How many years constitute a generation?" Greg asked.

Shelly furrowed his brow, but did not answer.

"I was thinking about my medallion the other night," Greg continued. "It makes reference to a hundred year curse for twenty-five generations. If these pendants were really made over 500 years ago, and back then a generation was, say, twenty years, then the time of the curse should be just about up."

It was just then that the background noise from the television grew louder. A Montreal homer in the bottom of the tenth gave the Expos a 5–3 victory; it also gave the Cubs their thirteenth straight defeat.

Greg looked up at his partner. "Our medallions speak of some kind of curse, your grandmother believed it had something to do with baseball, and the Cubs haven't won a thing since the day I was born. I bet it's the Cubs who were cursed."

Shelly's expression then brightened noticeably. "Well if your generational theory is correct, does that mean the curse is about to end?"

HARRY'S HOLLER

Sometime during the first half of the 1984 season, Harry Caray, and his color man, Steve Stone, became the most entertaining show in town. And Caray's theatrics quickly became part of the Chicago culture. This included his pre-game small talk: "They're here from Peoria, they're here from Decatur, and they're here from Galesburg." Such banter was inevitably followed by Harry's unique way of filling on-the-air dead time: "We got a nice message from the Kowalski family in Evanston, that's IKSLAWOK spelled backwards."

The next day hand-made signs sprouted in the bleachers like dandelions. "We're here from Alderon." Others simply said, YARAC and OG SBUC. The signs of course, merited a cameo on WGN's live television broadcast, and a reprise on the local evening news. With WGN's superstation reaching millions of people across the country, signs reading EW EVOL YRRAH began appearing at Major League ballparks from coast-to-coast.

Even more memorable, perhaps, was Harry's exaggerated home run calls, which were not intended to be descriptive, but theatre. Indeed, by the time Harry finished his signature quip, "It might be, it could be, it iiiizzzz," the home run ball had long since left the park and was bouncing along Waveland Avenue. In addition to his exuberant, slurred and unintelligible attempts to announce a bases-clearing double, or a game-winning RBI, there was also the unmistakable groan of abject disgust when a Cub batter failed to come through with men on base: "Heeeee popped it up."

The seventh inning stretch, which had become a routine, obligatory non-event at every other ball park in America, generated the excitement of a rock concert at Wrigley. The moment the last out was made in the top of the seventh, Cub fans began chanting, "Harry, Harry." Soon enough, Harry's big, florid, bespectacled head could be seen leaning out of the WGN broadcast booth. This was quickly followed by a gravelly voice that encouraged the fans to, "Let me hear you, now. Uh one, uh two, uh three ... Take me out to the ball game ... " And if things worked out well, as they were starting to do that spring, there would be enthusiastic shouts of, "Cubs win! Cubs win!" as the picture of the exuberant Cub players shaking hands with each other in the center of the Wrigley infield faded to a beer commercial.

Early in the year Greg Tover bought a season-ticket package of four box seats per game, most of which he planned to give to customers. On the first summer Saturday of the 1984 season, however, he gave two of the tickets to his partner, Shelly, with the suggestion that they meet at the ball park with their sons, P.J. and Henry. Two hours before game time, Greg and P.J. drove to the Howard El, parked the car and boarded the train. Greg chose this route, not only to avoid the congestion at the ball park, but to provide his son with a little family history. When they passed the stop at Foster Avenue, Greg told his son how he had once mistakenly taken the wrong train from Wrigley Field, got off at that very station, and had to walk three miles home.

"What else did you do when you were a kid?" P.J. wanted to know.

Greg looked at his son, then at several people—most wearing Cub caps—on the crowded El. They had overheard P.J.'s question and were trying not to seem as if they were waiting for the answer.

"Things were a lot simpler back then," Greg began. "We played baseball in the summer and football in the fall. Then we waited for the snow to melt and spring training to start." Several of Greg's fellow passengers broke out in chuckles; a black man playfully elbowed his own son and gave him an "I told you so" expression.

P.J. played Peewee football in an organized league on a well-maintained field. "Where did you play football?" he asked his dad.

"We played in the park," Greg explained. "We marked off the field with our jackets and sweatshirts, chose teams, and played. Everyone had a helmet; a few of the rich kids had shoulder pads. That was all there was to it." Then Greg remembered an incident worth retelling. "Once I got tackled face-down right in the middle of a huge puddle. So many people jumped onto the pile that I couldn't move. For a minute I thought I was going to drown in two inches of water."

All of the passengers within earshot laughed. P.J. just looked admiringly at his father.

Shelly drove to the game, but took a detour through his old neighborhood to show Henry where he had grown up. His parents had moved to a suburban condominium just after Henry was born, and now Shelly was compelled by some familial urge to show his son the neighborhood of his youth.

"When I was your age," Shelly lectured his son, "We didn't have power mowers like you do now. When I mowed the lawn, I did it by hand."

Shelly parked his car at the curb and stared nostalgically at the old bungalow. He had forgotten that the house was so small. It was the postage stamp-sized lawn, however, that caught Henry's attention. "This is the huge lawn you had to mow?" he asked, smiling.

"I think they must have cemented over some of it," Shelly answered, also smiling.

Father and son left the car and looked down the narrow tree-laden street. It was "One Way" now, but Shelly remembered it being wider. "Are these the steps you played 'pinners' on?" Henry said, pointing to the front of the red brick bungalow.

Shelly nodded. "And it was on this very sidewalk that your Aunt Sheila fell down while roller skating, and had to get five stitches in her knee."

"Did you ever have stitches?" Henry asked.

Shelly looked incredulously at his son, surprised that Henry didn't know the answer to that question. "Half a dozen of them," Shelly answered. "In my tongue."

Henry gagged.

"You see the school yard at the end street?"

Henry shook his head, but it didn't matter.

"We used to play baseball there every day of the summer. I was diving into second when a guy with the ball leaped at me trying to make a tag. He landed on my head, and I bit my tongue. The next thing I knew one of the guys said, 'your tongue is falling off.'"

Henry gagged again. "Didn't it hurt?"

"I didn't even know it happened. But all of a sudden there was blood all over the place. We weren't sure what to do so we walked across the street to the candy store where we used to buy our baseball cards. The owner was a real nice man." Shelly groped for his name. "Plotkin," he finally said with enthusiasm. "His name was Mr. Plotkin, and he kind of looked after us. Anyway, Mr. Plotkin called Gramma Patrice, and by the time I got home, she had already managed to borrow a neighbor's car to drive me to the doctor. Grampa Teddy met us there and gave me his medallion to hold for good luck while they sewed me up."

Shelly showed Henry both his medallion and his Bar Kochba pendant. "In a few years these will be yours," he smiled.

Henry smiled back.

By the time they got to the ballpark, Greg and P.J. had already arrived. Their seats were in the first row of boxes three-fourths of the way down the third base foul line. Shelly recalled the days when he and the other kids spent half the game trying to sneak into box seats such as these.

The crackle of the Wrigley loudspeaker interrupted Shelly's nostalgia. The announcer was giving the fans the starting line-ups. Shelly looked at Greg. "Who was the guy…"

Greg knew both the question and the answer. "Pat Pieper," he interrupted. "'Tention, tention, please,'" he reminisced.

The Cubs quickly fell behind the Cardinals 7–1, and everyone feared it would be a long day. Going into the bottom of the sixth, the Cubs were still trailing 9–3. By then Cardinal center fielder Willie McGee was on his way to a four-hit, six-RBI game. In the process he would achieve one of baseball's rarest feats: hitting for the cycle. The NBC announcers, who were broadcasting the game on national television, had already awarded McGee "Player-of-the-Game" honors.

"There's still hope," P.J. said. "The wind is blowing out." No sooner were the words out of his mouth than the Cubs erupted for five runs. But the score remained 9–8 going into the bottom of the ninth, and it looked like "curtains" for Chicago when former-Cub Bruce Sutter was brought in to pitch. The first batter he faced was second baseman Ryne Sandberg. As 40,000 fans squirmed uneasily in their seats, Sandberg stroked a waist-high Sutter-splitter over the left field wall to tie the game. The crowd was first stunned, then on its feet cheering.

Their joy was short-lived. St. Louis responded with two runs in the top of the tenth. It could have been worse. With two out, and runners going with the crack of the bat, a lazy fly drifted in the direction of the Tovers' seats. A fellow with a beer in one hand and a hot dog in the other dropped them both, and was about to reach over the red brick wall that separated the box seats from the field of play, to snatch a souvenir. Henry could see what was about to happen and immediately thought to himself, "Cub fans are supposed to be smarter than that." Then he screamed at the fan with all his might: "Back off!"

The fan hesitated just long enough for Sarge Matthews to reach up and make the catch. Sarge gave an appreciative smile in the direction of the scream and pointed a long index finger in Henry's direction. Then he took the ball out of his glove, flipped it to the knowledgeable, young fan, and trotted to the dugout for the bottom of the tenth.

Sutter was still on the mound, and the Cubs' eighth and ninth hitters were due up. Suddenly, a pallor of hopelessness fell upon the field like a thick fog. Even when Sandberg was advancing to the batter's box with two outs and a man on first, no one really believed that lightning could strike twice.

It did. Sandberg sent another Sutter-splitter into the left field bleachers for his second game-tying homer in as many innings. The blast sent the Wrigley faithful who were at the ballpark, listening on the local radio station, and watching the game in every corner of the country into a state of giddy ecstasy. And when Leon Durham raced home with the winning run in the eleventh to give the Cubs an improbable 12–11 victory, all Harry Caray could holler was, "Holy Cow!"

Bull's Boner

Despite the Cubs' success, Greg Tover and Shelly Barr felt a sense of uneasiness during the 1984 season that their ten-year old sons didn't share. It was Shelly who volunteered an explanation as to what was troubling them.

"This isn't really a Cub team," he suggested to his partner one afternoon while there was a lull in office activity at Jewel Electronics.

Greg concurred. "Except for Ryno and Jody ... and Durham, I don't feel like any of these guys are really Cubs."

"What about Smith?" Shelly suggested.

"I'll give you Smitty, too," Greg conceded. "But it's not like the old days of Banks and Santo and Williams."

"And Kess and Beckert and Hundley," Shelly said wistfully. "Those guys were real Cubs. They were like family."

"Same with Fergie and Holtzman," Greg reminisced. "I mean Cey is a Dodger," Shelly complained. Then his jaw hardened. "I still hate the Dodgers for moving out of Brooklyn."

Now it was Greg's turn to vent. "What, if all of a sudden, we got Seaver? Now he's on the White Sox, but as far as I'm concerned he's a Met and always will be." Greg paused for a moment." And I still hate the Mets. I gag every time I even think about '69. How am I supposed to root for a Met?"

"Bowa's a Philly, Sutcliff's an Indian, Sanderson's an Expo, and Trout—he was on the White Sox," Shelly chafed.

"Don't forget the guy we just got for Buckner," Greg reminded him. He stopped for a moment to remember his name. "Eckersly," he finally said. "We got Eckersley from the Red Sox."

"I'll tell you something else," Shelly interrupted. "I hate the Red Sox almost as much as I hate the Mets. They've been in three World Series since '45, and all they do is complain. They don't know from pain; they don't know from loyalty. These are the guys who booed Ted Williams for God's sake."

"I'll tell you something else I hate," Greg said. "Where do people get off calling the Cubs 'America's team'?"

Shelly nodded.

"Would you believe I've got a cousin in South Carolina who now tells me he's a Cub fan?" Greg continued.

"Where was he in the Fifties when we were thirty games out of first place every year?" Shelly asked.

"Probably rooting for the Dodgers," Greg answered.

Greg and Shelly could have added another reason for their uneasiness. As the summer progressed, and the Cubs improved their record to 80–54 by the end of August, arrangements had to be made for post-season play. Since NBC's deal with Major League baseball would cost each team about half a million dollars if week-day play-off games took place during the daytime, a contingency plan was arranged to limit the Cubs to three World-Series home games instead of the four that had been originally allotted to the 1984 National League champs.

Similarly, in the best of five League Championship Series, the Cubs would be limited to two home games, even if they had a better record than their Western Division opponents.

When the Cubs clinched the Eastern Division Championship on a two-hit masterpiece by Rick Sutcliffe at Pittsburgh's Three Rivers Stadium, the contingency plan went into effect. Sure enough, the Cubs had a far better record than their Western Division foes from San Diego, but only the first two games would be played in Chicago. The final three games, if necessary, would be played in San Diego.

October 2, 1984 was a warm, sunny day in Chicago. What made that day unusual, however, was not the weather but the fact that the

Cubs were playing their first post-season game in almost forty years. Cub fans were overcome with emotion to see Wrigley Field adorned in bunting, and hosting the national media. Ernie Banks was given a uniform and would be sitting in the Cub dugout as an honorary coach; Jack Brickhouse was given a seat in the broadcasting booth and would be allowed to announce an inning of the game. A Chicago family of Greek extraction actually brought a goat to the game in an effort to excise a curse that they believed was placed on the Cubs several decades earlier.

"We're playing in October," Shelly beamed, giving his son Henry a playful elbow. They got off the Howard El, walked down the stairs and found themselves in a sea of people milling down Addison Street.

Greg and P.J. were already munching on some peanuts when Shelly and Henry inched their way to their seats. Shelly took a moment to survey the ivy-covered walls, the huge hand-operated scoreboard, the emerald grass and the russet-brown infield before sitting down. "This is my favorite place on earth," he said to himself.

Shelly's thoughts were interrupted by a nudge from his partner. "Do you believe this?" Greg exulted. "I'm thirty-eight years old, but when P.J. and I walked through that tunnel and my eyes laid sight on the green grass of Wrigley, my heart started beating just as fast as the day my dad took me to my first game when I was eight."

"Yep. I remember my dad taking me to my first game," Shelly reminisced. Then he turned toward his son. "Grampa Teddy and I sat way out there," he said, pointing to an area in the center field bleachers that was now cordoned off to make a better background for hitters.

Sutcliffe retired the Padres in order in the top of the first, getting first baseman Steve Garvey on a called third strike to the delight of the fiercely partisan fans. The buzz had barely subsided when scrappy Cub lead-off man, Bob Dernier, shocked the capacity crowd by lining a homer to left. It began one of the most joyous games in Wrigley Field history. Before the day was over, the Cubs would hit four more homers and score twelve more runs. They slaughtered the Padres 13–0. And when they defeated San Diego the next day behind the five-hit pitching of Steve Trout, no one in Chicago doubted that the Cubs were going to the World Series.

Even after the Padres won the first game in San Diego, Cub fans were not particularly concerned. Indeed, when they watched the game on TV, and contrasted the Padres' sterile concrete stadium with the legendary ball park at Clark and Addison, their disdain for the Padres only increased. Cub fans literally laughed out loud when San Diego's electronic scoreboard showed an animated pair of "clapping hands" during a Padres' rally. "They don't even know when to cheer," the Wrigley faithful mocked.

In Game Four the Cubs bravely overcame Padre leads of 2–0 and 5–3. With the game tied at five, the Cubs brought in their ace reliever, Lee Smith. But when Padre first baseman Steve Garvey hit a two-run, walk-off homer, it was Smith who absorbed the loss. It gave Shelly Barr the same sick feeling he had when Willie Stargell blasted a dramatic, two-out, two-strike homer against the Cubs' best reliever in 1969. "Oh Brother," he could still hear Jack Brickhouse moan in disappointment.

Even with Rick Sutcliffe taking his fifteen-game winning streak into Game Five, Cub fans were now decidedly edgy. "If this game was at Wrigley, I know that we could bring our boys home," Greg complained. He breathed a little easier when the Cubs staked the big right-hander to a 3–0 lead, thanks to a two-run homer by Bull Durham and a solo shot by Jody Davis.

But then the Padres scored two runs in the bottom of the sixth to narrow the Cubs' lead to a single run. In the bottom of the seventh, with one out and a runner on second, light-hitting Tim Flannery hit a grounder to Durham. To the shock of Cub fans everywhere, the ball rolled right through the first baseman's legs for the most costly fielding boner since Hack Wilson's miscues in the 1929 World Series. "I think I'm going to be sick," groaned Shelly Barr. A few moments later three more runs had scored, and when they did, it was the Cubs hopes for a pennant that died as well. That the former Cub Bill Buckner would commit the same error as a member of the Boston Red Sox in Game Six of the 1986 World Series did not ease Shelly's pain, even after the passage of two years.

Greg Tover was more incensed than heart broken. "We didn't lose because of Durham's error. We didn't lose because we were on the road; we didn't lose because the Padres were better." His faced flushed with anger. "We lost because the Cubs are cursed. They are *really* cursed. And if it's the last thing I ever do, I intend to find out why."

SAMMY'S HOP

At the end of the 1976 season, the Cubs traded a young third baseman by the name of Bill Madlock to the San Francisco Giants for
three mediocre players. Madlock had just won two consecutive batting
championships for the Cubs, and would win two more—one in '81 and
the other in '83. In the course of his fifteen-year career, Madlock would
compile a lifetime average of .305. Having disposed of Madlock, the
Cubs would spend the next twenty-five years trying, without success,
to find a replacement third baseman.

In 1987 the Cubs traded ace relief pitcher Lee Smith to the Red
Sox in return for two unproductive starting pitchers. By then, Smith
was on his way to becoming the best "closer" in baseball history. In his
first year with Boston, Smith recorded twenty-nine saves in thirty-
five opportunities; that same year, without Smith, the entire Cub staff
recorded an equal number of saves in fifty-six opportunities.

At the end of the 1988 season, the Cubs, now desperate for a "closer,"
traded a twenty-three year old first baseman by the name of Rafael Palmeiro
to the Texas Rangers for relief pitcher, Mitch Williams. Williams, unfortunately, had so much trouble getting the ball over the plate that Cub fans
sang the rock song, "Wild Thing" every time he walked in from the bullpen. Palmeiro, on the other hand, would amass over 550 career homers, 1,775
RBI's and 3,000 hits.

In 1992 the Cubs literally gave away future Hall of Famer, Greg Maddox. The Cy Young winner publicly expressed a strong preference to remain in Chicago when his contract came up for renewal; it took a shocking combination of ineptitude and stinginess to allow him to sign with Atlanta. He would win three more Cy Youngs for the Braves, in the process becoming one of the most winning hurlers in modern baseball history. The Cubs subsequently obtained an unheralded pitcher by the name of Jose Guzman. The Cubs' General Manager boasted that he now had the starter to replace Maddox.

Despite their long, unrivaled tradition of front office incompetence, on March 30, 1992, the Cubs blundered into one of the best trades in baseball history—they sent George Bell to the White Sox for Sammy Sosa. The previous year Bell hit .285 with twenty-five homers and eighty-six RBIs. Sosa, on the other hand, batted an anemic .203 with ten homers and thirty-three RBIs. Sosa did lead Bell in one category: he had ninety-eight strikeouts to Bell's sixty-two. The Cubs acquired Sosa, not because they thought he was a better ballplayer, but because Bell had a pricey free-agent's contract that they wanted to unload.

Sosa was not an immediate hit. At season's end it would be Mark Grace who led the team in hitting, Ryne Sandberg who led the team in home runs, and Andre Dawson who led the team in RBIs. The following year, however, Sosa became the first Cub player in history to hit over thirty homers and steal over thirty bases. The team posted only its third winning season in over twenty years. Nonetheless, this was all it took to give the eternally-hopeful Cub fans reason for optimism as the 1994 season began.

That proved to be a mistake. Before the year came to an end, Harry Caray suffered a stroke, Ryne Sandberg retired, and the Major League baseball players went on strike.

The day after the season had been officially cancelled, Shelly Barr marched angrily into his partner's office. "No one could have loved baseball more than me," he fumed.

"Or me," Greg Tover said to himself.

"But now I'm through. I can't stand the greed, I can't stand the hype, I can't stand how the game has been compromised."

Greg nodded. Then came a stunner. "You won't believe this," he began simply enough, "but you know who I really feel sorry for?"

Shelly gave his partner an inquisitive stare.

"The White Sox."

"The White Sox?" Shelly repeated in disbelief.

"I think they're getting screwed," Greg said, his anger starting to mount.

"We're all getting screwed. So what?"

"So the Sox were the best team in baseball before the strike. So they were going to win the pennant. So despite wars and disasters, a baseball season has never been cancelled. Yet just when the Sox are about to stick it to the Yankees, the rug is pulled out."

Shelly looked at his partner askance. "You're not becoming a fair-weather fan, are you?"

Greg sniffed. "After over forty years, I've paid my dues. But now there's something about the Cubs that really annoys me."

It was only then that the same sense of discomfort hit his partner. "It's like the Cubs aren't the underdogs anymore?" Shelly blurted.

"Exactly! Now it's the Sox who never get a fair shake. And the Cubs get a pass no matter how bad they are." The dot-matrix printer near Greg's desk began to buzz, but he ignored it. "It's not that hard to figure," Greg continued. "The Trib owns the Cubs. You don't think they're going to be objective when they've got 40,000 seats to fill every game?"

Shelly squinted.

"And there's something else that's beginning to annoy me," Greg added.

Shelly squinted again.

"It's the fans with the Rolex watches who go to Wrigley," he began. "It's like they don't really care that much if the Cubs lose. There's no heartache, no pain. And the Tribune doesn't care either as long as those idiots keep pushing their turnstiles."

All of a sudden, Shelly felt abused. "You think the Trib is just stringing us along?"

"Like a Stradivarius," Greg said.

Despite Greg's grousing, Jewel Electronics kept its box seats at Wrigley, and the two partners continued to take customers to games. Like a jilted lover, however, the strike did not pass without leaving a psychological scar.

"I've promised myself that I'll never become as emotionally invested in the Cubs as I was before the strike," Greg explained to his partner one beautiful spring afternoon, in between scoops from a Wrigley Field "Frosty Malt." "And I've kept that promise for three years now by rooting for the Sox as well as the Cubs."

"Isn't that like being both a Protestant and a Catholic?" Shelly chided.

"Some people have two kids and they love each of them; Chicago has two teams and now I root for them both. Why should that be such a big deal?"

"Because part of being a Cub fan is hating the Sox," Shelly explained.

Greg chuckled. "I don't even remember why I hated the Sox. All I do know is that rooting for the Cubs gives me nothing but heartache."

Greg's promise not to become emotionally involved in the Cubs ended before the game was over. In one of the most glorious days in Wrigley Field history, a twenty-year old rookie flamethrower by the name of Kerry Wood struck out a record twenty Astros in the course of a one-hit, 2–0 Cub victory. No Cub had struck out as many batters since Jack Pfiester fanned seventeen Cardinals in 1906.

And though Sammy Sosa hit a team-leading thirty-six homers the previous season, he would hit almost that many by the end of June. By then, Mark McGwire of the rival Cardinals hit thirty-seven. And so began the greatest home run race since 1961, when Roger Maris outslugged the great Mickey Mantle for the distinction of surpassing the immortal Babe Ruth.

As the summer progressed, the homers kept coming and the suspense kept building. Through it all, McGwire maintained a dignified respect for Maris' achievement, and Sosa demonstrated an enthusiastic admiration for McGwire's quest. Their graciousness did much to diminish the lingering bitterness that had kept baseball fans away from the ballparks years after the players' strike had ended. Suddenly, things were good again.

"Boy, is he big," Shelly remarked, as he stared at the Cardinal first baseman through a pair of expensive Bushnell binoculars.

Greg grabbed the binoculars from Shelly and took a look for himself. "Was he always that big?" he asked rhetorically.

Shelly took the Bushnells back from Greg and trained them on Sosa, who was standing in the on-deck circle, calmly staring into the Cub dugout. "Take a look at Sammy," he said, handing the binoculars back to his partner. "Where did he get a body like that?"

Greg studied the Cub right fielder. His biceps bulged out of his blue, short-sleeved Cub jersey. "Must be spending a lot of time in the weight room," Greg mumbled.

A moment after Sammy stepped into the batter's box, he took a powerful swing, the ball cracked off the bat, and Sammy took a joyous hop in the direction of first base. A few seconds later the ball landed onto Waveland Avenue, bounced off the pavement, and crashed into a yellow brick building on the other side of the street. Not only did the homer give the Cubs the lead, it gave Sammy forty-eight dingers for the year—one more than McGwire.

Three innings later, McGwire tied both the game, and Sosa, by hitting a monstrous blast of his own. Neither tie lasted very long. In the top of the tenth, McGwire's two-run homer gave the Cardinals an 8–6 lead. For the umpteenth time, a capacity crowd left Wrigley Field disappointed.

At the end of August, McGwire and Sosa were tied again at fifty-five homers apiece—one shy of the National League record set by the Cubs' Hack Wilson in 1930. McGwire broke Wilson's record the very next day. A week later he tied Maris in the first of a two-game set against the Cubs at Busch Stadium in St. Louis. The next day Cub pitcher, Steve Trachsel, would become the answer to a trivia question when he gave up McGwire's record-setting sixty-second homer.

By season's end, McGwire would add eight more homers, finishing the 1998 campaign with an unheard-of seventy round-trippers. In any other season, Sosa's sixty-six home runs would have been hailed as a legendary achievement. Instead it will be remembered as an outstanding effort from a mere also-ran. As Shelly explained, "No one remembers how many homers Mantle hit in '61."

The Cubs were quickly eliminated by the Braves in the 1998 playoffs. They then returned to their days of utter futility. In 1999 they finished thirty games out of first place. In the first year of the new millennium, they finished thirty games off the pace once again.

Much to the chagrin of both Cub fans and Sox fans, the New York Yankees were better than ever. No one could have been happier than a seventy-six year old, life-long Yankee fan, by the name of Theo Merkle.

Theo and Chen Merkle spent the Labor Day weekend of 2001 alone at their home in Maple Grove, New York. The Yankees were again in the thick of the pennant race and so was Theo. Chen, however, was in the thick of a disturbing news story that was unfolding on C-Span. It showed virulent anti-semitic demonstrations at a misnamed United Nations Conference Against Racism and Bigotry in Durban, South Africa. The scene harkened back to a time, sixty-five years earlier, when Chen witnessed firsthand the abject evil that such misguided hatreds can produce. She snuggled on the couch next to her husband and shivered—not because she was cold, but because she was afraid.

"This is just how the world was before the war," she shuddered.

Theo looked down at his wife. Her eyes were red; her face was ashen. He wanted to offer words of comfort, but none was forthcoming.

"History is repeating itself," Chen sobbed.

Theo tenderly stroked his wife's head, but could not ease her pain.

"Say something," she entreated.

Theo hesitated. "The cowards, the hate-mongers and the tyrants will briefly have their day, but then they will be condemned to a fate worse than death itself. Like Hitler, they will spend their last days of freedom hiding underground like animals and their names will be reviled throughout eternity."

Chen was unconsoled. "I hear the same lies. I feel the hatreds. I am told the same excuses. I see the same explosions." Her voice trailed off in hopelessness.

"But, honey," Theo objected, "there are no explosions."

Then came 9/11.

One of the casualties on that terrible day was an old World War II bombardier by the name of Teddy Barr. Teddy was attending an apparel show at the World Trade Center while his wife went shopping.

They were planning to stay an extra day in New York to visit their daughter, Sheila, who lived on Long Island. Teddy was killed when the second Tower collapsed. Before his heart gave out, however, Teddy led over a dozen people through dust and smoke, to the safety of an emergency stairwell. Patrice was comforted in her grief with the knowledge that God had kept her husband alive all these years to undertake this one last mission for his country.

HENRY'S CHAT ROOM

In April of 2003 Patrice Barr suffered a stroke. Less than two months later, Shelly had the unenviable task of moving his mother into an assisted-living facility. In early June he, and his son, Henry, visited Patrice's condominium for the purpose of cleaning out her basement locker. It contained numerous mildewed boxes that obviously hadn't been opened since the day she and Teddy moved them there, from their north side bungalow, over twenty-five years earlier.

When the bottom fell out of the first box, revealing nothing but old clothes and useless memorabilia, Shelly stifled his sentiment. "Throw it all out," he told his son. Soon decades of out-dated apparel, faded photographs, dance bids, restaurant menus, cancelled checks, broken seventy-eight rpm records, and dime-store curios were stuffed into garbage bags and deposited in the back-alley Dumpster. Also discarded was a 1938 Wrigley Field scorecard, and an even older post-card showing the Brooklyn Bridge.

When Henry transferred the contents of the last box into a big black Hefty bag, however, something caught his father's eye.

"What was that?" Shelly wanted to know.

Henry shrugged.

"You didn't see anything?" Shelly asked.

Henry shrugged again. "What do you think you saw?" Henry asked.

Now it was Shelly who shrugged. "Nothing," he said with a distinct tone of resignation. "Just chuck the bag in the Dumpster with the rest of the junk."

Henry dutifully hoisted the plastic bag over his shoulder and headed for the alley, leaving his dad alone with a deep sense of pathos. A few moments later, Henry returned with an impish expression on his face, and a yellowed baseball in his hand.

"It says 'Cubs Cursed,'" he announced as he tossed the ball to his dad. "And it has the sign of the Tover axe and the Bar Kochba coin."

Shelly caught the ball and looked carefully at the faded words, barely visible on the cover of the age-darkened ball. "It's dated 10/14/08," he added.

"What does it mean?"

Shelly re-read the words, then reached for the medallion that hung visibly around his son's neck. "It means that the Cubs are really cursed, and that this ball and your medallion contain the clues for ending it." He paused for a moment to take a deep breath. "We better tell the Tovers."

Later that evening, in the first inning of a night game against the Devil Rays, Sammy Sosa took an awkward swing at an off-speed pitch and broke his bat. To the surprise of everyone at Wrigley, including the home plate umpire, the bat was corked. When Sammy was ejected from the game and suspended for a week, both the Tovers and the Barrs became convinced that this was all part of the Cubs' curse that was referenced on their 1908 baseball. They became convinced that it was now their mission in life to undo that curse.

The very next morning Henry Barr sent an email to his dad and the Tovers. "I've created a private chat room so we can share information. Here's what I think I know so far. The curse of Mirceal that is engraved on our medallions, and the curse on the Cubs that is written on our baseball are one and the same. The date on the ball is October 14, 1908. That's the day the Cubs won their last World Series. But here's a question: if they were cursed on that day, shouldn't they have *lost* the World Series?"

"Maybe they were cursed *after* the game on 10/14?" came an immediate reply.

"They beat Detroit. Maybe it was a disgruntled Tiger Fan who cursed the Cubs?"

"Maybe it was Ty Cobb?"

After Sammy Sosa served his suspension, things for the north-siders started to change for the better. Cubs' ace Kerry Wood and sophomore sensation, Mark Prior, could throw nothing but strikes. Young shortstop Alex Gonzalez was getting timely hits, and veteran Moises Alou was getting timely home runs. With youngsters Carlos Zambrano and Matt Clement providing quality starts, the Cubs had the best four-man rotation since Brown, Pfiester, Overall and Ruelbach pitched in 1908.

An email from Greg Tover suddenly popped up on Henry Barr's chat room. "Look at the attached article. The Cubs won the pennant in 1908 only because they beat the New York Giants in a one-game playoff. But there wouldn't have been a playoff if a Giant baserunner didn't forget to run from first to second." Then came a stunner. "The name of that baserunner was a rookie by the name of Fred Merkle. He was mercilessly skewered by the New York press as 'Bonehead' Merkle."

"Are you saying there's a connection between the Fred Merkle of the Giants and the 'Mirceal' on our medallions?"

"Yes!!!"

"How could that be? The Merkle of 1908 lived 500 years after the Mirceal on our medallions."

"Maybe he's a descendant?"

"But they don't have the same last name."

"If my grandfather could change his name from Bar Kochba when he came to America," Shelly reminded everyone, "then so could Mirceal."

Throughout the summer, each Cub game seemed to produce another hero in more dramatic fashion than the day before. On June 26th, Prior struck out sixteen Brewers. On July 2nd, Sosa homered in the ninth to give the Cubs a 1–0 victory. On July 5th, Gonzalez drove in the winning run in the bottom of the ninth to cap a Cub win after spotting the Cardinals a 5–0 lead. On July 9th, Wood struck out twelve Marlins. Ten days later Wood beat the Marlins on a two-hitter.

———————

P.J. Tover sent an email to the chat room after the July 19th Cub victory. "Halley's Comet appeared in both 1456 and 1531. The comet on our medallions must have been one of those."

"What does a spear in the comet's tail mean?"

Three people responded with the words, "Don't know."

"Transylvania is a Province in Romania. There was a coup in Romania in 1456; I'm betting that's the year of our comet."

———————

Clement threw a two hitter against the Giants on July 29th.

———————

"Get this. The 1456 coup was started by someone named Vlad Dracula."

"Are you telling us Dracula was a real person?"

"Dracula wasn't a vampire; he was a tyrant. Read the attached."

"Just read it. Dracula was defeated by his brother Mirceal."

"How long is a generation?"

"What's that go to do with anything?"

"The medallions refer to twenty-five generations."

———————

On August 22nd, Zambrano, propelled by Sosa's 500th Cub homer, carried a no-hitter into the eighth inning against the Diamondbacks en route to a 4–1 victory.

———————

"The reference on our medallions to 'year one in the revolt to redeem Transylvania' must refer to a counter-coup against the usurpers."

"Someone must have copied that language from the Bar Kochba coin."

"Maybe a Bar Kochba fought in the counter-coup?"

"I bet a Tover did, too."

"That's why the signs are on the medallions."

"The same signs are on the 1908 baseball. I'm betting that the names on the medallion are ancestors of the people who cursed the Cubs."

"Here's a terrible thought. If we are the descendants of the 1908 Tovers and Barrs, then the curse on the Cubs is our families' fault!!!"

"We are victims of our own curse!"

On September 3rd, after trailing the Cardinals 6–0, Alou drove in the winning run to climax a dramatic comeback.

"Mirceal had a son named Cristian who did not inherit the throne."

"Catch this: Cristian was born when Mirceal was one-month shy of twenty-two years old."

"So what?"

"If that constitutes a generation, then twenty-five generations is 547 years."

"Again, so what?"

"Well, if you add 547 years to 1456 you get 2003."

"The 1456 comet appeared on October 14—the same day that the Cubs were cursed in 1908."

"I think the medallion is telling us that something's gonna happen to the Cubs on October 14, 2003."

"You expect us to believe that 500 years ago someone etched a prophecy about baseball onto a couple of medallions?"

"Is there such a thing as a prophecy?"

On September 8th, both the Cubs and the White Sox were in sole possession of first place. This was the first time that both Chicago teams had been on top of the standings that late in the season since the South Side "Hitless Wonders" upset the powerhouse Cubs in the 1906 World Series. The city was about to become unhinged.

Aaron's Prophecy

Two weeks later, Shelly Barr set up a conference call with his son and the Tovers. A moment later Shelly patched Rabbi Aaron Levy onto the line. After a brief introduction he asked the rabbi an urgent question: "Is there such a thing as a prophecy?"

The rabbi suppressed an impulse to inquire why Shelly wanted to know. "Of course," he answered.

"Can you give me an example?" Shelly urged.

Again the rabbi suppressed an impulse to inquire. "Our prophets have foretold of a better world, one where swords are beaten into plowshares and spears into pruning hooks, a world where each man shall sit under his own fig tree and not learn war anymore."

Shelly was unable to stifle his groan of disappointment. "Is there any prophecy in the Bible that foretells something that actually happened," he asked impatiently.

"The Bible is not a fortune teller," the rabbi admonished. "The words of our prophets do not predict secular events; they pertain to momentous paradigms for repairing the world and guiding the destiny of the people of Israel."

The rabbi's words triggered a thought in Shelly's mind. "Would such a paradigm include the rebirth of Israel itself?"

"It would," the rabbi answered confidently.

"And is it so written?" Shelly asked with eager anticipation.

Rabbi Aaron Levy cleared his throat into the phone and quoted from the Book of Deuteronomy. "…the Lord thy God will return and gather thee from all the peoples, whither the Lord thy God had scattered thee and will bring thee into the land which thy fathers possessed."

"It's the ingathering of Jews to the State of Israel, exactly as prophesized 3,000 years ago!" Shelly interrupted.

The rabbi paused for a moment before continuing. "The Lord will cause thine enemies that rise up against thee to be smitten before thee; they shall come out against thee one way, and shall flee before thee seven ways."

"Seven ways?" Shelly asked.

"It's a reference to the seven Arab nations who attacked as one when Israel was reborn, but then retreated in disarray," he answered.

There was a silence.

"Is there anything more?" Shelly asked.

"What more do you need?"

"What will the future bring for Israel and her enemies?" Henry wanted to know.

"The enemies of Israel hold the key to their own future," the rabbi explained. "The greater their enmity for the people Israel, the greater will be their misery." He paused for a moment before continuing. "So it is written, so it will be done," he warned.

The Tovers and the Barrs thanked the rabbi for his time, and were about to say "goodbye." But then Greg Tover blurted out a question: "Who determines whether a prophecy is authentic?"

Rabbi Levy breathed a thoughtful sigh into the phone before answering. "I don't really know," he confessed, "except to say that it's a cosmic gift of our peoplehood."

"Do any other people have this gift?" P.J. asked impulsively.

Rabbi Levy breathed another heavy sigh into the phone. "I'm sure they do," he continued. "But to whom God gave this gift, and for what purpose will, I'm afraid, remain one of His mysteries."

Despite the clanging in his ears, P.J. heard the others thank the rabbi.

"Shalom," the rabbi responded before hanging up his phone.

"So prophecies do exist," P.J. told the others who remained on the line.

Though the White Sox couldn't keep pace with the Twins in the last three weeks of the season, the Cubs just got stronger. So did right-hander Mark Prior. Down the stretch, Prior won ten of his last eleven starts. He allowed only eleven earned runs and struck out an average of nine per game. Everyone agreed that if the playoffs came, this guy was not going to falter.

Henry Barr's chat room was obsessed with a different subject. "The curse on the Cubs was due to the misplay of Bonehead Merkle."

"The curse on our medallions was due to the tyranny of Vlad Dracula."

"Both curses were made by a Mirceal ancestor."

"So is it the family Mirceal that carries the power of the curse?"

"It must be. And the descendants of the 1908 Mirceal should know how the curse was made."

"I'm guessing that the 1908 Mirceal was a New York baseball fan who spelled his name Merkle. He cursed the Cubs because the blunder of his namesake cost the Giants a pennant."

"No!" He cursed the Cubs because the blunder of his namesake brought ridicule upon his proud family name."

"That's it! That's the significance of the words on our medallions that refer to an impreciation to restore the good name of Mirceal."

"But that imprecation was etched on the medallions centuries earlier."

"Don't you see?" The original Mirceal wanted the good name of his family restored after the coup of Vlad Dracula, and the New York Merkle wanted his good name restored after the blunder of Bonehead Merkle."

"Find the living progeny of the New York Merkle, and you will find a way to undo the curse."

On September 27th Prior won the first game of a day/night double-header against the Pirates. That win, combined with the Brewers victory against the Astros, clinched a Cub tie for the Central

Division Championship. Later that day, when Pirate third baseman Jose Hernandez rapped into a short-to-second-to-first double play to seal the Cubs' 7–2 victory in the nightcap, the Cubs were officially in the playoffs.

What followed was a genuine love-fest between the Cubs and their fans. Dusty Baker led his players in a triumphal walk down the right field foul line, around the outfield warning track, and back toward the Cub dugout. The players waved affectionately to the fans, and the fans enthusiastically waved back. Sammy, forgiven for his "corked" bat, uncorked a bottle of champagne and let it spray over the right field wall into the laps of his well-wishers. An hour later, the fans were still in the stands celebrating effusively. Tens of thousands of others were dancing on Waveland and Sheffield Avenues. The love-fest continued the next day when the Cubs retired Ron Santo's number 10. Thereafter, it would fly forever over the Wrigley Field bleachers along with Banks' number 14 and Williams' number 26.

The next day, Henry Barr sent a global email to his father and the Tovers. "I know how to find the New York Merkle. I'm modifying some telephone directory software to search every Merkle name in the city and suburbs of New York City. It will automatically dial their phone number and send them a recorded message."

"What will the message say?"

Henry gave his mouse a couple of clicks, and the following message instantly appeared on the chat room monitors: "Hello. My name is Henry Barr. If you own a bronze medallion which bears the names Tover and Bar Kochba, please email me at the address below. My cousin, P.J. Tover, and I have identical medallions."

"Cool."

"When will it be ready?"

"In about a week."

When the Cubs defeated the Atlanta Braves three games to two in the first round of the playoffs, it marked the first post-season series that the Cubs had won since their World Series victory against the Detroit

Tigers in 1908. Now only the Florida Marlins obstructed their path to the National League pennant.

"Does anyone in Miami even know they have a team?" P.J. Tover asked sarcastically, as he and his dad made their way to their seats for the first game of the League Championship Series. They were met there by Shelly and Henry Barr.

"We better win in five," Greg announced.

P.J. and the Barrs gave Greg a quizzical glare.

"If this series comes back to Chicago, we may not be able to go to Game Six," he explained. "I promised those tickets to our biggest customer."

The Cubs split the first two games at Wrigley, but took two-out-of three from the Marlins in Miami. Cub fans were ecstatic. They had won three and now only one game stood between them and the World Series, they were coming back to Wrigley, and Prior was well-rested and ready to go. The following afternoon, Greg Tover received some additional good news: his best customer was going out of town and couldn't use the tickets to Game Six.

SHELLY'S INSIGHT

About an hour before the start of Game Six, Greg and P.J. Tover got off the Howard El and began walking toward the corner of Clark and Addison. The streets and sidewalks were already thick with people. Makeshift bands played on every street corner. Vendors were hawking souvenirs along the entire length of Addison Street between the El Station and the ball park. Half a dozen African-American boys were rhythmically beating drumsticks onto the bottoms of plastic buckets turned upside down. A spare bucket was already filling rapidly with change.

Though there was still plenty of daylight left, the lights on the stadium roof were shining brightly. They burned P.J.'s eyes. And the noise on the street rang painfully in his ears.

The Tovers rendezvoused with Shelly and Henry, at the corner of Clark and Addison, then headed for the turnstiles.

"Any news from the Merkles?" P.J. asked his cousin.

Henry shook his head. "I only got the system working this morning," he apologized. "But in the meantime there's something else I figured out."

Henry withdrew his medallion from under his shirt and asked P.J. to do the same.

"Look at the diagram," Henry urged.

P.J. looked down.

"That sphere near the sun—it's a baseball, not a comet," Henry explained. "And the diagram—it's not some medieval symbol involving a spear and a cross—it's a baseball diamond."

P.J. stared at his medallion but was unconvinced.

"Look carefully," Henry pleaded. "The spear tip is home plate, the flattened ends of the cross are the bases. Don't you see?"

The Tovers and the Barrs slowly made their way through the narrow stadium concourse, into the dark tunnel under the grandstand and down the crowded aisles to their seats. Enroute P.J. bumped into a pillar because his eyes were fixed on his medallion.

Everyone rose for the *National Anthem*, then rose again when the Cubs took the field. "Look at the path of the comet," Henry yelled over the din, but his words were drowned out by the cheers.

Prior struck out Derrek Lee stranding Marlin runners on first and second. Henry repeated his exhortation but the fan noise again drowned out his words. When Cubs' center fielder, Kenny Lofton, singled to open the home half of the first, the crowd was on its feet, cheering again. And when Sammy doubled him home, the crowd roared with unrestrained glee.

P.J. clamped his hands over his ears as if in distress.

"Are you okay?" Greg asked after the noise subsided somewhat.

P.J. nodded. He popped three Advil into his mouth and washed them down with a beer.

Henry, meanwhile, thrust his medallion in front of P.J.'s face and implored him to follow the path of the comet.

When the Cubs' first baseman flew out to end the inning, the crowed quieted.

"Pretend the comet is a baseball, and the diagram is a baseball diamond," Henry urged. "Now tell me: where does the comet head end?"

Greg, P.J. and Shelly stared down at the medallion. "It's a home run," Greg answered blithely.

In a moment of epiphany, P.J. saw the answer to Henry's question. "No it's not!" P.J. insisted. "Dad, look again."

Greg and Shelly focused carefully on the path of the comet. Their eyes alternated from the medallion to the playing field. Greg traced an imaginary arc from home plate toward the comet head several times.

Slowly, Greg's face brightened like a sunrise. So did Shelly's. "The comet lands right where we're sitting," Greg announced with surprise.

"Don't you think that's more than just a coincidence?" P.J. challenged.

"What should I think?" Greg asked.

P.J. pleaded his case. "Twenty-five generations from 1456 brings us to the present year; the date of the revolt brings us to the present day; the diagram on the medallion brings us to this place—the very spot where we're now sitting. All of this can't be a coincidence."

In the bottom of the sixth, Sammy singled, advanced to second on Alou's single, and went to third on a double play. The Marlins brought in a new pitcher, and the first thing he did was throw a wild pitch to bring home Sosa with the Cubs' second run. The Wrigley Field crowd erupted with joy as Sammy crossed the plate. All 40,000 fans were on their feet cheering madly—all except P.J., Henry, Greg, and Shelly. They were staring intently at the diagram on the medallions, oblivious to the frenzy that surrounded them.

"Something is going to happen today," P.J. said to himself. "Something's going to happen right where we're sitting," he said aloud. Then he turned toward Henry. "The only question is: when."

"The comet head is right next to the sun," Henry observed. "The position of the sun must be a clue to the time."

The Marlins hit three easy fly balls in their half of the seventh— one to left, one to center and one to right. On making the final catch of the inning, Sammy threw the ball into the right field bleachers. The Wrigley faithful sang "Take Me out to the Ball Game" together as if they were family.

Henry was on his wireless. He was not making a call, but logging onto the internet. Greg and Shelly were peering over his shoulder. P.J. was alternately shielding his eyes from the lights and his ears from the noise.

The Cubs strung three hits together in the bottom of the seventh to extend their lead to 3–0.

Henry was feverishly typing in commands using the key pad of his wireless.

Prior finished his warm-ups.

"What year was the comet?" he asked P.J. .

The first batter for the Marlins lofted a routine fly to left.

"Five more outs," a jubilant fan in a nearby seat yelled to a friend.

"1456," P.J. said.

"We're going to the Series," the fan's friend yelled back ecstatically.

"The perihelion of Halley's Comet of 1456 occurred at 10:17 p.m.," Henry announced.

Juan Pierre doubled to left.

"What time is it now?" Greg asked.

"10:16," came P.J.'s ominous response.

The crowd was still and eerily quiet, but P.J. nonetheless had his hands clasped over his ears as if they were cheering loudly.

The Marlins' switch-hitting second baseman, Luis Castillo, dug his back foot into the batter's box and glared at the pitcher—a youthful smile creasing his smooth, tan face. Prior glared back, then went into his familiar, compact wind-up. Castillo lunged at Prior's offering and lofted a high lazy foul down the left field line.

"It's coming right toward us," Henry thought.

The crowd hushed.

P.J. could see exactly what was going to happen.

Alou drifted toward the wall.

Some of the fans in P.J.'s box rose to their feet.

Alou raised his glove.

"Back off!" P.J. screamed with all his might.

Everyone in the box was distracted by P.J.'s scream, but one—a fan wearing earphones who could not hear his warning.

"Back off!" P.J. screamed again. But it was too late. The fan, a twenty-six year old consultant by the name of Steve Bartman, deflected the ball from Alou's glove a fraction of a second before the Cub left fielder could make the catch.

"Kill that guy!" someone hollered. And then followed such a hail storm of garbage and debris that the hapless Bartman had to be escorted out of the stadium by a cadre of ushers for his own protection.

Alou stomped his foot in anger. The fans in the box were livid. P.J., however, was in a state of repose, comforted by the fact that the painful ringing in his ears had finally ceased. Despite Prior's anxiety, no one walked out to the mound to give him comfort.

Castillo fouled off at least a half dozen pitches until he coaxed a walk from the Cub pitcher. Rodriquez singled to spoil Prior's shut-out, but again, no one came to the mound to talk to him. The next Marlin hitter was their rookie right fielder, Miguel Cabrera. Despite the tense situation, he seemed calm and relaxed.

Cabrera took a level swing at Prior's offering, but hit only the top of the ball. It rolled toward the Cub shortstop and took a Sunday hop. Cabrera wasn't watching. He flew out of the batter's box and raced toward first in an effort to beat the relay that would complete a potentially inning-ending double play. The effort was hardly necessary. The Cub shortstop booted the ball. It was the worst error in Cub history, surpassing Bull Durham's boner in 1984, Don Young's miscues in '69 and Hack Wilson's blunder in the 1929 World Series. Then followed two doubles, two walks and a single. By the time the third out was made, eight runs had scored, and the season was effectively over.

The Tovers and thousands of other fans left the game early in a state of shock. "I feel as if someone in my family just died," Shelly heard his partner lament as Greg and P.J. made their way toward the aisle. The same feeling of sadness compelled Shelly and his son to remain in their seats 'til the bitter end.

In the bottom of the ninth, Shelly propped his chin in his hands and gave a vacant stare at the baseball field that he loved so much. The stands were now quiet, and the fans' collective sense of anxiety had dissolved into one of helplessness and despair. He reached for the medallion that dangled down the front of Henry's sweatshirt, and stared at it pensively.

"This medallion has been a blessing and a curse," he told his son. He held the pendant between his thumb and forefinger and turned it from side to side. Then he released the medallion and watched it fall limply onto Henry's chest.

Shelly glanced out at the playing field one more time. Kenny Lofton popped out to end the game. The Marlins gathered near the pitcher's mound for a ritual of hugs and "high-fives." The Cub players walked dejectedly down the left field line toward their clubhouse door.

Henry grabbed the medallion, looked at it briefly, then let it drop. "It's certainly no blessing," he grumbled to his father.

Shelly returned his eyes to his son and offered a final insight. "The

Cubs have been victimized by Merkle's curse for almost a hundred years," he began, "but it was always in our power to do something about it." Then a smile crossed his face for the first time since the disastrous eighth inning. "And that, after all, is a great blessing."

P.J.'s Vision

About the same time that 40,000 dispirited and demoralized Cub fans began filing out of Wrigley Field, Theo and Chen Merkle returned to their home in Maple Grove, New York, after a night at the opera. Theo reclined in his easy chair and loosened his tie. Chen removed a mobile phone from its cradle in the kitchen and interrogated her voice mail. She almost erased a pre-recorded message, but the names Tover and Bar Kochba caught her attention.

Chen was momentarily uncertain whether to share Henry Barr's message with her husband. In recent months Theo had been suffering from the same symptoms of old age that took the life of his revered matriarch, Angela. Now Chen feared that the startling news residing in the memory of her answering machine might trigger a similar systemic shock to Theo. But Chen's uncertainty quickly passed. An instant after the message ended, she walked over to her husband's easy chair, put the phone up to his ear, and pushed the replay button.

"Listen to this," she said.

Henry Barr's recording precipitated a series of emails and phone calls that resulted in members of the Tover, Barr and Merkle families meeting in the City of Chicago shortly after the 2004 New Year. It was the first time they had come together since Theo's accident in that same city over seventy years earlier. Because of Theo Merkle's baseball connections, the family members met at Wrigley Field and congregated around home plate. They brought with them the Bar Kochba coin, the Tover axe, three bronze medallions and a 1908 baseball.

Shelly looked out at the empty seats in the stadium he loved. His eyes slowly panned across the lumpy, unraked infield, the dormant brown grass, the drab ivy that clung lifelessly to the outfield walls and the blank center field scoreboard. In his mind's eye, however, he saw big number nine—Hank Sauer—jogging out to his position in left field on a hot summer day. A huge chaw of tobacco created a bulge in the cheek of Sauer's craggy face. His lips parted into an embarrassed smile as he sheepishly tipped his hat in an effort to acknowledge the fans' enthusiastic cheers.

Halfway between second and third, Shelly saw a youthful Ernie Banks glide gracefully to his left, scoop up a grounder and throw it to first in one fluid motion of athletic prowess. Then Ernie came to bat, a protective liner under his blue Cub hat, his fingers subconsciously twitching on the handle of his Louisville Slugger. With powerful wrists, Ernie quickly moved his bat from an upright position over his shoulder to a level plane as it swept across the plate. The ball cracked off the wood—propelled into the blue sky on a shallow arc until it landed into the eager hands of a left field bleacher bum.

On the opposite side of the batter's box stood Billy Williams. In Shelly's mind, nothing in Mona Lisa's smile or Juliet Capulet's description of a rose could ever be more beautiful than Billy's swing. "Oh, what I wouldn't have given to have a swing as sweet as that," Shelly mused. His imagination then recreated the countless times Williams sent a baseball screaming into the gap in right-center field.

At third base, Shelly watched Ron Santo—his uniform plastered with dirt—smooth out a tiny bump in the infield with the toe of his spikes. Shelly saw a wind-up, a pitch, and a shot in the hole between short and third. Santo dived to his left and speared the ball—then regained his feet in time to fire a strike to first. At game's end, Shelly saw Santo exuberantly clicking his heels on the way to the clubhouse.

Shelly's happy nostalgia was interrupted by Greg Tover's wife, Grace. She suggested that everyone form a circle around home plate and join hands. Theo's grandson, Truman, suggested that the axe, the coin, and the medallions be placed in the center of the circle. Shelly's sister, Sheila, suggested that they pass the 1908 baseball from hand-to-hand around the circle. P.J. Tover filmed everything on his camcorder.

When the patriarch of the Merkle family entered the center of the circle and began to speak, everyone listened. "We are gathered here today to reverse a curse that our ancestors brought upon the Chicago Cubs back in 1908. I do not know the words or the rituals that are required, so I have to hope that the bond of our friendship and the sincerity of our plea will be sufficient to accomplish our objective." Theo cleared his throat, started to resume his extemporaneous oration, but cleared his throat a second time instead.

Although accustomed to public speaking and making decisions, Theo Merkle suddenly found himself at a loss for words. Chen noticed her husband's hesitation and spontaneously tried to help, lest the uneasy pause degenerate into an embarrassing silence. "The words on your medallion refer to an imprecation to reinstate the good name of Mirceal," she encouraged.

Her comment, unfortunately, only made Theo more disoriented and confused. The color drained from his cheeks, his jaw tightened, and a smear of perspiration began to glisten above his brow. "The medallions refer to your family name in its original spelling," Chen prompted. But Theo's expression remained wan and his demeanor remained awkward. Then, just as suddenly, the awkwardness receded and color returned to his face. Theo cleared his throat yet again, but this time the words came forth.

"We are here to undo a curse that our families placed on the Chicago Cubs back in 1908," Theo began in a slow, measured cadence. When he saw several heads begin to nod, Theo continued at a swifter pace. "I therefore declare that any curse on the Chicago team bearing the Cubs' original name is now ended, concluded, and permanently extinguished; and that the team's good name is hereby restored!"

Chen attributed the somewhat stilted language of her husband's declaration to his momentary confusion, now passed. She gave him a reassuring smile. Theo took his wife's smile as a cue to continue, resulting in one final statement that everyone happily understood: "I further declare that next year there will be a World Series Champion in Chicago."

Greg Tover felt compelled to say something as well. He joined

Theo in the center of the circle, picked up the two-headed axe that was lying on the ground, lifted it in the air and stated in a loud clear voice: "subscribed and sworn by the Tover family."

Shelly Barr followed suit. He retrieved the Bar Kochba coin that had been set on home plate, balled it into his fist, and then joined Greg and Theo in the center of the circle. Shelly raised his fist into the air and made a similar pronouncement: "subscribed and sworn by the family Bar Kochba."

Theo put his arms around his two comrades; one a man of color, the other a passionate Jew.

"Our ancestors came from different traditions and hostile environments, yet all of us have found peace and opportunity in this land of ordered liberty," he said to himself. "May the blessing of peace and opportunity come to all who choose freedom under the rule of law, fairly enacted and justly enforced," he said aloud. "And may the wrath of God come down upon those who do not."

Instead of "amen," someone on the perimeter of the circle yelled, "Let's eat."

In the baseball season that followed, the Cubs failed to even make the playoffs, much less win a world championship. Even worse, they were plagued by an unprecedented and inexplicable spate of injuries that made Henry Barr doubt that the curse against the Cubs had really been lifted. He did, however, want to believe that it had.

"At least they didn't lose because of Merkle's curse," Henry told his father as they walked to their car after the last home game of the 2004 season.

"It doesn't matter," Shelly lamented. "We should have won in '03. No World Series victory in the future will ever be as sweet as the one we didn't win last year."

Henry could only nod his head in agreement.

Nonetheless, the following year there was, just as Theo Merkle declared there would be, a World Series Champion in Chicago. Since the Cubs' original name was the "White Stockings," however, it turned out that Theo's declaration in Wrigley Field had literally applied to the team that played on the south side of town—not the north side. So instead of undoing the curse against the Cubs, Theo Merkle had inadvertently restored the good name of their cross-town rivals. The stain of the 1919 Black Sox scandal had finally been removed in one glorious succession of post-season victories.

The White Sox won the pennant on October 16, 2005. That day was significant for yet another reason: despite a national election in Iraq, violence, devastation and misery were spreading across the globe from Tunisia to Indonesia. It reminded P.J. Tover of Rabbi Levy's warning to the enemies of the people Israel, explained in the course of the conference call two years earlier. Nonetheless, in his mind's eye P.J. saw an oasis in the desert with contented men—each reading his holy book—each under his own fig tree. For reasons P.J. did not understand, this vision caused his eyes to burn and his ears to ring.

Ten days later, the Chicago White Sox won their first world championship since 1917. All of their fans believed that the team's improbable victory was due to dominant pitching, superb defense, speed on the base paths and timely hitting—not to mention a few fortuitous calls by the home plate umpires. Only three families, each with identical bronze medallions, came to understand that the Sox owed their championship to the ingenuity of four die-hard Cub fans, and their tireless efforts to undo Merkle's Curse.

EPILOGUE

When P.J. Tover and Henry Barr came to realize why Theo Merkle's stilted declaration failed to expunge the curse on the Cubs, the cousins had decidedly different opinions on what to do next. Henry remained obsessed with the curse and wanted to remove it once and for all; P.J. wanted to forget the whole thing because the hundred year curse was about to expire on its own. When their disagreement became heated, they decided to let Rabbi Aaron Levy arbitrate the dispute. They met in the rabbi's study a week later, and explained their dilemma.

"The answer to this controversy resides in the last verse of Deuteronomy, Chapter XXV," the rabbi announced. Then he reached for a tome that rested on his desk, and thumbed briskly through the pages. When he found the desired passage, he cleared his throat and began to read from the holy book: "'... thou shalt blot out the remembrance ... from under heaven; thou shalt not forget.'"

P.J. and Henry looked at each other incredulously. "How can we simultaneously blot out a memory and not forget it?" Henry asked.

The rabbi smiled. "One who fails to remember will live out his life as a fool; one who fails to forget will live out his life as a victim. Therefore, not only can you do both, you must do both."

"But how does one know what to remember and what to forget?" P.J. wanted to know.

The rabbi smiled again. "When you are wise you will know the answer."

"And who'll teach us this wisdom?" Henry asked.

Now the smile disappeared from the rabbi's face, and his expression grew serious. "Wisdom is not taught, my friends. It is learned."

The rabbi's secretary interrupted their discussion with an urgent message. "I'll be right back," he told the cousins. "Maybe you can tell me what you've learned when I return."

P.J. and Henry were in an animated conversation when Rabbi Levy re-entered his study a few minutes later. "Well," he began, "what'll it be? Will the curse be removed or ignored—or dare I suggest—reinstated for another hundred years?"

"We still haven't decided," P.J. explained, "so at least for now, the fate of the Cubs is in their own hands."

"But we did agree on one thing," Henry volunteered.

"And ..." the rabbi prompted.

The cousins gave each other a knowing nod, then removed the medallions that were beneath their shirts and touched them together. "We'll give these to our sons when they get married."

Rabbi Levy nodded approvingly, and whispered, "Amen."

NOTES

Merkle's Curse, of course, is a novel. The preeminent families in the novel—Merkle, Tover and Barr—are entirely fictional. In the course of the novel, members of these families, and their acquaintances, encounter real people and participate in actual events. All such encounters and participations are also fictional. Similarly, with the exception of some expressions used by Cubs' broadcasters, and some references from the Bible, all quoted statements and thoughts expressed by any character in this novel are made up.

To those readers who desire an identification of some of the historical persons and events referred to in the novel, the following explanation may be of assistance.

Trajan was a Roman general and Hadrian was a Roman emperor. Mircea was a revered king of Wallachia. Dracula was a real person who may have served as the prototype for the vampire in Bram Stoker's novel. The dates and circumstances of Dracula's life, however, are invented.

Simon Bar Kochba led the zealot's revolt against Rome in 132, and may well have been perceived as the Jewish Messiah by the real Rabbi Akiba.

Constantine was an Emperor of Rome and Helena Augusta was his mother. Constantine claimed to have seen a cross of fire in the sky shortly before he defeated Maxentius, and later, Licinius. He was baptized on his death bed.

Athanasius was an Alexandrian priest, as was his antagonist, Arius. The Council of Nicea did take place, and it was attended by Bishops Eusebius, Paulinas, and Alexander.

Ferdinand was a King of Spain, and Christopher Columbus was, of course, an explorer who initially landed on a Caribbean Island in The Bahamas which he called San Salvador. Francis Drake was a real sea captain knighted by Queen Elizabeth and Peter Minuit was the Dutch representative of the West India Company who purchased Manhattan Island for twenty-four dollars.

Abner Doubleday and William Tecumseh Sherman were Union generals who fought in the Civil War; A.G. Spalding was a Chicago pitcher who retired to start a successful sporting goods company; Harry Pulliam was the National league President in 1908; Arnold Rothstein was a Chicago gambler; and Kenesaw Mountain Landis was the Commissioner of Baseball in the aftermath of the Black Sox scandal. Abraham Lincoln, William Howard Taft and Theodore Roosevelt were, of course, Presidents of the United States.

Murphy, Taft, Wheegham and the Wrigleys were owners of the Cubs; Comiskey, Frazee and Dunn were owners of the White Sox, Red Sox and Orioles, respectively; Branch Rickey was the General Manager of the Brooklyn Dodgers in 1947. Burt Wilson, Jack Quinlan, Jack Brickhouse, Lou Boudreau, Vince Lloyd, Steve Stone, and Harry Caray were, at various times, broadcasters for the Chicago Cubs. Pat Pieper was the team's field announcer for many years.

With few exceptions, the Major League baseball players, coaches, managers and umpires mentioned in the book played, coached, managed, and umpired in the manner essentially described, but all of their conversations, as well as their off-field activities, are entirely fictional. It should be pointed out, however, that certain events, such as a pop foul in the tenth inning of the "Sandburg Game," did not happen; others, such as the performance of the Cubs and their players during the 1953 and 1957 seasons, may be charitably described as hyperbole.

Babe Ruth's parents, George and Kate, did commit him to a Baltimore orphanage, which is where he spent most of his childhood. Jackie Robinson did grow up in poverty in Pasadena. He was abandoned by his father, Jerry, and raised by his mother, Mallie. Ruth received encouragement from a Catholic priest by the name of Father Matthias; Robinson had an older sister named Willa Mae who did look after him when he was a child. The wives of Babe Ruth and Lou Gehrig were also real people.

To some extent, the events portrayed and the actions taken by the various characters in this book represent my personal interpretation of history based on a combination of research, speculation, and imagination. Sometimes, however, liberties had to be taken to provide the proper back-drop for the storyline. This is, after all, not a work of scholarship, but a novel.

Finally, Steve Bartman was a real Cub fan whose conduct at the Cubs-Marlins game at Wrigley Field on Tuesday, October 14, 2003 was destined to happen because of Merkle's Curse.